THE
DEAD CRY
JUSTICE

Books by Rosemary Simpson

WHAT THE DEAD LEAVE BEHIND

LIES THAT COMFORT AND BETRAY

LET THE DEAD KEEP THEIR SECRETS

DEATH BRINGS A SHADOW

DEATH, DIAMONDS, AND DECEPTION

THE DEAD CRY JUSTICE

Published by Kensington Publishing Corp.

THE
DEAD CRY
JUSTICE

ROSEMARY
SIMPSON

www.kensingtonbooks.com

KENSINGTON BOOKS are published by

Kensington Publishing Corp.
119 West 40th Street
New York, NY 10018

All Kensington titles, imprints and distributed lines are available at special quantity discounts for bulk purchases for sales promotion, premiums, fund-raising, educational or institutional use. Special book excerpts or customized printings can also be created to fit specific needs. For details, write or phone the office of the Kensington Special Sales Manager: Kensington Publishing Corp., 119 West 40th Street, New York, NY, 10018. Attn. Special Sales Department. Phone: 1-800-221-2647.

Library of Congress Card Catalogue Number: 2021940065

ISBN: 978-1-4967-3334-4
First Kensington Hardcover Edition: December 2021

ISBN: 978-1-4967-3335-1 (ebook)

10 9 8 7 6 5 4 3 2 1

Printed in the United States of America

*La plus belle des ruses du diable est de vous persuader
qu'il n'existe pas.
(The devil's finest trick is to persuade you that he does
not exist.)*
—Charles Baudelaire, *Le Spleen de Paris (Paris Spleen)*

CHAPTER 1

Prudence MacKenzie was no closer to finding an answer to the problem she'd gone to Washington Square Park to solve than she'd been when she'd arrived.

A packet of sandwiches wrapped in butcher paper and brown twine lay on the bench beside her; an enormous red-gold dog stretched its shaggy length at her feet. Nesting birds darted in and out of the tree canopies and a riot of early wild-flowers lined the gravel paths and dotted the open spaces where the warm May weather had turned the grass a brilliant green. Everything in this pastoral retreat at the bottom of Fifth Avenue was alive with new purpose.

Except Prudence.

She sighed, rubbed the sole of one booted foot over Blossom's thick, feathery coat, reached absentmindedly for the sandwiches, then let her hand drop to her lap. She wasn't hungry.

Her eyes drifted over a group of well-dressed young men entering the Gothic main entrance of the fifty-year-old building that housed the Law School of the University of the City of New York. For a moment, she imagined herself one of them, laughing and talking about nothing in particular as they climbed its marble steps and disappeared into narrow corridors lined with lecture halls.

On a long-ago outing with her father, she'd listened from one of those same hallways to the resonant voice of a bearded, solemn-faced professor booming off the walls of a wood-paneled amphitheater. As student after student stammered answers the lecturer unabashedly ridiculed as incomplete, illogical, or preposterously wrong, Judge MacKenzie's arm had tightened reassuringly around his daughter's shoulder. Even at fifteen years of age Prudence could have held her own with the learned men of the law who had no patience with ineptitude. But at the time of that visit, no woman had as yet been called to the bar in New York State.

Four days ago, on May 5, 1890, the university's governing council had met and voted to admit women to the study of law. One of the councillors had sent a note to Prudence's Fifth Avenue home, politely requesting a few minutes of her time, writing that he had been her father's friend and colleague from the years before she was born. She'd invited him to tea.

"We need this class of women to succeed," he'd explained between bites of Cook's excellent seed cake. "Already there's opposition to our decision. Columbia's dean is declaring to anyone who will listen that females will only be allowed to enroll in that institution over his dead body. Or words to that effect."

"What will happen to the Woman's Law Class?" Prudence asked, referring to a series of private seminars recently sponsored by the university. There'd been articles detailing the new venture in the *Times*. "I've heard nothing but praise for Dr. Kempin."

"She's a good lecturer. We wouldn't have endorsed her otherwise. But she's going back to the University of Zurich, and the course she's been offering was never meant to substitute for what we demand of our matriculated male students. No admittance criteria. Forty-eight hours of instruction over a six-week period. You can't compare that to what the law school requires."

"I understood her students take an exam."

"They do. But what they earn is a certificate of attendance rather than a diploma. The program of study doesn't go beyond a bare minimum of legal issues applicable to the fair sex. Dr. Emilie Kempin may have begun by wanting to establish her own law school for women, but what she ended up with is a stopgap measure at best."

"Thirteen states have admitted women to the bar," Prudence reminded him gently. It was a topic she and the late Judge MacKenzie had enthusiastically followed during the years when she'd joined him in the library every evening while he recounted the details of the cases before him. "Kate Stoneman was licensed to practice in this state four years ago. Without the benefit of a law school education."

"But no other woman in New York has followed her example," Edgar Carleton said, brushing crumbs from his beard. "Your father told me more than once that he was confident you could pass the bar exam without ever setting foot in our classes. He said you'd apprenticed at his knee since you were big enough to lift one of his lawbooks. I believed him then, Prudence, and I believe him now."

"There are extenuating circumstances." She hoped he wouldn't ask why she hadn't followed Kate Stoneman's example and applied to take the bar exam despite a lack of formal study.

"What happened to Mr. Hunter was in all the papers. I know he's your partner at Hunter and MacKenzie, Investigative Law." He pronounced the name of the firm with the gravity normally accorded only the city's most long-established law firms. Ex-Pinkerton Geoffrey Hunter and his society-girl partner were slowly but surely gaining the grudging respect of the city's police, newspapers, and legal community. "I also understand he's making a slow but assured recovery from the bullets he took in February."

"He almost died."

Prudence heard the words as a whisper in her heart and hoped the lawyer sitting opposite had not caught the emotional edge of what had been weeks of desperate uncertainty.

Carleton sipped his tea, giving the judge's daughter time to turn her full attention back to the argument he'd come to make. Years of teaching and practicing law followed by appointment to the university's governing council had taught him to be wily and patient. Prudence MacKenzie had already proved to the rigid world of New York society that she could venture outside the bounds of what was considered appropriate behavior and remain a lady in fact as well as name. In his considered opinion, it was time for her to take the next step.

"We need the women of this first class to persevere through graduation. They'll have to support each other both within the lecture halls and in the larger community. Stand their ground without flinching. I believe that calls for a strong leader to hold them together, Prudence. Someone of their own feminine persuasion because we can't predict how the male students will receive them."

"I've heard some of the stories about what happened elsewhere," Prudence said. She grimaced. "Glue on the seats so the women's skirts stuck to the wood, pig's blood in their inkwells, the tallest men in the class sitting directly in front of them to obstruct their view of the lecturer. Threats whispered in the hallways, withdrawing rooms locked or filled with discarded furniture so they couldn't answer calls of nature." True or not, there had been rumors of more dangerous harassments, incidents even the women who suffered them were reluctant to bring out into the open.

"That kind of behavior will not happen at New York University." Even its council members used the nickname by which the University of the City of New York had been popularly known from its inception.

"What are you asking me to do?" She thought she knew what Edgar Carleton wanted, but her father had taught her to be sure of her facts always.

"Join the other women of this groundbreaking class, Prudence. You'd be its strongest, most well-prepared member, male or female. See it through to graduation and the bar exam. Help us prove to the naysayers that our resolution to admit women is a sound one."

There it was. The direction and acceptance she'd longed for. The choice she was now reluctant to make because she knew it would change her life forever in ways she could not predict.

"Will you think about it?"

"I will," she promised. Her first instinct had been to refuse outright, but Judge MacKenzie's voice in her head had counseled a more moderate course. *Don't burn your bridges, Prudence.*

"May I expect an answer in a week's time?" Carleton had asked.

And Prudence had agreed.

Blossom sighed and resettled herself, long snout pillowed on her front paws, ears alert for a command or a threat. She was a beautiful animal, intelligent and devoted to the four- and two-legged creatures among whom she lived, immensely fond of the huge white horse whose stable she shared. But like many of her ilk, she'd only ever given her whole heart to one human. Kevin Carney of the red hair and tubercular lungs. Street child. Denizen of alleyways and an unheated shed in the backyard of a brothel. Dead now. Mercifully reprieved from a suffering that had lasted far too long. She'd transferred her allegiance to the humans who'd cared for Kevin during his final days, but her heart had remained her own.

The dog welcomed the gentle rub of the woman's boot along her back and wondered when she'd share the package of sandwiches. Blossom had a particular fancy for ham roasted with cloves and coated with honey. She was a canine with a definite sweet tooth.

Somewhere behind her, Prudence heard the whir of a rolling hoop and the ticktock tap of the stick that kept it upright. Children's voices trilled in high falsettos as nursemaids chided and chivied them through their afternoon walk in the fresh air. Elderly couples climbed slowly down the marble steps of their elegant redbrick Greek Revival townhomes on the north side of the square, tugged along by small dogs yipping excitedly.

Newly arrived immigrants had filtered into many of the neighborhoods south of Washington Square, drifting into the park to get away from the crowded, airless tenements that crushed several families into spaces hardly large enough for one. It was said you could hear every language spoken in every country of the world if you stood long enough on a New York City street corner. Or lingered in one of its parks.

The children, the old people, and the pinch-faced newcomers eddied around the well-dressed woman and her dog. They cast curious glances but did not approach the bench on which she sat. Every now and then someone's eye caught hers, and a smile was exchanged or the dog's tail thumped. Prudence, lost in her thoughts, hardly noticed the silent, polite nods as her legally trained mind concentrated on the dilemma she'd come here to resolve.

Once, not too long ago, she would have leaped at the chance to study law at New York University. She'd even contemplated following Kate Stoneman's example to take the bar without academic credentials.

Over time she'd become diverted from what had seemed a well-defined path. Her father died. Her stepmother tried to parlay Prudence's grief and accidental addiction to laudanum into iron control of her life and fortune. Then Geoffrey Hunter had introduced her to the world of the private inquiry agent and trained her in the ways of the famed Pinkerton National Detective Agency. They'd been successful; the bar had taken a back seat to the challenge and thrill of solving crimes. Of stopping wrongdoers in their tracks. As she'd told Edgar Carleton, there were extenuating circumstances.

None so devastating as Geoffrey's near brush with death.

It changed Prudence's world as nothing else had done since the loss of her father. Sitting day after day beside Geoffrey's bed in his suite at the Fifth Avenue Hotel, she'd relived over and over again the moment his bullet-ridden body crashed into hers, the helplessness and loss of hope when his blood saturated her clothing and stained her hands. She'd assisted at the kitchen table surgery that saved his life, teeth clenched against waves of nausea as she watched forceps extract deadly bits of misshapen lead from his body. Sat bolt upright through the long night of moving him by wagon and train. The threat of infection and gangrene, the specter of amputation.

And finally, when Geoffrey opened his eyes and the doctor cautiously pronounced him out of immediate danger, came the need to talk. How difficult it had been. So much had been left unsaid.

One decision had been made. Prudence's aunt Gillian, the Dowager Viscountess Rotherton, had sailed back to London a few weeks ago without her niece. They had argued, mildly at first, then ferociously. Lady Rotherton had threatened, ordered, and finally been reduced to flattering her sister's daughter into considering a life among England's titled aristocracy. With her fortune, Lady Rotherton assured her, Prudence could easily marry a title. Wouldn't she like to be a countess? A duchess?

No, Prudence told her, she wouldn't.

What she hadn't said was that she couldn't bear to leave Geoffrey. Not even with nothing between them settled. Not even with the long silences that grew stiffer and more uncomfortable with every passing day. The feeling that she was waiting for something to happen was like a slowly creeping paralysis.

The offices of Hunter and MacKenzie stayed closed. Josiah Gregory's desk remained cleared, his scarcely touched Remington typewriter covered, the telephone unplugged from the wall. Faithful secretary that he had always been, Josiah was in Geoffrey's hotel suite when Prudence arrived in the morning and he was still there when she left every evening.

Then Edgar Carleton had invited and urged Prudence to enroll in the first New York University Law School class to admit women. The waiting was over.

A grimy, barefoot urchin in tattered shirt and ragged pants streaked across the grass, swooped within inches of the bench on which Prudence sat, and snatched up the package of sandwiches she hadn't yet opened.

Blossom sprang to her feet before the boy managed more than a few steps beyond the reach of her jaws, but she glanced at her mistress before leaping to sink her fangs into his leg. And read a denial of permission in Prudence's upraised hand. Blossom sat, but her body trembled with the eagerness to chase.

The two of them watched the boy zigzag his way through the people strolling the square and then scamper across the graveled space between where the grass ended and the huge University Building blocked his way.

"Now what?" Prudence asked aloud. She walked quickly to the path that snaked along the far side of the park, the dog following her, tail wagging furiously. "I can still see him, Blossom. It looks like he plans to make a run for it." She caught herself laughing and put one hand over her eyes to shade them from the sun. "He's disappeared. That's impossible. I can see right down past the side of University Building into Waverly Place and there's no sign of him. Where did he go?"

She started off at a brisk pace, the red-gold dog trotting beside and then in front of her, plumed tail stiff, muzzle stretched out to find the scent she'd caught as the boy darted past her clutching the snack she'd been anticipating.

"Not so fast, Blossom," Prudence ordered.

The dog obediently slowed down, stopped, and turned to wait for her human to catch up.

Hand to her side to ease her tight stays, Prudence reached for Blossom's collar and felt the large animal's considerable weight lean against her legs. Solid, strong, reassuring.

"Shall we find him, girl? Shall we catch our little thief?" It would be a welcome distraction from what she didn't want to think about anymore.

"My father said students rarely went into University Building's basement, even when he was here. It's supposed to be haunted, although I don't know why any respectable ghost would want to hang out in damp, smelly storage rooms."

Blossom wagged her tail.

"I think our boy has found a way in and decided he's safer with the ghosts than out on the streets. He's probably right."

And there, around the corner from the park, was a set of narrow concrete steps leading down from the sidewalk to an iron door with a broken padlock hanging from its hasp. An inch of empty space separated the edge of the door from the frame, the hinge too rusty to allow it to close all the way without someone pulling it tight. A boy on the run might not have known that, might have assumed the door would slam shut behind him. Might not have waited to find out.

Blossom smelled a narrow ribbon of ham and honey wafting through the air. She whined, but quietly, so as not to alarm her prey.

"I agree," Prudence said. "Let's go in after him."

CHAPTER 2

Prudence pried open the heavy iron door and motioned the large dog inside, leaving a gap just wide enough to squeeze through without attracting attention from a passerby.

The cellar stretched off into unbroken darkness, but at this end of what looked to be a huge storage room filled with piled-up furniture, shafts of weak daylight filtered through a row of grimy, sidewalk-level windows. Prudence felt her way gingerly along the wall, trying not to shuffle her feet noisily on the concrete floor as she sidestepped bits of unrecognizable debris.

She made one of the hand gestures Danny Dennis had taught her. Blossom obediently fell back to walk beside her.

Inch by inch, step by step, the woman and the dog crept into blackness. Prudence could hear nothing but her soft, hesitant footsteps, her own and Blossom's breathing. Wherever he'd disappeared to, the boy they were after had found refuge in silence. She couldn't tell whether he was hiding nearby or had scampered deep into the bowels of the building. Feeling her way along the wall with one hand stretched out in front of her, Prudence counted on Blossom to scent danger and alert her to it by a warning growl or low bark.

She almost cried out when her extended arm struck an obstacle. It was another iron door, though not as heavy or difficult to push open as the one leading to the street. Flakes of rust showered to the floor as Prudence felt for a handle. The door opened on corroded hinges, the scrape of unoiled metal against metal setting her teeth on edge. Was the noise loud enough to alert whoever was on the other side that someone was coming?

Her eyes gradually accustomed themselves to the dimness; what had at first seemed dark as pitch resolved into a grayness not unlike a heavy winter fog. When she looked down at the damp floor, she saw the shine of pooled water, smelled mold and the ripe rottenness of decay.

She hesitated, then nodded reassuringly to herself as Blossom's warm snout found her hand.

"All right, girl. Here we go," she whispered as a faraway flicker of candlelight shone briefly before being shielded from view. Not snuffed out or she would have smelled a puff of smoke as the burning wick was extinguished.

Blossom growled, but when Prudence glanced at her through the gloom, she saw the dog's ears had not flattened and her formidable fangs remained hidden. Not a warning then, not a precursor to attack. More a shared acknowledgment that what they were seeking lay not far ahead of them.

Prudence froze in place, waiting for the glimmer of candlelight to flare again, realizing as she bided her time that, like the first room through which she and Blossom had come, this larger storage space was also dimly illuminated in places by shafts of weak daylight. Small windows that looked as though they hadn't been opened in years were set at regular intervals immediately below the ceiling, their panes sooty with layers of dust and greasy smut.

When Prudence would have taken a step, Blossom placed herself in front of her human, blocking the way. Every muscle of the dog's body tensed, every sense directed toward the unknown with the concentration of a stalker careful not to disturb nearby prey. Prudence's hand stroked Blossom's head, and she felt rather than heard the answering swish of the feathery tail. *Not too much longer.*

When the candle flame danced before their eyes again, it was almost blindingly bright. Prudence could hear a whispery voice pleading with someone, though so faintly she could not make out the words.

There was no response. Just the lone murmur entreating a silent someone. Begging for some kind of acknowledgment?

With the singlemindedness of the expert tracker she was, Blossom moved directly toward the tiny blaze of yellow light. Not waiting for a command from Prudence, confident that her human would follow behind. She seemed to be communicating that neither of them was in any danger from the street child they'd tracked into the university's cellars.

A rustle of paper reached their ears and the rich odor of ham, cloves, and honey rose above the grimy damp. Someone had unwrapped the package of sandwiches Prudence had been too preoccupied to eat.

A sixth sense warned the boy he'd been found.

As Blossom and Prudence emerged from behind a wide cement column halfway down the room, he leaped to his feet and stood facing them, elbows bent in front of a skinny chest, hands fisted like a prizefighter's. Lit from below by a candle lantern, he cast fearsome shadows that danced above his head and climbed the wall behind him. But he was only an eleven- or twelve-year-old boy bravely confronting a menace he thought he'd safely eluded.

"We're not going to hurt you," Prudence said, her words echoing off the low ceiling, then losing themselves in the towering mass of moldering wooden desks, chairs, and bookcases. Crates of disintegrating leather-bound tomes.

An odor of unwashed human flesh and old blood underlay the smell of the sandwiches.

"Don't be afraid."

Eyes focused on the boy, determined not to react to the absurdity of his pugilistic stance, Prudence at first missed what had drawn Blossom's attention. Until the dog whined as if in pain.

A girl lay curled up on a crude pallet made from tufts of horsehair stuffing pulled from ripped chair cushions, her face so covered in dirt and dried black blood that it was difficult to make out her features. Long blond hair spilled over her shoulders down to a small waist below which a filthy, ripped skirt had been carefully arranged over her bare legs for modesty's sake. Like the boy, she was barefoot, her feet scarred with old wounds and scabbed with new injuries. Her fingers curled into the palms of her hands. Old and new purple and black bruises mottled the skin of her bare arms.

Blossom crouched beside her, yipping a high-pitched whine that sounded so like an attempt at speech that Prudence half expected the girl to open her eyes in response.

Nothing.

Neither the boy nor Prudence moved. Then, very gently, Blossom's tongue flicked over the girl's chin until a convulsive twitch of injured nerves jerked feebly through a tiny patch of white flesh.

Prudence dropped to her knees, two fingers of one hand searching the girl's wrist for a pulse. She felt the boy try to push her away, then Blossom heave herself upright. A moment later she heard a familiar warning growl; a weight that had fallen against her back was relieved, and she understood that Blossom was holding the boy at bay, allowing Prudence to examine the girl without interference.

"Wake up," she urged, letting go the wrist where a thready pulse skipped uncertainly. "Can you hear me? Wake up." Prudence raised one of the girl's eyelids, as she had seen his doctor do so often when Geoffrey lay unconscious, but she wasn't sure what she was looking for other than an absence of blood.

The girl's skin was hot to the touch in places, cold and clammy in others, as though her body fought its way alternately through freezing chills and burning fever.

Prudence shrugged off the light spring shawl she was wearing, covering the inadequately clothed girl who was stubbornly holding on to life despite what must have been a terrible beating. Looking up, she saw the boy's wide-eyed stare flit from her to Blossom, then back again. Frightened yet defiant. His fists had fallen to his sides, but they remained clenched, as though, given half a chance, he'd use them to pound his way back to the girl he'd been protecting. The unwrapped sandwiches lay at his feet atop the butcher paper.

"She's badly hurt." Prudence watched the boy's face for signs of comprehension and agreement. "I can help, if you like." She thought she caught a gleam of understanding in his dark brown eyes, but he neither nodded his head to acknowledge what she had said nor replied. She wondered if he spoke English, or if he was one of the flood of immigrants arriving daily in the city with nothing but willing hands and a desperate need to escape their homelands. She waited, then repeated what she had said in schoolgirl French, the only other language she could attempt to speak. "*Elle est gravement blessée.*" Still no sign that he understood.

Blossom whined again, and Prudence made up her mind. She didn't dare leave the girl alone in the basement with only the boy for company, and she wasn't sure he could be sent outside to ask for help. Blossom was her only resource.

"Go get Danny," she instructed the dog. "Fetch Danny."

For a brief moment Blossom seemed to hesitate. Then she nuzzled Prudence's hand, barked warningly at the boy, glanced one final time at the girl who lay on the floor beneath her human's shawl. A streak of red-gold flashed through the dimly lit basement, and she was gone.

"Now we wait," Prudence said to the boy, settling back onto her heels, reaching for the sandwiches. She held one out to him until he took it, then wrapped the other in the butcher paper and laid it within reach of the girl's hand to signal that no one would take it from her. "She'll be hungry when she wakes up," Prudence said conversationally, though privately she thought the injured jaw Blossom had been licking might be broken. The important thing was to keep talking until Danny Dennis arrived, keep talking so the sound of her voice would calm the boy and mesmerize him out of thoughts of flight.

"The dog's name is Blossom," she went on, holding the boy's eyes with her own. "She lives in a stable with a large white horse called Mr. Washington who pulls a hansom cab driven by my friend Danny Dennis. Danny is an Irishman. You'll like him. He's big and bluff and sometimes rough in his speech, but he's kind to animals and children. Blossom's young master lived on the streets, as I imagine you do also. He was very ill, so Danny took him in and nursed him until he died of a consumptive pneumonia. Blossom stayed on and sometimes she spends a night or two in my stables, but she always goes back to Danny and Mr. Washington."

Cradling her patient's head in her lap, Prudence stroked the thin, bruised arms as she talked, lightly touching the girl's forehead from time to time to check for fever. Sometimes the skin beneath her fingers seemed to burn; at other times it was as if the girl had died and her body begun to cool. She knew a victim of illness or physical abuse desperately needed liquids. On the doctor's instruction, Prudence had spooned beef broth, tea, and watered whiskey into Geoffrey's flaccid mouth for hours, every swallow a step toward recovery. But there was nothing she could give this sufferer. Prudence was one of the very few women in New York City who didn't carry a tiny bottle of laudanum in her reticule.

"Why don't you sit down here with me?" she asked the boy, smiling what she hoped was an unthreatening invitation to join the vigil at the girl's side. "She'll be able to see you better when she opens her eyes." *If she opens them.* Prudence moved the candle lantern closer; there was only a finger's width of stub left and no other source of light nearby. No light bulbs hung from the basement ceiling; the university's governors hadn't bothered to electrify the building's basement.

She tried to judge how long the candle would last and hoped Blossom would find Danny parked at his usual stand near Trinity Church. She counted off the blocks between the end of Wall Street and Washington Square. Not far. Not far at all.

But the wait stretched on interminably.

When Danny came, it was with a rush of heavy footsteps and Blossom's joyous barking to announce their arrival. Fresh spring air coursed through the stagnant basement; he'd left the door to the street flung wide, the one connecting the two basement rooms propped open.

"Now then, miss, what have we here?" Danny asked, his brogue deeper than usual at the sight of Miss Prudence MacKenzie crouched on a dirty cement floor with a badly injured young woman's head on her lap and a belligerent street boy scrambling to his feet beside her. "Calm down, lad. Blossom, see he doesn't try to do anything foolish."

Danny bent over Prudence, lifting the shawl from the body stretched out beneath its dubious warmth. "She's in a bad way, miss," he said. "But I've seen worse." He stretched the truth a bit because he read anguish on Prudence's face. "Not to worry. We'll soon have her where they'll be able to fix her up." Unless she died in his cab on the way to Bellevue. New York City's streets were crowded, sometimes nearly impassable. It would take precious time to carry this girl to the city's trauma hospital for the poor and indigent. Time she might not have.

"Not Bellevue, Danny," Prudence said, guessing that was where he assumed she wanted them to go. "She needs to be tended by a woman doctor." Prudence knew what damage an enraged sexual predator could inflict on a girl as young as this one. "I don't think she can be more than thirteen or fourteen years old." Her mind raced through a list of the charities to which she donated money or time. "There's a clinic for women down near Five Points. It's run by Quakers; the doctor in charge is a woman. I volunteer there occasionally."

"I know the one you mean, miss," Danny said, lifting the girl's light body in powerful arms that daily drove the city's largest white horse from one end of Manhattan to another and sometimes across the new bridge into Brooklyn. "Friends Refuge for the Sick Poor, it's called. I chop wood for their stoves sometimes." *And crack a few drunken heads when need be.*

"That's it," Prudence agreed, laying the shawl over the girl again. "We'll have to hurry."

"Understood, miss." Whistling to Blossom, Danny strode from the cellar, kicking aside or flattening debris beneath feet almost as large as his horse's.

The boy stood in fascinated, immobilized terror while the Irishman marched off with the injured girl in his arms. Prudence took him by a sleeve, and with Blossom nudging at his legs, tugged him along until he broke into a run when Danny momentarily disappeared from sight.

The May sun was blindingly bright after the darkness of the cellar. Prudence stumbled up the cement steps to the sidewalk, Blossom bounding along between her and the boy, snuffling encouragement when she faltered, diligently herding him toward the hansom cab pulled up next to the curb. Danny laid the girl's body across Prudence's lap, head resting against her rescuer's shoulder. Without being told, without a word of protest, the boy squeezed himself beside Prudence onto the cab's leather seat, hands twitching nervously beneath the woolen blanket Danny tucked in tightly around them.

Instead of leaping up to ride beside Danny as she usually did, Blossom pressed herself into the narrow space at their feet, head resting on the boy's knobby knees.

The fingers of one small, dirty hand crept out from under the blanket to twine themselves in red-gold fur.

"We're off," Danny shouted as he vaulted onto the driver's seat high above and behind them. "Hold on tight now."

Mr. Washington, who rarely needed more than a flick of the whip over his broad white back, took off at a steady trot toward the clinic where Quaker women devotedly cared for their less-fortunate sisters.

CHAPTER 3

The Friends Refuge for the Sick Poor occupied what had once been the luxurious upper-middle-class home of a New York fur wholesaler. Four stories of solid brick faced with pale gray granite had been repossessed by a pitiless creditor when the wholesaler went bust in the Panic of 1873. By the time a generous donor to Quaker humanitarian causes bought the building, it had deteriorated into a rundown shell of its former self.

"That's the only reason we were able to open the clinic here," Dr. Charity Sloan had told Prudence the first time she visited the Refuge. "We use most of the two lower floors for waiting, treatment, and operating rooms. The large parlor has become a dining hall to feed the hungry and the smaller sitting rooms are offices. The topmost floors we've turned into an overnight dormitory, convalescent ward, and sleeping quarters for the staff. The kitchen is in the basement."

Prudence had contributed a generous sum to the building's ongoing restoration, donning an apron twice a month to join other volunteer ladies who admired the work the Quakers did. One of them, she recalled as Danny maneuvered the cab through the congested Lower Manhattan streets, had expressed an interest in the Woman's Law Class.

Despite the weight of the unconscious girl lying across her lap, the press of the boy's body against her side, and the clop of Mr. Washington's shoes on the cobblestones, Prudence couldn't banish from her mind the dilemma of the decision she had to make. The closer the cab got to the Refuge, where she could safely hand over to Dr. Sloan's care the children she'd found in the University Building basement, the more she thought about the friendship that had developed during the hours she and Helen Gould had worked side by side assisting Dr. Sloan.

Now almost twenty-two, Helen was the eldest daughter of the notorious speculator and railroad magnate Jay Gould. Despite their immense wealth, the Goulds remained on the fringes of New York society, snubbed by the Vanderbilts and well outside the exclusive company of Mrs. Astor's Four Hundred. Helen busied herself with family obligations, the arts, education, and charities.

Prudence had liked the young heiress from the first time they'd met at the Refuge; she had a way of looking directly at you that was disarmingly honest. "Call me Nellie," she'd urged. "Everybody in the family does." But Prudence hadn't been able to think of the dignified, rather solemn young woman as anything but Helen. Now she wondered if her fellow volunteer might also have been approached by Edgar Carleton. The Goulds might not be welcome in the rarified ranks of high society, but Helen, intelligent and determined, had made no secret of her interest in the law. Once she found out that Prudence's late father had been a well-known judge, that was all she wanted to talk about.

The more Prudence contemplated talking to Helen Gould about the pros, cons, and consequences of the law school invitation, the more she warmed to the idea. They were nearly the same age, had both been well educated, and were beginning to distinguish themselves from their peers by living lives outside the narrow restrictions of society. And if Helen had considered seriously the idea of studying law, they had that in common, also.

Was it beyond the realm of speculation that she and Helen together might break down barriers against women in legal circles? Might they be among the first women to graduate from the Law School of New York University?

"We're here, miss," Danny Dennis shouted from his perch atop the hansom cab, pulling Mr. Washington to a halt in front of the Refuge. A cluster of women in tattered skirts and well-worn knitted shawls waited on the steps and sidewalk to be admitted to the clinic that never turned anyone away, day or night. They watched intently as Danny lifted the girl out of the cab and carried her toward the door, moving aside to let the newcomer pass before them into the doctor's waiting room. Like recognized like, though each of the victims of life on the streets or with a violent man preserved her distance.

"This way, Mr. Dennis," directed a thin woman dressed in the self-effacing gray favored by many Quakers. A voluminous white apron covered her from neck to hemline and a starched white kerchief hid most of her hair. "I've sent for Dr. Sloan. She's in the house somewhere, so it won't be long."

Prudence followed, one hand holding firmly onto the boy, the other reaching out to ensure that Blossom stayed by her side. It had been a long time since the stink of the animal's alley-way existence clung persistently to muck-encrusted fur; nowadays she carried the faint scent of fresh stable hay and her coat shone like a brilliant autumn sunset. Danny Dennis cared for her with as much devotion as he did Mr. Washington. But she was a very large dog and her presence could be intimidating.

"Rebecca, we'll need a basin of warm water, some clean towels, and a pair of scissors," Dr. Sloan announced from the door-way, nodding approval that her newest patient had already been stretched out on an examining table. "What have you brought me, Prudence?" she asked, stopping for a moment to kiss her friend lightly on both cheeks. She smiled at Danny Dennis, nudged Blossom affectionately with one knee, and laid a diagnostic hand on the boy's forehead. "I think we'll send you gentlemen to the kitchen with Blossom to look after you while we see to the young lady," she directed. "You know where it is, Danny. Tell Cook I said to feed all of you and make sure the boy drinks a glass of milk."

While Dr. Sloan examined the girl's bare feet and legs, Rebecca cut off the ragged skirt and torn bodice, finding neither petticoat nor undergarments. The body exposed to view was as black and blue as a prizefighter's after a bare-knuckle bout, the skin crusted over in places with old wounds that looked as though someone had scored her with a knife. The gridlike patterns reminded Prudence of the crosshatched hams served studded with cloves at Christmas and Easter. She'd never seen anything remotely like it on a human being.

"Where did you find her?" Dr. Sloan asked, running her fingers firmly but delicately over the girl's head, chest, belly, arms, and hands. "No broken bones that I can feel. It's hard to make out her features under all the dirt, but there doesn't appear to be anything but superficial dried blood on her face. I'll take a closer look after Rebecca has washed her."

"She was in the basement of University Building in Washington Square," Prudence explained. "The boy was hiding her there. Her skin felt burning hot when I touched it, then cold, as if she were in the throes of chills and fever."

"Unconscious?"

"The whole time. I spoke to her, but I don't think she was able to hear me."

"You may not want to remain while I finish what I have to do," Dr. Sloan said, hands poised in midair over the girl's lower torso. Her drawn, professionally composed face radiated sympathy and understanding.

"I think I need to know everything if I'm to help," Prudence said, but she took one step back from the table and tightened her throat against a surge of bile rushing up from her stomach. She'd never seen this type of examination done, but it couldn't be worse to watch than preparing a body for burial or looking at remains in the Bellevue morgue. Both of which she'd survived.

"She's been viciously violated," Dr. Sloan said, turning away from the table to wash her hands in the basin of soapy water Rebecca would use to cleanse the girl's body. The acrid smell of carbolic filled the air as the doctor shook droplets of the strong-smelling water off her hands and dried them. "More than once. It's probably useless to attempt to count how often. I could feel old scar tissue and new tears in both her orifices. Most of the brothels won't tolerate that kind of behavior from their clients, but there have always been rumors of private clubs that exist solely to meet every perverted lechery their members can dream up. I'm going to speculate that this girl was some monster's victim until she managed to escape to the streets. Then instead of shelter, she found more abuse. Sometimes the gangs of homeless children watch out for one another, but mostly they do whatever they have to in order to survive."

"They prey on each other?" Prudence asked incredulously.

"If that's what it takes. I've known twelve-year-old boys to pimp their sisters on street corners and in alleyways. Older or younger, it doesn't seem to matter. When the girls get pregnant or so diseased they can't work anymore, they bring them here to me. The more fortunate ones. It's no secret that abandoned children of all ages are left to fend for themselves. We shouldn't be surprised at what happens to them when nobody cares."

"I've seen Jacob Riis's photographs," Prudence said, "and he's worked with us on several cases. The illustrated article in *Scribner's Magazine* caused a sensation when it came out last December."

"People talked about almost nothing else," Dr. Sloan agreed. "And then they very conveniently forgot. So nothing much has been done. Sometimes I doubt it ever will be."

"How old do you think she is?"

Dr. Sloan leaned against the examining table to support her lower spine as she bent over her patient. Her back ached all the time now; someday she'd have to find the time to get a colleague to take a look at it. But the other Quaker doctor who donated her time to the Refuge rarely had a free moment either. "I'd say thirteen or fourteen. Possibly as old as fifteen. Her breasts are budding, but I doubt she's experienced the onset of her monthly bleeding. The thinner the girl, the later the menses. And this child is clearly half-starved."

"And the boy?" Prudence asked.

"Without an examination it's hard to tell. He's younger, probably by at least a year or two."

"Eleven or twelve perhaps?"

"That's as good an estimate as any," Dr. Sloan agreed. Hand once again supporting her stiff, tender back, she smiled at her helper.

"I'll see to washing her and finding a clean nightgown and a bed," Rebecca said. "You go on to the kitchen now and get thyself and Miss MacKenzie a cup of tea. There's nobody waiting who can't be seen to by a nurse."

"Tea solves everything, does it?" Dr. Sloan teased.

"It may not solve all our problems, but it makes the worst of them more bearable." Rebecca's affection for the doctor was genuine and long-standing.

"I want to take a look at the boy anyway," Dr. Sloan said, steering Prudence out of the treatment room, as if taking time away from patients to drink a cup of tea needed to be justified. She halted when they were halfway down the corridor, the door behind them shut and no one else in sight or within earshot. "I think the girl regained consciousness while I was examining her, Prudence. She was trying to hide it, but she seemed to be aware when I lifted her eyelids. Very dark brown eyes, almost black. Unusual coloring for a blonde. Something else." Charity Sloan hesitated. "I'll know for certain after Rebecca has washed her, but I have the impression that there are tattoos where the natural eyebrows should be."

"I didn't see that. Are you sure she came awake?"

"Patients try to conceal things from their doctors. Usually unsuccessfully. I've never understood why, but it's a fact of medical life."

"The boy hasn't spoken a word since Blossom and I first chased after him."

"You and Blossom?"

"He stole the sandwiches off the bench I was sitting on in Washington Square Park."

"And that's how you found yourself rummaging around in the basement of University Building?"

"Yes," Prudence said. "It's a bit more complicated than that, but you've got the gist of it right."

"Do I need to know why you were in Washington Square Park in the first place?" Dr. Sloan asked. Her diagnostic head-to-toe evaluative glance took only a moment to complete and left Prudence feeling studied to the bone.

"The university has voted to admit women to its law school," she said.

"About time."

"I agree."

"So will you be part of its first class?" Dr. Sloan went straight to the point.

"I don't know." It was on the tip of Prudence's tongue to mention *extenuating circumstances,* but she'd already used the phrase once recently, and now it suddenly seemed both weak and cowardly.

"How long do you have to make up your mind?"

"A week."

"Time enough for our girl to begin healing. And for both the children to decide whether they trust us enough to reveal who they are and what happened to them." Dr. Sloan chose her words carefully; the new science of studying the human mind and behavior was imprecise and controversial. "Fear can cause a temporary muteness in which the injured individual takes refuge as a kind of protection from the consequences of what he's done or what's been done to him," she explained. "You have to understand that it's not stubbornness or contrariness. Punishing the silent patient exacerbates the problem; it's not that he or she *won't* speak, it's that he or she *cannot*. Whatever cruelty the individual suffered has had severe effects that are both physical and of the mind. Medicine doesn't understand the phenomenon, but it can't deny its existence."

"Will they ever speak?" Prudence asked as she and Dr. Sloan resumed their walk through the clinic hallways and down to the kitchen.

"Eventually, when enough healing has taken place to lessen the fear. When some measure of trust is established between doctor and patient. Or victim and rescuer. My first piece of advice would be not to separate the boy and your dog."

"Blossom?"

"Danny's told me her story. She bonded to one waif of the street. I think it likely she's as capable of mending this broken boy as any physician. Perhaps more so, if I'm to be honest. It's something to consider, Prudence."

Danny greeted them with a broad smile and a wood box filled with freshly-cut kindling. There were chores around the Refuge that were easier for a strong man to do than for the ladies to accomplish. Not that they didn't try their hands at everything. It was just the way things were.

"He's had a bowl of porridge, half a loaf of bread with dripping, and two glasses of milk," Cook reported. She turned from the pots she was stirring to wave a wooden spoon in Blossom's direction. "A soup bone for the dog."

Blossom's tail thumped the bare wood floor. She grasped a well-chewed bone between her two front paws, waiting politely for the command to resume what she had been doing. When Prudence signaled permission, she lowered her head and got back to the business at hand. But quietly. Humans didn't like to be interrupted.

Cook set a fresh pot of tea and two more cups on the well-scrubbed worktable where she rolled out dough and sliced onions, potatoes, carrots, and cabbage for the potage that was the mainstay of every meal. Slices of plain yellow cake studded with raisins lay on a chipped dish. The Refuge accepted donations of everything and anything that could be useful.

Danny pulled out chairs for Dr. Sloan and Miss Prudence, seating them as stylishly as though they were in one of the city's finest restaurants instead of the basement of a free clinic that welcomed and treated abused women of the night. And their married but no less abused sisters.

The boy stared at the remains of his bread and dripping, one finger carefully gathering the sticky crumbs and conveying them to his mouth.

"How is she?" Danny asked, as much for the boy's sake as his because he'd carried the girl's slight weight in his arms.

"Better than might have been hoped for," Prudence answered.

"No broken bones," Dr. Sloan contributed. "A lot of bruising that will be painful as it heals, but there isn't any reason to believe she won't recover. In time and with care." She'd been speaking to Danny, but now she turned her attention to the boy, leaning forward to talk directly to him as she poured tea, stirred in milk and sugar. "Care the Refuge is more than willing to provide for as long as she needs it."

The expression on the boy's face didn't change, and he didn't look up from the plate he was studying, but Prudence thought she caught the flick of an eyelid and what might have been the beginning of a sigh of relief. When she raised her cup to her lips, she read in Charity's eyes the same conclusion. The boy understood English, at least enough to realize that the girl he'd gone to such lengths to protect had come to a place of safety.

Prudence wondered if his slight shoulders felt lighter for knowing he could put down some of the burden he'd been carrying. She reached a cautious hand across the table in his direction, and immediately pulled it back when he fisted his fingers and dropped them into his lap.

"Would you like to see her?" Prudence asked. "I'm sure Dr. Sloan will allow it."

Nothing. No sign he understood what she had said. He was playing it cautious, she decided. And perhaps rightly so. They were all strangers—she, Dr. Sloan, Danny, even the cook who had fed him. And it had to have been one or more strangers who had beaten and abused the girl who had by now been bathed, dressed in a soft nightgown, and tucked into a clean bed upstairs. What would he do next? Where would he go?

"Blossom and I will take this one back to the stable with us," Danny announced, as if he had read Prudence's mind. "I often sack down there myself. Mr. Washington's good company, the hay is soft, and the blankets get a thorough shaking out every time they're used." Blossom had once been nearly eaten alive by fleas and ticks, insects Danny couldn't abide and against which he waged continuous war. He often boasted that his stable was as clean as Mrs. Astor's parlor. "If that meets with your approval, Miss Prudence?"

"It does," she said, catching Dr. Sloan's pensive nod as she sipped her tea and contemplated the uncommunicative boy whose dumbness she'd assured Prudence was most likely temporary. "He'll need a bath, some fresh clothes, and a pair of sturdy boots."

"Mr. Josiah sends me the castoffs he collects for the street urchins and hasn't room to store in your office closet. There's bound to be something he can wear." Without actually touching it, Danny cupped a large hand over the boy's head, nodding toward Blossom. A few splintered chips lay scattered on the floor, all that was left of Cook's soup bone. When no one was looking, the boy had reached out to hold tightly to the dog's soft, red-gold fur.

"I'll take him upstairs to say good-bye before you go," Dr. Sloan offered. She stood, motioned to Blossom to follow her, and began to walk out of the kitchen.

The boy hesitated, but only for a moment. The last Prudence saw of him was a pair of stubbornly set shoulders, ragged britches, and dirty bare feet disappearing through the doorway.

"This is kind of you, Danny," she said.

"There but for the grace of God . . ." he answered.

CHAPTER 4

The Jay Gould mansion was at Fifth Avenue and Forty-seventh Street, more than twenty blocks north of the Fifth Avenue Hotel where Geoffrey Hunter occupied a luxurious suite.

As Prudence's hansom cab made its way uptown from the Friends Refuge near Five Points through the noisy congestion and traffic snarls of one of the city's busiest thoroughfares, she chided herself for putting off the conversation she knew she would have to have today with her partner. And wondered why she was so reluctant to tell him about Edgar Carleton's invitation to be among the city's first women law students.

It wasn't as though everyone hadn't known the moment would eventually arrive, especially since demands for admission had become more frequent as law schools around the country began to open their doors to female scholars. The University of the City of New York prided itself on staying ahead of its close rival, Columbia College, claiming a position in the vanguard of modernism as the twentieth century approached. Electricity and the telephone were already transforming everyday lives, and just recently a German named Benz had astounded the world with what he called the Benz Patent Motor-wagen, a self-propelled horseless carriage.

Why shouldn't social change for women, including the controversial and all-important vote, advance as rapidly as the inventions pouring out of scientific and engineering workshops all over the world? Prudence could feel barriers being breached all around her. It was an exciting time to be alive.

Two lanterns flanked the portico of what had once been the grand brownstone home of one of the city's former mayors, a mansion whose interior had taken a year to redecorate to Jay Gould's specifications. Prudence's friend was its mistress now; Helen's beloved mother had died a year and a half ago, leaving her eldest daughter to oversee both her father's comfort and the upbringing of the family's two youngest children.

The Friends Refuge didn't have a telephone yet; Prudence had decided on the ride uptown that Helen would just have to forgive her unannounced visit.

"I'm so glad to see you." Helen Gould, dressed in the suitably subdued mauve of second-year mourning, embraced her friend warmly, head cocked to one side like an inquisitive bird. "I'm sure what I heard about your being in the midst of a gun battle aboard a train on its way to Canada was a complete fabrication," she said. "Not even you could have become embroiled in anything like that!"

"Not a fabrication at all," Prudence assured her, as Helen led the way from a large reception parlor into the private, much smaller domain where she wrote letters and managed everything from the household's accounts to the children's lessons. "Not even an exaggeration."

"And Geoffrey?"

"Badly wounded, but recovering."

"I suppose what they say about Pinkertons applies to ex-

Pinks as well," Helen said, seating herself at her desk and motioning Prudence to a comfortably upholstered armchair.

"What is that?" Prudence asked. Geoffrey had told her more than once that Allan Pinkerton had taken great pride in crafting the agency's reputation for solving seemingly impossible cases by dogged persistence.

"Something about following a suspect to the far ends of the earth if necessary and never sleeping. It has to do with their logo, that huge eye staring out at you. Father says it's one of the best he's ever seen."

And Jay Gould should know, Prudence reflected. The Pinkerton National Detective Agency had earned much of its fame defending the profits of railroad magnates like Helen's father.

"I know that's not what you came to talk about," Helen said. "I read the announcement about the university governing board's decision in Tuesday's paper. Very small, and you could have missed it if you weren't reading carefully, but it was there in black and white. They can't change their minds."

"I didn't see it."

"One of the editors must have decided it was better to bury the item rather than have to deal with a flood of letters from readers frothing at the mouth about the impertinence of women," Helen explained.

"I'm being recruited," Prudence said bluntly. "I'm not sure how I feel about it."

Helen took a piece of embossed stationery from a desk drawer, uncapped a gold-nibbed fountain pen, and drew a vertical line down the center of the page. "*Pros* on one side, *cons* on the other," she announced, ever the intrepid organizer. "What does your partner say about losing you to lectures and lawbooks?"

"We haven't discussed it," Prudence confessed. "I haven't told him yet."

"Oh, Prudence." Helen laid down her pen. "That puts a different light on things."

"He's not fully recovered. We've closed down the office. Temporarily."

"You have to tell him."

"I know."

"I don't envy you the task," Helen mused. "But it must be done. The sooner the better. Certainly before he hears about it himself. Or that efficient secretary of yours tells him."

"What I really came for was to find out if you plan to apply. Or if someone has already contacted you," Prudence said.

Helen opened one of the small drawers of her French writing desk, took out an opened envelope, and handed it to Prudence.

"This is very flattering, Helen." Prudence scanned Edgar Carleton's short letter. "Have you answered him?"

"Not yet. I wanted to savor the thrill of it before I had to refuse."

"You know you'd take to the law like a duck to water. You've got one of the most analytical minds I've ever had the pleasure of arguing with."

"If this had come before we lost Mother, I would have jumped at it."

"Surely the children can spare you now." She couldn't remember the ages of Helen's younger sister and brother.

"Anna will be fifteen next month and Frank turns thirteen in December. They're growing up very quickly, Prudence, but it's not entirely because of them." Helen sat up straighter in her chair, clutching a lace-edged handkerchief in one hand. "Papa became noticeably frail during the Texas trip last month, though he claims he always feels better out west than here in New York. I spoke with Dr. Munn soon after their return. It's very bad, Prudence."

"I'm so sorry, Helen. I hadn't realized . . ." The financial world had been led to believe that Jay Gould had turned over the day-to-day management of most of his business affairs to his eldest son, George, in response to the illness and loss of his beloved wife. Followed by a particularly painful bout of dyspepsia. An ailment that was not uncommon amongst men of his age, but hardly a mortal affliction. Now, if Prudence interpreted *frail* correctly, Helen was hinting at a far more serious condition. And, she remembered, there had been rumors no one had been able to confirm. At least one reporter had speculated that Gould's weakened condition was due to consumption, the disease that had taken her mother when Prudence was a child of six.

"No one outside the family has been told. Father insists on his privacy. He especially doesn't want business competitors to find out. But I don't believe anyone who sees him on one of his bad days could remain in ignorance."

"Young as I was at the time my mother fell ill, I knew something was very wrong," Prudence said. Memories of Sarah MacKenzie's hollow-cheeked, flushed face sped through her mind. The invalid's cough. The brave smile. "If there's anything I can do . . . ?"

"I'll stay here at home with him and the children. Or at Lyndhurst. I imagine we'll be spending more time in Tarrytown. It's quiet. All you hear is birdsong. And the Hudson River up there isn't crowded with ships coming and going and jockeying for space at crowded docks." Helen smiled wistfully. "The city is changing, Prudence. Do you ever go out to your summer home on Staten Island just to get away from the throngs of people?"

"I was in Washington Square Park this morning for that very reason." She told Helen about the boy who had snatched up her packet of sandwiches, the girl she had rescued from the basement of University Building, the examination that had revealed so much misery and horror. "I cannot even imagine what she's been through," Prudence concluded. "It's beyond anything I've ever known."

"We're among the fortunate ones," Helen agreed. "Which is why we both volunteer at the Refuge. *From those to whom much is given, much is expected.*"

"I've always liked the Gospel of Saint Luke more than any of the others," Prudence said.

"I may not be able to spend as many hours with the Friends in the coming months as I would like. But I've told Dr. Sloan she can always count on me for anything she needs."

Helen's generosity was as quietly unobtrusive as her father's. Very few people knew that Jay Gould, vilified as a rapacious financial speculator in countless newspaper cartoons, had another side to him, a generosity seen only by his family and the needy to whom he opened his purse strings.

"I'm sure that's a great comfort. The women she treats are among the poorest in the city."

"You'll stay in touch, Prudence?"

"I will, Helen."

The two women clung briefly to one another.

Prudence found Geoffrey pacing steadily if slowly up and down the long, carpeted hallway outside his hotel suite, urged on whenever he flagged by the implacable Tyrus, whose last name was the same as that of the man whose family had once owned him.

"Mistuh Ned sent me on over," the octogenarian explained to an amused Prudence. "Said Mistuh Geoffrey need me more'n he did. Might be true. Mebbe not."

"I'm sure you're doing him a world of good," Prudence said, noting that despite the exhausted but grimly determined look on Geoffrey's face, he appeared stronger and steadier on his feet than yesterday. "I can take over if you'll stay to help him back into his rooms."

"He only got one more up and down to finish out," Tyrus said, waving a gnarled hand in Geoffrey's direction. "Ain't no point quittin' early. Just give you more to do the next day. You go set yourself down, Miss Prudence. I'll see to bringing him in when we're good 'n' done."

"I'll phone down for coffee," Prudence said.

Nobody ever attempted to argue with Tyrus.

"Has Josiah been by yet today?" Prudence asked over the strong, chicory-laced coffee Geoffrey preferred to all other blends and regularly ordered sent to the hotel's kitchens from New Orleans.

"Once this morning to bring the mail, then again a little while ago to reassure himself that Tyrus was here to harry me up and down the corridor." He wondered how long it would take his partner to beat around the conversational bush and reach the topic she was avoiding.

"We agreed that we wouldn't take on any new cases until you were ready to come back."

"You and Josiah agreed," Geoffrey corrected.

"I don't recall that you strongly objected."

"I haven't *strongly* done anything since February." How quickly they moved from polite nothings into verbal sparring these days. "I don't have much to occupy my time except read-ing the newspapers. I saw the article you haven't referred to. Don't you think it's time we talked about what it means, Pru-dence?"

"I've just come from visiting Helen Gould."

Geoffrey waited, determined not to make things too easy for her. The key to unlocking the secret places of Prudence's heart, he believed, was that she would eventually do it herself. She couldn't, and shouldn't, be forced into anything.

"We're both being recruited to join the first class to include women among its members. Beginning in September with the fall semester."

"Congratulations. But I'm not surprised. You're probably the only woman in New York City who could sit for the bar tomorrow and pass with flying colors. And Helen has supported the Woman's Law Class from the beginning. The governing board knows what it's doing. They can't afford a failure. Hence the recruitment effort."

"Helen won't be joining the class," Prudence said.

"So the rumors are true?" The first reporter to note a precipitous decline in the health and vigor of the financial world's favorite villain had launched a flood of speculation that had never entirely abated. "Is it what's been suspected?"

Consumption was considered a death sentence, despite the new medical innovation of mountain sanitoriums where patients were believed to breathe more easily. Reports of cures had been greeted with hopeful skepticism. There had been so many nostrums that promised to vanquish the disease. They'd all failed miserably. A few of the desperate had begun to flock to the Adirondacks where Dr. Edward Trudeau, himself a former sufferer, had opened a rest home at Saranac Lake. For everyone else, there was no hope at all.

"She's determined to remain at his side," Prudence confirmed. "She thinks the family will leave the city for Tarrytown whenever possible. And stay away longer."

"I'm sorry for Helen. She's the type of woman who bears more than her share of burdens without complaint," Geoffrey said. It was on the tip of his tongue to add that Prudence was another of that long-suffering and under-appreciated group, but the lift of her head told him that while she might accept a compliment on her friend's behalf, she wasn't in the mood to welcome one on her own. "But you're not in Helen's situation," he added firmly.

"No, I'm not," Prudence conceded. "However, something else has come up."

Geoffrey glanced at the correspondence lying on the desk where he had managed to put in an hour's work after Josiah's early-morning visit and before Tyrus pulled him away to hobble along the hotel's carpeted hallway. "I didn't see anything particularly urgent. At least nothing we couldn't in good conscience refer to another inquiry agency."

She told him the same story she'd recounted to Helen Gould. The stolen sandwiches, she and Blossom in pursuit of the thief, finding the abused girl. Mr. Washington's swift progress to the Refuge down near Five Points, Danny Dennis's offer to shelter the boy. Dr. Sloan's assessment of what her patient had suffered. The mutism that might or might not be temporary. She tried to explain the overwhelming sense of responsibility that had settled over her as Helen had explained what the approaching death of her father would mean to the life she had envisioned for herself. A weaker woman might be crushed by it. But not Helen. And if Helen could put her aspirations on hold because someone else needed her, what did that say to Prudence?

"I feel I have to do something," she finished.

"You already have," Geoffrey said. "You've taken the girl to a place where she can heal without being judged. That's more than most rescued women can hope for. And I can't think of anyone better qualified than Danny to mend a broken boy. Not to mention Blossom and Mr. Washington. What child wouldn't want to camp out in a stable with a huge horse and a dog that's almost as big as a small pony?" He smiled, and when the dark expression on Prudence's face lightened, chuckled softly. "I'm sure Josiah would agree with me."

Their secretary had a soft spot in his heart for the street urchins he and Danny employed as fleet-footed messengers and snoops.

"Except to open your purse, which I'm sure Helen will do also, your part in this little drama is over, Prudence." He set down his coffee cup, straightened the blanket Tyrus had tucked around his legs, and clasped his hands into stillness. It was not unlike the way Judge MacKenzie had waited for attorneys to argue their cases before his bench. "There's no reason why you can't accept Edgar Carleton's invitation."

"I don't want to be one of those women who passes the bar but never steps into a courtroom," Prudence blurted out. "That's what happens. One barrier is knocked down, but another takes its place. I won't be stuck behind a desk, writing briefs for someone else to deliver. The disappointment would be too great, Geoffrey." She paused for a moment, then met his eyes. "I get so tired of fighting for what is rightfully mine. And every other woman's." She looked away again. "But I don't expect you to understand that. No man can."

"I understand what it means to fight for something you believe in, Prudence. I lost a culture and a family because we differed fundamentally on the value of human life. The entire country is still suffering the effects of the war."

She took a folded piece of notepaper from her reticule. "Mr. Carleton wrote this after he came to see me. He sent something similar to Helen."

"Very persuasive," Geoffrey commented. "I think we should leave Helen out of this discussion. Her situation is not pertinent to yours. Do you agree?"

Prudence nodded. Geoffrey was a trained lawyer whose analysis of a case was not unlike the late Judge MacKenzie's approach. It was a structure in which the judge had nurtured his daughter from their earliest sessions in the library that had been a place of refuge for the motherless child and the lonely young woman into which she had grown.

"I've already debated the case with myself," she said, no longer bandying words with the man who never failed to magnetize and mystify her.

"And did you win?" Geoffrey asked. He dared not smile while he waited for her answer.

"Can we adjourn for the day?" Prudence asked. "I need to sleep on it."

"Closing arguments tomorrow?"

"Closing arguments tomorrow," she agreed.

And felt a wave of relief wash over her.

Whatever had been wrong between them had been set right. Wherever she went, she would not go alone.

Daylight came early in May. Prudence was still asleep when Danny Dennis pulled Mr. Washington to a halt in front of her Fifth Avenue mansion the next morning.

"Miss MacKenzie is not available to visitors," Ian Cameron protested when Danny demanded to see her. The cabby's vigorous pounding on the door had sent the maids scurrying and brought the butler as near to a run as he could manage. He'd served the MacKenzie family since before the judge's daughter had been born and he wasn't about to allow her to be disturbed, even by someone who was as near to being a member of the household staff as you could get without actually living in.

"She'll want to hear this, Mr. Cameron," Danny insisted. "You'll have to trust me."

"Cameron?" Prudence queried from the top of the staircase leading to the second floor. She'd thrown a silk dressing gown over her nightclothes and let the loose braid of her hair fall across one shoulder. She glimpsed Danny Dennis in the open doorway, and behind him, in the street, the hansom cab pulled by Mr. Washington, Blossom perched in the driver's seat. "What is it? What's happened?"

"He's gone, Miss Prudence. The boy disappeared during the night. I don't know how he managed it, but Blossom didn't wake me. She let him go."

"Dear God in Heaven," she breathed.

CHAPTER 5

Except for delivery drays and pallid-faced laborers hurrying to job sites as the sun rose over the city, New York's streets were empty. The pickpockets, pimps, and prostitutes who usually thronged alleyways and brothels below the exclusive Ladies' Mile district had completed another night's work and collapsed into their own or someone else's beds. Sober householders were not yet awake, though in the basement kitchens of their brownstones, cooks and servant girls stirred the fires, filled kettles with water, and sliced yesterday's bread for their breakfast. Here and there, white-uniformed street sweepers shoveled piles of garbage and debris into green wagons pulled by horses who moved slowly along the curbs and not infrequently foundered, lying there until they, too, could be hauled away.

This was not the bustling, wide-awake city where fortunes were made and lost on the opening and closing bells of the stock market, where millions in gold and specie lay accumulating interest in bank vaults, and where powerful men meeting in opulent rooms thick with cigar smoke and the aroma of imported French brandy hatched schemes to industrialize the country and crisscross it with railroad tracks.

Danny Dennis was driving Prudence into the heart of New York City's underbelly.

The Refuge steps were bare at that hour, but as Prudence descended from the hansom cab, she glanced down into the areaway where deliveries were made. Three young women lay heaped together like dirty laundry, arms flung over their faces, stockingless feet in broken leather shoes sticking out from under their skirts. Ragged snores told her they were not dead.

The Quaker woman named Rebecca answered her knock, a ring of large keys in one hand. She stepped onto the stoop, glanced at the clinic's early and still-unconscious clients, then ushered Prudence inside.

"Is the doctor expecting thee?" she asked, relocking the front door. Rebecca's clean gray dress, spotless white apron, and severely pulled back hair signaled that here was a woman who woke and set to work before anyone else in the house stirred.

"No, she isn't," Prudence said. "But I do need to speak to her. It's urgent."

When she reappeared a few moments later, Rebecca carried two cups of steaming hot coffee. One she gave to Prudence. "Thee will need something to warm the stomach," she said. "And so will Mr. Dennis. Dr. Sloan will be down as soon as she's able."

Soft footfalls on the uncarpeted stairs announced that the doctor was on her way.

"The boy disappeared from Danny's stable sometime during the night," Prudence explained to Charity Sloan. Like Rebecca, the doctor was immaculately if hastily turned out.

"When was the last time Danny checked on him?"

"Around midnight. He'd given the boy the cot he uses himself, but he found him curled up in the hay with his head on

Blossom's flank. He covered the two of them with a blanket, then went off to sleep in the tack room. The stable was still quiet when he woke up. Neither the dog nor any of the horses made a sound when the boy left, though he couldn't have sneaked out without attracting their attention."

"He doesn't want to be found," Dr. Sloan said thoughtfully. "Patients who could barely walk have gotten out of their beds here in the middle of the night and slipped away into the darkness because they were afraid the men who had beaten them would guess where they'd taken shelter."

"He was definitely hiding when he stole my sandwiches," Prudence said.

"Even if he's mortally afraid of someone, he may try to find a way to contact the girl we know he's been protecting."

"I've wondered if they might be brother and sister. Is that possible, judging from what you've seen of them?"

"I wouldn't rule it out. Their coloring is distinctive and similar," Dr. Sloan said. "But it's only speculation unless or until one of the children confirms it. Shall we go upstairs and see if our girl is awake and able to talk?"

"Will you tell her the boy's vanished?"

"Not yet. I won't lie, but I think it's enough right now to say that he slept in a stable last night, in the care of a hansom driver who's well-known around the city for helping out stray children."

"And if she asks a direct question about him?"

"Then we'll have to tell her the truth." Dr. Sloan gathered her long skirt into one hand for the climb to the third-floor wards. "Don't be too disappointed if she won't talk, Prudence. With the kind of trauma she suffered, it's a wonder she's still alive."

"But you said no broken bones."

"Other things kill us in addition to physical wounds. People die when there's not a mark on them." One of the most difficult things she had to do was close the eyes of a patient who should not have expired. Too many of the women she treated couldn't bear the hopelessness of life for another day.

"They share the same dark brown eyes," Dr. Sloan considered as they made their way upstairs. "Very large, very expressive. I would almost say Italian, except that the facial features and the very pale skin are not what I've come to expect from that group." Immigrant women of many nationalities made their way to the Refuge, but lately there had been a larger than usual influx of southern Europeans.

"I tried my not-very-expert French on them," Prudence said. "No response. Mademoiselle would have been horrified at how much I've forgotten over the years. She was something of a tyrant in her day. I suppose all governesses are."

"We have only a very few private cubicles," Dr. Sloan explained as she led Prudence past the larger of the two wards into which the third floor had been divided. "Otherwise it's curtains to pull around the beds of the dying to give them a semblance of privacy. Rebecca put her in the cubicle where she sometimes sleeps herself when a patient needs to be checked every few hours."

Eight iron bedsteads lined the walls of the room, four to a side, a narrow central aisle separating them. The air had the heavy fug of overcrowded sleeping quarters. The room's single window had been tightly shut against the night air, a dark curtain drawn over it to block light from flaring torches outside the street's brothels and saloons. Every bed was occupied. Some evenings the Refuge resorted to pallets on the floor. Usually when pay packets meant the men's fists were as unbridled as their thirst.

Dr. Sloan nodded toward the white drapes at the far end of the room. Prudence followed her across the spotless floor, wondering if it was the indefatigable Rebecca who ensured that cleanliness was indeed next to godliness in this house of charity.

A still form lay beneath a blanket pulled up over her head as if to block out the restless moans and weeping of the room's other occupants. Too still and not quite bulky enough to be altogether convincing.

The doctor didn't hesitate. She'd snatched back the coverlet before Prudence realized what she suspected.

"Gone." The bed lay empty before them, the sheets holding a fading imprint of the girl's slight body. Dr. Sloan's voice was as flat as the look on her face. "The boy you think may be her brother probably came straight here from Danny's stable. I'm sorry, Prudence, but I'm not surprised."

"How could this happen?"

"My guess is that we'll find the basement door has been jimmied. I had a new, stronger lock installed the last time there was a break-in attempt, but the reality is that you can't keep out someone who's determined to get past your defenses. They always find a way. We've thought about keeping a dog on the premises. At least we'd have warning that our security was being breached. And we'd buy time for whoever is in danger of being attacked to get away. Though that wasn't the case here."

Dr. Sloan's hands fisted over her lower back, as if she were in pain. Prudence thought her voice sounded vaguely slurred. Laudanum?

"Are you all right, Charity?"

"Just tired. I never seem to get enough sleep." The hands fell away. Dr. Sloan straightened the afflicted back and smiled reassuringly at a nightgowned figure clambering unsteadily from one of the beds. "Did you hear anything during the night, Elsie?" she asked. "Did anyone come into the room who had no business being here?"

"Just a boy, Doctor. He and the girl crept out together quiet as a pair of mice. But a mother always hears when children get up in the night, don't she?"

The patient tottered toward the hallway, at the end of which was a newly installed water closet. Some patients, put off by the noise and rush of the flushing water, preferred to squat over more familiar chamber pots.

"Elsie had seven children," Dr. Sloan volunteered. "All dead now. She drinks to forget. Sells the only thing she's got left for the price of a glass of gin. She was a good wife and mother while she could be, but the heart went out of her when the last child died."

"Her husband?"

"Gone. Or dead. She doesn't know. But if she heard the boy come for the girl last night, then we can be sure that's what happened."

"I wonder why she didn't try to stop them," Prudence asked.

"They don't interfere in one another's lives down here," Dr. Sloan explained. "It's something people learn very early on. You make your choices and you pay the price. Without complaint, for the most part. Every day can be harder than the one before or the one after, so you focus on the present because the past is too much to bear and the future is anything but certain."

Elsie came back into the dormitory, climbed into her cot, and pulled the covers up.

"Is there anything else you can tell us?" Prudence asked softly. She walked to the woman's bed, a shiny coin on her outstretched palm. Laid it on the pillow.

A work-roughened hand with broken fingernails snatched the coin out of sight. Two bruised and blackened eyes peered up at Prudence.

"There ain't nothing more to tell. In he come and out they go. Not a word said between them. I reckon she knew he'd be here 'cause she weren't sleeping. She was up on her feet before he did more'n reach out and touch her shoulder. Miss Rebecca'd laid out clothes for the morning for her; she already had 'em on. Don't know where she put the nightgown."

"Thank you, Elsie." Prudence placed a second coin on the

pillow. It, too, disappeared in the blink of an eye. She'd given the woman enough for at least a week's decent lodging, but whether she spent it on a room or bottles of gin wasn't something Prudence could or would dictate. Charity shouldn't have strings.

"I'm surprised Tyrus isn't here," Prudence said. She'd interrupted Geoffrey at his breakfast and was now nibbling on toast and drinking coffee while waiting for a waiter to bring up the eggs and bacon he'd insisted on ordering for her.

"He's due after lunch today. Ned is apparently scheduled for a boxing session this morning. I don't envy the poor fellow. Tyrus will have him bobbing up and down and doing short jabs with the gloves until he's splashing through puddles of his own sweat."

"What a horrible thought." Prudence spread more butter on her toast. "But I suppose it's all for the good if it keeps him sober and clean. He says he swore off the whiskey and cocaine at his last birthday."

"I would have, too, if I'd celebrated half as hard as I heard he did. Tyrus threatened to use a stomach pump on him." Geoffrey poured more coffee and swiped the last bit of egg yolk off his plate. "What do you intend to do about your vanished children?"

"I'm not sure there's anything I can do. I wouldn't know where to begin to look for them. Dr. Sloan had only the usual suggestions. Leave descriptions at a police station in the area. And the morgue. Put advertisements in the newspapers offering a reward for information that leads to finding them. Danny has already spread the word via his sweepers. They've run away from something or someone, and they're desperate not to be found."

"Who's that, Miss Prudence?" Josiah put away the key he'd used to let himself into the suite. He stacked the morning papers and put a white cardboard bakery box on the table.

"Crullers," he said, cutting the string with a flourish of his pocketknife. Josiah had been known to detour blocks out of his way for the right bakery.

"You weren't here yesterday when I told Mr. Hunter what happened to me in Washington Square," Prudence said. She reached for a cruller. "Geoffrey, you explain it."

When Geoffrey had finished and returned to his coffee, Josiah thumbed through one of the newspapers he'd brought, then folded it into a small square. "Look at this." He pointed to an article whose headline screamed DO YOU RECOGNIZE THIS BOY? And in slightly smaller print below, *The City Asylum for Orphan Boys and Foundlings wants to know.*

"What is it, Josiah?" Prudence asked.

"I heard one of the newsboys calling it out," Josiah explained. "So I scanned the article on my way here. The Asylum staff found a dead body on their stoop early this morning when someone opened the front door to bring in the milk bottles. A boy of about twelve or thirteen years old. Described as a street urchin. Blond hair, dark brown eyes. Nothing on him to suggest a name or nationality. That sounds a bit like the boy you were talking about, Mr. Hunter. At least the blond hair and brown eyes are a match."

Prudence choked on her cruller. When Josiah finally stopped pounding on her back, she waved her hands at him for the newspaper, read the article for herself, then passed it to Geoffrey.

"You can't go to the Asylum alone, Prudence," he said firmly, knowing that was what she was planning to do. "It's even closer to Five Points than the Refuge."

"I'll go with you, Miss Prudence," Josiah volunteered. "Danny can drive us."

"We need him on the streets. This may not be our boy. And the article doesn't say anything about a girl, so she's still missing. No, not Danny. I'll telephone Cameron to have Kincaid drive us in my carriage," Prudence decided, picking up Geoffrey's desk phone from a nearby table.

"I may need some help, Josiah," Geoffrey said quietly, getting to his feet with the aid of his new cane. He wore trousers and a dress shirt beneath his chamber robe, but slippers on his feet instead of shoes.

"Do you think this is wise, sir?" Josiah asked.

Prudence had turned her back on them to place her call. Telephoning was still an iffy proposition; voices faded in and out and strong crackling noises raced up and down the line like the squawks of angry chickens. She cupped one hand over the mouthpiece the better to concentrate on making herself understood.

"There's room in Miss Prudence's carriage for all of us. Tyrus has me walking almost as well as I did before the shooting. And I'm tired of being treated like an invalid. It's long past time I got back out into the world. It doesn't hurt to have an extra man along in the Five Points."

"Miss Prudence won't like it."

"I don't intend to ask her permission, Josiah."

"I didn't think you would, Mr. Hunter. The idea never crossed my mind."

CHAPTER 6

The body found on the front stoop of the City Asylum for Orphan Boys and Foundlings had been washed, wrapped in a shroud that left the head exposed, and placed in a pine box with a hinged bottom so it could be used again. The boy lay with hands folded across his chest, eyelids stitched closed, mouth also stitched but fallen slightly ajar to reveal mottled brown teeth. Balls of cotton saturated with camphor oil had been placed beneath the neck, elbows, knees, and feet. May was proving to be warm this year.

"We've come in response to this article," Josiah explained to the attendant who ushered them into an uncarpeted parlor just large enough to accommodate the coffin and a few wooden chairs. He held out the newspaper folded open to the headline that had caught his eye.

"We're hoping the young man can be named and returned to his family for burial," Victor Bayliss said, making way for them to stand beside the open box.

Prudence held a scented handkerchief to her nose to mask the pungent smell of camphor and a hint of decay.

One hand leaning heavily on the carved head of his cane,

Geoffrey reached out to his partner with the other. Brave though Prudence was, and stoic though she attempted to be, he knew that the sight of a dead body never failed to unsettle her.

The boy's hair had been washed and combed to a bright, golden sheen. A scattered yellow glow of fine stubble on cheeks and chin indicated the beginnings of what would have been a beard had he lived to grow into full manhood. He was a handsome fellow, or had been at one time in his life. Now he was a shell devoid of vitality, barely a memory of what had been forever lost.

Prudence used a gloved finger to pull the rough canvas shroud down far enough to reveal the once-gaping slit that policemen called a victim's second smile. Like the eyes and mouth, it had been sewn closed with thick black thread.

"He didn't suffer long," she remarked.

Victor Bayliss coughed, and when Josiah looked at him, shook his head. Whatever injuries to the body lay hidden beneath the shroud were unfit to discuss in the presence of the gentler sex.

"It's not him." Prudence raised her eyes to meet Geoffrey's, an unmistakable look of relief on her face. She lowered her voice to a near whisper. "This is not the boy Danny and I brought to the Refuge. He looks a great deal like him; in fact, I'd almost venture they were brothers or cousins, but he's not the one."

"Do you still have the clothing in which he was found?" Geoffrey asked. He handed a Hunter and MacKenzie, Investigative Law business card to the attendant.

"Is someone looking for him?" Bayliss ran an appreciative finger over the expensive embossed lettering, then tucked the card into a waistcoat pocket.

"The clothing?" Geoffrey repeated, ignoring the question.

"We'll wash and repair the pants and jacket for another boy to use," Bayliss said stiffly.

Geoffrey slipped the man a coin. "I'll buy them from you." He didn't explain why he wanted the clothes or volunteer that the boy might have something to do with a case under investigation. Let the attendant draw whatever conclusions he wanted. As long as they got what they needed.

Taking Prudence by the elbow, Geoffrey escorted her out of the stuffy little space with its dead occupant. Josiah cast a last, lingering look at the body, then followed close behind. Victor Bayliss shut and locked the room after them.

"I wonder if you'd be kind enough to give us a tour of the Asylum?" Prudence asked, turning away from the front door. On her gloved hand rested two five-dollar gold eagle coins. Uncommonly generous for so casual a gift. "Perhaps the boys would enjoy a treat. Children have a sweet tooth, don't they?" She turned to Josiah. "Could we add the Orphan Boys and Foundlings to our charities?"

"I'll make a note of it, miss," Josiah said, silently applauding the ruse. Without actually stating it, she'd managed to imply that she was a wealthy socialite who might be persuaded to add the Asylum to the list of worthy institutions her family was prepared to support. And if the attendant inferred from her name that a father or brother was the MacKenzie on the firm's business card, so much the better. Not everyone read the society columns.

"Do you have a courtyard where I can sit down for a few minutes?" Geoffrey inquired, leaning heavily on his cane. "I'd prefer that to a tour."

"Would the visitors' parlor do, sir?" Victor Bayliss asked. "I'm afraid the outdoor spaces are likely to be noisy right now. We send our boys into the fresh air twice a day for their good health." He beamed proudly at this proof of enlightened concern for the well-being of the abandoned children in his care.

"I don't mind the noise," Geoffrey said, "and I definitely prefer a garden to a parlor."

"One of our older boys will escort you," Bayliss conceded,

returning his attention to the young woman whose patronage he was determined to secure.

"I'll join you on the tour," Josiah declared. One of his self-assigned duties was to look out for Miss Prudence whenever possible. She had a way of getting herself into trouble that worried him. This visit to the Asylum wasn't yet a case, per se, but unless he was mistaken, it was headed in that direction.

What Prudence would always remember from her tour of the City Asylum for Orphan Boys and Foundlings was the dreary gray and brown austerity of the place and the sound of footsteps echoing through cavernous rooms devoid of any but the crudest wooden bedsteads, tables, and chairs. Windows were few, uncovered by curtains or drapes, but letting in very little light, the panes coated with a tarlike residue from the coal fires used for heating and cooking. The air grew thicker and harder to breathe the more deeply they penetrated into the building. She smelled boiled cabbage and full slop jars, the sweat of unwashed young male bodies, and the stench of despair.

"This is the schoolroom where the younger boys learn their letters." Victor Bayliss ushered them through rows of splintery desks and benches. A slate blackboard stood at the front of the room, and a schoolmaster's large desk shared a dais with a three-legged stool on which rested a dunce's hat and a leather riding crop.

"No books?" commented Josiah, eyes darting around the soul-destroying space.

"We reserve those for our older boys," Bayliss said. "The younger ones learn by rote. It sharpens the memory."

"How can they form their letters without paper, pen, and ink?" Prudence asked, nodding toward the empty inkwells and the lack of anything to write with or on.

"We start them off with small slates and chalk." The attendant pointed to a pile of crudely cut slates stacked in a corner.

"I'd like to see where they sleep," Josiah said.

"It's quite a climb to the top of the house," Bayliss protested.

"Dormitories are important." Prudence chimed in. "Children who don't sleep well seldom thrive." She had no idea if that were true or not, but it seemed logical. "I hope each of your boys is able to occupy a bed to himself?"

"We find the smaller children do better two or three to a bed," Bayliss said, obviously not pleased to be questioned.

"I suppose it reminds them of when they lived *en famille.*" Prudence smiled encouragingly at him, as if she knew about living conditions in the crowded tenements from which most of the orphans and foundlings came.

"Exactly." Slightly mollified by her apparent approval, Victor Bayliss led the way to where ranks of narrow beds were lined up side by side in what had once been attic storerooms.

As they passed one of the less filthy windows at a turn of the staircase, Prudence glanced out into the courtyard below where a tangle of boys was surging back and forth kicking a rag ball in a fiercely competitive game that had them shouting and flailing furiously at one another as they ran.

To one side, beneath the only tree in the yard, Geoffrey sat talking to two older boys, both hands propped on his cane, an intent expression on his face.

"How many youngsters do you have in the Asylum?" Prudence asked before their guide could catch a glimpse of her partner and wonder what he was being told that provoked that look of determined purpose on his face.

Josiah edged closer to the wall, effectively blocking the window until Victor Bayliss had passed. He and Miss Prudence always worked well as a team.

"He ain't the first one they found like that," the sixteen-year-old redhead named Neil was saying. He'd already explained to Geoffrey that the only reason he was still at the

Asylum was because he was good at settling down the littlest newcomers. He was hoping to be kept on as a helper for a few months longer, until the feeler he had out to a nearby brothel brought him a solid offer of bed and board and a few coins for running errands. The madam, he confided, was either a cousin or his mother. He wasn't sure which, and she wouldn't say.

"The thing is, this one and the other boy looked about the same," Neil's fifteen-year-old companion contributed. Clearly of mixed parentage, Willie couldn't wait to be set free from the Asylum where all he'd ever known was sneers and ill treatment. He'd been left there in a basket and grown up without an inkling of who or what he was. "Both yellow-haired with real dark brown eyes. You don't see that much. The Swedes got mostly blue eyes." He drew a finger across his throat. "Sliced hard and deep where it counts."

"How many have there been?" Geoffrey asked. He had a fistful of nickels, and each time he asked a question, he dropped one into an outstretched hand.

"Just the two," Neil said.

Willie nodded agreement.

"When was the first boy found?" Clink. Another nickel.

"Three days ago. The staff is spooked about it. They're afraid the Asylum will get a reputation worse than it already has." Willie tore off a small piece of the ragged shirt he was wearing and rolled the nickel into the worn fabric. "Can't have it making a noise," he explained. "Not if I want to keep it."

"Kids are always dying around here," Neil contributed.

"The first one was all twisted up, legs and arms every which-away," Willie said, rolling his hands around each other. "Looked to me like he tried to crawl away down the sidewalk. Didn't make it."

"Some of his bones were broken," Neil added. "I could tell by the way the arms and legs hung all floppy when we picked him up."

"We're the two oldest boys here now, so we got to bring the

bodies in off the street. Mr. Bayliss wouldn't wait for the coppers to come. Said it made the Asylum look bad to have dead kids lying around outside." Willie shook his head and made a puffing noise with his lips.

"What does it mean, Mr. Hunter?" Neil asked.

"What do you think it means?" Geoffrey said.

Neil shrugged. "I don't got blond hair and brown eyes."

"Me neither." Willie studied the coffee-colored surface of his skinny forearm.

"What it means is somebody's looking for a kid he's got to kill," Neil said thoughtfully. "Maybe he's been paid, but he hasn't found the right one yet. So he's gonna keep on trying."

"The kid ratted somebody out or poached in the wrong territory," Willie speculated.

"No good," Neil argued. "Whoever's killing blondies around here don't know who he's looking for. He's working off a description and hoping for the best."

"Why kill them at the Asylum?" Geoffrey asked.

"You can get a meal at the back door most of the time," Neil explained. "Not from Mr. Bayliss; he's as mean and stingy as they come. But Cookie carries a bible in his apron pocket and he's always talking about helping your neighbor and reaping what you sow. Stuff like that. He's the one who gives out the food, when there's anything left."

"Our Cookie ain't the only one," Willie explained. "Pretty much all the street kids know where to go when they need a handout."

"Mr. Bayliss don't know about it. He'd put a stop to it otherwise."

"So homeless boys who haven't managed to earn enough for a meal that day might come by the Asylum after dark in case food is being distributed?"

"That's it," Neil confirmed. "Sometimes there's five or six of 'em hiding in the shadows. Waiting."

"Which means that someone looking for a boy down on his

luck and desperate would know to hang out nearby and wait for him to show up?" asked Geoffrey.

"That's what I'd do," Neil answered. "Sometimes the restaurants give out slops in their back alleys, but you can't count on 'em like you can the Asylum."

A bell clanged at the far end of the courtyard. With one final kick of the ball, the boys began pushing and shoving their way into two lines.

"Got to go now," Willie said. "Mr. Bayliss locks you up in a cage in the cellar if you're late getting back inside."

"With the rats," Neil added. He, too, had wrapped bits of cloth around the coins Geoffrey had given him. "Much obliged," he said, one forefinger tugging at a lock of red hair.

"Stay safe," Geoffrey murmured.

The boys had already hustled away and didn't hear him.

"What made you so certain the dead boy wasn't the one gone missing from Danny's stable?" Geoffrey asked. They'd climbed back into Prudence's carriage and given instructions to Kincaid to take them to Wall Street, to the office Geoffrey hadn't visited since the mid-February shooting that nearly took his life.

"Information I decided not to share with our Mr. Victor Bayliss. There's something about the man that grates on my nerves," Prudence said.

"I've known his type," Josiah commented. "Full of the milk of human kindness. As long as anyone he deems important or influential is around to praise him. A monster to the children he secretly hates and terrorizes."

"Willie let slip that he locks them in a cage in the basement for misbehavior as slight as being late," Geoffrey said. "The other boy, Neil, said there are rats down there."

"Rats nibble on your toes and your earlobes while you're asleep," Josiah said quietly. "If you're lucky, you wake up before too much damage is done." He couldn't repress a shudder.

"The boy from Washington Square has two very badly bent fingers on his left hand," Prudence said, holding her own hand out to demonstrate. "Dr. Sloan believes they were broken and never set properly. Which means it wasn't just the girl who was abused." Prudence lowered her left hand, covering it with the right. "If he really is frightened for his life and the girl's, and if two other boys have been killed because they were mistaken for him, then no one should know about the crooked fingers. They might be the only certain way to identify him."

"Could he move them?" Geoffrey asked.

"I'm not sure," Prudence answered. "Dr. Sloan didn't have the chance to give him a thorough physical examination. Everything happened so quickly."

"He appears to be older than you first thought him to be," Geoffrey said. "If the boy who was just killed is any indication."

"Dr. Sloan thought the girl might be thirteen or fourteen, even as old as fifteen, and the boy perhaps as young as eleven. He's small for his age."

"Which may be working in his favor," their secretary contributed. He was an undersized man himself, compact and light on his feet, but always so impeccably dressed and dignified in his bearing that lack of height was not what people remembered about Josiah Gregory.

"The killer who's stalking him clearly isn't working from a photograph," Geoffrey said. "A boy from a well-off family would have had his picture taken. That tells us something about his background."

"But why is the boy being pursued and not the girl? That doesn't make sense," Prudence said.

"Any number of reasons," Geoffrey answered.

Josiah pulled out the stenographer's notebook that was as much a part of him as the brightly embroidered waistcoats he wore beneath his dark suit jackets.

"The most obvious one is that the killer or whoever hired him believes the boy will lead him to the girl, and that he should be easier to find than she," Geoffrey began.

"Or perhaps he believes she's already dead and the boy has information that could lead the police to crack the case," Prudence theorized.

"I doubt there's any kind of ongoing investigation," Geoffrey said. "Even Neil and Willie said that street kids disappear or get killed all the time. Nobody cares once the bodies are out of sight."

"Then how do we go about finding him?" Josiah asked, jotting down notes in the shorthand scribble only he would be able to read and transcribe. His smooth-shaven cheeks flushed bright red when Prudence and Geoffrey both turned to look at him. Josiah occasionally forgot that while he was more than an employee, he was something less than a full-fledged investigative colleague.

"The boy doesn't hold the key to whatever's going on," Prudence declared. "It may appear so because he's the one we believe is being targeted. But that's deceptive reasoning."

"Explain, please," Geoffrey prodded.

"It's the girl who's really the core of the puzzle. Find out what was done to her, and by whom, and all of the rest of the pieces will fall into place. The boy is incidental to the story."

"No one is incidental to his own life," Josiah whispered, unable to keep quiet but hoping neither Miss Prudence nor Mr. Hunter had heard him.

"We'll find both of them," Prudence promised. She laid a hand briefly and very lightly on Josiah's sleeve, remembering at the last moment that he didn't like to be touched. "And save them, if we can. We have to hope it's not too late."

Geoffrey thumped his cane on the carriage's front panel to signal Kincaid to pick up the pace. If he could.

The New York City streets were as frustrating a mélange of urgency and hurdles to overcome as he suspected solving the disappearance of two damaged young people was likely to prove.

He wondered what Tyrus would say when he arrived for the afternoon's exercise session and found the hotel suite empty and his patient flown the coop.

CHAPTER 7

"Did you have a hard time persuading him?" Geoffrey asked as Prudence's carriage rumbled across the Brooklyn Bridge on its way to Long Island and Jacob Riis's home in Richmond Hill.

"It was surprisingly easy," Prudence answered. "I think my telegram caught him off guard. I sent it yesterday evening with instructions for the delivery boy to wait for a reply. So he had to send an answer."

"Did you remind him that today was Sunday?"

"I did. I wrote that since I assumed he would not be working on the Lord's Day, I hoped he would allow me a short visit."

"But you didn't tell him why?"

"Of course not."

"You're becoming more devious with every case, Prudence."

"I've learned from a master."

"Touché. I'll take that as a compliment." His face paled and his lips tightened as the carriage jolted over the rough descent from the bridge.

"You didn't have to come, Geoffrey," Prudence said. Every time he winced, it sent a pang of anxiety through her. "You need rest, and this is a long shot. We may be making the trip for nothing."

"I think it's the best chance we have of locating your two missing children without traipsing through every alley on the Lower East Side. And less dangerous." He stretched out the leg that was refusing to heal. The only time the bullet lodged in bone didn't throb was when he was asleep and couldn't feel it. "Are you sure Jacob is keeping the photographic plates at his home?"

"Russell Coughlin swears that's where he stores whatever isn't specifically contracted for by the *Herald*. Apparently Riis's article in the Christmas edition of *Scribner's* got him a book contract. He's been putting in longer hours than usual writing it and choosing the illustrations. Russell said he asked where he stored the glass plates he prints from. Jacob laughed and told him he'd filled up his cellar and attic with them and just hoped the ceilings in his house didn't cave in from the weight."

"Why doesn't he print out the photographs and get rid of the plates?"

"He has photographs, too," Prudence said. "Hundreds of them, according to Russell. Maybe thousands. Reporters never throw anything away because they all dream of writing a book someday. Russell may not stay at the *Herald* much longer. He says Riis is already talking about leaving, too."

"He sees himself as more a social reformer than a reporter."

"He does. I'm sure of it. He only took up photography after he was assigned to the police beat because he couldn't get any-one else to go with him into the slums at night. He nearly set himself on fire with that magnesium flash until he figured out what he was doing."

"I won't say he's not good at it," Geoffrey decided. "But he has an accidental eye. He tries to catch whatever his subjects are doing when the magnesium flames up. And he's the first one to tell you he can't always time the flare. His photographs may be more powerful for being unposed."

"All I hope is that he'll allow us to look through the prints and plates he's taken of street children."

"Going back how far?"

"A month? I'm guessing the children we're looking for haven't been out on the streets much longer than that."

It might turn out to be a very long afternoon, but while Geoffrey didn't believe half of what newspapers printed, he agreed that no one could quarrel with a photograph.

Elisabeth Riis served strong Danish coffee and buttery cookies that crumbled on the plate and melted in the mouth. The mother of two living sons and two daughters between the ages of thirteen and nearly three, she had created the kind of comfortable home that was a refuge to her husband. Obsessed by what he saw daily on the streets and in the tenements of New York City, Jacob fled to Richmond Hill for rejuvenation. And never ceased to find it in the laughter of his children and the calm, supportive love of his wife.

"Jacob's photographs and plates are not organized," she told Geoffrey and Prudence, shaking her head in despair at her husband's lack of method in cataloging the images he prized.

"I know where everything is," Jacob Riis argued. "I can lay my hands on whatever you ask for." He smiled at Elisabeth. "Eventually."

"The children need me, so I'm going to leave you to it." Elisabeth stacked empty plates and cups onto a hand-painted wooden tray. "I'll bring sandwiches and more coffee later on." She smiled at Prudence. "Trust me, my dear, you'll need them."

"Tell me again what your two runaways look like, Miss MacKenzie," Jacob said when his wife had left the room. He fiddled with the round eyeglasses perched securely on his nose. "Blond hair and dark eyes? Are you sure about that?"

"Positive. I was with both of them in that basement for at least forty-five minutes or an hour until Danny Dennis got there. Then I assisted Dr. Sloan at the Refuge while she examined the girl, and later sat across the kitchen table from the boy. I wish I could draw them for you. I can see them in my mind's eye, but I've no skill with pen or pencil when it comes to sketching faces."

"We don't think they could have been on the street for very long," Geoffrey put in.

"What makes you say that?" Riis asked.

"Street children acquire an ingrained scruffiness that comes from not being able to wash off the daily dirt they acquire," Geoffrey began, drawing on his years of Pinkerton experience. "Their fingernails are black and their hair looks like it's been hacked off with a dull knife. Which is usually the case. The longer they live rough, the more unkempt they get. From the descriptions Prudence was able to give us, these two still showed traces of having once been cared for."

"Who is *us?*" Riis asked. Like most reporters, he guarded his private news sources jealously and trusted none of them completely.

"Josiah Gregory, our secretary," Geoffrey said.

"He accompanied us to the City Asylum for Orphan Boys and Foundlings," Prudence explained. "The body left on their stoop wasn't the boy we were looking for."

"I remember Josiah." Riis said. "From when we worked together on the postmortem photographs of that young woman whose husband married and killed for profit. Your secretary may be of more help to you with this case than I can be."

"I don't understand," Prudence said.

"Have you ever inquired about his childhood?" Riis asked.

"He's always seemed to me to have sprung out of nowhere a fully formed adult, perfectly groomed and immaculately turned out. I can't imagine him kicking a ball around or getting into the kind of mischief boys delight in," Geoffrey said.

"He keeps extra shoes and clothing for the ragamuffins who run errands for us and for Danny," Prudence contributed. "He's always said they were donations, but I've never thought to ask from whom. Or why anyone would imagine we'd want handouts like that."

"I wouldn't be surprised if he spent his own money to buy them out of used clothing bins down on Hester Street. New clothes would be like wearing a target on your back for a street boy. Josiah knows that. He couples generosity with caution," Riis said.

"And knows so much about what life in alleys and doorways is like because he was once a street urchin himself?" Geoffrey concluded.

"Our Josiah?" Prudence couldn't fathom it. She pictured Josiah during their tour of the Asylum and suddenly realized that he'd seemed to know the place as only a former inmate would.

"That's why he never lets down his guard. He's afraid of being caught in the kind of mistake you or I would never make," Geoffrey said.

"We mustn't let on we know," Prudence decided. "That would be cruel, after all the trouble he's taken to conceal it."

"Don't shut him out of the investigation," Riis counseled. "But don't question whatever help he's able to give, either." He dismissed the enigma that was Josiah Gregory from his mind. "Do you want to tackle the prints first or the plates?"

"Definitely the prints," Prudence decided. "The glass plates you photographers use are almost impossible for anyone else to read."

"It takes practice," Riis agreed. "I have boxes of prints in my study. Most of them weren't any good for the book, but I did sort them. After a fashion."

"What does that mean?" Prudence asked.

"Children, alone and together. Groups of adults. Families doing piecework in the tenements. Street scenes."

"We'll start with the children," Geoffrey said. "The boy is small for his age. Prudence had him pegged as eleven or twelve. I think we could say that Dr. Sloan cautiously agrees."

Young voices drifted into the house through windows open to the soft May air. Shouting, laughter, the gallop of small feet running over a grassy lawn. Elisabeth's voice calling out to *be careful*. So unlike the sounds of the dangerous streets and filthy tenements where it was more than likely the boy and girl they were searching for had gone to ground.

Geoffrey's cane tapped rhythmically and Prudence's skirts swished over the wooden floor as Riis led them across a wide hallway to the room in which he worked every night after laboring all day for the *Herald*. A narrow aisle led from the doorway to a desk nearly buried under stacks of paper. Every other available foot of space from one corner of the room to another was crowded with boxes piled waist high.

"We'd best get started," he said.

In the end it was Riis who found the photograph he'd taken of the fragile-looking girl with the unusual coloring and the fierce boy who'd come charging at the photographer moments after the magnesium flash lit up the alleyway where they'd been crouched behind overflowing barrels set out for the night soil carriers.

He'd remembered them as soon as Prudence confirmed the combination of blond hair and dark eyes, but he wasn't sure what he'd done with the photograph he'd taken. Or even whether it existed on paper or on a glass plate that could be anywhere. So he'd said nothing, for fear of getting their hopes up. Sometimes, despite the magnesium flash, images turned out to be too dark to make out. There were days when he had as many failures as successes.

He'd almost despaired of locating it until he came across a set of recent pictures taken that same late afternoon of a street gang. Boys not lucky enough to be selling newspapers banded together to survive on what could be stolen from carts and scavenged from back alleys behind restaurants. Riis hadn't forgotten the shock of the thin figure roaring up at him from behind the foul-smelling barrel. The girl had emerged at almost the same moment, her white dress streaked with human waste, bare toes clinging desperately to the slippery cobblestones.

"Here they are," Riis said, handing the print to Prudence. "There's an overexposed white spot in the upper right corner and the background is out of focus, but you can make out their faces clearly."

"Where did you take it?" Geoffrey asked after Prudence had passed the print to him and he'd turned it over to search for a penciled notation of date and place. Riis hadn't bothered to scribble those down because he'd known the photograph wouldn't be included in the book he was putting together for *Scribner's*. He had hundreds of pictures of impoverished orphans. There was nothing special about this boy and girl.

Except that Mr. Hunter and Miss MacKenzie had come looking for them on a Sunday afternoon.

"Let me think a moment," he said, fiddling with the glasses that were always slipping down his nose. "An alley behind a restaurant. That's all I can tell you."

"It's them, all right," Prudence confirmed. She put the pile of pictures she had been examining into the nearest box. "Is this the only one you took?"

"It was an accident. The boys I was taking pictures of had run off. I didn't know anyone was hiding behind the barrel, and that was what I'd decided to concentrate on next. Nobody downtown believes the stories I tell of what I've seen, but they can't deny the pictures I bring them. Sometimes the magnesium sizzles for a second or two before it goes off. That's what happened here. These two jumped out during that very short delay and then the flash startled them, so they froze just long enough for the image to be captured before I realized what had happened. I almost threw the plate away."

"That doesn't make photography seem like much of a science," Geoffrey said.

"A good photographer has to know all about chemicals and measuring light and counting exposure seconds. It's definitely meant to be a science, but it doesn't always turn out that way." Riis was the first to admit he didn't consider himself an expert.

Prudence had taken back the print and was studying it carefully. "Do you have a magnifying glass?" she asked.

Riis passed her one from the debris on his desk. "What are you looking for?"

"Anything that will identify the place this picture was taken. Which alley? Which restaurant?"

"I went into the alleys behind five or six restaurants that day. I thought I might write about how street gangs survived on the scraps they found. Other people's garbage. All of them were so young. So thin. And sick-looking. They ran off as soon as I gave them a few coins, and that's when I decided to document the waste barrels. The smell was nauseating, but I've gotten used to worse things in the tenements. I hardly noticed it while I was concentrating on the boys."

"So the barrels of waste wouldn't have come from a restaurant?"

"More likely tenement privies that had been emptied. When the wagon hauling the barrels gets filled up, the crew drives to the river to dump what they've got then comes back to take on a new load."

"They dump the filled barrels into the river?" Prudence asked, horrified.

"They empty the waste out of the barrels they've got, then fill them up again. Barrels cost money, Miss MacKenzie. Nobody throws them away."

"So we could be looking for a restaurant whose alleyway backs up behind a tenement building." She bent over the photo again, moving the magnifying glass from left to right, top to bottom, making small throat-clearing noises of disgust.

Geoffrey guessed she was finding unmistakable evidence of what had caused Riis to point his camera into that particular section of the alley.

"I think I see oyster shells on the ground," she said, giving both the photo and the magnifying glass to Geoffrey. "Can you take a look and tell me if I'm right?"

"Every restaurant in New York City serves oysters," Geoffrey said, peering where her finger pointed. "Oyster shells, cigar butts, and things I'd rather not guess at."

"Does that jog your memory, Mr. Riis? A restaurant where the boys in that gang fished oyster shells out of the garbage to scrape off bits of flesh a diner might have overlooked?"

For answer, he pawed through the documents on his desk, then pulled one out and began to skim through it. "Sometimes I do a journal entry of what I've seen and photographed," he explained. "If I think it might make good material for my magic lantern shows. I remember wondering if that gang of young boys—none of them could have been more than nine or ten years old—would appeal to the church audiences I lecture to. So here it is. I composed a description when I got home that night. It doesn't say anything about the boy and girl you're looking for, but it does mention that someone from the restaurant kitchen came out to run me off. He was afraid the sparks from the flash would set the building on fire."

"What was the name of the restaurant? Prudence asked. She held her breath as Riis closed his eyes to search his memory.

"*Vesuvius*," he said triumphantly. "*Vesuvius*. Only about a dozen tables but the food is wonderful. Everyone in Five Points knows where it is."

"Why is that?" Geoffrey asked.

"Fat Rico Bernardi is the owner. He's got a reputation."

"For something other than operating a restaurant?"

"He owns the building and runs his business from a back room, but I doubt he's ever set foot in the kitchen except to taste what's in the pots."

"I'd like to take this with me," Prudence said, holding up the all-important photograph.

"Be my guest. The plate is somewhere in the attic and the picture isn't one I'll be using, so you're welcome to it."

"I can't thank you enough, Mr. Riis."

"You make life interesting, Miss MacKenzie."

"Will you give our excuses to Mrs. Riis? I'm sure her sandwiches would have been delicious."

"But now that you've got what you came for, you need to be on your way." Riis smiled and held out a hand. "A word of caution, though. Don't go to Fat Rico's place alone. I mean the two of you shouldn't go alone. Especially if you plan to ask questions. Take some muscle with you."

"Muscle?" Prudence asked.

"Explain it to her, Mr. Hunter. You were a Pinkerton. You know what I mean."

Geoffrey nodded. He knew exactly what Jacob Riis was warning them about.

CHAPTER 8

In the end, they opted for debts owed rather than muscle. Which meant involving Ned Hayes and the protection he'd long been accorded by Billy McGlory. The do-gooders had finally managed to close down the Armory, one of the city's most notorious concert saloons, and Billy had declared himself done with running drinking establishments of any kind. Nobody believed him. Now he'd reportedly bought a respectable hotel across the street from Tammany Hall. People said it was only a matter of time before it acquired as bad a reputation as the Armory had enjoyed.

"He stays in touch," Hayes informed Prudence and Geoffrey when they asked about going into Five Points under the umbrella of McGlory's safekeeping. Everyone on the wrong side of the law in New York City knew that nobody laid a hand on the ex-detective who had saved the saloonkeeper's life and been thrown off the force for his trouble. "We have a whiskey together once in a while. Billy's a man of contradictions."

"All we need is to get in and out of the alley behind Fat Rico's restaurant without being robbed or having our throats slashed," Geoffrey said. His Pinkerton years had stripped away whatever illusions he might have harbored about the humanity of underworld bosses and gang leaders.

"You'll be all right as long as you stay with me," Ned told them.

"I don't know how Jacob Riis manages it," Prudence wondered.

"He's safe. The Five Pointers know he doesn't have any money and the only weapon he carries is a camera. It's like being a nun down there. The sisters are protected by holy poverty and their habits; Riis is set aside from the crowd by the equipment he lugs around. There's a strange kind of respect for pictures. It's as if the images transform the reality of what they capture. Like the postmortem galleries make a fetish out of dying. Or Matthew Brady's battlefield scenes enshrined the worst moments of the war. Nobody understands photography, but everybody recognizes its power."

"You're turning into a philosopher, Ned."

"Could be. It's definitely not the drink talking. I have a hard time slipping away to lift a glass with Billy once in a while. Tyrus keeps me on a tight leash."

"You look healthier than I've seen you in years," Geoffrey commented.

"I feel better. Less inclined to drink myself to death. Sorry, Miss Prudence, but that's what all of us drunkards end up doing. Tyrus has brought me back from the brink so many times that I'm starting to think life might be worth hanging on to for a while longer."

"You were one of the few honest New York City detectives on the police force," Geoffrey reminded him. "And among the best."

"I'm not contemplating trying to get reinstated," Ned assured him. "Even if I wanted to carry a shield again. Which I don't. It's an open secret that the police force needs reforming. But I don't see anybody on the horizon who's capable of doing the job. Every precinct house is as corrupt as it's always been."

"Tell us about Fat Rico's restaurant," Prudence asked.

"Just don't call him *Fat* to his face. Respect is their life's blood to men like Rico Bernardi. You show disrespect and you're dead. That simple." Ned drained the last dregs of coffee from his cup and took a final bite of the sweet German pastry Josiah served whenever Hayes came by the Hunter and MacKenzie offices. "We'll be crowded, but it's safer to take Danny Dennis's hansom. Your carriage is too ostentatious, Prudence. It screams wealth and privilege. Danny stays with the cab while we go inside."

"Mr. Riis said we needed muscle," Prudence recalled. "Wouldn't Danny fit that bill?"

"Danny needs to keep an eye on Mr. Washington," Ned replied cryptically. He didn't want to plant a mental image in Prudence's mind of the huge white horse being set upon and carved up for dinner by a gang of starving street urchins.

Vesuvius didn't open for regular business until shortly before lunchtime, so when Danny pulled Mr. Washington to a halt in front of the restaurant, patrons hadn't begun to gather at its doors. Ned had told them it was a toss-up as to whether the saloon side or the dining room made more money. In his opinion the beer was watery and the whiskey like rubbing alcohol. But the pasta dishes, cooked to the fat man's liking, were the tastiest in the city.

"He's expecting us," Ned said, knocking a coded tattoo on the saloon door.

Prudence wasn't sure what she had expected, except that the word *restaurant* didn't adequately describe the dark space she was ushered into as the door closed behind their small group. A scantily dressed and theatrically made up woman led them through a maze of tables that badly needed cleaning.

A wide bar backed by rows of bottles stacked against a wall of mirrors dominated one side of the huge room. No barstools, but a brass railing around the bottom provided a place for customers to prop a foot. The tables surrounded what was either a dance floor or a performance arena, Prudence wasn't sure which. And decided as they crossed the open space that it didn't make much difference. She'd made it a point to read all the newspaper articles she could find about Billy McGlory's Armory Hall when Ned Hayes first introduced the saloon-keeper's name into a Hunter and MacKenzie case. She didn't doubt that what had gone on there was replicated here and in the Tenderloin's countless other establishments of ill repute. What looked dangerous in daylight turned deadly by night.

Fat Rico Bernardi was the biggest individual Prudence had ever seen, including Phineas T. Barnum's eight-foot-tall Chinese giant and the seven-hundred-pound Fat Lady who had recently died. But *freak* was a label no one dared apply to the man who had agreed to see them only when reminded that Billy McGlory never forgave or forgot a debt. Whatever it was or how long ago it had been incurred.

"It's good of you to meet with us, Rico," Ned said, executing something between a bow and a hug in Fat Rico's direction, since it was impossible to shake hands with him in the ordinary way.

The saloon's owner reclined in an easy chair that was as wide as a regular bed was long. And still his legs sprawled out like crudely cut trunks from enormous oaks and his arms lay flat across acres of chest and belly. The black suit and white shirt he wore had been tailored from yards of soft wool and fine linen, and on each of his ten sausagelike fingers shone diamond and gold rings. For all the blubber, he was, or had been, a handsome man. But the sparkling black eyes peered out from rubbery circles of dark flesh and the once-perfect white teeth had turned discolored and rotten in a mouth that never ceased sucking on itself. Gurgling and smacking noises came as steadily from between Fat's lips as the grind of a hand organ accompanying the antics of a dancing monkey.

"Any friend of McGlory's . . ." Fat Rico didn't bother finishing the phrase. His eyes focused on Geoffrey's cane long enough to assess its potential as a weapon, then passed on to the woman. "What can I do for you?"

"We're looking for two children, Mr. Bernardi," Prudence said. She could feel Ned stiffening beside her. She'd been told that the fat man didn't like pushy women who didn't know when to keep their mouths shut. Geoffrey's cane tapped a warning. "I have a picture of them to show you," she continued, ignoring the signal. "Will you look at it?"

"I'd rather look at you," Fat Rico said, but he beckoned her forward with a beringed forefinger and what was either a smile or another of the odd lip smackings.

Prudence held out the picture Jacob Riis had taken in the alley. When the distance proved too much for Rico to negotiate, she edged closer. The smell of the man was like the scrapings of a hundred dinner plates left in a garbage can no one had bothered to empty for a week or more. She held her breath and leaned over him. "The girl was being treated at the Friends Refuge when she disappeared overnight with the boy."

"Never seen 'em before," Fat Rico said, barely glancing at the photograph. "Don't like kids, anyway."

"You were a child once yourself, Mr. Bernardi."

"Watch your language, Miss MacKenzie." Fat Rico waggled a caution with the same forefinger that had invited her to approach him. "Pretty young lady like you don't have no business down here. Unless she's of a mind to change her line of work and stay a while." This time the lip smacking turned into an unmistakable leer.

"We'd like to spend a few minutes in the alley out back," Ned Hayes interrupted. The thought of Fat Rico touching Prudence was enough to turn a man's stomach. Not that the monster could move enough to do anything but crush her with his bulk. "That's all we need, Rico, but I wouldn't set foot there without checking with you first."

"Not if you know what's good for you."

"We've been told you let the street kids forage for scraps," Prudence informed the big man. "Are you sure you don't know who this boy and girl are?" She was perilously close to a line nobody acquainted with Rico wanted to cross.

"I don't hang out in the alley watching 'em, and they don't come in here. So how's it that I'm supposed to know one brat from another?"

"No one thought you would, Rico," Ned soothed. "Miss MacKenzie's just so worried, she's not making sense."

"Women never make sense."

"Not so's you'd notice," Ned agreed. "So we're all right to take a look?"

"Don't stay too long. I got customers coming." Fat Rico rang a small bell that tinkled loudly in the empty saloon. "I'm going upstairs," he said. "What the hell's that?"

The fat man's head moved an inch or two from side to side and his nostrils flared in and out like a pair of bellows. He pointed one ham-sized fist at the huge red-gold shaggy dog whose head was just visible peering out from behind Prudence's skirts.

"Her name is Blossom," Prudence explained, making one of the discreet hand signals Danny had taught her. Blossom rose to her feet, wagging her tail politely as she came out into the open. Head cocked, she considered Fat Rico for a moment, as if trying to decide what part of the animal kingdom he belonged to. Then she barked a brief greeting. "We hope she'll be able to tell us if the children we're looking for were out in your alley."

"Dogs don't talk," Fat Rico informed her. "Who said you could bring a mutt in here?"

"She's very well mannered, very well behaved."

"We'll put her to sniffing out their scent," Ned said, stepping between Blossom and Fat Rico. A man who didn't like children probably didn't care much for dogs, either.

"Get rid of her before I send for my cook. There's people down here who eat dog. Mostly puppies, but they could make an exception."

"How does he get upstairs?" Prudence wondered as she, Geoffrey, Ned, and Blossom followed the scantily clad woman through the saloon's back hallways and kitchen into the alley.

"His chair or bed or whatever it is has wheels on it," Geoffrey explained.

"They roll him into the same dumbwaiter they use for hauling barrels of beer up from the cellar," Ned said. "Ropes and pulleys."

"I've never heard of anything so strange," Prudence said. She was fascinated by the logistics of moving Fat Rico around.

"Don't underestimate him," Ned said. "He's got more kills to his credit that any other man in the Five Points. Most of them done on his way up, before he started putting on the pounds. Now he gives orders, and whatever he says to do gets done."

"Someone will take him out one of these days," Geoffrey predicted. "He knows it."

"I'll lay you odds it's the guy he's groomed to be second-in-command," Ned agreed.

"That's a sucker's bet. No matter what the odds."

"She's picked up something." Prudence had let Blossom off her leash and held a piece of the girl's clothing to her nose. "I don't see any barrels, but she's definitely interested in something."

They watched as Blossom tracked back and forth over a small strip of unpaved alley. A pile of lumber protected a space just large enough for two young bodies to occupy if they were crouched down behind it. Hiding. Sleeping perhaps. When she'd finished, Blossom barked once, then sat down, alert eyes fixed on Prudence. Waiting for praise and another command. Danny had trained her well.

Geoffrey stayed where he was while Ned walked over to Blossom, ruffled her ears, and patted her head. "Good girl." He paced the area she'd sniffed out, then paced it again. "They didn't leave anything behind," he said. "Except their scent. This has got to be where Riis took that photograph."

He rejoined Geoffrey and Prudence, Blossom trailing along behind.

"My guess is that they spent a few nights here before the boy found them shelter in the University Building basement," Prudence said, trying to recreate the pattern of their street lives. "Does scent linger that long, Ned?"

"For a dog like Blossom, yes. Especially if the subjects she's after are as fragrant as those two must have been. It hasn't rained in the last week, so I think we can assume the scent she picked up was theirs."

"Now the question is whether they'll be back," Geoffrey said. "If I had to make a prediction, I'd say no. We're bound to have been seen poking around. They'll be warned off as soon as our description gets out. And one of the urchins they might have run with will sound the alarm if they come back into the neighborhood."

"So it's a dead end," Prudence said. "We've made no progress at all."

"I wouldn't say that. When you're a police detective you put together dozens of seemingly unrelated bits of information until a pattern begins to emerge. I know the Pinks operate in the same way," Ned said.

"They do," Geoffrey confirmed. "So what we know is that your two runaways frequented this part of Five Points. Jacob Riis photographed them last Sunday, according to his notes. Then something spooked them into making a run for it."

"Even though the girl was in desperate straits," Prudence added.

"And that leads us to the possibility that she was abused somewhere in the area. She escaped her abuser but was so badly injured that she couldn't go very far. Hence the hiding place behind Fat Rico's. Either the boy or the girl felt safe there, meaning one or the other of them had used it before. Sometime in the past, we don't know precisely when or for how long, but it couldn't have happened without the permission of one or more of the gangs that run these streets."

"You're not talking about the adult gangs?" Prudence asked.

"No." Geoffrey shifted his weight off the bad leg. The cane helped, but only so much. "The gangs I'm talking about are the children dumped out on their own by circumstance or tragedy. Too many children for a manless woman to feed, so she shoves the older ones out the door. Or the parents die and the kids decide to risk making it on their own rather than be separated and locked up in an orphanage."

"I used to see them all the time when I was a detective," Ned explained. "Running in packs. Stealing whatever they could lay their grubby little paws on. Barefoot, scrawny, uneducated, half-starved. The boys beating up on each other, the girls brutally misused when they're hardly out of babyhood. Sometimes a gang would stay together long enough for ties to be formed. A pair of children would start looking out for one another. They'd choose a substitute mother and father from among themselves, someone who could impose a semblance of order on their lives and lay out the few rules they might be willing to obey."

"And you think the boy who stole my sandwiches might have been part of a gang like that?"

"Perhaps. What I can tell you," Ned continued, "is that no child can survive by himself out here. They get to recognize one another by their street monikers, and many of them eventually forget the names a parent gave them. So now that we know where your boy and girl were hiding, even if it was only for a short time, Danny can direct his band of urchins to this specific area. They'll know who to approach and how. If there's information, they'll find it. They're the only ones who might be able to crack the kid gangs. They don't trust adults. For good reason."

Every time she thought she had encountered the worst one human being could do to another, Prudence felt herself slapped in the face by evil so profound, she could not have imagined it. She had been brought up to believe children were wanted and cherished. Yet the simple snatching up of a packet of sandwiches had revealed a world in which children were as disposable as household vermin.

"I had no idea." Prudence sighed. "No idea."

CHAPTER 9

"You might as well go, Prudence," Geoffrey said, handing her back the note she had just shown him. "It sounds as though this professor is inviting you to sit in on a lecture as a way of acknowledging the board's decision and welcoming you. And there's nothing else to be done about your missing children until Danny's runners bring back more information."

"I haven't decided whether to apply. I told Edgar Carleton I'd let him know after I'd thought about it."

"It seems a polite gesture. I assume Hiram Vogel also knew your father?"

"I don't think so. I never heard his name mentioned."

"Mr. Vogel is relatively new to the faculty," Josiah put in. He adjusted the pillow under Geoffrey's bad leg and set the early-afternoon editions of the newspapers within easy reach. "He began lecturing at the law school a little over a year ago. He's young, unmarried, and out to make his reputation in the field of economic law."

"How do you know all that?" Prudence asked.

"I read the papers, miss." He didn't add that he had a gift for remembering everything he read and nearly every conversation he heard. "Shall I order tea or coffee?"

"I won't stay," Prudence decided. "I'll only fidget if I do."

"He doesn't say what the subject of the lecture is," Geoffrey remarked.

"Probably something I've heard half a dozen times. My father started teaching me torts while I was still in the cradle."

"Go be nice to the man, Prudence," Geoffrey said. "You're in a rare mood today."

"I feel at sixes and sevens. That's what one of my governesses used to call it."

"We'll find your missing girl and boy," Geoffrey soothed. "And you'll make the right decision about the law school invitation."

"You're the one who reminded me I could pass the bar right now if I'd a mind to," Prudence snapped. She folded the note from Professor Vogel and tucked it into her reticule.

Josiah held out a fresh stenographer's notebook and a newly sharpened pencil.

"What's that for?"

"You may want to take notes, miss."

Prudence accepted the notebook but waved off the pencil. She'd started carrying a fountain pen recently, one of the newest models with its own ink reservoir and gold-banded cap. It did leak onto her fingers sometimes, but it was more impressive than a yellow wooden pencil stub.

"I'll walk," she informed Josiah before he could ask if she required Danny Dennis's cab. "It's a beautiful spring day and not that far to Washington Square."

"God help any slow-moving pedestrian who gets in her way," muttered Geoffrey when his partner was safely out the door.

Josiah said nothing, which was how Geoffrey knew the secretary shared his employer's opinion.

* * *

Prudence showed Professor Hiram Vogel's' note to the resident janitor standing at the arched entrance to University Building. It wasn't unlike displaying your invitation at one of the exclusive balls hosted by a member of Mrs. Astor's Four Hundred. You were an insider permitted entry to society's most restricted club or you were relegated to the outer darkness inhabited by social pariahs. No middle ground.

"If you'll follow me, please, Miss MacKenzie." The janitor bowed politely and led Prudence into the warren of hallways and classrooms where lectures were delivered. Very few students passed them on their way to class.

"I hope I'm not late," Prudence said. "Mr. Vogel did say two o'clock." And the janitor had been looking out for her arrival. Which was reassuring. There wasn't another woman in sight.

According to Josiah, the school's janitor lived with his family in one of University Building's apartments and was famously touchy about any criticism of how he performed his duties. He'd carved out a comfortable life for himself, one hand perennially extended for the coins discreetly pressed into his palm by students and faculty alike.

"I wonder if you have problems with street people squatting in your building when the police precincts are full," Prudence said. She had no idea whether the neighborhood station houses opened their cellars to vagrants in the spring and summer months the way they did during the coldest winter nights, but it was the only discreet way she could think of to find out if he'd known about the boy and girl hiding in the basement.

"No one enters the building after hours, miss," the janitor said sharply. He jangled a ring of keys hanging from his belt. "I check the hallways and lock all the doors every night."

"I'm curious because the square seems much more crowded than I remember it being a few years ago. The park, too."

"It's not a place to be walking alone after dark. But nobody enters this building who doesn't belong here. I see to it." He halted at the door to one of the amphitheater classrooms. "This is where Mr. Vogel lectures." One hand on the knob, stocky body blocking her view through the door's frosted glass window, he waited.

Prudence fumbled in her reticule for the small purse of coins she kept ready for the tips she and every other New Yorker accepted as an inescapable part of city life. The janitor opened the door and closed it behind her as soon as she'd taken a step into the room. She heard his footfall echoing down the hallway.

The amphitheater was dim, almost dark, the wall of windows along one side of the large room obscured by black paper shades pulled down to the sills. But it wasn't empty. Prudence could make out the shapes of broad shoulders in every one of the rows slanting upward from the lecture platform. She stood for a moment, nonplussed, allowing her eyes to accustom themselves to the lack of light, uncertain whether to make her way toward the aisle of steps leading into the rows of seats or remain where she was.

Suddenly there was a noise like thunder as the paper shades snapped up to the tops of the narrow, arched windows and a hundred booted feet stamped on the wooden risers. When Prudence looked away from where blindingly bright afternoon sunlight was now streaming into the lecture room, she saw a sea of dark-suited young men staring down at her. Unsmiling mustachioed faces eyed her reflectively, as though she were an object they were contemplating purchasing. Here and there a hand rested on a gold watch chain stretched across a silk vest.

Not a word, smile, or nod of greeting.

Every detail of her person was being taken in and assessed: the length and fit of her walking dress, the shine of the boots peeping out from beneath her skirts, the stitching on her gloves, the gold earrings that hung from her ears. She felt as though layers of clothing were being stripped away right down to her corset and petticoat.

"I see you managed to find your way to us, Miss MacKenzie," a voice boomed behind her.

Prudence turned so swiftly, she almost stumbled. Her face flushed scarlet; she could feel heat staining her cheeks.

A tall, bearded man stood behind her, a stack of papers cradled in one arm, the other gesturing her toward where she could see a single open space midway up the rows of standing students.

"I'll be lecturing on a topic I'm sure will be of interest to you, touching as it does on the history of proposed, but until now defeated, legislation that would profoundly affect both the economic and moral climates of our fair city and state." Mr. Vogel ran appreciative fingers over the neatly barbered brown mustache that concealed the shape of his mouth.

"Gentlemen, I present to you Miss Prudence MacKenzie, who is joining us today in recognition of our board of governors' recent decision to admit ladies to our ranks this fall. You'll be studying some of the late Judge MacKenzie's decisions as you tackle the always-thorny issues of criminal law." He deposited the pile of papers on the desk and moved behind the podium, gesturing the ranks of students to be seated.

Feet shuffled, coattails flipped up as the young men settled themselves, and here and there a plume of smoke rose from a newly lit pipe. Mr. Vogel did not allow cigarettes, cheroots, or cigars while he lectured, but the fragrance of pipe tobacco did a decent job of overlaying the heady body odors that accumulated behind closed windows.

"If you'll take your place, please, Miss MacKenzie."

Eyes followed Prudence's progress as she climbed carefully up the steps to the aisle seat that had been left empty for her. Skirt clenched firmly in one hand, she concentrated on not tripping, not stubbing the toe of her boot, not meeting any of the appraising stares that never turned away for so much as a second. She didn't look or smile at the young man beside whom she finally sat, focusing all her attention on the figure striding back and forth along the dais below.

Something about the way he pulled his watch out and peered at it for a very long moment suggested the lecture was off to a late start. And that it was her fault. She set Josiah's notebook on the narrow desktop running in an unbroken line down the row of seats and willed herself to be invisible. Sent her eyes and ears somewhere else while she prepared to endure the next two hours and hoped the lecture would distract from her presence.

It was not to be.

Five minutes into Mr. Vogel's presentation, she realized that the man who had so politely invited her to his lecture had set her up for what was intended to be such a humiliating experience that she would never want to set foot in his classroom again.

"The popular romantic novels devoured by impressionable and empty-headed young ladies would have you believe that the fallen women depicted in their pages are one and all the victims of criminally predatory men," he began, voice pitched to carry to the farthest corner of the room. "Not so, gentlemen. And lady. Not so. We know without a doubt that these denizens of the street and houses of ill repute have chosen to enter this oldest of the professions for reasons of greed and concupiscence. To fuel their hunger for morphine and demon drink while satiating their erotic passions and bestial lusts. I say bestial, because although that is a term we do not usually associate with the fairer sex, these women—old, young, still healthy, or raddled by disease—must be accorded a wholly different place in society than that reserved for the decent wives, sisters, and daughters we all cherish."

Pens scratched across paper and nibs tapped against the edges of the inkwells as Hiram Vogel launched himself into his topic with the full expostulatory fury of the righteous. Prudence knew the points he would make before he got to them. She'd read them in the newspaper articles that summarized lectures given in halls and churches all over the city by reformers determined to stamp out the evils of prostitution. Every effort by those who argued that legalizing the sale of sexual encounters would make it possible to curtail the spread of disease had been met by fierce opposition.

"To legalize these foul encounters is to endorse them. We cannot and should not remove the stigma of sin if we are to preserve the godly society we all desire. I ask you now to enter through your mind's eye the depraved dens of carnality and licentiousness in which these fallen women perform their evil on the hapless men seduced by the wiles of Eve's most wicked daughters."

Vogel ranted and droned on for another hour and a half, as relentlessly bombastic as a smug politician who knows the votes he's bought are secure. Prudence closed her ears to the sniggers that greeted his lurid descriptions of what he termed inherently unchristian acts performed in the city's brothels. She kept her eyes fixed firmly on the lecture platform, refusing to look around her at the faces she knew were avidly watching for her slightest reaction. Determined not to give them the satisfaction of seeing her squirm, she sat like a stone statue until knuckles rhythmically tapping applause on the rows of desktops signaled that the lecture was over.

Students who normally rushed for the door at the end of class meandered their way out, pausing frequently to exchange muttered comments that Prudence couldn't decipher, but was certain concerned her. She busied herself closing Josiah's unused notebook and putting away the pen whose cap she hadn't removed. The overfilled inkwell in front of her had oozed a thick rivulet of black across the desktop, and when she stood up and looked down at the seat she had occupied, she realized there must be a large smudge of coal dust on the back of her skirt.

Mr. Vogel watched Prudence make her cautious way down the steep steps toward where he waited. She clenched her teeth tightly against the arguments she yearned to fling at him, intending to pass by the raised dais with no more than a polite nod of the head.

But he was having none of it.

"So, Miss MacKenzie. Shall we see you here in September?"

"I'll be in touch with Mr. Carleton," she answered. "As promised. I'm sure the women who decide to apply for admission will find your lectures instructive."

"Am I to take it you will not be among their company?" he pressed.

"The study of law is a challenge I'd be loath to dismiss," she hedged.

"But perhaps not a task best suited to the delicate minds and spirits of young ladies."

"There's nothing delicate about a woman's mind," Prudence retorted. "It's every bit as strong and capable as a man's." She could feel an angry flush creeping back along her cheeks, and took a deep breath to calm herself. This was a confrontation she couldn't win.

"We'll see, won't we?" Mr. Vogel said. He brushed the fingers of one hand along the mustache and luxuriant brown beard that proclaimed the superiority of manhood.

Standing on the raised dais, he loomed over the slender young woman who refused to be cowed. It was a stance meant to intimidate, but his adversary was made of sterner stuff than he had anticipated. To his surprise, Prudence MacKenzie hadn't fled the lecture room when he'd described in unnecessary detail the scandalous behaviors of the streetwalkers who nightly plied their trade from Five Points to the Ladies' Mile. Nor had she exhibited the signs of imminent fainting that might have been expected from a well-bred and unmarried girl exposed to such shocking revelations. Instead, every time he met her eyes, she had stared blandly back at him. Sometimes a dot of brilliant red shone on her cheeks, but that was the only indication he could read of discomfort or embarrassment.

Still, he thought he had made his point. The law was not for women.

"I found your lecture intriguing, but familiar." Prudence refastened an undone button on one of her gloves. "There was nothing in your arguments I hadn't already read in the *Times.*" She met his eyes without flinching.

She paused at the door to the hallway.

"Good day, Mr. Vogel."

He didn't answer.

Prudence chose the same bench to sit on in Washington Square Park that she had occupied on Friday. Fewer people strolled the pathways, and no children rolled hoops or tugged at the skirts of their nursemaids. The last wave of students hurried out the gothic doors of University Building, laughing and calling out evening plans to one another.

The janitor appeared at the top of the steps, watch in hand, as a nearby church bell tolled the hour. He slid his timepiece back into a vest pocket, took one long, appraising look around the square, then disappeared. A late-afternoon stillness settled over the trees and the green grass. Even the birds were silent.

Though she wouldn't give him the satisfaction of knowing it, Hiram Vogel's crude strategy had worked. Prudence would not be coming back to the University of the City of New York in the fall as a law student, but not because she had discovered that the law was an unfit occupation for a woman. She had a different commitment in mind.

Edgar Carleton would be disappointed at her rejection of his offer, but there were other young women in the city who were more than capable of taking her place. Accomplished women. Determined and persistent. Strong enough to look men like the disgusting Vogel in the face and not be browbeaten into submission. All that was needed was a handful of them to forge the way for others to follow. Helen Gould could have done it, but Helen had a dying father and motherless siblings to take care of.

Prudence jotted a note to herself on Josiah's stenographer's pad. *Contact Helen again. Ask her to help Edgar Carleton find suitable candidates he might not have thought of.* Hiram Vogel would meet his match in the women who enrolled in his classes, even though Prudence would not be among them.

The lecture that was meant to shame her had instead given Prudence pause for thought. The law would wait for her, but an abused child-woman and her fledgling champion could not. They needed her more than Prudence needed the university and a piece of paper she was confident she could obtain on her own. Vogel had unknowingly supplied the clue that was the impetus for her decision.

The girl she'd rescued and taken to the Refuge needn't have come by her injuries selling her body on the street. Vogel's vivid descriptions of the city's houses of prostitution and their clientele made it seem more likely she had been kidnapped or sold into a brothel. Used and abused and unable to gain her freedom until something happened that allowed her to escape. Or someone helped her. *Then* had come the streets. And the hiding.

The brothel was key, Prudence believed. If what she had heard in the lecture hall was even partially true, madams switched and swapped girls as casually as they changed their stockings. Houses existed to serve specialized perversions, and the madams who ran them knew the demands of one another's patrons.

Hiram Vogel had tossed out a string of names in his diatribe against the women who made a profession of running brothels, none of which Prudence remembered. But one name, from a case a year and a half ago in which she and Josiah had nearly lost their lives, had immediately popped into her mind.

Prudence had always wondered what she and Madame Jolene would have talked about had they met a second time, but she'd never had the chance to find out. She'd had to argue forcefully with Geoffrey that a professional inquiry agent went wherever a case called her, and she'd won the initial battle, but that first visit had also been her last. She'd never had reason or opportunity to repeat the victory. Until now.

Her mind made up, Prudence marched resolutely out of Washington Square Park toward a stand of hansom cabs. With luck she'd be in the Hunter and MacKenzie offices before Josiah gathered the mail and the late-afternoon newspapers for his last visit of the day to Geoffrey's Fifth Avenue Hotel suite.

If Prudence couldn't pry Madame Jolene's address out of Josiah, there was always Danny Dennis and Mr. Washington. Perhaps not this evening, when the brothel was bound to be at its busiest, but definitely tomorrow. Early, she thought, and with a list of questions Madame Jolene might never have been asked.

What did you wear to a brothel?

CHAPTER 10

"Geoffrey will have my hide over this," Ned Hayes grumbled. "I don't see why you have to take a chance on ruining your reputation, Prudence. If anyone finds out, there won't be a society parlor in the entire city where you'll be welcome."

"I've done it before, Ned," she reminded him. "And I got away with it. Colleen attached a veil to the hat I'm wearing, so no one seeing us go into Madame Jolene's will have any idea who I am. And there's no need to tell Geoffrey what we're up to." He'd been the one to take her to Madame Jolene's that first time, but only because Prudence had forced his hand. "Hurry up and finish your coffee."

She'd decided the night before that going to Josiah or Danny Dennis for the address of one of the city's most famous madams was too risky. Josiah was hard put to keep her secrets at the best of times and Danny might refuse outright. Either of them could believe that, for her own good, he had to tell Geoffrey what Prudence intended to do. And that would be the end of it. She didn't know how her partner would manage it, but somehow he'd ensure that Prudence and Madame Jolene would not meet again.

So she'd written a note to Ned Hayes that had him on her doorstep thirty minutes after it was delivered. Not exactly blackmail, but so close as not to make much difference. All she'd had to do was refer to a recent escapade Ned had boasted about. And threaten to inform Tyrus that his master had once again slipped the leash. And reveal how he had done it.

"He hardly lets me out of his sight as it is," Ned had complained, giving in, as Prudence had known he would.

Sober though Ned might be at the moment, his friends were never surprised when he fell off the wagon. With Ned it was always a matter of luck and timing. You hoped he'd be dry when you needed him, and Tyrus was your ally when his master had to be rescued.

"Tell me what I should know about Madame Jolene," Prudence insisted.

"What did Geoffrey say about her that time?" Ned asked, delaying the inevitable.

"Not very much. We were trying to locate a midwife who performed abortions, and he made the mistake of telling me that he knew a brothel keeper who could provide the information we needed. He felt she'd cooperate because of what you and he had done for her in connection with a previous case."

"I've known her ever since my days on the force," Ned began. Unsuitable as it was to take a lady to a brothel, it was undeniably intriguing. Sobriety, especially with Tyrus watching his every move, could be boring. "She runs an exclusive house and only sees a few select clients herself, but she was a greenhorn when she got off the boat. With no skills and no way except the obvious to keep body and soul together."

"Is that unusual, for a madam to have clients?" Prudence asked. She hadn't forgotten a word of Professor Hiram Vogel's lecture, including the unfamiliar vocabulary that was rolling off her tongue as though she'd been using it all her life.

"It's political," Ned explained. "She pays protection like everybody else, but she has ins at city hall and at the highest levels of the police department. She's as safe from raids as money can make her. Word is she counts several bankers among the house's regulars, the usual clutch of politicians, and a handful of Mrs. Astor's precious Four Hundred."

"How did she do it, Ned? How did she get to where she is today?" Vogel had emphasized that the life of a prostitute was short, brutal, and unforgiving. Death from disease and abuse was her inevitable end. Women who worked the brothels were only marginally safer than those who strolled the streets.

"The immigration officer who processed her through Castle Garden was new at his job. He had no idea what language she was speaking, so he put it down as French. Probably the first thing that popped into his head. It was Gaelic, of course, but Madame Jolene knew from the beginning that a French whore would be vastly more popular than an inexperienced girl from the bogs of western Ireland."

"Do you know her real name?"

"No one does. And the story I just told you is as much conjecture as anything else. Even after she perfected her English, Madame Jolene continued to claim she was French."

"My French is rather good," Prudence said. "My governess made sure of that."

"Madame Jolene won't understand a word you say. And she'll have some grand excuse for why she insists on speaking only English. With the worst imitation French accent you've ever heard." Ned had almost forgotten how vehemently he'd tried to talk Prudence out of this scandalous scheme.

He was genuinely fond of Madame Jolene. Over his years as a police detective, and afterward, they'd exchanged more than a few favors. Each of them was an outsider, one by choice, the other by circumstance.

Ned had never lied to the men and women he arrested, and he had never subjected a prisoner to the violent beatings known as the third degree. Madame Jolene, recognizing one of the few honest souls of her acquaintance, had conspired more than once with Tyrus to nurse Ned back to sobriety after a binge.

"I think the girl we were looking for in the alley behind Fat Rico's may have been kidnapped and sold into a brothel," Prudence said. "Danny's runners haven't found any trace of her on the streets yet."

"And you think Madame Jolene will know who she is?"

"It's worth a chance. It's the only lead I have so far."

"You do realize that if we're caught I'll be paying for this little adventure for a long time to come." Ned winced as he tallied all of the sparring bouts, jumping rope, and sit-ups Tyrus would goad him to perform. "That old man will have me sober as a judge, healthy as a horse, and miserable for the rest of my life."

"Then we have to make sure neither Tyrus nor Geoffrey gets wind of where we're going or why. And if Madame Jolene does recognize the girl from Jacob Riis's photograph, we'll concoct a plausible story about where we got the information."

Prudence pinned her hat on her upswept hair and lowered the veil over her face. Her mind raced from one possible explanation to another, none of them sound enough to pass muster. Geoffrey could smell a lie as soon as it was uttered.

They just wouldn't get found out.

"I don't know how I ever let you talk me into this," Ned groused.

If Madame Jolene was surprised to find a former New York City police detective and a veiled society woman on her doorstep shortly after the last client had stumbled out of the house in the early-morning hours, she concealed it well. One of the secrets to her success was the ability to mask her feelings behind a stunningly beautiful face that had changed very little over the years since she'd left the pious poverty of Ireland for the rapacious streets of the new world.

Dressed head to toe in black, even to the patterned jet beading on her dressing gown and high-heeled slippers, Madame Jolene ushered Ned and Prudence into her private parlor and sent the ex-boxer who worked as her bouncer to stir the kitchen fire and heat up what was left of the coffee she drank as though it were water. Not a sound disturbed the silence of the house. The women of the brothel worked by night and slept by day. Their madam never sought her bed until after she'd tallied the night's receipts and updated the private notes she kept on important clients whose identities and personal idiosyncrasies were meticulously chronicled.

If Prudence had nurtured romantic notions of a sporting house as depicted on the gaudy covers of popular novels and in the penny press, she was swiftly disabused. The morning debris through which the bouncer had led them was mute testimony to the cold commerciality of the night's transactions. Empty glasses and bottles of cheap whiskey crowded every tabletop, cigar butts spilled out of ashtrays, and the stink of wet, chewed tobacco lingered over a half-dozen brass spittoons. Here and there a woman's flimsy undergarment decorated the back of a chair or a client's forgotten hat lay trodden underfoot on the floor. The closed shutters and pulled drapes let in just enough light to bathe the scene in what preachers called the hellish red of devil fire. Crimson was the color of passion. Hot and exciting. Tawdry and faded when lust had been satiated.

Madame Jolene made no excuses for the state of the rooms where clients waited to mount the stairs with the girl of their choice or whoever was available. It amused her to know that Ned's companion was almost certainly appalled at what she had seen, and that her visitor's imagination must be furiously picturing the scenes that had left behind so much proof of human wreckage. Before nightfall all would be clean and orderly again. Madame Jolene prided herself on beginning each business cycle with a level of decorum in the public rooms that some establishments did not bother to maintain. She charged higher prices, but the house and the girls who worked in it delivered on every penny.

Prudence hesitated before lifting her veil, then mentally shrugged her shoulders. Her light gray eyes met Madame Jolene's gaze with frank interest and a determination that was not lost on the madam. Reading people was a necessary skill in both their professions.

"You didn't say what's brought you here, Ned." Madame Jolene shifted her attention to the ex-detective who had earned both trust and friendship over the years.

"It's Miss MacKenzie's story to tell." Ned settled himself in one of the tufted velvet armchairs that gave the madam's private office the feel of a luxurious sitting room. He gestured in Prudence's direction, thinking that they looked like two decorous widows met for mutual consolation.

"I appreciate your agreeing to see us," Prudence began. "I wasn't sure you'd remember me."

"I had occasion to appear several times before your father," Madame Jolene told her guest. "He was a fair man. A decent judge." It was the highest praise she could offer.

She glanced at Ned Hayes and decided not to ask why Geoffrey Hunter hadn't accompanied his partner.

"I'm looking for a girl somewhere between fourteen and sixteen, who appears much younger than her real age," Prudence said. She'd heard her father's honesty reluctantly praised more than once by miscreants who had appeared in his courtroom. "I discovered her in the basement of a building in Washington Square. She'd been beaten and badly misused." The nod of Madame Jolene's head told her that the madam understood the euphemism. "I took her and the boy I believe has been protecting her to the Friends Refuge down near Five Points."

"Dr. Sloan," Madame Jolene confirmed. "She never turns away a woman who needs her. Unlike some other doctors who won't soil their hands with our kind."

Prudence wondered how many times in her working life the madam had seen the bruising and tearing of young flesh. "I sent the boy to spend the night in a stable with a hansom cab driver I trust. The girl stayed at the Refuge. But overnight, she disappeared. According to one of the women in the ward, the boy came for her and she left with him. Willingly. The woman thought she had been waiting for him because she was already dressed when he arrived."

"What names did they give you?" Madame Jolene asked. She knew better than to think that they had been anything but assumed identities made up on the spur of the moment.

"Neither of them said a word. Dr. Sloan explained that it wasn't unusual for a victim of assault to retreat into silence."

"And you think I might know something about your girl?"

Prudence held out the photograph Jacob Riis had taken in the alley behind Fat Rico's saloon restaurant. "This is what they look like."

The girl's dark eyes were pools of despair, fear, and pain, her light hair a nimbus of light around her battered face. A breath-takingly delicate beauty shone through the bruising. The resemblance between her and the boy at her side was unmistakable.

"Are they sister and brother?" Madame Jolene asked.

"We don't know," Prudence answered.

"I think we can assume they are," Ned put in. "Until we find out otherwise."

"What part do you play in all this, Detective?" Madame Jolene asked, using the title he'd lost when he'd been forced to resign from the police department.

She handed the photograph to Ned, who studied it intently for a moment before returning it to Prudence. Sometimes a picture spoke to you in a way reality could not.

When neither of them answered, Madame Jolene understood that Prudence had inveigled Ned into bringing her to a place she might never have been able to find were she entirely on her own. And that he had been anything but pleased by the forced complicity. The judge's daughter had the kind of spunky pluck one didn't expect from a society girl.

"I believe she might have been kidnapped or sold to a brothel," Prudence explained.

"How would someone like you know about things like that?" Madame Jolene asked. She didn't bother to deny that the theft and buying of women's bodies were everyday occurrences in a city like New York.

"I attended a lecture," Prudence said. "The descriptions were very graphic."

"It's a lucrative business," Madame Jolene said blandly. "Like any successful venture, it can't afford to be affected by concern for the human casualties left in its wake."

"These are children," Prudence said.

"The younger they are, the more valuable," Madame Jolene informed her. "To men of a certain inclination." She sounded as un-French as any ordinary New Yorker.

Despite the iron control she was maintaining, Prudence felt her face flush. She had tried not to let her thoughts venture into the intimate details of the sexual abuse Dr. Sloan had told her the girl had suffered. Beatings and knifings were so commonplace in the city that you could read about them in the sensationalist press every day, but no one ever talked about what was done to women in private.

"There are houses that cater to every whim you could imagine," Madame Jolene explained, eyes focused on the play of emotion across her visitor's face. "Places where the girls are all Swedes or Italians, for example. Or where they mix the races, if that's your preference. I won't bother to describe the other impulses and fancies."

"How can I go about finding her?" Prudence persisted. "Or at least identifying the brothel from which she escaped?"

"You can't," Madame Jolene said bluntly. "You're dangerous to business, Miss MacKenzie. Ned should have explained that to you. You can't be trusted not to run to one of the do-gooders trying to shut us down. All of us, including someone like me who makes it possible for a woman not to be pregnant every year of her wedded life. Or die in childbirth because her body is too worn out to survive another miscarriage or botched delivery. A man who can't control himself needs somewhere to go if he doesn't want to kill his wife. And we provide that service."

"I'd hardly call it that," Prudence said, although that had been one of the arguments bruited by those in favor of legalizing prostitution.

"We're here to stay," Madame Jolene asserted. "Whether you like it or not. Whatever excuses are offered for the trade. The simple fact is that men can't do without us." She shot a glance in Ned Hayes's direction.

"Leave me out of the discussion." He had his own views about the commerce between casually lustful men and economically desperate women, but none of them applied to the situation Prudence was trying to remedy. The girl she was determined to save had never consented to the merchandising of her body.

"I'm asking for information," Prudence said. "Whether you recognize her or know of anyone who would beat a young woman like her so badly." She fixed her gaze on Madame Jolene's unmarred face. Did the madam remember what it had been like to earn a living on her back when she was the age of the girl in the photograph? She held out the black-and-white print again. It was the only leverage Prudence had.

Madame Jolene turned away from it once, then sighed and seemed to change her mind. She nodded at Prudence, who laid the picture on the small table between them. It took on a life of its own there, impossible to ignore, like the pleading dead eyes of a postmortem image. "Something's been done to her face. Hard to make out under all that dirt and bruising, but I'd say your girl is a specialty item. Expensive to maintain. Someone's considerable investment. I've never seen her in the flesh. That's the truth, Miss MacKenzie, whether you choose to believe it or not. But I have an idea or two about what you should do next."

"I'd be grateful for any help you can give. I had a friend make a drawing you could show your girls." Prudence's governess had insisted that she learn the fundamentals of sketching, but Josiah was a far more competent copyist. The penciled picture of the girl in the photograph was as lifelike as the image printed from Riis's glass plate negative.

"The obvious things first." Madame Jolene turned brusquely businesslike, ticking off her suggestions on exquisitely manicured fingers. "I can show the sketch to my girls. It's just possible one of them has come across her. They tend to move from house to house, always searching for a better situation. Or a john who will buy them out of the life and set them up for himself alone. That's every girl's dream."

"I don't know how long she's been . . ." Prudence couldn't find the right word, despite Hiram Vogel's lecture.

"It doesn't matter. Once in the life, you never get out of it. Even the girls who dip in when times get rough and pull back when they've got a little money saved." Madame Jolene shook her head. "There's no getting out," she repeated. "The other thing I can do, but it's trickier, is speak to a few of the women I do business with. We know each other's regulars almost as well as we know our own."

"Would they help?"

"None of us profits from this kind of abuse," Madame Jolene said, gesturing toward the photograph. "A girl beaten that badly isn't able to work until she's healed. And that can take a while. Clients don't like to see the evidence of another man's temper. It puts them off their own pleasure. Bad for business."

"What do you do about that?" Prudence asked, curiosity winning out over discretion.

"We hire men like the one who met you at the door this morning. George Bright is an ex-bare-knuckle boxer. His fists make a very persuasive argument. It seldom takes more than one encounter."

Ned Hayes cleared his throat. "She needs to hear the whole truth, Jolene," he said.

The madam hesitated.

"Miss MacKenzie is stronger-stomached than she looks," Ned assured her. "And she won't stop asking questions until she gets the right answers."

"A man can buy anything in New York City," Madame Jolene said. "Everything is for sale. Everything."

"Even a woman's life?" Prudence demanded.

"Especially that. Women and girls are among the cheapest things a man can purchase."

"The prices go up with the degree of violence being bargained for," Ned contributed. In his short career with the New York City Police Department he'd seen a lifetime's worth of brutality.

"Do the women, the girls, know what lies ahead for them?" Prudence asked.

"Usually not," Madame Jolene said. "But by that time the drugs and alcohol have so worn down their will to live that it makes little difference in the end. Death comes as a release."

"I find that hard to believe," Prudence said. Then she remembered the beautiful warmth of a laudanum haze and the refuge of a sleep from which too many of its users never awoke.

"I do have one more thought," Madame Jolene said briskly. She was losing patience for the education of a naïve society girl, despite Ned Hayes's assertion that the lady was tougher than she looked. "It involves more than asking questions."

"I'm ready," Prudence said.

"Nellie Bly isn't writing for the *New York World* anymore," Madame Jolene said. "They covered her expenses but didn't pay a penny extra for that around-the-world exploit she pulled off. The paper's circulation increased by leaps and bounds and Bly's name and picture are plastered on everything from table napkins to jewelry boxes, but she isn't making any money off the hoopla. She's supposed to be writing a book about the experience." One of her clients had bartered the interesting twist in the famous reporter's career for services rendered.

"What does that have to do with anything?" Ned asked.

"She got her start as a reporter by having herself locked up in an insane asylum, don't forget. She was after a story about the institution's abuses and figured that was the only way to get it. I wouldn't be surprised if Nellie agreed to go underground to find your girl for you."

"Pretend to be a prostitute?" Prudence asked. Appalled, but immediately fascinated by the possibility and what it meant.

"New Yorkers might be as mesmerized by tales from inside a brothel as they were by the stories she wrote about the asylum on Blackwell's Island. Or the dispatches from her trip around the world. She could name her price. Any of the papers would pick her up."

Prudence remembered every word of those riveting articles. Nellie Bly's challenge to Jules Vernes's famous book had been followed by readers everywhere. "Do you think she would?"

"All you can do is ask," Madame Jolene said. "I'm surprised she hasn't thought of it herself."

And as easily as that, Prudence understood what she had to do next.

CHAPTER 11

Under the byline *Nellie Bly*, Elizabeth Jane Cochrane became the most famous woman reporter in America. Before she was twenty-five years old, she had captured the public imagination by having herself committed to the Women's Lunatic Asylum on Blackwell's Island to expose cruel and inhumane conditions in the hospital. When she bested Jules Verne's fictional exploit *Around the World in Eighty Days*, the *New York World* printed her telegraphed dispatches from foreign ports as soon as they came in. Her picture was plastered on every conceivable object from china teacups to children's school satchels. Everyone knew what she looked like.

"Which means I'm finished investigating stories under-cover," Nellie told Prudence as the two women stood in her cluttered parlor, trying to decide which chairs to sweep clean of the stacks of paper spilling everywhere. "The book I've written about the escapade will be out at the end of July, and I've got my fingers crossed that it sells well. I won't go back to the *New York World* after the way they treated me, and I failed miserably at the lecture circuit." She snatched up a handful of newspaper clippings and thrust them in Prudence's direction.

"Apparently it's all right for a woman to traipse around the globe by herself, but she can't demean her ladylike qualities by stepping onto a lecture stage. It's too manly." She spat the words in pent-up frustration.

"I thought the tour started off with packed houses and receptive audiences," Prudence said. She hadn't gone to the first event at the Union Square Theatre because she and Geoffrey had been deep in the final stages of a case. In mid-February, by the time of the second lecture, he had been shot and almost killed. The furthest thing from Prudence's mind had been the hoopla surrounding Nellie Bly's seventy-two-day round-the-world adventure.

"New York was wonderful to me. The rest of the country not so much. All of these venerable newspaper editors seem to think I'm some kind of threat to the smooth running of the society they're trying to protect. They believe I'll convince other women to shake out their skirts and leave hearth and home. I'm a bad example of the feminine virtues, Miss MacKenzie. You'd do well to avoid my company."

"On the contrary, Miss Bly. I think you and I would get along together very well."

"Nellie, please."

"And you must call me Prudence." Unlike her friend Helen Gould, this woman urging her to call her Nellie seemed to fit the moniker.

Nellie held out her hand. "Pleased to make your acquaintance, Prudence."

It was a firm grip, brisk and businesslike, yet Nellie Bly's afternoon at-home dress was the epitome of style, her waist so tightly corseted that Prudence wondered how she could breathe. She was a young woman of contradictions, but so was her visitor.

"I apologize for calling when you're obviously busy," Prudence said. She looked around for a spot to set down the newspaper cuttings where they wouldn't be lost amid the drifts of paper, then decided it probably didn't matter where she put them. There didn't look to be any rhyme or reason to the piles of foolscap and notes scratched on torn bits of blank newsprint.

"I'm glad for the distraction," Nellie said. "The book is on its way to the printer and before that I did four long pieces for the Sunday edition of the *World*. It's time to work my way out from under all of this." She nudged a brightly illustrated board game with one elegantly booted foot. "Around the World with Nellie Bly," she said. "Recommended as the perfect way to spend an exciting evening without having to leave the comforts of your home. That's where men want us to stay, you know."

"Things are beginning to change for women," Prudence said, thinking of what would soon be happening at the law school in Washington Square.

"Not fast enough." Nellie swiped a tufted velvet sofa clean of its debris and gestured to her guest. She perched herself on the edge of a matching armchair. "Now," she said, "what brings a lady like you so close to the Tenderloin?" Nellie's apartment was located near enough to the busy theater, gambling, and saloon district to be a world away from the Fifth Avenue residential elegance in which Prudence had grown up and still lived.

"I'm looking for two children," Prudence began. "Someone told me you were the best person to ask for help."

"Children!" Nellie laughed. "I'm not the motherly type. As my critics haven't hesitated to point out to me and everyone else who reads the papers." She stirred the mess at her feet. "Being unmarried means being unnatural. Did you know that?"

Undeterred by Nellie's disgruntlement with the state of the world, Prudence plunged into the story she had come to tell. "I think the girl is somewhere between fourteen and sixteen, the boy perhaps two years her junior. But they both look much younger." When Nellie chuckled at the sandwich episode and nodded her head appreciatively at the description of Fat Rico, Prudence knew she had snagged her interest. She finished up with the tale of the dead boys found at the City Asylum for Orphan Boys and Foundlings.

"Someone has a grudge against a particular blond, brown-eyed boy," Nellie agreed, cutting off Prudence's speculation about what she had stumbled into. "But you're right that he's not at the heart of whatever's going on. The girl is."

"I have a photograph of them," Prudence said.

"This looks like some of Jacob Riis's work." Nellie traced the image of the alleyway with one manicured forefinger. "The trash cans, the filth on the ground, the way the eyes stare at you."

"He took this behind Fat Rico's," Prudence explained. "The cook there hands out scraps at the end of the day."

"Every restaurant and saloon cook in Manhattan with half a heart does the same thing," Nellie told her. "It's an open secret that the streets in some neighborhoods are full of dead and dying kids. Once in a while someone opens up a warehouse to shovel them into, but it rarely lasts for very long. There isn't any money to be made in orphans and foundlings. Or in abused women."

"The Quakers take them in, whenever they can," Prudence said. "And there are Catholic nuns working in the Five Points area. I've seen them."

"So there are," Nellie said. "But what they manage to accomplish is a drop in the ocean. And just as likely to be swallowed up by the tide. *Cui bono*, Prudence. That's how you'll find out what happened to your missing girl."

"Who profits?"

"Do I have to spell it out for you?"

"No. I know she was the victim of someone's depravity," Prudence said. "And that there has to be money paid to conceal whatever's going on." The flush she'd fought so hard to repress at Hiram Vogel's lecture surged up her neck and across her cheeks.

"Now you've turned as red as a pair of flannel underdrawers.

You'll never get where you need to go if everyone can read what you're thinking." The ability to keep a straight face no matter what was happening around her was one of the keys to Bly's ability to work undercover. She was as much an actress as a reporter.

"I know about prostitution, Nellie," Prudence said fiercely. "I wasn't born yesterday."

"And now you're letting yourself get angry. You have to keep the emotions under tight control. Otherwise they run away with you. And you lose the story."

"Is that what you think this is to me? A story?"

"Everything is a potential story, Prudence. Everything," Nellie said pragmatically. "Unfortunately, this one won't sell. Nobody cares about dead kids. And men buying women's bodies is too much a part of New York's commercial life to surprise or interest anyone."

"I've read some very disturbing stories in the newspapers," Prudence said.

"Those stories aren't really about the women," Nellie explained. "Not if you read them carefully. They're all about the do-gooders who campaign vigorously to restore virtue to city life and pretend to be shocked by what they find. The preachers and the reformers want to read about themselves, Prudence. They want to see their names in print and hear them on people's lips. They couldn't care less about the girls and women they profess to want to rescue."

"Dr. Charity Sloan runs a clinic down near Five Points. That's where I took the girl to be examined and treated."

"And if you study Dr. Sloan's Refuge carefully, you'll find that her name is never in the papers, she doesn't seek out publicity, and nobody preaches at the women. She patches up broken bodies and provides a safe place to sleep. Food, shelter, medical help, and understanding. With no quid pro quo. That alone is more than these women are used to being offered."

"So what you're telling me is that there's no story here."

Prudence peered at Jacob Riis's photograph of her missing children as though willing them to speak to her.

"Even if I were still working at the *World*, I wouldn't take it to my editor," Nellie said. "He'd laugh me out of his office. There's no hook. When something happens every day, whatever it is quickly loses the power to attract attention. Readers get used to it. They buy fewer papers. Circulation goes down. Reporters get fired."

"What am I to do then, Nellie?"

"You came here to ask me something. What is it, Prudence?"

"You're famous for the stories you dig up that no one else reports on. I thought you'd want to help me find these children."

"Did you know I'd written a novel?" Nellie asked, switching subjects abruptly.

"No."

"I did. *The Mystery of Central Park*. It bombed. The reviews were terrible and it never sold more than a few copies."

"What does that have to do with my children?"

"Only that I'm thinking about taking another stab at fiction writing," Nellie said. "I've been approached, and I'm seriously considering it."

"The *World* would have you back, I'm sure."

"So Joseph Pulitzer says. I have an open invitation. All I have to do is accept it."

"But you won't?"

"He didn't pay me any kind of bonus for making the *New York World* the most-widely-read newspaper in the country," Nellie said. "And I'm not getting one thin dime for having my picture stare back at me from every shop window I pass. Do you know what it means to someone like me to be recognized everywhere I go? I'd never have gotten the Women's Lunatic Asylum story if they'd known I was a reporter."

Prudence felt opportunity slipping out of her grasp.

"What you came here to ask me to do is to go underground

again. To disguise myself as a prostitute and worm my way into one of the brothels to find the information you want. Or peddle my wares on street corners and in alleyways. Isn't that what you had in mind, Prudence?" Nellie's grim bluntness contrasted sharply with the aura of gentility she had cultivated over the years. It was what had surprised many an interview subject into saying too much.

"Put that way, I can't believe I ever considered it," Prudence said, suddenly appalled at her own temerity. Pictures she didn't realize she had been repressing ran across her mind's eye like the jerky images of a magic lantern show. Nellie's scantily clad body wrestling off sexual advances with a variety of faceless men. Nellie's face superimposed over the nearly nude models on the popular French postcards sold at tobacco shops and newsstands. "I didn't think through what it would mean," she apologized.

"You have to consider every detail when you set out to expose what men have gone to considerable lengths to conceal," Nellie said. "And this is both a non-story and something too personally dangerous to get involved in." She smiled then, to take some of the sting off what she had been saying. "Neither of us is married. If it came to it, would you even know what to do?"

She couldn't help herself. Prudence burst into laughter, and the tension that had been building between her and the reporter dissolved.

"So fiction is the only place left for me," Nellie continued, returning to the point she'd been making about how she intended to earn a living now that she was a household image as well as a name. "I'm good with words and I can churn them out as fast as anyone else in the news business. I've always been able to earn my own way. I'm not quitting now." She paused for a moment, meeting Prudence's eyes. "And I have something to prove. Obviously."

"But there won't be time to spare for anything else," Prudence said, anticipating the argument Nellie was making.

"No. And I think I'd get in your way. I'm a nine-days wonder, Prudence. I can't go anywhere without people gawking
and then rushing over to ask questions or demand an auto-
graph. I would have liked to help you. I think we could have
worked well together, even if finding those children isn't the
kind of story I could sell."

"We've got crossing sweepers out looking for them," Prudence said. "Staking out the alleys behind Fat Rico's and the
Refuge. In case they go back to where they felt safe for a
while."

"I have another idea," Nellie said. "Take the photograph you
showed me around to the police precincts where the children
could have sought shelter in the basement during cold nights.
Their looks are distinctive enough so that somebody might remember them. That would at least narrow down your search
area." She scribbled something on a scrap of newsprint. "If that
doesn't work, this is the name of a detective friend of mine at
Mulberry Street Headquarters. He's got a special interest in
crimes against girls and women. You can trust him, Prudence.
He's not on the take because he doesn't need to be, and I don't
know how much longer he'll stay on the force. But for now, he
might be your best bet."

"Warren Lowry," Prudence read aloud. "The name sounds
familiar."

"The case was in all the papers. Two years ago his sister disappeared from the family home in the middle of the night.
Never seen or heard from again. No sign of a break-in, no ransom demand. When the police stopped investigating, Lowry
joined the force and bought and worked his way up to detective rank. I've seen him in action, Prudence. He's very good.
No one talks about it, but everyone knows he only became a
copper so he could continue looking for his sister. He follows
every lead that comes his way, but so far, none of them have
panned out."

"And the police department lets him do that?" From what

Ned Hayes had told her about the New York City Police Department, you stepped out of line at your peril. But his, she remembered, had been a special case. Ned had saved the life of
one of the city's most notorious saloonkeepers and refused to
regret it. The drink and the drugs hadn't helped, but plenty of
coppers hadn't known a sober day since they first put on long
pants. Ned's real offense was to show compassion toward a fellow human being. It made the other cops look bad. And that
they could not forgive.

"Lowry pulls his weight. He's got a reputation for closing
every case that gets assigned to him. Except his own. So they
cut him some slack.

"I think you'll like him, Prudence."

CHAPTER 12

"I'm looking for Detective Warren Lowry," Prudence told the desk sergeant at the Mulberry Street Headquarters of the New York City Police Department.

"Take this to the second floor, miss," he said, handing over a scribbled pass. He looked around for a uniformed officer, but most of the morning's roster were already out on the streets. The remaining few were gulping down coffee to dispel last night's whiskey fumes and in no shape to escort a lady. "Ask anyone up there to direct you."

The hallways of Police Headquarters were dingy, noisy, and peopled by men in uniform, men in handcuffs, and men with blackened eyes, bloody noses, and cut lips. Despite her intentionally drab navy blue secretarial suit, every one of them eyed her up and down appreciatively as Prudence threaded her way along the first floor and up to the second.

Smelly spittoons stood at the end and midpoint of every corridor, surrounded by wet brown rings of near misses. Cigar and cigarette smoke billowed out from behind half-closed office doors, and everywhere was the rumble of male voices. Questioning, denying, arguing, threatening.

By luck or accident, which were probably the same thing in this place, she decided, Prudence found Detective Lowry's office without having to accost any of the shirt-sleeved men wearing holstered guns strapped below their shoulders. Unlike every other office she had passed, Lowry's door was closed. She studied the name painted on the opaque glass for a moment, rapped smartly, then twisted the brass doorknob before she could change her mind.

The man who looked up from a stack of paperwork as she stepped into his office rose to his feet, reaching for the gray jacket he'd discarded in the stuffy spring heat of a building where windows were rarely opened. She caught a glimpse of pale hair, bright blue eyes, and the tanned, weathered skin of an outdoorsman before she turned to close the office door behind her. Quietly. Carefully. Angling for time.

"May I help you, miss?" a low-pitched voice asked. "Are you looking for someone in particular?"

Prudence turned to face him. "Detective Warren Lowry?"

He nodded, then gestured toward one of two visitors' chairs.

Not warmly welcoming, but not abruptly dismissive, either, she decided, opening her reticule to take out the slip of paper Nellie Bly had given her.

"So you're here about a case I might find interesting?" he queried, folding the note into neat quarters before handing it back.

His hair was more silver than blond, Prudence decided. Prematurely so, because although the skin around Lowry's startlingly clear blue eyes was wrinkled, the rest of his clean-shaven face was smooth. She judged him to be in his late twenties or early thirties, a man's best years, according to some ladies' magazines.

"I'm searching for someone," she began. "Two someones. Miss Bly isn't able to help, but she thought you might be willing to assist, even though I can't prove the disappearance is a crime. Not yet, that is." The explanation sounded inept, confusing.

"How is Nellie?" Lowry asked, the use of her first name acknowledging his friendship with the famous reporter. "I haven't seen her since the beginning of the lecture tour."

"She's decided she can't work undercover anymore because of all the publicity," Prudence said. "And she's considering writing another book. A novel."

"I wish her well. And success. She deserves it." Lowry waited for his uninvited visitor to get to the heart of why she was sitting in his office this May morning. One finger tapped impatiently on the document he had been reading.

"I've interrupted important work," Prudence said. "And I apologize. I wouldn't have bothered you if I felt I had anywhere else to go."

"Why don't you start at the beginning, Miss MacKenzie?" Lowry said.

He had recognized who Prudence was as soon as he'd read her name in Nellie's note. Judge MacKenzie had been known throughout the police department and the court system for the strict fairness of his decisions and the old-fashioned courtliness of his manners. His daughter was equally well celebrated, but for different reasons. A young woman who lived alone without the supervision of a family chaperone broke one of the most rigid codes of society, and her professional alliance with an ex-Pinkerton had scandalized Mrs. Astor and the Four Hundred. Whenever Prudence MacKenzie's name appeared in the gossip columns, even by innuendo, it was with the titillating hint of impropriety.

"There's one other thing," Prudence added, when she'd completed her tale of stolen sandwiches, disappearances, and murdered orphan boys. She slid a grimy scrap of paper from beneath her glove where she had tucked it against the palm of her hand. "One of the street boys who runs errands for us brought this to my house this morning as I was leaving."

"Do you know where or what this is?" Lowry asked, reading aloud the names of two intersecting streets.

Prudence shook her head. "The boy said it was from Danny Dennis. With his compliments. He drives a hansom cab," she added.

"Everyone who works the streets knows Danny," Lowry said. "If he's directing you somewhere, it's for a good reason." He reached for the hat hanging from a coatrack beside a bookcase whose shelves held legal tomes as well as criminal case files and books on evidence detection and preservation.

"Shall we go, Miss MacKenzie?"

"Can't we walk?" Prudence asked when Warren Lowry raised his arm to signal a hansom cab.

"It's safer this way," he said, bundling her into the first cab to reach the curbside.

Designed to accommodate two adult passengers, hansom cabs weren't meant to be shared by strangers. Prudence put as much distance between her and the detective as she could, but when they turned to speak to one another, their faces were only inches apart.

"The last time I was in this neighborhood," Lowry said, "there were saloons on three of the corners and the fourth was a falling-down tenement slated for demolition."

"To make room for another saloon?" Prudence asked.

"Probably." *Or a brothel.*

It was a toss-up whether drinking establishments or bordellos were more lucrative. Between the taxes they paid and the protection money handed over to politicians and the police, saloons and bawdy houses put hundreds of thousands of dollars into public and private pockets every year. Nobody knew exactly how much, but no one except religious reformers wanted to stop the steady stream. And what harm did they do? Drinking, gambling, and whoring were consensual sins that didn't hurt anybody but the sot, the compulsive high roller, or the john. Not in the same category as robbery or murder.

The tenement they were looking for was typical of the buildings hastily erected to house the wave of newcomers in the years when famine and war flooded the city with European immigrants and refugees from the defeated South. Barely twenty-five feet wide, tenements sat cheek-to-jowl with other tenements, each occupying a narrow lot with an arm's length of space between them.

Jacob Riis had described in his *Scribner's* article what he had found on his nightly excursions to document the lives of tenement dwellers. As Prudence and Detective Lowry opened the building's shoddy front door and stepped inside, she was struck by the full force of what she had read and seen only through the lens of the photographer's camera.

The stink of urine, rotten vegetables, and spoiled meat assaulted them like a heavy fog, impossible to avoid breathing, making the eyes water and the nostrils contract.

Each of a tenement's five floors was split into tiny apartments whose occupants fought and wept and slept behind doors so thin they might not have been there at all. Only the front and rear rooms had windows, she remembered. Everywhere else the residents lived in darkness feebly relieved by oil lamps or candle stubs.

"Are you sure you want to do this, Miss MacKenzie?" Lowry asked.

"I'm sure," Prudence answered. "We've come too far to turn back."

Lowry raised a powerful fist and knocked commandingly on the closest door. A silence like death fell over the first floor. A door creaked open above them. Fierce whispering broke out, then boots scampered down the upper hallway.

"Some of them run whenever the police come anywhere near," Lowry said. "Can't blame the poor devils. There isn't a one among them who hasn't done something we could lock him up for."

"Try again," Prudence urged. She thought she had heard movement inside the apartment.

This time the door opened before Lowry finished knocking. A tiny face peered around the jamb at waist height. Dark eyes large with fright, stringy hair in which Prudence could see insect life crawling, nails bitten to the quick on filthy hands except for one spotlessly clean-sucked thumb. Barefoot, a too-large ragged dress covering her from neck to knobby knees.

Prudence squatted until she and the little waif were at eye level.

"Hello," she said. "My name's Miss MacKenzie. What's yours?"

"Lila." The girl stared at Prudence's pale straw hat with navy ribbons as though she'd never seen anything like it.

"Lila, I'm looking for some friends of mine." Prudence held out Jacob Riis's photograph. "I think they may be in trouble and I want to help. Do you recognize them?" Too big a word. "Have you seen them?"

Lila shook her head, eyes snapping from the photograph back to the fascinating hat.

"Are you sure? Look again."

Warren Lowry's hand came down lightly on Prudence's shoulder. She saw Lila's lips tremble and open just enough to reveal stained baby teeth and gaps where the ones that had fallen or been knocked out hadn't been replaced by new ones yet. Then he was on his knees beside Prudence.

"Would you like to try on the lady's hat?" he asked.

Lila's face lit up like one of Jacob Riis's magnesium flashes. She nodded her head *yes,* looked behind her into the dark, then shook *no.* Tears welled in her eyes.

Prudence slid out the long hatpin holding the boater in place and balanced the modish creation on one outstretched hand. "I have a mirror in my reticule," she said, hoping her maid hadn't taken it out for some reason. "We can put the hat on your head and I'll hold up the mirror so you can see what you look like."

"A princess," Lowry whispered.

"Just for a moment," Prudence promised reassuringly, sensing a disapproving presence lurking behind the girl.

"What do I got to do?" Lila asked. Even at her young age, she knew from experience that nothing was freely given.

"You've seen my friends, haven't you?" Prudence urged.

A barely perceptible nod of the head.

"Can you tell me where?" Prudence whispered. "And when?"

Lila's grubby little hand reached out to touch the wondrously beautiful hat.

Lowry's fingers encircled Prudence's wrist, drawing back the tantalizing offering.

Lila gasped in disappointment, then leaned onto Prudence's shoulder and whispered into her ear.

"You're sure?"

When the girl nodded, Prudence secured the straw hat on her head, tied the ribbons into a big bow beneath her chin, and held up the mirror from her reticule. Just before she got to her feet she pressed a nickel into the grimy little palm.

Lila disappeared behind the closed door amid a burst of startled, angry screeching. Then silence as the child must have handed over the nickel she'd been given.

"In the cellar out behind the building," Prudence said as Lowry rose to his feet and helped her up with one firm hand at her elbow.

He loosened the gun in his shoulder holster as they made their way down the hall and out the back door to the small, beaten earth yard in which nothing grew but a pair of stinking privies.

"I don't see an entrance into a cellar," Prudence said, walking the width of the building and back again.

"What she called a cellar might be just a dugout in the ground." Lowry edged behind the privies. "Nothing here either."

"I'll look again," Prudence said. "Maybe I missed it."

This time, when she passed a heap of rubble piled precariously against the side of the building, she used a piece of board to shove away some of the larger stones. And discovered that they had been strategically placed to hide a hole that didn't look large enough for anything but a dog or a small child to wriggle through.

"I've found it," she called, dropping to her knees to lift away what she could manage before Lowry nudged her aside. His large hands and powerful arms made short work of what she'd been struggling with.

"Why go to all the trouble of piling rocks in front of a cellar door?" Prudence asked when it became obvious what they had found.

"Stand back," Lowry said, not bothering to answer. Gun in hand, he yanked open the pair of narrow doors. Debris littered three concrete steps leading into blackness. "We need a lantern."

"I don't have another hat to trade for one," Prudence said.

Then she spun on her heel and raced off across the yard without explanation. When she came back, she was dragging a skinny street child by the neck of an exceptionally dirty shirt. In one hand he held on to a turnip as if for dear life. The other slapped futilely at the woman manhandling him at arm's length. He stopped struggling the moment she turned him loose into the grip of the tall man he knew instinctively was a copper.

"I heard him behind me," she explained. "He ran when I turned my head."

"I don't think a beat officer could have done any better, Miss MacKenzie."

"That's his dinner he's holding on to." She took in the bony frame of the child whose age she couldn't begin to guess, and realized when she heard him cough that anything she could do for him would be too late and too little. Rickets, consumption, and who knew what else.

Lowry's hand crept into his trouser pocket and came out with five nickels. He held them in the palm of his hand, loosening his grip on the boy's arm only when he was certain he wouldn't dart away again.

"This will buy you more than a turnip for dinner," he said.

The boy's eyes lit up, but he said nothing.

"We're looking for some friends of ours," Prudence told him, holding out the photograph she'd shown to Lila. "We think they may be in trouble. Somebody told us you'd know where they are."

"Do you have a candle down there?" Lowry asked, pointing toward the gaping cellar doors.

The boy nodded.

"All right." He hefted the nickels until they shot out scintillas of brightness. "These are yours when you've shown us the cellar and answered our questions."

The cellar was not much bigger than a room in one of the building's apartments, its walls scabrous with damp filth, the floor littered with bits of collapsing walls. There was barely enough headroom for an adult to stand upright. Ten steps in one direction, ten in another. It would be bitterly cold in winter, Prudence thought, foul-smelling in all seasons.

"*Il diavolo* came one night. The devil. We was all asleep," the boy who had told them his name was Marco said. He'd struck a safety match to his precious candle and deposited the turnip in a dented pot teetering over a primitive cookstove like the ones soldiers had used during the war. "That was afore we started pilin' rocks against the door and makin' a tunnel through 'em."

"To keep *il diavolo* out?" asked Lowry.

Marco nodded. "He took a yellow-haired kid away with him. Somebody tole us a copper found him on the street with his throat cut."

"What was his name?" Prudence asked.

Marco shrugged.

"Then what happened?" Lowry prodded.

"*Il diavolo* came back."

"Did he take anyone else?" Prudence asked

"Everybody runned. 'Cept me. I can't run so fast now. That's why you caught me, miss."

"You almost got away," Prudence said.

"Yeah, but almost ain't good enough."

"Were they ever here, this boy and this girl?" Prudence held the photograph as close to the candle flame as she dared.

"You already aksed me that."

"I'm asking again. I hope you'll help me keep them safe from *il diavolo*. He'll cut their throats, too, if he catches them." She had no idea if what she was saying was anything close to making sense, but she had to try.

Lowry took his hand off the nickels that lay in the dust in front of Marco's crossed legs.

"The boy was here," Marco said, staring at the fortune he was about to earn. "Bedded down with us. He was real good at stealin' from the carts. Earned his keep. We showed him where to go for food on a bad day. Restaurants where the cooks hand food out the back doors. The Asylum. Places like that."

"When was this?" Lowry asked.

"Not too long ago. Around when *il diavolo* came the first time. Only stayed two or three nights. Left when we tole him about the blond kid what got his throat cut. Didn't come back."

"Did he tell you his name?" Prudence found a mint in her reticule. She held it out.

"Long name. Fancy like. Tole us to call him Zander."

Marco crunched down on the mint. It was the first sweet he'd ever tasted.

CHAPTER 13

One glance at his welcoming smile was enough to reassure Prudence that Geoffrey didn't know about the visit to Madame Jolene. She told herself it shouldn't matter what her partner might have to say about the propriety of a lady stepping foot inside a house of ill repute, but she didn't want to test those particular waters. There was also the excursion into Five Points and what she and Detective Lowry had learned at the tenement. She'd done that without consulting Geoffrey, either.

All of the rules changed when you were a woman.

"You haven't told me how the law school lecture went, Prudence," Geoffrey said. He was walking back and forth in his parlor exercising the bad leg, using the cane as little as possible, but not able to do without it entirely.

Prudence's cheeks flamed. She'd been doing a lot of that lately, she chided herself, remembering that Nellie Bly had said a successful investigator needed to be able to hide all of her feelings all of the time.

Edgar Carleton had sent her a note of horrified apology yesterday. Someone had leaked the story of Hiram Vogel's embarrassing oration and the stony reception of his students. She'd not yet answered Carleton's expression of regret. The hurt was too recent, too deep.

Eventually she would have to relate the whole humiliating experience to Geoffrey. But not today.

"The lecture was adequate," Prudence replied. "Boring. I heard better instruction at my father's knee. Deeper scholarship and far more experience in the courtroom."

"Still, it's a step in the right direction." Geoffrey concentrated on placing each foot with careful attention to maintaining his balance when pain shot up the leg where one bullet remained deeply embedded in bone. "You've broken the ice for the group of women who will follow you in the fall. Is it known yet how many will be admitted?"

"Perhaps as few as three or as many as five or six," Prudence said, remembering her conversation with Edgar Carleton on the subject. And that she intended to contact Helen Gould again to help recruit candidates.

And where was Josiah? He usually paid both morning and afternoon visits to his employer, delivering mail, newspapers, and boxes of pastry, none of which she saw stacked neatly on any of the room's tables.

Before she could ask about their secretary's whereabouts— and incidentally change the subject—familiar male voices echoed in the foyer.

"We ran into one another on the Avenue," Ned Hayes explained, ushering Detective Lowry into the suite, introducing him to Geoffrey and Prudence. "He joined the NYPD after I'd left, but we consulted every now and then just the same." Which was Ned's way of saying that for private reasons Warren Lowry had tapped into the ex-detective's storied connection with the New York underworld.

"I didn't expect to see you again so soon, Miss MacKenzie," Lowry said, executing a gentleman's bow over her hand.

Too late to pretend they'd never met before. "I was about to acquaint my partner with what we discovered this morning," she said. Half a truth, in this case, being better than the entire complicated narrative. She had no intention of saying anything about the visit to Madame Jolene's.

"This morning?" Geoffrey asked. "Or do you mean yesterday?"

Ned Hayes seemed to shrink into himself like a gradually deflating balloon.

"One of Danny Dennis's urchins came to the house today with a Five Points address scrawled on a scrap of paper," Prudence explained to Geoffrey as the gentlemen seated themselves. "I was on my way there but I stopped at Mulberry Street Headquarters first. I thought if the boy and girl had slept in the station house basement someone might recognize them from the photograph."

"I told Miss MacKenzie it wouldn't be safe for her to go into that neighborhood alone," Lowry picked up smoothly, ignoring Geoffrey's scowl. "It's a tenement building that's slated for demolition, though nobody's been evicted yet."

"The boy we're looking for camped out in the cellar with a band of street children," Prudence said. "We talked with one of them. He was vague about when precisely the boy was there, but he recognized him from Riis's photograph. He was positive about that. And he also gave us a name. Zander. Which I presume is short for Alexander."

"The disturbing thing is that we've been able to corroborate that someone else is looking for Miss MacKenzie's runaways," Lowry said. "The boy we interviewed called him *il diavolo*." He didn't insult an ex-Pinkerton's intelligence by reminding Geoffrey that *il diavolo* meant *the devil*. "He took a blond boy out of the cellar. Found later in an alley with his throat cut."

"It's another area we can send Danny's street kids," Prudence went on. "Detective Lowry says there's a chance the orphan gangs in that neighborhood might trust them."

"Is the New York City Police Department taking an interest in Miss MacKenzie's project?" Geoffrey asked. The question and the tone of voice were scathingly close to an insult aimed squarely at both Prudence and the man Nellie Bly had sent her to.

"I have private reasons for looking into cases involving missing children," Lowry replied smoothly. He met Geoffrey's stare and matched its mute belligerence.

The air crackled with the tension of two poker-faced men assessing each other's worth.

"I know your story," Geoffrey finally said.

Lowry didn't ask how his personal life had become familiar to Prudence's partner. The newspapers had been full of his sister's disappearance for weeks after it happened, the articles only petering out with time and no leads to keep the investigation active.

When the doorbell rang Ned jumped up to answer it, wondering as he went if he could think of an excuse to get out of what was shaping up to be a tense afternoon. If he'd known that Warren Lowry and Prudence had already begun to investigate the missing children case together, he never would have brought the detective up to Geoffrey's suite. Lowry had always been popular with the ladies, he remembered, and becoming a copper hadn't blunted his society manners. At least Prudence had had the sense to keep quiet about Jolene.

Ned needed a drink.

The package was inscribed *To the attention of Miss Prudence MacKenzie,* but delivered by private messenger to Geoffrey Hunter at the Fifth Avenue Hotel.

"This is odd," Prudence said, when Ned had taken the long, rectangular box from a bellboy and deposited it into her hands. It was tightly wrapped in layers of brown paper and tied with multiple knots of twine. For good measure, the brown paper flaps had been glued together. "I'll need a scissors or a knife to get into it."

"Do you recognize the handwriting?" Detective Lowry asked. He cut through the string with a wickedly sharp pocketknife that he then used to slit the wrapping paper. It fell open neatly, as though the folds hadn't been long in place. "Take another look, Miss MacKenzie."

But her eyes had gone immediately to the box itself, thick red cardboard embossed with wide gold wreaths of curling leaves, flowers, and corkscrewed vines. Centered down the length of the lid, underlined with a theatrical flourish of more twisted vines, were the words *The Doll House.*

Prudence ran an appreciative fingertip over the deeply incised gold letters.

"The handwriting, Miss MacKenzie?" Lowry insisted. He had folded the brown paper into a neat square, leaving the inscription uppermost.

"I don't think I've ever seen it before," Prudence said. Impersonal block letters spelled out her name and Geoffrey's in an easily readable but unidentifiable script. "I should imagine it was done by the store's clerk."

"Mr. Hunter?" One professional courteously consulting another.

"The only distinguishing trait about the handwriting is the way he's crossed the letter *t*. Here in my name, and in the words *Fifth* and *Hotel*. The same strong horizontal bar each time, as though he's slashed the line angrily with his pen."

"I concur," Lowry said. "Very careless of our mysterious gift giver."

"But definitely a man," Geoffrey said. He took the wrapping paper from Lowry and placed it on his desk, examined the box Prudence was holding for anything suspicious, then handed it back to her.

"Very good odds against its being a woman," Lowry agreed.

"Shall I open it, gentlemen?" Prudence asked. The box was so beautifully elaborate that the doll inside had to be exquisite. She raised the lid and lifted aside layers of blood-red tissue paper patterned with more of the gold vines.

The doll stared up at them out of deep green glass eyes

fringed with long, stylized lashes. Feathery painted eyebrows arched in perfectly symmetrical semicircles across a wide forehead. Pursed lips painted a delicate coral emphasized a tiny mouth beneath circles of matching cheek color. Thick blond hair fell in soft curls halfway down the doll's back.

"She's dressed to go to an entertainment of some sort," Prudence said, lifting the creature from its tissue paper nest. "These are the clothes of an adult woman, altered just enough to be suitable for a young girl." It was the fashion to dress children above the age of eight or ten as though they were miniature men and women, in costumes so elaborate and restrictive that anything resembling vigorous, healthy activity was well-nigh impossible.

"It doesn't look like something a child would be given to amuse herself with." Ned's clever cardplayer's fingers danced over the toy that was too expensive to be enjoyed.

"This is a bisque fashion doll," Prudence explained. "Probably made in France of unglazed porcelain, judging by the features. The French are experts at making the skin look nearly human. Everything, including the clothing, is stitched by hand, and always reflects the latest art of the couturier. The end product is meant to be displayed on a shelf or sit in a young girl's lap on special occasions, not to be played with. For that there are far less fragile baby dolls. These fashion dolls are too valuable for any but the wealthy to afford, though similar fashion dolls made from less costly materials are popular."

"I would never have imagined you as the type to cherish a doll collection, Miss MacKenzie," Detective Lowry said.

"My mother was the collector," Prudence said. "She acquired several dozen of these French bisque dolls over the years, displayed in a specially designed glass cabinet. And once she became an adult and married, no one could forbid her to handle them all she liked. We had doll tea parties together. Before she fell ill." And there Prudence stopped. Most of her mother's precious dolls had been gotten rid of by her father's second wife. Only a very few remained in the Fifth Avenue mansion where the judge's daughter now lived alone except for a staff of devoted servants.

"Is there a note in the box?" Geoffrey asked. "This had to have been sent by someone who knows you. Perhaps also remembered your mother's fondness for the dolls?"

"Nothing," Prudence said, shaking out the last piece of tissue in which the figure had been wrapped. She examined the doll closely, scrutinizing the construction of its body, the lines of its painted features, and the materials and seams of the clothing it wore. When she'd finished, she placed the doll back in its red box, leaving the issue paper open around it. "I'm not sure what this is meant to be," she said.

"What do you mean, Prudence?" Geoffrey asked. His partner had not seemed herself from the moment she arrived at his suite this afternoon. Now she was visibly annoyed.

"At first glance this looks like an imported French bisque fashion doll. But on close inspection, and if you know what you're looking for, it's an obvious fake. I can't imagine that whoever sent me this wouldn't know I'd discover the discrepancies."

"Explain, please," Detective Lowry said.

"The French have a very exact way of stitching their seams," Prudence began. "It's not just Monsieur Worth's designs that keep clients flocking to him from all over the world. It's the workmanship, the training their seamstresses undergo, the hours of painstaking labor they put into their creations. The best of the fashion dolls reflect that same level of craftmanship."

"And this doll doesn't?" Ned plucked it from its nest of tissue paper. Now that Prudence had declared it a counterfeit, he could treat it as any other piece of evidence. But proof of what? A pair of missing abused children and a bogus fashion doll. Were they somehow connected?

"Don't get me wrong," Prudence said. "I'm not saying this doll isn't an expensive toy. It is. But it's not what it pretends to be. The French porcelain is unglazed, which is what gives their dolls such a lifelike complexion. Ned, hold that doll up to the light coming in the window," she instructed. "Do you see the shine, the way the light is reflected instead of absorbed? That's only one of the differences, but it's crucial."

"Do you know this shop, Prudence?" Geoffrey asked, holding out the box lid with the words *The Doll House* on it.

"I've never heard of it."

"There was no return address on the wrapping paper, and there's nothing else on or in the box itself," Lowry said.

"Maybe you have a secret admirer," Ned commented. His mother had had a doll that lay atop the counterpane of her bed by day and on her pillow at night. She'd kept it from girlhood, a worn-out thing made of corn husks and calico. Like her, it had disappeared from his life at the end of the war.

"Something about her is familiar," Prudence said, reclaiming the doll from Ned, sitting with it on her knees, fingers wrapped around its tiny hands, rocking it back and forth as though it were alive and needed soothing. *Something about the face? The way the thin eyebrows curved so perfectly?* Even women who plucked their eyebrows seldom removed more than a few stray hairs.

"You're muttering to yourself," Geoffrey said quietly, coming to sit beside Prudence.

"I would swear I've seen this face before," Prudence said. "The more I look at it, the more it grows on me."

"I imagine most of these dolls look very much alike."

"This one is hand painted, Geoffrey. Not as skillfully as the French manage, but it's still very well done. And in anything hand painted, there are always tiny differences from one piece to another."

"Did your governess make you paint china cups and saucers?" he asked, eyes twinkling and a dimple appearing in his right cheek.

"I can tell when you're teasing me," Prudence said. "The dimple gives you away every time." Her stomach had finally untwisted itself. "I did paint bits and pieces of chinaware, if you must know. Every young lady learns useless skills."

"Is there anything in particular that seems familiar?" Geoffrey ran a finger lightly over the doll's cheeks, then cupped his hand over various portions of the face, the better for Prudence to study the features.

He knew by his partner's sudden intake of breath that she'd figured it out.

"The girl I took to the Friends Refuge had plucked eyebrows, Geoffrey. I don't know why it's taken me so long to realize it. Even though she was bruised and dirty, you could tell that the eyebrows had been shaped. They were very, very thin, less than half the width you usually see on a young face. Plucked to look artificial, if that makes any sense. Too perfect to be natural. And there was something else. I can't be sure, but I seem to remember that only one of her eyes had lashes. Very long and now that I think about it, as artificial as this doll's. They must have been glued on. But why?"

"Now it's all beginning to make sense," Detective Lowry interrupted. Neither of them had noticed him approach near enough to overhear their conversation. "Do you agree, Ned?"

"If it's what I think you mean, I do." Ned's face settled into the grim lines it had acquired when he wore a badge. He reached for his hat. "I know where to get some answers," he said ambiguously. "Somewhere none of you would be welcome. Or should be seen."

He left without explaining himself, Lowry following briskly in his wake.

"This isn't a gift, Prudence," Geoffrey said, removing his hand from the doll's face. "It's a message. Now all we have to figure out is who sent it. And why."

CHAPTER 14

"This looks like a private home," Prudence said as her carriage pulled to a halt on a fashionable, shady street well within the Ladies' Mile and just off Fifth Avenue.

The redbrick house was narrow, three stories tall, and only a fraction of the size of the MacKenzie mansion. But an opulent neatness about its shiny black door, elaborate wrought-iron fencing, and two tiny squares of emerald-green grass spoke of moneyed and meticulous attention to detail. A brass plate proclaimed THE DOLL HOUSE.

"I hope clients are seen without appointment." She took Geoffrey's arm as if she needed his assistance to climb the stoop.

"We should be all right." He had to lean on his cane to negotiate the steps. "Can you manage?"

Prudence clutched the box containing the bisque fashion doll in one arm and held on to Geoffrey with the other. It was awkward, but not for anything would she let him think she was afraid he might falter or trip.

They'd debated making this visit under false identities, then reluctantly concluded that the trail they were following precluded that. Prudence's name had appeared more than once in the society gossip columns, linking her, as the only daughter of the late Judge MacKenzie, to an ex-Pinkerton of Southern lineage. The tone of the columns leaned heavily toward cozy tittle-tattle, with a hint of sensationalism and scandal to ensure continued reader interest.

"We build on that," Geoffrey had suggested. "You're a bored young woman of wealth and family who has taken up poking her nose into other people's business as a hobby of which you'll inevitably tire. And I'm a disillusioned, equally affluent dilettante who dabbled in the Pinks before finding it to be too much like real work."

"So bits and pieces of what can be corroborated, gravied over with the clichéd behaviors expected of our type and class?" It appealed to the delight Prudence took in disguising herself as someone she wasn't, as close as she would ever get to the magic spun by famous actresses like Sarah Bernhardt and Lillie Langtry.

"Our names might not be recognized, but if they are, we'll give the impression that whatever success the agency has achieved has been grossly exaggerated by the press. We're harmless dabblers. Amateurs tolerated by society because our antics amuse Mrs. Astor and her ilk."

"I like that," Prudence had agreed. "I may have to apologize for dragging us into this, Geoffrey, especially if it turns out to be one of those messy family situations without any legal recourse for the children involved."

"I think it's much more than that," Geoffrey had answered. "As for legalities, we'll leave that stone unturned for the moment."

So Prudence had put on her latest Charles Frederick Worth Parisian walking suit and Geoffrey had dressed to a gentleman's sartorial nines. The warmth of their reception would prove whether or not the dissimulation had worked.

Prudence tugged on the brass bellpull and tugged again as Geoffrey reached for the polished door handle.

"Shall we?" he asked as the door swung open into a wide front hallway. Glass doored cabinets narrowed the walk space, each of them boasting an array of exquisitely crafted dolls. Every cabinet was secured by an unobtrusive but secure-looking keyed lock.

Prudence tried to do a quick head count. At least thirty to forty of the breathtaking creations in this one space alone, she estimated. There were no price tags attached to any of them.

"Sebastian Marks. At your service," a slender, clean-shaven man announced from a parlor adjoining the entryway. He wore a European-styled suit that was softer in line and more supple in fabric than its American counterpart. His blond hair curled softly over a rolled shirt collar and a diamond stickpin the size of a thumbnail gleamed from the folds of a darkly patterned silk neckpiece. He appeared to be on the wrong side of forty, but so well preserved and perfectly tailored that it was difficult to pinpoint his age. He extended a soft white hand in Geoffrey's direction, then bowed over Prudence's gloved fingers.

Geoffrey could have proffered an agency card, but he didn't, introducing himself in an indistinct, slightly slurred voice, as though he'd had one too many healthy jots of brandy in his morning coffee. He had recognized something about Mr. Sebastian Marks that catapulted him into one of the roles the ex-Pinkerton often played to extract information when a casual witness crossed a line into potential suspect.

When Prudence heard him murmur her name, she acknowledged the presentation with a slight nod, but said nothing. The grander the lady, the more unapproachable she was to anyone not of her station.

Neither removing her pale gray gloves nor giving the man a second glance, Prudence and then Geoffrey followed Marks as he led them into a parlor where another fifty or so dolls sat propped up in identical glass-fronted cabinets. Bisque beauties stared at them out of unblinking eyes in every conceivable shade of blue, gray, green, hazel, and dark brown. Prudence turned slowly in place, as if thoughtfully appraising the choices offered her, then regretfully shook her head. Moved away, rejected all of that beauty, judging none of it fine enough for her sensitively honed tastes and bottomless purse.

The front parlor opened into a rear display room, its walls also lined with glass-fronted cabinets containing an array of elaborately costumed dolls. A stack of folded white linen cloths lay atop the polished surface of a long mahogany table. Prudence had seen something like that before, in shops that sold exclusive wares so delicate they had to be individually presented atop elegant napkins edged in lace or tatting. This, she presumed, was where a doll would rest while a client considered its purchase, never handling it until after the sales transaction had been completed.

She couldn't make out what Marks and Geoffrey were discussing as she circled the exhibit, taking advantage of a moment when their backs were turned to test the handle of one of the cabinets. It didn't give even a fraction of an inch under the pressure of her fingers. So the locks were more than decoration. And the glass served a dual purpose. It allowed the dolls to be viewed and it ensured that any attempted theft would be thwarted by the sound of a shattering pane. For all the museum-like feel of the place, it was obviously a successful business catering to a limited clientele.

Perhaps it was time to bring out the doll that had appeared without warning at Geoffrey's suite. Josiah had made a special trip to a butcher shop to obtain a length of plain brown paper that bore no identifying marks. The original wrapping had been stored in the office file. One of the Pinkerton axioms was that evidence, once collected, was never put in jeopardy of being lost, stolen, or in any way altered.

"I wonder if you would take a look at the doll I've brought with me," Prudence said, interrupting Geoffrey in midsentence, offering Marks the box she carried.

Sebastian Marks inclined his head gracefully. "We don't provide appraisal services," he replied. "But I can certainly give you an informal evaluation." He stripped off the brown paper, pursing his lips and frowning when the distinctive red box appeared, then quickly recovering his aplomb.

"It's one of your dolls," Prudence volunteered. "At least the packaging comes from The Doll House." She pointed to the scrolled golden letters surrounded by twisted vines, the profusion of red tissue paper when he lifted the lid.

"This is not one of our imported bisque dolls," Marks said after a brief examination that included removing the figure's silk stockings and miniature dancing slippers. "This doll was not made in France. Not even in Germany. Nor was its clothing. I'm afraid you've been swindled, Miss MacKenzie."

"How can you tell?" Prudence asked, all wide-eyed innocence.

"You're not a collector then?" Marks turned the doll over in apparent disgust. "There is always a maker's mark on the genuine article. Like fine silver." There was no maker's mark on the sole of either porcelain foot.

"The doll was originally a gift," she explained. "Not to me. It's rather too worn for that. To someone else. How I came by it is immaterial. But given your assessment of its lack of worth and provenance, it's certainly not something I intend to keep."

"You may leave it with us, if you wish. It's not the first item I've seen that fails to pass muster. In cases like this, we make whatever repairs are necessary, then donate the doll to one of the many philanthropic organizations in the city. It's not valuable, but some poor child may derive pleasure from it."

Prudence pretended to hesitate, glanced at Geoffrey as if for guidance in making up her mind, then sighed and shook her head. "I have a favorite charity myself," she said, taking the doll from Marks and nestling it back in the bright red box.

"Oh, Mommy, look! The lady is buying a dolly for her little girl. Please, please, may I have one, too?" chirped a tiny voice from the doorway.

"The door was open," apologized the girl's mother. "Shush, Phoebe." She held her child's hand tightly in her own to keep her bouncing daughter from rushing across the room. "The gentleman is busy."

"Do you have an appointment, madam?" Sebastian Marks asked. It wasn't a question he had posed to Prudence and Geoffrey, but Phoebe and her parent, while well dressed, did not occupy the same rung of the social ladder as Miss MacKenzie and her escort.

"I'm Mrs. Gerald Harris Taylor." She tightened her grip on Phoebe's fingers. "You may have heard of my husband's bank. Taylor First Guarantee Trust?"

And with that declaration Mrs. Taylor condemned herself to the outer darkness of the parvenu. No one in society would dream of clarifying who he or she was. It was always assumed that mention of the surname was explanation enough. Still, since the nouveau riche were notoriously lavish in their spending, the new arrivals were invited to peruse the dolls on display, with the caution that the excitable Phoebe not touch the glass of any of the cabinets.

"How utterly bizarre," Prudence murmured under her breath, but just loudly enough for Sebastian Marks to hear and agree with a sycophantic nod of his head.

"As I was saying, Miss MacKenzie, we would be most happy to dispose of this"—he hesitated, searching for a word that would not offend—"this facsimile," he finished.

"While I'm here, I might as well purchase something for the daughter of a dear friend," Prudence said, strolling toward one of the cabinets with an elaborately casual glide. "She has a birthday in a month or so. Girls her age adore their dolls. I can't decide whether to get a collectible or something her mother would allow her to play with. Do you have a suggestion, Mr. Marks?"

"Collectible," he answered. "Definitely collectible. It's never too early for a young lady to learn to treasure her acquisitions."

"And it would certainly make my obligation as her godmother that much easier," Prudence said. "I wouldn't have to shop at all, would I? Simply rely on your good taste whenever there is occasion for a gift."

"The Doll House has many such arrangements with our clientele."

Prudence took Geoffrey's arm and tugged him away from the table where their red box lay open. "Come help me pick out one of these beauties," she said, dismissing Marks with a wave of her hand. As she had hoped, he immediately approached the shop's other customer and her awestruck daughter.

"May I be of assistance?" they heard him ask.

"I have a rather special request," Mrs. Taylor replied. "My friend assured me that The Doll House would be able to accommodate my wishes."

Prudence and Geoffrey eased closer to the open pocket doors separating the two rooms. Standing just out of eyesight in front of the closest cabinet, they could hear every detail of the conversation in the adjoining parlor.

"It's delicate." Mrs. Taylor let go Phoebe's hand and the child immediately skipped away toward the hallway where a single low cabinet held baby dolls made expressly to delight little mothers.

"Phoebe was a twin, you see," she began.

"My sympathies," Marks said in a soft undertone, anticipating what she was about to tell him.

"Diphtheria. They both fell terribly ill, but only Phoebe survived." Opening her reticule, she took out a black-bordered cabinet card printed with a photograph of the dead child.

"So beautiful," droned Marks. "But then your Phoebe is exquisite, so one would expect her twin to be equally lovely."

"They were a few days shy of their fifth birthday," Mrs. Taylor continued, her eyes tear brightened by a loss from which she would never recover. "And inseparable, the way twins are."

"I understand. How terrible for Phoebe to lose her sister."

"My friend told me that The Doll House makes dolls to order."

"We do. But you must understand that since they are made in our shop, they cannot be of the caliber of collectibles. For that one must rely on French imports. And German products, too, although we do not rate them as high."

"I have in mind a commission for Phoebe that would copy her dear sister's sweet face, so that when she plays with the doll, it will be as though Penelope had not left her. Is that possible?" Mrs. Taylor held out the cabinet card again.

"I would have to consult with one of our master craftsmen," Marks said, tucking the card into his waistcoat pocket. "But we do accept such commissions. From time to time." He coughed discreetly.

"Price is no object," Mrs. Taylor assured him.

"We would insist that you allow your daughter to sit for a portrait."

Mrs. Taylor hesitated.

"Purely to allow us to capture the true tint of skin, hair, and eyes that would make the doll as much a duplicate of Penelope as you would want her to be. Since the sisters were twins." The cabinet photo was in black and white. "Our portraitist is both talented and expeditious."

"I don't know. . . ."

"You would accompany your daughter, of course. And remain with her throughout the sessions."

"If it could be done at our home?"

"It's a question of getting the best light. Good artists can be temperamental about that. We would include a miniature of the completed portrait in the final package, if that is your wish."

Mrs. Taylor was clearly moving toward committing herself.

"I found the dolly I want," Phoebe trilled, dancing from the hallway to her mother's side. She tugged on Mrs. Taylor's skirts, looking up her pleadingly. "You must come see it. Please, Mommy, please."

Prudence stepped into the open doorway just as Sebastian Marks laid a caressing hand lightly on Phoebe's richly red brown curls. She watched as he smiled conspiratorially at Mrs. Taylor. The deal was as good as made.

"I'm sure Sebastian Marks was disappointed you didn't buy anything, Prudence." Geoffrey leaned his cane on the opposite seat of the carriage. "Damn this thing. It's always in the way."

"I don't know any little girls," Prudence said. She'd told Kincaid to roll the carriage to the end of the street, but not to turn onto Fifth Avenue. "Did you notice that he tried to keep our doll?"

"It was smoothly done," Geoffrey agreed. "I wonder why."

"I never accepted his offer to refurbish it for donation to a philanthropy. In fact, I clearly remember telling him I had my own charities. I thought, when he rewrapped the box, that he would hand it back to me, but he didn't. I had to ask for it. Pointedly."

"The whole visit was odd. A shop that looks like a private museum. A clerk dressed far above what his wages would allow. Nothing to attract clients except word of mouth."

"I hope little Phoebe gets her twin doll," Prudence said. "That was such a sad story her mother told."

"Marks said our doll wasn't one of their imported treasures, the proof of that being the absence of a maker's mark," Geoffrey said. "I wonder if they put The Doll House maker's mark on the custom dolls they craft on commission."

"Do you think he was lying to us?"

"I think he was very cautious about how he worded things. If they don't mark their special creations, then what's to tell them apart from any other unmarked doll?"

"So ours could have originated in The Doll House workroom, but for some reason he doesn't want us to know that?"

"Why? He was quite willing to design something for Mrs. Taylor that will no doubt be very expensive. Custom commissions of almost everything are usually signed by the craftsman or the company that originated them."

"It's how you know you've got a one-of-a-kind piece," Prudence corroborated. "Now that so many things are being made in factories or sweatshops, a maker's mark takes on added value."

"What do you know about sweatshops?" Geoffrey asked. She never failed to amaze him.

"Jacob Riis," Prudence answered. "His photographs. What he lectures and writes about."

"There they are," Geoffrey interrupted. Kincaid had knocked the handle of his whip atop the carriage roof in a prearranged signal. "Just coming out of The Doll House."

"I didn't see a carriage or a hansom cab waiting."

"They're walking this way. Toward Fifth Avenue."

"FAO Schwarz in Union Square. I read in the *Times* that it's supposed to be the toniest toy store in the city. She's probably taking Phoebe there." Prudence's hand closed over the handle on the carriage door.

"Prudence, what are you doing?"

"Wait and see," she said as she stepped onto the pavement, waving delightedly at Mrs. Taylor and her daughter.

"So glad I was able to catch you," she trilled, smiling down warmly at Phoebe as she approached the pair. "I just had the most marvelous idea for a gift, inspired by your conversation with Mr. Marks. We were in the next room, of course, and he didn't take the trouble to lower his voice. I wonder if you'd be kind enough to share some details with me. I'm rather in a hurry and I don't want to have to order my coachman to turn the carriage around in this narrow street."

"I'd be happy to, Miss . . . ?"

"Wonderful," Prudence replied, not volunteering her name. "So I understand that to make a custom doll, it is necessary to sit for a portrait."

"To get the skin and hair and eyes correct, is what he said. A photograph isn't as close a likeness as the artist needs."

"And where will the sittings take place?"

"At the artist's studio," Mrs. Taylor answered. "But there will only be two sittings. Which I find extraordinarily convenient, not to have to give over one's sitting room or library for weeks on end."

"I'm getting a Penelope doll," Phoebe said, eyes wide with wonder. "For our birthday."

"I'm sure it will be a beautiful doll." Prudence turned her attention to the little girl. She'd paid her only passing attention before, but now she studied her with an eye for what made her different from other little girls. Phoebe's hair was a bright red-brown, entrancing in the way the tones changed as light danced off her curls. Her eyes were a pure hazel, the shade of an autumn leaf before it lost its green hue. With a clear, pale complexion unmarked by freckles or spots of bright color, she was a strikingly winsome child who would no doubt grow up to become a stunningly attractive woman.

"I gather this is not a usual commission."

"Not offered to the average client, I would say," preened Mrs. Taylor. "My friend who recommended The Doll House had taken her little girl there and spoke most highly of their offerings."

"So she also commissioned a special doll for her daughter?"

"She never took delivery of it." Mrs. Taylor leaned forward to speak in a whisper that Phoebe would not overhear. "She had just begun a fashion doll collection for her when the child disappeared. It was a terrible thing to have happened. She only mentioned The Doll House to me when I spoke of wanting to do something unique for Phoebe. She showed me the doll she bought before her daughter was lost. It looked nothing like her *memento mori* photograph. I don't think she would have kept it had there been a resemblance. We all grieve differently."

"Disappeared?" Prudence repeated. "Your friend's child disappeared?"

"She wasn't my friend at the time. I didn't meet her until quite a while after it happened. They tried to keep the story out of the newspapers, and away from the police, but the assumption was that the girl had been kidnapped. The private detectives they hired believed the child was killed very soon after being taken, either accidentally or on purpose. No ransom was ever demanded. Her parents were heartbroken. They're in Europe now, and none of their friends expect them to return. Too painful."

Phoebe's shoes tapped on the pavement.

"I'm sure you're anxious to be on your way," Prudence said, her mind suddenly churning.

"We're going to FAO Schwarz," Mrs. Taylor said. "It's Phoebe's favorite store."

Mother and daughter strolled toward Fifth Avenue, then disappeared from sight around the corner. The carriage door opened.

"Geoffrey," Prudence said as she climbed inside. "I've just had the strangest conversation."

CHAPTER 15

The red-and-gold embossed Doll House box lay on the Hunter and MacKenzie conference room table, the doll beside it. Josiah had smoothed and folded the tissue paper into a neat square and retrieved the original brown wrapping paper from the file.

"Have you ever heard of a doll being created to look like the little girl who owns it?" Geoffrey asked.

"My mother tried to interest me in her collection and encouraged me to play with the dolls, but I was never fascinated by them," Prudence said. "So I'm not sure I'm the right person to be answering your questions." Didn't Geoffrey have sisters?

"We're missing something," he said.

"I feel it, too," Prudence agreed. A tantalizing wisp of thought just out of reach. "Should we set one of your ex-Pinks to watch the Taylor house and notify us when Phoebe and her mother go to her portrait sitting?"

"What would that give us other than the name of the artist hired for the commission?"

"I keep thinking about the story Mrs. Taylor told me."

"The friend whose daughter was kidnapped?"

"The woman bought her daughter a doll. Then the child was stolen and never returned. No information about what happened to her. Dead or alive." Prudence shaped her sentences carefully, following the sequence of events as she recreated them from Mrs. Taylor's sketchy recounting.

"Not every child who receives a gift from The Doll House disappears," Geoffrey said. "I'm not saying there couldn't be a connection, Prudence," he backtracked quickly. "It's just that it's unlikely." This felt like groping with blind fingers in dark mud, hoping to snag something. Anything.

"I wonder if she brought her daughter with her to pick out the first doll," Prudence continued. She focused her thoughts on a mental image of a tiny, perfect little lady wandering from one glass-fronted cabinet to another, stopping finally to point delightedly at the doll that spoke to her. While the shadowy figure of Sebastian Marks followed every movement.

"Russell Coughlin remembered the incident," Josiah Gregory said from the open doorway. "He wasn't the reporter assigned to cover it, and the parents did everything they could to kill the story, so the kidnapping never made headlines, but he said it wasn't something he was likely to forget. Largely because the crime was unsolved. No clues. No body." He held his stenographer's pad in one hand. "I'll transcribe the notes I took and put them in the file."

"Was that all the information he had?" Geoffrey asked.

"He said there wasn't much more to tell."

"I don't understand how the disappearance of a child could be ignored," Prudence said.

"It's a big city." Geoffrey shrugged. "There are more crimes committed every day than the police can investigate. Only the most sensational of them get reported. And we have to take into account that society families don't want to see their names attached to anything that might reflect badly on them. They have ways of keeping even remotely scandalous news items away from the general public. They buy silence."

"Nellie Bly said no one wanted to read about abused women. No editor would buy that story if she tried to sell it to him." Prudence thought about what else Nellie had said. "If something happens all the time, it's not newsworthy. Does that also apply to a kidnapped child? Do children go missing from families who care about them as often as girls and women get beaten and abused?"

"The streets are a terrible place to live, Miss Prudence." Josiah hadn't returned to his desk in the outer office. Since the visit to the City Asylum for Orphan Boys and Foundlings he'd taken a deeper interest in this case than in any of the others whose records he kept.

"It's as though we're running in multiple directions at the same time." Prudence sounded as bewildered as she felt. "I've gone from two possibly abused runaways to chasing after gangs of street children, a free clinic that shelters women as well as treating their illnesses, an orphanage anxious to hide the fact that bodies are being dumped on its premises, a filthy alley in Five Points, a reporter who claims there's no story in anything I told her, a brothel keeper who said much the same thing, a tenement basement, and now a doll that appears out of nowhere but is probably linked to an expensive boutique that has nothing to do with the streets." She stopped to catch her breath.

"A brothel keeper, Prudence?" Geoffrey queried.

She'd spoken without thinking and said more than she intended. Revealed the one thing she'd deliberately kept from her partner. And now Prudence had to talk her way out of it. With Geoffrey, the plain truth was always the best way through a rough patch. She'd known that from the beginning. She should have told him, flat out, where she'd gone and why. Better still, where she *planned* to go. They might have had words about the propriety of barging her way into a brothel, but there wouldn't have been this awful pall of guilt hanging over her.

"Professor Vogel at the law school talked about the fancy

houses that pay protection to the police and the city politicians. I thought a madam might know something about how a girl came to be in one of those places if she didn't start by selling herself on the streets. So I went to see Madame Jolene because she's the only madam whose name I knew. You're the one who introduced me to her, Geoffrey. Remember? You and Ned Hayes and Russell Coughlin helped keep her house open after one of her girls was killed. You said she was a decent, caring woman. Despite how she earns a living." Prudence tried for a lighter tone. "I knew I wasn't going to be shanghaied and sold into white slavery."

"I assume Ned took you?"

She wouldn't have given up his name, but it was too late to deny it. And if Geoffrey asked Ned, he wouldn't lie. "Yes. I blackmailed him into it."

In the long silence that followed, neither Geoffrey nor Prudence moved or took their eyes off one another. Josiah stared at the floor, concentrating on not dropping the pad and pencil in his hands.

"Was she able to tell you anything you didn't already know?" Geoffrey's voice was flat, expressionless. "Did you meet Big Brenda, the cook? Did you and Jolene and Ned sit in the kitchen and drink coffee and eat cake with the women who work there? Were they even dressed to receive a respectable visitor?"

Every name, every image was a challenge.

Prudence could feel the same anger rising in her throat that she'd experienced listening to Hiram Vogel's diatribe on prostitutes who had no one but themselves to blame for their degradation.

"She claimed not to recognize the picture I showed her, but she suggested I contact Nellie Bly, and then Nellie thought of Detective Lowry." That was the way investigations worked. One seemingly unimportant conversation after another, painstakingly sought-after bits of information gradually forming themselves into a recognizable pattern. She shouldn't have to explain her actions.

"I can't stay out of places I need to investigate just because I wear skirts instead of trousers, Geoffrey. I can't avoid speaking to certain people because I'm supposed to be too fine and delicate to learn about the kind of human misery no one wants to admit exists." Prudence thought for a moment. "Except Jacob Riis. His photographs won't let us turn our backs on the people who live in slums and alleyways."

"We're not talking about Jacob Riis's social crusade."

"I won't be held back. I've told you that before." Every step she'd taken on her own had brought hurdles to meet and overcome; every success had been a vindication of the chances she'd taken. Prudence wasn't the same pampered and protected young woman she'd been two years ago when Geoffrey Hunter rescued her from a stepmother who was bent on forcing her into a laudanum addiction. She wondered if he realized that as she grew stronger, she also, inevitably, edged out from beneath his watchful gallantry. Feelings she had been resolutely pushing aside were at war with each other. She wasn't sure how much longer she could hold them in check.

"I was studying women's faces as we drove back from The Doll House," she said. She refused to discuss Madame Jolene any longer, dismissing outright the notion that her partner had the right to criticize a professional decision purely on the grounds that she was female. If he chose not to follow her lead, so be it. But she wouldn't continue to argue the point. "None of them looked even remotely doll-like."

"Perhaps she's meant to be an ideal image," Josiah volunteered. He knew what Miss Prudence was doing and applauded the tactic. The last thing he wanted to witness was an argument that could escalate into something serious.

"I'm sure that's true," Prudence agreed. "Just as the clothing on the best French bisque dolls is as close to a Worth creation as the dollmaker can devise."

"Why spend all that time and effort and skill on something so expensive no child can play with it?" Josiah asked.

Geoffrey laid the Jacob Riis photo next to the doll, covering up a portion of the picture so that only the girl's startled face was exposed. He moved the photograph closer, then farther away, changing the perspective of his scrutiny, studying the doll alone, the photograph alone, both of them together.

With each movement of his hand, with every minute that passed without rancor, the tension in the room decreased a fraction until at last Prudence felt the tight ache in her shoulders loosen and the lump at the base of her throat dissolve. This wasn't the first time she and Geoffrey had clashed, but it had come close to being the most divisive. Something just below the surface of their relationship was coming to the boil. She thought of a trick her father had chuckled over when he recounted tales of how he had once mesmerized juries into finding his clients not guilty. *Imagine yourself beside the placid waters of a deep lake on a serene summer morning. Nothing disturbs you, nothing ruffles your belief that all is right with the world. Carry that same confidence into your argument. A jury that wants to accept what you tell them as true is halfway to acquittal.*

"We're missing something," Geoffrey said again. This time he caught and held Prudence's eyes with his own. Black, unreadable pupils staring into a calm gray gaze.

Prudence bent over the doll and the photograph, her fingers near Geoffrey's as she retraced his movements. Close, but not touching.

"Her eyebrows have been plucked to an impossibly thin line. Her face isn't as dirty in the photograph as it was when Blossom and I found her in the basement. Here. Look." She sketched in the air the perfect arcs above the doll's eyes, matching them to the image Riis had captured. "I wish we had a name to give her. Calling her *the girl* is so impersonal."

Josiah's manicured hand came to rest on the lower half of the doll's face. The eyebrows were perfectly drawn half circles; thin brushstrokes imitated the fall of individual lashes on the upper and lower lids. Prudence placed another piece of paper over the photograph so that only the top part of the girl's face was revealed. Now there was no mistaking the similarity.

"We've come at this from the wrong direction," Geoffrey said. "It's the girl who's been made to look like a doll, not the other way around."

"Her clothing," Prudence said, hiding everything in the photograph except the girl's dress. "The skirt is torn and filthy, but you can make out the remains of ruffles and what must have been falls of lace on the sleeves. Did we bring her dress back from the Refuge, Josiah?" She tried to remember what had happened to the garments Dr. Sloan had cut from the girl in order to examine her body, but all she could recall was the sight of bruised and broken flesh and the intrusive intimacy of the probing that had confirmed multiple instances of violence. Rapes. Were there worse things you could do to a woman's body?

Josiah shook his head. "It wasn't a case then, Miss Prudence. If it's at all wearable, someone at the Refuge will have washed and mended it by now. Quakers don't waste anything."

"The Refuge isn't on the telephone. I do remember that much," Prudence said.

"One of Danny's boys can be sent over."

"I'd rather go myself," Prudence said, placing the doll back in the box, tucking the folded tissue paper beside it. She reached for the wrapping paper with her name and Geoffrey's address printed in bold black letters on it, hesitated, then placed it also in the box, securing the lid with a piece of knotted twine.

"We'll go together." Geoffrey unhooked his cane from the back of a chair.

"I want to show Dr. Sloan the doll," Prudence said. "She may be able to see things we can't."

"You shouldn't go into Five Points in your own carriage, Miss Prudence," Josiah reminded her. "Not unless you want to attract a lot of attention."

"I don't," she said. "I think that from now on we want to draw as little notice to ourselves as possible."

Geoffrey extended a gentlemanly arm as they left the office. Prudence slipped her hand into the crook of his elbow, feeling a muscle tense and then release as her fingers came to rest on the wool of his coat. They were a team again. But who knew for how long?

CHAPTER 16

"Officer Haden brought her in a couple of hours ago," Rebecca said, leading Prudence and Geoffrey to one of the Friends Refuge examination rooms.

"Why here?" Geoffrey asked. The tap of his cane on the bare wood floor made a staccato accompaniment to their hurried footsteps. "Why not Bellevue? That's where most of the city's indigent casualties are taken."

"Officer Haden has been working the Five Points for a long time," Rebecca answered. "The women say he looks out for them as much as he can. Bellevue can be frightening and impersonal to the younger ones."

"How old would you say this girl is?" Prudence asked.

Rebecca shrugged. "Not much more than fifteen or sixteen. If that."

"Is Officer Haden still here?"

"He left the girl with us, then brought Detective Lowry back from Mulberry Street. They're both with Dr. Sloan."

Geoffrey's jaw muscles tightened. He glanced at Prudence, eyes flashing black lightning. "What is Lowry doing here?"

"He always comes when the patient is this young," Rebecca

said. "He slips something under the table to any patrolman who notifies him when a girl of the age he's looking for gets so badly beaten she ends up here or at Bellevue."

"His sister, Geoffrey," Prudence murmured. "His sister's disappearance is the one case he hasn't been able to solve."

Rebecca nodded. "He's gentle with them, but he asks questions until they haven't anything more to tell."

"What kind of questions?"

"Who their procurer is. How long they've been on the street. The name of the madam if the girl operates out of a brothel. Then he shows them a picture. As far as I know, none of the girls he's interrogated have admitted to knowing the one he's searching for." She handed a white cotton apron to Prudence and helped her drape it over her skirt. "It's sad, really. Two years and nothing to show for it."

"Would you reckon him a friend to the Refuge?" Geoffrey asked.

The Quaker woman considered the question for no more than a second or two. "We only allow women volunteers, but Detective Lowry helps out when funds run low. And he lets it be known that anyone who harasses Dr. Sloan or her staff will have to answer to him."

"Something else I learned about him after talking to Nellie Bly," Prudence said. "He has a private fortune. That's why the family expected a ransom demand when his sister disappeared."

"He's very generous," Rebecca said. "Dr. Sloan calls him our financial angel of mercy."

She tapped softly on the examination room door then opened it without waiting for a response.

The girl lying on the table seemed to be lapsing in and out of consciousness, her eyelids fluttering but only occasionally opening, lips clamped tightly shut, fingers jerking spasmodically as her hands fisted, then released. Fisted again. The clothing she'd been wearing when Officer Haden carried her into the Refuge had been cut off and heaped onto a chair. Horse manure coated a pair of fragile dancing slippers. A basin of bloodied water stood ready to be emptied, stained wet cloths draped over its sides. The room smelled of alcohol, liniment, and the effluvia of the street.

Dr. Sloan nodded a silent greeting, taking her eyes off her patient only long enough to glance at Officer Haden and Detective Lowry, who were standing several steps away from the table to keep watch over the victim but afford her what privacy they could. "I don't think she'll be capable of answering questions until she's had a little more time to recover. If you gentlemen will wait outside, I'll join you shortly."

Lowry touched one finger to his forehead as he passed in front of Prudence. Dr. Sloan's Quaker assistant disappeared into the hallway behind the two policemen, closing the door softly as she left.

"It's not your girl, Miss MacKenzie. She's been similarly abused, but over a more extended period of time, I would say. Some of her injuries are of very long standing."

"How can you tell?" Prudence asked, approaching the table. She could sense Geoffrey following closely behind.

"Many of what look like stains on her skin are the permanent discolorations that come with repeated beatings. She has more internal scarring, and I would say she's suffering from the mental and emotional consequences of abuse." She touched one of the girl's trembling hands. "I think her mind forces her to relive what's been done to her body. Over and over again. She's caught in a nightmare from which there is no awakening."

"Rebecca said she was probably fifteen or sixteen years old." Prudence studied the battered face, wondering how anyone that young could withstand so much mistreatment.

A spasm rolled across Dr. Sloan's features. Her hands gripped the edge of the table as she bent forward to hold her breath against a stabbing pain that bent her nearly in two.

"Are you all right?" Prudence asked. She slipped a supportive arm around Charity's waist, holding her tightly as Geoffrey moved the chair holding the patient's clothing behind her, setting the filthy garments on the floor as Prudence eased her down. Dr. Sloan's face had gone grayish-white. Her teeth bit into her lower lip. "Shall I send for someone?"

"Give me a moment. Just a moment." The doctor gestured toward the laudanum she'd set out for her patient. Geoffrey handed her a glass into which she poured an amount not unlike the doses he'd often seen Ned Hayes consume. "Again," she murmured.

Prudence stared in horror. Even during her worst moments, she'd never consumed as much laudanum at one time as Charity Sloan had just ingested.

The sound of soft panting filled the room. It was like listening to the final moments of a suffering animal. But gradually the rhythm changed and the panting eased into more regular breathing. When Dr. Sloan stood up, her skin had nearly returned to its natural color. "I would appreciate it if you would keep this incident between ourselves," she said. "I especially don't want Rebecca to be told. She'd only worry, and there's nothing to be done."

Geoffrey recapped the bottle of laudanum, removed the chair to where it had stood against one wall, and replaced the girl's clothes on its seat. Whatever was afflicting the Refuge's doctor was something only a medically trained professional could diagnose or deal with. He wondered if physicians were good judges of their own ailments.

"If you're sure?" Prudence murmured.

"I am." Dr. Sloan stood beside her patient as steady and upright as though nothing had interfered with her examination. "Have you come bearing gifts?" she asked, smiling toward the box Prudence had set down on the table. Shifting the conversation away from herself. "The Doll House?" The gold embossed lettering glittered against the bright red cardboard. "We don't usually treat children here."

"It can wait," Prudence said. Then she looked, really looked at the face of the girl lying before her and changed her mind. "The eyebrows are the same." She drew the doll from its tissue paper nest and placed it on the table. "And so are the painted-on lashes."

Dr. Sloan removed a brass mounted magnifying glass from its leather carrying case, squinting to hold it in place against one eye while with gentle fingers she lightly smoothed the patient's skin. "The lashes you see below the bottom lids aren't drawn on the skin with ink or pencil," she said. "They're tattooed."

"That must have been excruciating," Prudence said. She could feel the multiple pricks of a tattoo needle moving across her eyelids.

"The eyelashes were pulled out before the tattooing was done," Dr. Sloan continued. "You'll notice that there aren't any natural lashes on the upper lids, either. But I can see traces of spirit gum. She wore false lashes." The laudanum she had given her patient had relaxed the girl into a deep sleep. Her fingers no longer twitched and her hands lay open and unfisted at her sides. "The eyebrows were tweezed out, also. And then tattooed to simulate individual hairs."

"How long ago was it done?" Prudence asked. "Can you tell?"

"Eyebrows usually regrow in a couple of months," Dr. Sloan said. "But if they're constantly being replucked, the skin can become so damaged that regrowth is much slower." She moved the magnifying glass in a slow arc, pausing frequently to study what she was seeing. "I can't be certain, but I think this girl's eyebrows and lashes have been removed multiple times. The eyelids are slightly red and puffy around the rims, as though they've itched enough for her to rub them repeatedly." She handed the magnifying lens to Prudence.

"I can't imagine anyone pulling out her own eyelashes," she said, shuddering as the magnified eyelids came into focus.

"I doubt she did it herself," Dr. Sloan said.

"Oriental women have a method they call threading," Geoffrey contributed. "It takes out several hairs at once, even a whole row, but not as deeply as using a tweezer."

Neither Prudence nor Dr. Sloan asked how he had come by this arcane bit of knowledge.

Wordlessly, Prudence passed the magnifying glass to him. When he straightened, he brushed a finger over the tattooed eyebrows. "Sailors are sometimes inked with solutions that leave raised scars on the skin," he said. "This was done with a purified ink to avoid that."

"How can you purify ink?" Prudence asked, appalled at the idea that the liquid she used to write letters could also be employed to mark skin permanently.

"You distill out the dangerous substances. I've never seen it done, only heard it described," Geoffrey said. "The most basic tattoo ingredient is carbon mixed with oil to make a kind of slurry. You prick it into the skin with a needle and wipe away the blood as you go."

"Why would anyone want to do that to himself?" Prudence touched her own tender skin as if to reassure herself it was still undamaged.

"I've never been tempted," Geoffrey said.

"Do you suppose she was drugged when they did it? Or did someone put a gag in her mouth so her screams wouldn't be heard while they held her down?"

"I hope it was the former," Dr. Sloan said. She replaced the magnifying glass in its case and raised the sheet covering her patient's legs. "The hair has been eliminated from her arms and legs." She let the sheet fall. "As well as from other places on her body. Some women use a pumice stone for delicate areas, but whoever desecrated this girl intended to make the removal more permanent."

"I can't imagine the pain," Prudence said.

"Do you have your observations from the examination of the girl Prudence and Danny brought to the Refuge?" Geoffrey asked.

"I do," Dr. Sloan replied, picking up a folder from the desk where she wrote notes and dispensed practical remedies. "I think you'll find what you're looking for."

Geoffrey scanned the carefully written account that Dr. Sloan had penned, noting the detailed description of the young woman's bruised and battered flesh and the frank and medically correct phrasing that described the most intimate findings.

"Are they the same?" Prudence asked. She held one of the patient's hands in her own, alert to the slightest pressure that might indicate the girl was conscious.

"I don't think I used the word *tattooed,*" Dr. Sloan said. "There wasn't time to go back over my notes before she disappeared that night. Busy as we were, I left her file on my desk, intending to get to it later, but later never came." She frowned as if to reprimand herself. "Until today."

"The notes indicate an absence of naturally growing hair on her body," Geoffrey said, reading aloud some of what the doctor had written.

"What have we stumbled into?" Prudence asked.

"I think it's time we put that question to Detective Lowry," Geoffrey said.

"I told Rebecca to show him into my office and fetch some tea." Dr. Sloan listened once more to her patient's heart and lungs, counted her respirations, and pressed her fingers into the flesh of her lower legs. "One of our women can sit with her for a while. She won't come to any harm. The laudanum has lulled her into a deep sleep."

The woman who answered Dr. Sloan's bell was dressed in Quaker gray and white, and so like Rebecca in looks and demeanor that Prudence thought they must be sisters.

With a last, lingering glance at the examination table, Dr. Sloan led Prudence and Geoffrey out of the room.

"Is she all right?" Warren Lowry said, rising to his feet, teacup in hand.

"Sleeping for the moment." Dr. Sloan waited for Geoffrey and Prudence to settle themselves before opening the folders she'd carried from the examination room. "What can you tell us about her, Detective Lowry?"

"Only what Officer Haden was able to determine when he found her."

"Which was?" Geoffrey asked.

"He came upon her in an alleyway. Heard a whimpering and then the hiss of a cat, so he took out his billy club and went to investigate. A billy club is the truncheon our officers carry," Lowry explained to Prudence. "She was lying behind some trash barrels, either trying to hide or crawl away, he couldn't make out which. But he could tell immediately what she was, and that she'd been beaten within an inch of her life. So when he got close and saw that she wasn't much more than a child, he picked her up and brought her here. Then he came to get me."

"He didn't try to question her?" Geoffrey's eyes remained fixed on Detective Lowry.

"She was conscious but bloody around the mouth and nose, so he decided to leave well enough alone. Brought her to the Refuge and then hotfooted it to headquarters." Lowry took out the small notebook no investigator was ever without. "I've sent him back to the alleyway to look around for anything she might have carried in there and dropped. Or any sign she wasn't alone. He'll let me know if he finds something."

"Have you seen her before?" Geoffrey asked. "I know you have yourself informed of any case involving a young woman of the streets. You must come across the same girls several times over."

"This one is new to me. I'll check when I get back to Mulberry Street, but I'd venture to guess she's never been picked up."

"She hasn't done anything you could charge her with," Prudence asserted. "She's a victim, not a criminal."

"She is a victim, but she's also a whore, Miss MacKenzie. Do you doubt it?"

"I don't disbelieve for a moment that something terrible happened to this girl to force her to sell her body to stay alive," Prudence retorted. "A horrible crime was committed against her person. A crime for which no one is likely to be pursued or punished. Do you call that justice, Detective Lowry?"

"She's awake, Doctor," a gentle voice interrupted. No one had heard the Quaker attendant's soft knock, nor the click of the door opening.

"I'll ask my questions now." Lowry directed his statement to Geoffrey, bristling as if they two were the only ones in the room.

"Only if she's well enough," Dr. Sloan said, blocking the way out with her slender body. "I won't have her suffer a setback. She needs rest, sleep, the comfort of knowing she's safe here. You may not interfere with her healing."

"I won't, Charity," Lowry said. "You know me better than that."

"Mr. Hunter?"

"This is Detective Lowry's case," Geoffrey snapped. "I won't meddle unless he asks me to."

"Gently," Dr. Sloan admonished. "Gently." She sent Prudence a look that communicated both amusement and exasperation.

Men! it seemed to say. *Even the best of them act like jealous boys sometimes.*

The girl scribbled an address into Detective Lowry's notebook and whispered her name. Then, as if terrified by what she had revealed, she refused to say another word. Covered her face and sobbed into her hands until she collapsed into spasms of hiccuping that had her gasping for breath until she finally lost consciousness.

Dr. Sloan coaxed a spoonful of laudanum between her lips, massaging her throat until she swallowed it. "That's enough," she ordered as two women wearing full white aprons and starched nursing caps wrapped Ottilie Urquhart in soft linens, lifted her onto a wheeled bed, and took her away.

"I'll notify the parents," Detective Lowry said into the silence of the examining room. "They shouldn't have to wait a moment longer for their daughter's return."

"I'd like to come with you," Prudence offered. "I recognize the address."

"Do you know the Urquharts?"

"I know *of* them. I've read the name in the society columns. But no, we've never been formally introduced." She didn't bother to add that she went out into society as infrequently as she could, refused as many invitations as possible without giving grievous offense. If Lowry knew about her family's immediate past, he gave no indication.

"There may be a problem," Geoffrey said. "I think I'd better be there, too."

"I agree." Dr. Sloan swayed as though her feet were about to give way beneath her.

"You're exhausted," Prudence said. "It's time you let someone else take over. Once we've spoken to Ottilie's parents and they've taken her home, you have to promise me you'll look after yourself. I'm ordering bed rest, Doctor."

"I'll do the best I can," Detective Lowry said. "And Miss MacKenzie is right. It might help to have a woman with me when I talk to Mr. and Mrs. Urquhart. Whatever they've imagined as their daughter's fate, it can't have been as shocking as what I'll have to tell them."

"Will you be all right on your own?" Geoffrey asked Dr. Sloan.

What was he implying? Prudence wondered. Surely Ottilie was no longer in danger?

Geoffrey took from its shoulder holster the Colt revolver Prudence hadn't known he was carrying. He handed it to Dr. Sloan, who checked the safety and the chamber as efficiently as though she'd been handling firearms all her life.

"I'll pray I don't need this," she said, "but I'm glad to have it tonight."

"We don't know who may have seen Officer Haden bringing Ottilie to the Refuge," Geoffrey explained. "Word gets around in the Five Points. We have evidence that someone is looking for the boy and girl who were hiding in the law school basement. We have to believe the same is true of Miss Urquhart. She's escaped from a horror that some monster is desperate to conceal. He can't afford to let her live. And talk."

"Which she will," Detective Lowry said. "Eventually."

And that's why a Quaker doctor hid a gun in her skirt pocket, Prudence thought.

Thank goodness she seems to know how to use it.

CHAPTER 17

Robert Urquhart received them with ill-concealed annoyance and bad grace, clearly displeased that his visitors had had the effrontery to challenge the butler's statement that neither he nor his wife was available. It was that quiet, private hour at the end of the day when the family bathed and dressed for the formal dinner always served precisely at eight on nights when there were no pressing social engagements to attend. Urquhart's custom was to gather his thoughts over a glass of imported whiskey, assess what had been accomplished since breakfast, and plan for tomorrow. He did not tolerate interruptions to any part of his routine.

But the MacKenzie name still carried weight in New York society, even though the judge was dead and his daughter a frequent subject of gossip. What she was doing on his doorstep in the company of a police detective piqued his interest almost as much as their presence vexed him. Urquhart never burned his bridges if he could help it. He ordered the visitors ushered into the main parlor, then waited fifteen minutes before joining them.

"Miss MacKenzie. I remember your father, of course. He's greatly missed."

"That's very kind of you, Mr. Urquhart." She nodded politely. "Allow me to present my friend and colleague, Mr. Geoffrey Hunter."

"Mr. Hunter's exploits are not unknown in the city."

Geoffrey's near death aboard a train speeding toward Canada and the escape of the murderous thief he was pursuing had made headlines in all the New York City papers.

"I'm Detective Warren Lowry, New York City Police Department, Mr. Urquhart. I'm sorry to intrude on your evening, but the matter is both urgent and personal." It always amused Lowry that it took mention of his family name to overcome the social stigma of being a policeman.

"Then we'd best get to it," Urquhart said, a wave of one hand inviting them to be seated. The sooner whatever it was had been dealt with, the sooner he could get back to his whiskey and cigar.

Despite it's being early May, a fire had been lit to dispel the mansion's damp chill. Its bright flames provided a welcome contrast to the darkly formal furniture and somber portraits adorning the walls. Everything was expensive, massive, and ugly.

"I think you'd better prepare yourself for an unexpected development in the case of your missing daughter, Mr. Urquhart," Detective Lowry began.

"It's been well over a year," Urquhart interrupted. "We hired private detectives after the police department failed to find any trace of her. In their professional opinion, Ottilie was killed during or immediately after the abduction. You may recall, Detective, that we never received a ransom demand."

"She's been located, Mr. Urquhart. Your daughter is alive."

"Impossible!" Robert Urquhart lurched to his feet, knocking a Chinese porcelain vase from a small table. "There must be some mistake. To raise false hopes now that we've accepted her loss is cruel." The muscles in his jaw twitched and spasmed as he fought to control himself.

"We don't believe there is any doubt, Mr. Urquhart. The individual in question told us her name and wrote her address in my notebook." Lowry thumbed rapidly through the pages. "Is this your daughter's writing? Do you recognize it?"

Urquhart's hand holding the detective's notepad trembled. "It can't be. Not after all this time. Not after what they told us."

"It may help if we know what the inquiry agents you hired were able to learn," Geoffrey said. He rose to his feet with the aid of his cane and slipped the notebook from Urquhart's unsteady fingers, handing it back to Lowry.

"If what they believed was true, they maintained she was better off dead." Urquhart's voice had the dull tone of a heavy wood door slamming shut in an empty room.

"We appreciate how hard this must be for you." Prudence's gray eyes radiated sympathy and understanding.

"It's not fit for a lady to hear," Urquhart protested. "Not fit."

Detective Lowry glanced at Prudence, who shook her head.

"Perhaps only another woman can truly understand what the detectives feared for your daughter," she said persuasively.

Urquhart's features hardened. He picked up the vase from where it had fallen on the thick Turkish carpet, rotating it slowly as he searched for cracks. One forefinger nudged it into precisely the space it had occupied before the announcement that had caught him off guard.

"We were informed there was reason to believe our daughter had been the victim of a white slavery ring." He swung around to stare self-righteously at Prudence. "I suggest you ask one of these gentlemen to explain the concept of white slavery, Miss MacKenzie. It is not a topic I care to discuss."

She didn't flinch. "I know that young women are often tricked or abducted into a life of addiction and prostitution, Mr. Urquhart. I'm aware of what is done to them and the toll it takes on body, soul, and mind."

"You can't be," he argued. "No lady of good family can have any idea of what goes on in certain quarters of the city. It's inconceivable."

"A young female who identified herself to us as Ottilie Urquhart is being cared for by Dr. Charity Sloan at the Friends Refuge for the Sick Poor," Detective Lowry said, effectively curbing Urquhart's rant. "That's a Quaker-run clinic in the Five Points area."

"My daughter would never frequent such a place."

"She was found in an alleyway, badly bruised and beaten. Unable to tell the policeman who rescued her how she came to be there. It was only after she was brought to the Refuge that she managed to reveal who she was." Lowry laid out the facts of the case in clear, precise terms that Urquhart would not be able to misunderstand.

"What did she tell you?" The query seemed to have been wrenched from some closely guarded place of inner torment.

"Only her name and this address. The rest we inferred from the police officer's report and the doctor's examination. Laudanum was administered to ease her physical pain and quiet her mind."

"I don't believe anything you're telling me," Urquhart said.

"Shouldn't we verify the story, Father?" The young man standing just inside the open parlor doorway closed the double doors behind him. "I'm R.L. Urquhart," he said. "As I'm sure you've already been told, our detectives searched for my sister for almost a year after the police department botched the investigation into her disappearance." He neither shook hands with Lowry and Geoffrey nor acknowledged Prudence's presence with anything more than a perfunctory nod in her direction.

"I don't want your mother or sisters to become aware of this development," Urquhart said. "They've suffered enough as it is."

"I agree." R.L. placed himself at his father's side. "However, I do think we'll have to dispel this notion that Ottilie has been

held captive all this time before a reporter catches wind of it."
He consulted his gold pocket watch. "If we order the carriage
now, we can be back from this Refuge place before dinner.
Mother and the girls need never know we've left the house."

"We have a carriage waiting outside," Prudence offered.
There was something methodically cold and unfeeling about
the way the Urquhart men were attempting to head off what
would certainly be a scandal if the girl at the Refuge proved to
be who she claimed. Women known to have been victims of
sexual predation never recovered from the stigma. Their
abuser's violent cruelty began their destruction, but it was completed by the ostracism of the society that should have supported and healed them.

"We'll take our own carriage," R.L. informed them. He
tugged the bellpull to summon the butler, giving a series of
brisk, tersely worded instructions before moving into the foyer
and toward the front door. "I'll instruct our coachman to follow you. I doubt he knows where to find this place in the Five
Points."

As she passed into the entrance hall, Prudence glanced up the
wide staircase that curved toward the mansion's upper floors.
She caught a glimpse of a lady's skirt disappearing down the
second-floor corridor. When she paused to listen, she was positive she heard the distinctive rustle made by expensive silk.

"Prudence?" Geoffrey touched her lightly on the arm.

"He's wrong if he thinks his wife and daughters won't guess
what's going on," she whispered, nodding toward the head of
the staircase. "Why else would a member of the New York
City Police Department come to their home?"

The girl who called herself Ottilie Urquhart was awake
when they arrived at the Refuge.

"We managed to get some broth down her," Rebecca told
them. "She's drowsy because of the laudanum, but she'll be able

to answer questions. Dr. Sloan requests that thee not proceed without her. She's finishing up with another patient, so it will only be a few minutes."

"What is this place?" Robert Urquhart asked, looking around at the unadorned wooden walls, the splintery floor, and the secondhand furniture.

"We serve the mistreated and ill-used women of the neighborhood," Rebecca explained. "And their children, when they have any." Which was her way of informing him that the women sheltering in the clinic were more often than not prostitutes who aborted unwanted pregnancies before they could develop into anything but a temporary nuisance.

The Urquharts, father and son, waited together and slightly apart from Detective Lowry, Geoffrey, and Prudence. Jaws set and backs stiff, they intended to dismiss the imposter as quickly and definitively as possible, then take their leave and never return. A small fortune had been paid to private detectives who had searched every corner of the city for the missing Ottilie. Their final report concluded, without a doubt, that she was dead. Whoever this girl was and whatever her motives, the hoax would not succeed.

"I'm sorry you've had to wait, gentlemen." Dr. Sloan greeted Robert and R.L. Urquhart with professional courtesy, then smiled a warm, personal welcome to the three who had brought them. Fatigue had deepened the lines on her face and darkened the puffy circles beneath her eyes, but the Quaker doctor rarely if ever surrendered to the exhaustion that had recently become her constant companion. Strong tea and an unshakeable belief in the divine spirit within each of the women who came to her for help and healing kept her on her feet. "Mrs. Urquhart isn't with you?"

"My wife is in delicate health," Urquhart said, uncertain how to address this person who claimed to be a doctor and dressed like a cleaning woman.

"I understand," Dr. Sloan said. "We shall try to make this meeting as painless as possible for all concerned."

Rebecca excused herself, murmuring that she would rejoin them in a few moments. Prudence had seen her look questioningly at Dr. Sloan and noted the doctor's answering nod.

"We've placed Ottilie in our contagion room so you'll have some privacy," Dr. Sloan explained. The contrast between her thin, tensile strength and Rebecca's stocky sturdiness was strikingly apparent as she led them toward the offices and examining rooms at the back of the building.

She paused before a closed door, then knocked softly, her concern for how the Urquhart men would react to what awaited them written on her face.

A shaded kerosene lamp cast dim light over the figure sitting propped up by pillows in an iron bedstead cushioned by clean white linens and a hand-knitted coverlet. Her hair had been washed and dried, a hint of darker gold at the roots making a startling contrast with the much lighter curls hanging loosely over the girl's shoulders. Her face had been cleansed of dirt, blood, and tears. Round bruises resembling the marks left by fingertips stood out starkly against skin that appeared to have been artificially lightened.

To Prudence's eyes, Ottilie's complexion resembled nothing so much as the colorless pallor of porcelain before paint was applied. She was sure, when they compared notes, that Geoffrey would agree.

After an initial glance at the girl in the bed, Detective Lowry, notebook at the ready, never took his eyes from Robert and R.L. Urquhart. His pencil noted their horrified recognition, and then, just as quickly, the shuttering of their eyes and the hard thrust of bone against facial muscle as they realized what lay before them. And the impossibility of ever admitting it.

Rebecca carried Prudence's Doll House box into the crowded little isolation room and handed it to Dr. Sloan.

Ottilie's eyes flicked from her father and brother to the un-opened box and back again, pupils so wide with fear that Prudence could read the terror that set her entire body trembling.

Rebecca's broad hand reached out to stroke the girl's clasped fingers, kneading her way through the tremors until the quivering eased.

"I won't show them until you tell me it's what you want," Charity Sloan said. "We talked about facing down fear with truth, but no one will allow it to happen unless and until you are ready."

In that moment Prudence understood where Ned Hayes had gone when he'd left Geoffrey's suite so hurriedly. Back to Madame Jolene's. Perhaps to find Billy McGlory. On the trail of answers to questions Prudence hadn't known to ask because what he and Lowry and probably Geoffrey suspected was so far beyond her realm of understanding that not one of the three of them had wanted to drag her into such a deep pit of barbarity.

Ottilie Urquhart closed her eyes as tightly as a spooked child, then nodded her head. Rebecca's hold on her fingers tightened as the sound of rustling tissue paper filled the room.

As soon as the doll was lifted free of its box and laid on the bed, it became apparent to everyone there what had happened to the girl who had disappeared from a quiet park and the sur-veillance of her governess over a year ago. Geoffrey had said it first. No longer considered human, she had been tweezed, bleached, tattooed, starved, drugged, and beaten into the living facsimile of a doll.

A plaything.

Abused, consumed, exploited, degraded.

But not yet destroyed.

"I've never seen this girl before in my life," Robert Urquhart said. "She isn't a member of my family." He stepped away from the bed, then turned back to speak directly to Dr. Sloan's pa-tient. "She's not my daughter. Not now, not ever."

"I don't know who she is," R.L. declared, "but she isn't my sister."

Dr. Sloan looked at both men as though she pitied them. No condemnation, no judgment, just compassion for their blindness and sorrow for their repudiation of the debt of kinship. "She'll remain here with us, then. We'll take good care of her."

As if either of the Urquharts cared a fig for what happened to trash picked out of a filthy alleyway.

"Will you tell Mrs. Urquhart and your daughters?" Prudence asked. Her anger slashed like a knife through the bitter fog of disappointment and defeat that filled the room like asphyxiating smoke from a badly stoked fire. "They know."

"Stay out of my family's business, young woman," Robert Urquhart snarled. "Or I'll see to it that not even your father's name and reputation will be enough to protect you."

"I think it's time you left," Geoffrey said. He held his cane like a weapon, but out of respect for this Quaker house of healing, did not raise it.

Detective Lowry closed his notebook and unbuttoned his jacket, revealing the butt of the revolver he wore in a shoulder holster.

Prudence wondered what had happened to the gun Geoffrey had given Dr. Sloan earlier.

Without another word, Ottilie Urquhart's father and brother left the room where she had waited for them and the Refuge that had taken her in.

"Wake up, Miss Prudence. Wake up." Colleen's urgent whisper pierced Prudence's bone-weary sleep as effectively as a splash of cold water. "Mr. Hunter's downstairs. He says it's important."

"What time is it?"

"Not quite six yet. Cook's just setting out the staff breakfast."

"Why is he here? What's happened?"

"He wouldn't say, miss. Just that I was to get you up. German Clara's readying a tray of coffee for the parlor." Colleen held out Prudence's dressing gown. "There's not time for anything else. Mr. Hunter said you was to hurry."

Prudence patted down the loose hair around her nighttime braid, slid her arms into the sleeves of her silk wrapper, and eased her feet into the slippers Colleen handed her.

"I'm ready," she said, standing up and heading for the door. Out of the corner of her eye she saw Colleen's right hand sweep to her forehead, her heart, left and right shoulders. A wave of melancholy swept over her, stronger and blacker than anything she'd felt since her father's death. Catholics consoled and armored themselves with the sign of the cross many times throughout their day. What did Episcopalians do?

Prudence sped down the stairs as quickly as she dared, one hand clutching the banister as the slippers on her feet scudded over the Turkish runner. Cameron held open the door of the formal parlor as German Clara passed through with a laden tray. The butler's face was solemn. German Clara wore a look of avid curiosity. Everyone in the house knew that something awful must have occurred.

"What is it, Geoffrey?" Prudence asked.

"The worst," he said. "Or perhaps only what we should have expected. Charity Sloan sent a note to my hotel suite before dawn. I've been to the Refuge."

"Without me?" A spasm of sudden anger made Prudence's voice shake.

"There wasn't time. And I had to be sure," he apologized.

"You'd better tell me straight out."

"Dr. Sloan gave Ottilie another dose of laudanum after we left. She thought it would help her sleep through the night."

"But it didn't?" Prudence said. She had a terrible sinking feeling that she knew what Geoffrey would say next.

"No. Sometime after everyone else had gone to bed, Ottilie

got up and found the closet where they store the cleaning supplies. She swallowed the arsenic they use to keep down the rat population." His voice softened. "It's a terrible death, Prudence. I wish I didn't have to say that it's also effective. Always fatal."

"Dear God in Heaven," Prudence gasped, fumbling her way to one of the silk upholstered sofas. Geoffrey placed something in her hand. A steaming cup of the coffee whose aroma filled the room.

"Drink that," he said, helping her lift the cup to her lips. "I wish it could be something stronger."

"Has anyone else been told?"

"If you mean the Urquharts, no. Nor will they be. For a Quaker, Dr. Sloan has a finely honed sense of retribution. Robert Urquhart will never be certain that the daughter he has disavowed will not turn up on his doorstep someday."

"And R.L. will have to look over his shoulder for the rest of his life for exactly the same reason," Prudence said. "He doesn't deserve to be called her brother." She managed another swallow of the hot coffee. "I'll dress as quickly as I can."

"Dr. Sloan said you needn't come to the Refuge. She and Rebecca will see to what has to be done."

"No, Geoffrey. Ottilie is as much my concern as the girl whose brother stole my sandwiches and kicked open this nest of vipers. I'll pay for her funeral and buy a decent cemetery plot. If anyone questions the arrangements, Dr. Sloan can say it was a donation from an anonymous benefactor. But I won't abandon her."

"It wasn't an easy death," Geoffrey said. "You may want to remember her the way she looked before."

"Do you have a cab waiting outside?"

"Danny Dennis."

"Somehow he's always there when things go badly wrong." Prudence set down her cup. "Give me ten minutes."

"Are you sure?"

She hadn't heard that much feeling in his voice since they'd begun the spate of trivial bickerings that seemed to be driving a wedge between them. She wanted to ask if Detective Lowry had been notified of Ottilie's death, but a flash of intuition kept her from inquiring. Perhaps Dr. Sloan would volunteer the information without having to be prompted.

"Are we sure it was arsenic?"

"Ottilie carried the box containing the powder back to bed with her, tucked herself in, then mixed the poison in her water glass and swallowed it down. There's no doubt. You'll see for yourself if Rebecca hasn't cleaned her up." Which he devoutly hoped would not be the case.

"Drink some coffee," Prudence said as she left to go upstairs. "It's going to be a terrible morning."

The last thing she saw before the door closed behind her was a look of anguish on Geoffrey's face.

Not for himself, she knew, but for what he would be bringing her to confront.

CHAPTER 18

"Your girl's name is Bella, short for Annabelle," Dr. Sloan said. "Ottilie didn't know the family name."

"What made her decide to talk?" Prudence asked. She had stood in silence over Ottilie's body until Geoffrey drew the sheet across the girl's face and folded Prudence into his arms. She'd wept until there were no more tears to shed.

"I think she'd already made up her mind that she was going to end her life." Charity Sloan studied the two sheets of paper she'd folded into a tight square and tucked into her apron pocket. "I went to check on her one last time before going to bed, and she was awake."

"Despite the laudanum?" Prudence asked.

"She must have ingested substantial doses in the past, enough to build up a tolerance." She gave Prudence a knowing look. "That does happen, you know. The patient needs increasingly larger doses to achieve the same effect. Eventually, the craving is pushed beyond the body's limit to endure and he or she dies."

"What else did she tell you?" Geoffrey asked. He'd seen Prudence tremble before when laudanum was discussed; her brief brush with addiction would haunt her for the rest of her life.

She shot him a grateful glance. He reached for her hand, held it lightly in his.

"I wrote down as much as I could," Dr. Sloan said. She smoothed out the sheets of paper torn from the pad on which she usually wrote prescriptions. "Rebecca had gone to bed and I was afraid if I left Ottilie's side for even a second, she'd lapse into silence again. The confidential moment can be a rare thing for someone who has suffered abuse. So when the story of what had happened to her began to pour out, I listened until she had no more to tell.

"Ottilie was taken from a park near her home, when her governess was distracted for a moment. I think the abduction was planned well in advance. She described the smell of the handkerchief that was held against her mouth and nose and the feeling of swooning into darkness."

"Chloroform," Geoffrey said.

"Yes. It has a very distinct odor and the effect is almost instantaneous. She woke up in a dark room, hands and feet bound, not knowing how much time had passed or where she was. After that, the tale grew more garbled and difficult to understand. There were periods of wakefulness and more applications of the chloroform. Laudanum, too. She described a sensation of detachment from her surroundings and what was being done to her. She remembered swimming back to consciousness once and thinking her skin was on fire."

"That must have been when her eyebrows and lashes were being plucked." Prudence shuddered. "I can't imagine how agonizing it must have been."

"Every hair on her body," Charity Sloan reminded her.

"How did she gain her freedom?" Geoffrey asked. It was important to know if Ottilie's escape was somehow tied to that of the girl they could now call Bella.

"She described what happened whenever she was summoned to serve the man she had to address as *Master*," Dr. Sloan began, glancing frequently at the papers on which she'd written her patient's story. "She would be stripped, her body inspected, then bathed. Any stray hairs plucked, although she also said that this was done more extensively on a regular basis. She had no way of knowing how often because she never saw daylight. On what she said were termed *party nights*, her face was carefully made up, her hair curled and styled, finger- and toenails polished. Perfumed oil was rubbed into her skin. Then she was dressed in what she called her costume. She was blindfolded, then led along corridors and down stairs to a very large room whose walls and windows were covered with velvet draperies. Her doll name was Barbara."

"Doll name?" Prudence asked. Despite the horror of what Dr. Sloan was relating, the account was mesmerizing, unlike anything she had heard before.

"Apparently each of the girls had been renamed and made to look like a different doll. The only things they seemed to have in common were the artificiality of their faces, the chemical whitening of their skin, and the exaggerated clothing they were given to wear. Every so often one of them would manage to whisper something to one of the others. Usually nothing more than her name. Dolls who broke the rules disappeared."

"This is monstrous," Prudence said. She swallowed the bile rising in her throat. Felt Geoffrey squeeze her hand reassuringly.

"I've heard worse," Dr. Sloan said. "Much worse."

"Go on, Doctor," Geoffrey urged. "What else did Ottilie tell you?"

"You can imagine what went on at these gatherings. Ottilie skipped over the details, as if she knew I did not need to hear them. One particular element stood out, though. At some point in the evening, each master paraded his doll before the others, then sent her to stand on a raised dais in the center of the room to be admired and appraised. It appears that a master could put his doll up for sale or trade once he tired of her."

"So each of the victims belonged to a certain individual?" Geoffrey's jaw muscles tightened. "Like slavery."

"That's what she understood. When a doll was sold, she joined her new master at his couch and the doll she replaced was sent to the dais. If no one bought her, she was led from the room. Ottilie thought that a master could commission a doll to his specifications or buy one ready-made. She said there were always extra dolls in what she called the *waiting room*. A master could select one or more to buy or to use for the evening." Tears stood in Dr. Sloan's eyes. She'd steeled herself long ago not to allow them to fall.

"How did she learn all this?" Prudence asked. "You said the dolls weren't allowed to talk to one another."

"Over time," Charity said. "Ottilie listened and absorbed whatever she heard while she was being bathed and plucked and clothed. She watched and tried to remember everything that took place in the party room. She was kidnapped a year ago, remember. It took a very long time, but she gradually pieced together the story she told me. I have no reason to doubt its accuracy. She recognized Bella when she saw the photograph you'd left in the box containing the doll Rebecca placed beside her when the Urquharts paid their calamitous visit."

"Her escape?" Geoffrey asked again, bringing Dr. Sloan back to what was immediately important.

"I'm sorry," Charity apologized. "I didn't mean to ignore your question." She traced a closely trimmed fingernail along the lines of hurriedly scrawled notes. "A day or so ago—she couldn't be certain exactly when—she was being readied for what she assumed was another party night. But at some point during the preparation, there was an interruption. I should add that Ottilie said the rooms where the dolls were prepared were medically equipped like our examination and treatment rooms. They called it the doll hospital. There was a whispered conversation, then she was hurried back to her room and locked in. The dollmaker who was working on her was angry that his efforts would be wasted. He cursed under his breath and handled her roughly."

"And forgot to lock the door?" Prudence guessed.

"Not that time," Dr. Sloan corrected. "But another dollmaker she called the costumer came to retrieve the clothing she was wearing. This was hours later, so the dress was badly wrinkled with a rip along one seam. In her panic, Ottilie had lost control of herself and stained the skirt. The costumer shouted at her that she'd ruined the gown, then stripped off the shoes and stockings Ottilie was wearing and stormed out, leaving her on her bed in the soiled dress. Ottilie said the sound of the key in the lock was different. Fumbling. She waited until she was sure no one was still awake, then she tried the knob. It turned in her hand. She tiptoed out into the hallway, crawled through a window onto the roof of a shed, dropped to the ground, and ran until she collapsed in the alleyway where Officer Haden found her. She said she wandered for most of a night and that she thought she had been confined somewhere on the outskirts of the city. I think she was trying to find her way home."

"So it's only been thirty-six hours since Ottilie escaped?" Geoffrey calculated.

"But Bella and the boy we think must be her brother were in Washington Square a week ago and in the alley behind Fat Rico's restaurant before that. And we know that Zander spent time in the tenement basement Detective Lowry and I visited." Prudence counted off the days on her fingers. "Can we assume they hid out together for as long as a week or ten days? And that Zander was alone on the streets before that?"

Geoffrey nodded. "If Zander really is Bella's brother, and if he did somehow engineer her escape, the blame for it must have fallen on these costumers and dollmakers Ottilie talked about."

"And in this instance, the fear of punishment led to paralyzing mistakes and dangerous sloppiness."

"So a week or two after Bella disappeared, Ottilie also escaped."

"Both girls were wearing the doll costumes," Dr. Sloan mused. "I think Ottilie's bolt for freedom was a spur-of-the-moment chance that had to be taken without thought for the consequences."

"I wonder if there have been other breaks," Prudence said. "Other girls who made it to freedom but didn't survive long enough to tell their tales."

"More likely they were discovered and eliminated before they could find help." Geoffrey let out a deep breath. "We know that someone is tracking Zander. That for some reason he expected the boy to show up at the City Asylum for Orphan Boys and Foundlings. Neil and Willie are witnesses to the fact that our killer has murdered two other boys there who resemble the description he's been given. And he hasn't troubled to hide the bodies."

"It's as if leaving the dead boys on the street is a way of taunting his prey every time he miscalculates," Prudence said.

"The first Asylum killing happened ten days ago." Geoffrey summed up for Dr. Sloan what he had learned at the City Asylum for Orphan Boys and Foundlings.

"Another boy was dragged out of the tenement cellar before that and later found with his throat slit," Prudence said. "I wonder how many children have had their brief lives brutally shortened by the masters." She held both hands to her cheeks for a moment. "I don't know what else to call them."

"The Doll Club." Charity Sloan folded the notes from which she had recreated Ottilie's story. "It was one of the last things she said to me before she fell asleep. Or pretended to sleep. She claimed that the man she had to call Master belonged to an organization known as The Doll Club."

"Such an innocent-sounding name," Prudence murmured.

"Was she certain?" Geoffrey asked. He doubted everything until offered proof he could accept.

"I don't know," Dr. Sloan admitted. "By this time I think she may have been regretting that she'd opened up to me. I didn't try to hide the fact that I was writing down much of what she said. But she didn't forbid my giving information to the police and I never mentioned that I might. I've learned by sad experience that almost all of the women I treat want the authorities kept out of their lives. Sometimes it's the first thing they beg for."

Prudence pressed a thick bundle of folded bills into Dr. Sloan's hand. "This is to bury Ottilie with as much dignified secrecy as you can manage," she said. "And for whatever else the Refuge needs at the moment."

"Rebecca has already washed and dressed her," Charity said. "It's not unusual to see a coffin carried out of here on a cart. We'll do it today."

"No name," Geoffrey cautioned.

Charity Sloan rose from her chair and crossed to the small fireplace where a few coals glowed. She ripped in half and then in half again the two pieces of paper that were all that was left of Ottilie Urquhart's identity. The coals flamed briefly, then the prescription blanks subsided into ash.

It was over.

There were no mourners at the burial of the most recent nameless woman to die at the Friends Refuge for the Sick Poor.

Dr. Charity Sloan was too unsteady on her feet to quit her bed, and Rebecca refused to leave her side.

Prudence and Geoffrey waited in their office for the ex-Pinkerton they had hired to report back on any unknown person spotted in the vicinity of the grave. No one appeared. He hung around out of sight as the gravediggers filled in the hole. They finished, tamped down the mound, shouldered their shovels, and took themselves off for a well-earned drink. Another hour passed. Still no one. It looked, he told his employers, as if their plan had worked. Ottilie Urquhart could be presumed to be still alive somewhere. No city death certificate had been signed. There was no proof that she had died.

Lowry was in the Hunter and MacKenzie office when the ex-Pink made his report. The detective looked ten years older than he had two days ago when Prudence first met him. When Nellie Bly had told her his story.

His sister had never been found. There had been no grave over which to weep, no headstone to mark her presence on this earth. There was little true comfort in the rituals of mourning, but going through the protocols for death could make real and final what the heart wanted to deny.

Every case in which a young woman figured must tear the soul out of him all over again. This one was particularly excruciating.

Detective Lowry unpinned his New York City Police Department badge from his vest, then slid the gold shield into his coat pocket.

"No new report will be written," he said. "The account Officer Haden composed when he found the young woman has been destroyed. The entire incident never happened."

"You're sure?" Prudence asked.

"The department is known for burying what it doesn't want the public to find out," Lowry promised. "It's what coppers do best."

"We have contacts and informants we can't share with you," Geoffrey said. "I'm sure you understand why."

"I'm not an ex-Pinkerton, Mr. Hunter, but I know the New York City underworld. Ned Hayes wasn't always discreet when he was in his cups. Whatever I do, and whether you want my assistance or not, it's off the record." He looked pointedly at Geoffrey's cane leaning against the desk within easy reach. Then he wrote an address and telephone number on the back of a card. "My butler can be trusted with telephone messages and telegrams. He'll find me if it's urgent. Best not to contact me at Mulberry Street Headquarters."

Geoffrey passed the card to Prudence, who ducked her head to conceal her surprise. Detective Lowry was a near neighbor. She tried to remember what Nellie Bly had said about him. What she'd found out herself by asking a few discreet questions. Wealthy parents. Mother then father deceased within a year of their daughter's abduction. Connections to Mrs. Astor's Four Hundred. A Fifth Avenue residence and a country estate somewhere up the Hudson.

She'd have Kincaid drive the carriage past the address. Inconspicuously, of course. At a time of day when she could be reasonably certain the detective would not be there.

As he left, Detective Lowry smiled at Prudence in a way that told her he had read her mind.

CHAPTER 19

"We've used Russell Coughlin before," Prudence said, referring to the *New York Herald* reporter who had provided information and access to the newspaper's morgue in return for the inside track on a big story. "He's ambitious enough to get the job done and trustworthy at the same time."

"Not a combination you run into very often," Geoffrey commented. "But I agree. If we're going to comb the society columns for mention of a girl named Bella or Annabelle, we'll need his help. She may be too young to have been a debutante, but there are always items about families retiring to their country places for the summer. And in those stories the children's names are often listed."

"So-and-so home from such-and-such a boarding school," Prudence agreed. "A certain daughter preparing for the upcoming season. I don't think Annabelle is as common as some other names. We might get lucky."

"Detective Lowry sent a telegram. Just the one word." Josiah Gregory read it aloud from the doorway of Geoffrey's office. "Nothing."

"So Bella was never reported missing, At least not to the New York City Police Department," Geoffrey said.

"I wish we knew when Ottilie saw her in The Doll Club." Prudence looked up from the telegram she was drafting to Russell Coughlin. "Dr. Sloan said she called her a new doll, so it's logical to assume that Bella was kidnapped sometime after Ottilie had been taken. That still means there's about a year's worth of newspapers to comb through."

"Why don't I take that over to the *Herald* myself?" Josiah suggested. The urgent bustle of a newspaper made him feel more alive than sitting at his desk in the front office of Hunter and MacKenzie. Even the noise and the dizzying combination of tobacco smoke and printer's ink was better than trying to conquer the complexities of the Remington typewriter. Pounding on its keys made the tips of his fingers ache every time he used it.

He returned an hour later laden with *spritzkuchen* and *bienenstich* from the German bakery he favored, but also the news that Russell Coughlin had given Josiah a letter that would gain him access to the newspaper's morgue. He himself would not be available for the next couple of weeks.

"Did he say why?" Prudence broke off a bite of the sweet *bienenstich*, savoring the taste of almonds and honey, licking vanilla cream from her fingertips. Ignoring Josiah's frown.

"Undercover was all I could get from him." Josiah set out china plates, silver forks, embroidered linen tea napkins. "I get the impression that with Nellie Bly not writing for the *World* anymore, other papers are trying to gain the investigative advantage."

"I didn't get anywhere with these," Prudence said, tapping on a stack of *Town Topics* magazines she'd found stuffed into a seldom used file drawer. "Aunt Gillian insisted on subscribing to this rag while she was here. It's a glorified scandal sheet. Not a single Annabelle in any of the issues. I don't know how they found their way to the office."

Josiah rescued the magazines from the trash basket. "I'll give them another read," he offered.

"You won't have time if you have to comb through the *Herald*'s archives by yourself," Prudence declared. "I'll come with you. With the two of us working, we should finish by mid afternoon at the latest. Geoffrey?" There were bound to be several flights of hard to navigate steps leading down into the bowels of the *Herald* building, but Prudence was determined not to imply that Geoffrey's injury in any way impeded his investigatory prowess.

"I think I'll pay Ned a visit. It isn't like him to become involved in a case and then disappear. We haven't seen or heard from him since Lowry appeared on the scene. That was two days ago."

"He may be having one of his spells," Prudence said. It was how Tyrus referred to Hayes's tumbles from the wagon of sobriety.

"That's another reason to check on him. He claims that crimes like the one we've uncovered don't bring on the thirst, but we both know better than to believe him. I've never met a decent policeman yet who didn't have nightmares. Ned has demons riding on his shoulders he can't bear to talk about, so he tries to drown them."

The basement archives of the *New York Herald* were dark, dusty, and noisy with the clacking thud and screech of the newspaper's presses.

"I can see why they call it the morgue," Prudence said as she made her way along the rows of shelves crammed with labeled boxes and piles of newspapers tied together with twine. "Look out, Josiah. There's a bowl of water on the floor."

"The rats down here are said to be nearly as big as the cat

who chases them. You'll probably see bones and bits of fur, too," he warned her.

"Shall we start with January of last year, just to be sure we don't miss anything?" Prudence suggested.

"I'll take January, you comb through February," Josiah agreed, pulling two large boxes from one of the shelves. "There's a table and a couple of chairs over in that far corner."

"The building may be electrified, but these ceiling bulbs are too dim to do us much good."

"Somebody's left an oil lamp on the table. Let's hope the reservoir isn't empty."

For the next two hours the only sounds in the *Herald*'s morgue were the rustle of newsprint, disappointed sighs, and the heavy thump of cardboard boxes being heaved back into place or pulled off shelves.

"I should have brought the bakery carton," Josiah grumbled. He'd reached September and was starting to lose hope. It wasn't that there weren't plenty of column inches about the comings and goings of New York society; there was more than enough material to fill a dozen engagement diaries. But it had all begun to be repetitive. Boring. He was finding it harder and harder not to yawn as he skimmed over yet another list of notables who had been observed at Delmonico's. "If I have to be re-minded of Mrs. Astor's fabulous diamonds one more time, I'll gag," he muttered.

"Josiah." Prudence's ink-stained fingers stilled. She bent closer to the newspaper she was skimming, breath held, eyes staring fixedly at an article so small, it could be mistaken for a want ad. "Josiah, read this," she said, pointing to a headline that was barely larger than the ordinary print below it.

"*Our reporter has learned that Master Alexander Nicholson will soon be attending Brereton Oaks Military Academy. Is Annabelle to have a new governess? And how will Hudson Valley society survive the upcoming social season when so many of our finest families deprive us of their presence to flood into the*

City?" Josiah fumbled Annabelle's name, repeating it with a touch of disbelieving wonder in his voice.

"It appears to be a reprint of an item from a newspaper I've never heard of," Prudence said. *"The River Valley Record."*

"Probably a weekly or bi-weekly paper that covers local stories and carries more advertisements than news," Josiah said. He'd taken out his stenographer's pad to copy the information he almost couldn't believe they'd found. Their own special needle in an enormous haystack. "No telling who added it to this edition to fill out a short column." The item was at the very bottom of a page, spectacularly unimportant, easily overlooked.

"No date. No byline," Prudence added. "Someone upstairs is bound to know what town the *Record* is published in." She was hurriedly folding and boxing the newspapers stacked on the table in front of her. For a brief moment she thought about tearing out the tiny article and stuffing the bit of paper into her reticule, but a glance at Josiah's busy pencil told her that would be unnecessary. And probably unethical when the whole point of a newspaper's morgue was to preserve a record of the written word.

Ned Hayes wasn't at home.

"He gone all night, Mr. Hunter," Tyrus told him. He rubbed his gnarled hands worriedly. "He ain't done that for a while now. No, sir."

"What time did he leave the house yesterday?" Geoffrey asked.

"Not 'til after dark. Fact is, I never did see him go. Gave him his supper, like I do most nights. Waited for him to get hisself into bed 'afore I turned off all the lights and checked the doors. Next thing I know it's mornin' and he ain't here."

"He'll be back, Tyrus. If worse comes to worse, I'll go out and find him for you."

"Thought I might could do a little of that myself."

"Stay here," Geoffrey instructed. "I have a feeling about this.

I don't think Mr. Ned is on a bender this time, but he may need you anyway when he gets back."

"He workin' that disappear gal case with y'all?"

"Could be."

"Mr. Ned don't got no secrets from ole Tyrus."

"I'm sure he doesn't." But Geoffrey thought that Ned Hayes's entire life was a string of secrets.

"Ned was seen going into the Hotel Irving around midnight," Danny Dennis said, bending down from the high perch of his hansom cab.

He'd pulled Mr. Washington over to the curb as soon as he spotted Geoffrey leaning heavily on his cane at one of the entrances to Union Square Park. It had been nothing short of a miracle that Miss MacKenzie's partner survived the bullets shot into his body at close range in February, but he was far from healed enough to be limping along a congested New York City street through crowds of people who were all in a godawful hurry.

"Was he alone?" Geoffrey asked, climbing into the cab. His leg pained him unmercifully.

"He was alone when he got there, but he might have met up with somebody inside," Dennis replied. "The hotel was respectable until McGlory bought it. Now he's turning the place into another Armory Hall. Word is he won't be in business there very long. It's one thing to run a joint like the old Armory on Hester Street, but the Irving is right across from Tammany Hall and Tony Pastor's vaudeville theater. The powers that be won't want Billy for a neighbor if his bouncers fill up the street with empty pocketed drunks and dissolutes."

"Any idea whether Hayes was expected?"

"All the bouncers know who he is. It's open the door and usher him in and *have a good time, Mr. Hayes.* He's always to be made welcome at any of McGlory's joints. The word went out a long time ago."

"Do you think he's still there?"

"Could be. None of my boys saw him leave, but they weren't keeping a particular eye out for him, either." Danny pulled Mr. Washington to a stop. "Want me to wait, Mr. Hunter?" It wasn't a long walk to the office down near Trinity Church, but from the lines of pain on the ex-Pinkerton's face and the firm grip he kept on his cane, it wouldn't be an easy one. "Mr. Washington could use a little time with his feed bag."

"If it's not too much trouble, Danny. I don't think I'll be very long."

He found Ned Hayes drinking coffee and playing two-handed poker with Billy McGlory in the office that had once housed the hotel manager. Chips and coins and paper bills littered the table in what looked at first glance to be disorganized piles. Ned was as good as a professional card shark at fleecing his opponent, but in McGlory he'd met his match. The lack of expression on either man's face told Geoffrey that the two opponents were enjoying the hell out of each other.

"Mr. Hunter," exclaimed McGlory. The diamonds in his cufflinks, tiepin, and rings twinkled in low-level light from the green shaded lamp suspended above the table. "Welcome. Will you have something to wet your whistle?" Cups of coffee stood at each player's elbow and a white-aproned waiter was gathering up the remains of a substantial and very late breakfast.

"Did Tyrus send you after me?" Ned asked, eyes never leaving the cards fanned out just enough so he and no one else could read them. "I knew I should have sent him a telegram this morning."

McGlory chuckled deep in his throat.

"I could use some more coffee," Ned said, gesturing toward the heavy tin pot resting on an iron trivet above a small candle.

"This is the last hand," McGlory declared. "Neither one of us is going to walk away with any more than we sat down with." He drained his cup and turned it upside down on the saucer. "I've got a business to run here, Ned. Can't wear out a deck of new cards so you won't have to go home to that old tyrant who bosses you around like he owns you."

"I didn't come here to play cards." Ned laid down a royal flush.

"What did I tell you?" McGlory asked, putting down his own royal flush one card at a time.

It was an impossible feat, so rare that most poker players, even the professionals, had never seen it happen. But Geoffrey had known Ned's nimble fingers to pull off other outrageous stunts and he wouldn't put anything below McGlory's ability to do the same. He wondered if the two of them read each other's minds.

"What did you come here for then?" McGlory asked, shaking out his shoulders and stretching his neck. "You never did say."

"Information." Ned cracked his knuckles and raked in his winnings. Half the pot. Just about exactly what he'd come in with, give or take a couple of dollars.

"I don't sell information. You know that." McGlory adjusted his stickpin and shot his cuffs. "And nobody's ever won any from me either."

"There's always a first time."

"Not today."

"I think what Ned's beating around the bush to get to is a case we've picked up that has us buffaloed," Geoffrey explained. Not more than a very few people in New York City felt comfortable with Billy McGlory. Ned and Geoffrey were the only detectives in that select group.

"Who's your client?"

"We don't have one. This is something Miss MacKenzie stumbled into all on her own."

"I can't picture Miss Prudence stumbling over anything." McGlory had a soft spot where Prudence MacKenzie was concerned. Not that he'd ever admit it openly. But he'd made sure that her stepmother and uncle by marriage got what was coming to them and never lost a wink of sleep over it.

"It's a long story," Geoffrey said.

"More coffee then." McGlory raised a finger to the waiter hovering near the door. A fresh pot of coffee, clean cups, a pitcher of warm milk, and a bowl of sugar lumps appeared almost before he put his hand down. "Try not to take the rest of the afternoon, Ned." He changed his mind when he saw the glint of the born storyteller gleam in Ned's eyes. "Maybe you better tell me, Mr. Hunter. Business is already picking up out there."

Geoffrey stuck to the facts as they had discovered them, waving off Ned's frequent interruptions. He started with the sandwiches in Washington Square Park and ended with Ottilie Urquhart's suicide. "Both those girls escaped from the same hell," he finished. "I'd lay odds on it."

"And you wouldn't lose," McGlory said. "Have you ever heard of the Viking House?"

Geoffrey shook his head.

"Ned?"

"Is that the place where the girls all wear horns on their heads and nothing much else?"

"They're all bona fide Swedes, Danes, and Norse goddesses," McGlory said. "If you believe what the clients are told. Every last one of them blond in all the places where it matters. They use so much bleach in that house, the madam orders it by the gallon."

"What does that have to do with Miss MacKenzie's case?"

"Only that any request a man can make will be answered somewhere in New York City. You just have to know where to look for it. You want a Danish princess to sit on your lap, you go to the Viking House. You want a dark-skinned beauty, you take your money to Miss Birdie's Parlor."

"And if a customer wanted a girl who'd been made up to look like a porcelain doll?" Geoffrey asked.

"Private club," McGlory replied. "There are some things you can't easily get away with, even in New York City. For those tastes, private clubs exist. Expensive, exclusive, and very secretive."

"What do you know about this one?"

"Porcelain dolls?"

"Very young women with tattooed eyebrows and lashes and whitened skin. Hairless where they shouldn't be. Dressed like the bisque fashion dolls sold to society women as collectibles." Geoffrey recounted briefly his visit with Prudence to The Doll House. "It was an education. I don't think I'd ever thought much about dolls before. But there had to be close to a hundred of them displayed in glass cases. Maybe more. They were all handmade, so each one was subtly different from all the others."

McGlory went very still for a moment. "Ned?"

"I agree with you, Billy. It has to be a private club of some sort. Like the ones that exist for fancy boys and sodomites."

"Old men have their predilections, too," Geoffrey added. "And they're usually rich enough to indulge them."

"I haven't heard anything on the street. But I'll give you some free advice. Stay out of this, whatever it is. Anytime you mix with the muckety-muck, you come out on the short end of the stick. What I'm doing with this place isn't in the same class as what I suspect you're getting yourselves into. Tammany and Tony Pastor might eventually shut me down, but they won't contract out my killing." McGlory picked up his winnings and folded the bills into his pocket, leaving the coins on the table. "Now if you'll excuse me, gentlemen, I have a business to run and a living to earn."

McGlory locked the office door behind them, then disappeared into the thickening crowd eager to get a head start on the evening's attractions. Just as he had at the Armory, Billy mounted a show nearly every night that was guaranteed to whet the most esoteric appetite and please the lowest taste.

"Tyrus wanted to come out looking for you," Geoffrey said as they emerged into daylight.

True to his word, Danny Dennis had put on Mr. Washington's feed bag while he waited for Geoffrey to finish his business. The big white horse's ears flicked at the sound of familiar voices. He shook his head when Danny removed the bag, scattering bits of half-chewed grain underfoot.

"McGlory was lying," Ned said as they climbed into the cab. "He was hiding something when he said he hadn't heard anything on the streets. He stiffened up and closed in on himself the first time you mentioned anything about kidnapped girls and fashion dolls."

"I caught that," Geoffrey agreed. "It's not like Billy to show any kind of reaction."

"Everybody has his limits. The most efficient knifeman can be some old lady's beloved grandson. He doesn't think twice about getting rid of a troublesome mistress if the price is right, but he won't touch a woman of a certain age if she reminds him of his grandmother. No matter how much you offer to pay him."

"So what's Billy's limit in all this?"

"I'm not sure. Could be he just wants to keep his head down for as long as he can with this new hotel saloon, but that doesn't explain it entirely. He's never turned me away before. Not like this."

"I think there's someone else who can help us, Ned. At least she can confirm what we suspect." Geoffrey tapped his cane against the roof of the cab and when the trapdoor slid open, told Danny where he wanted to go. "She's got a reputation for looking out for her girls. And we heard firsthand what she thinks of other madams who put up with the kind of brutality she won't tolerate. If we put the case to her the right way, she may give us a name."

Ned didn't have to ask who Geoffrey meant. He knew.

CHAPTER 20

The *River Valley Record* occupied a small redbrick building on the west side of the town square in Francton-on-Hudson, a quiet, tree-shaded borough that fell on hard times after its thriving river port silted up. Twenty-five years later, it hadn't recovered.

Ten minutes, the stationmaster had told them. They couldn't miss it. Big gold letters spelling out the newspaper's name scrolled across the front windows.

"It's not the only town along the Hudson that's dying," Josiah said as he and Prudence walked from the train station. "Anything can cause a river to shift its channel and erode its banks. A storm that blows in from the sea, a bad winter freeze, too much boat and barge traffic, sometimes just the passage of time."

"The *Herald* article we found mentioned a social season. All the best families decamping for New York City."

"There may be a grain of truth in it if some of Mrs. Astor's coterie have summer estates in the area."

"Less than an hour north of the city? I'd say there's a good chance."

"My impression is that society people tend to cluster to-gether," Josiah said. "Like seeks like. Hence the season in New-port. I've never heard of Francton. If any of the Four Hundred lived in the vicinity, the town would be mentioned in all of the gossip columns. My guess is that the *Record* is talking about hangers-on who dance attendance on the fringe of Mrs. Astor's elite circle. They don't quite make it, but they never give up hoping an invitation will appear in the mail someday."

The remark made Prudence realize how little she knew about Josiah. He wore beautifully tailored suits, was never less than perfectly barbered, and ran the Hunter and MacKenzie of-fice without a hitch. The ideal secretary. She knew nothing about his personal life. She hadn't asked, but then again, he'd never volunteered. After their visit to the Asylum she'd thought he might have spent time in an institution for abandoned chil-dren. Now she wondered if he came from a family not unlike the ones he was describing. Like a chameleon, he seemed to adapt to wherever he found himself.

"There it is, the *River Valley Record*." Prudence read the name aloud. A well-worn wooden bench stood on the sidewalk and a mongrel dog lay curled up in a patch of sunlight. She counted the empty storefront windows around the square. "A third of the shops are out of business. I wonder how the news-paper's kept from going under."

"Shall we find out?"

"My grandfather founded the *Record* fifty years ago," Chester Olney told them. A small man who barely reached Prudence's shoulder, thin back sharply hunched, head perma-nently twisted to one side, he talked around a cigar clamped in the corner of his mouth, the occasional ash dribbling onto a printer's leather apron pocked with tiny burn holes. "He was owner, editor, reporter, typesetter, printer, and carrier in those early days. There's been an Olney publishing the paper ever since."

"And now it's your turn," Prudence said, touched by the man's family pride.

"The *Record*'s in our blood, Miss MacKenzie. Unfortunately, I'll be the last." He handed her the framed photograph of a young man wearing the Union uniform and a captain's insignia. "I'd planned to keep it running long enough for my son to take over, but that won't happen now."

The photograph occupied pride of place atop the editorial desk. On the wall above it hung an officer's sword and a letter expressing condolences. A row of medals had been pinned to a strip of blue velvet and mounted under glass with the letter.

They drank coffee that tasted like old tar and took a tour of the premises, Prudence thinking all the while that what she was seeing bore no resemblance to the mighty fortress that was the *New York Herald*. This small building consisted of a single room, the walls unplastered brick, the floor slabs of stone set into beaten dirt, worn down unevenly over the years as a succession of Olneys traveled back and forth from copy desk to typesetter's bench to the now-antique printing press.

"I know you didn't travel all the way up here from New York City to sightsee around a weekly rag like the *Record*," Olney said, wiping ink from his fingers after he'd demonstrated typesetting to an intrigued Prudence. "You'd best put aside your good manners and tell me what I can do for you."

Josiah took out his notebook, thumbed through to what he'd copied in the *Herald*'s morgue, ripped out the page, and handed it to Olney. "It's about this story that first appeared in the *Record*. The *Herald* reprinted it in its October fifteenth edition of last year."

Olney read it through, smiled, and handed it back to Josiah. "My star reporter wrote that piece. What about it?"

"We're interested in the two people mentioned in the article, Annabelle and Alexander Nicholson."

"Why?"

Josiah turned to Prudence, unsure how much she wanted to reveal.

"This is off the record, Mr. Olney," Prudence said, extending one of the firm's business cards. She'd picked up the expression from Russell Coughlin, remembering that he'd told her it guaranteed confidentiality. "Do we agree on that?"

"I won't name you as the source of any information I use," Olney said. "That's as far as I'll go."

"How familiar are you with the city?" Prudence asked.

"I have a degree from the University," Olney replied. "Like most undergraduates I spent more time out of the lecture halls than in them."

She repeated the story she'd told Madame Jolene, Nellie Bly, and Detective Lowry, adding the sad tale of Ottilie Urquhart's suicide. "She told the doctor who treated her at the Refuge that the girl we were seeking was named Bella. Short for Annabelle. There's no record in the city police reports of any Annabelle being abducted or disappearing within the last year. That led us to believe that rich or at least respectable parents might have hired private detectives rather than go to the police. Our last recourse was the gossip columns where the only Annabelle we found was the one you wrote about—Annabelle Nicholson."

"As I said, I didn't write that item." Olney relit his dead cigar. "My wife did. She's the star reporter I mentioned. I don't think I could fire her if I tried."

"Will she talk to us about the Nicholsons?"

"I'll ask," he answered, picking up the receiver of a wooden box telephone. "She's on her way over," he said a few moments later. "Friday afternoon she checks in with the sheriff. We publish a crime report in every edition. Let me see if I can answer some of your questions while we're waiting."

"I don't really know where to begin," Prudence said. "Except with this." She showed him Jacob Riis's photograph of the two young people in the alley behind Fat Rico's restaurant.

Olney studied it in silence, cigar smoke wreathing his head. He held a magnifying glass over the faces, moving it in and out to bring the features into sharper focus. "It looks like them, but I haven't seen either of the Nicholson offspring in two or three years. Children change."

"What can you tell us about the family?" Josiah asked, pencil poised to take notes.

"George Nicholson, their grandfather, was a war profiteer. He speculated in railroads but made most of his money through government contracts. Dried beef and hardtack. Only George was in a hurry to get rich, so rumor has it that the beef wasn't dried long enough and the hardtack wasn't always baked through. Which meant the meat rotted and the crackers sprouted weevils."

"That wasn't unusual, from what I've heard and read," Prudence said. It had been one of Judge MacKenzie's great vexations that very few war profiteers were brought to justice for what he considered unpardonable crimes against an army of poor conscripts and idealistic volunteers.

"Too many good men died," Olney said, glancing at his son's picture. "People who started out on the bottom became adept at graft and manipulation. They ended up on top, richer and more powerful than they had any right to be. War turns a society topsy-turvy."

"You're a reformer, Mr. Olney," Josiah commented.

"I'm not a big enough frog, Mr. Gregory. And my pond is too small. I write a decent editorial every now and then, but few people read it. Circulation is low." He puffed on the stub of his cigar, sending another cloud of Virginia-cured tobacco smoke into the already-thick air.

The bell over the front door tinkled as a tall, wide-shouldered woman surveyed them for a moment, then took off her gloves, unpinned her hat, and strode purposefully in their direction.

She nodded briskly toward her husband, shook hands with Prudence and Josiah, dragged a chair over from near the unlit wood-burning stove, and settled in with a determined efficiency that had Josiah nodding in approval.

"I was telling them about George Nicholson and his wartime contracts," Chester Olney explained after he'd briefed her on the story Prudence had recounted.

"George built the place he christened Lanternlight with the fortune he made cheating the government," Pearl Olney said. "By that time he had a son and a daughter from his first wife. He married two more times, but neither of those wives produced any living children. Ira Nicholson, the son by the first wife, is about forty years old. His sister, Effie, was five years younger, but she's gone now, too. The children you're asking about are hers, Alexander and Annabelle."

"We pegged their ages at between thirteen and sixteen," Prudence said. "Though they don't look that old."

Pearl thought for a moment, juggling years and figures in her head. "That's about right. Annabelle is the older of the two. Alexander is two years her junior. Nice youngsters, both of them. More like their mother than their uncle."

"Who was their father?" In Prudence's world, bloodlines were discussed with the same passion as Frederick Worth's fashions.

"That's where the scandal comes in," Pearl said. "Effie's lover was Ira Nicholson's tutor. Nobody knows why, but he stayed on in the house after Ira went back to Yale. They eloped in the middle of the night. We found out later he never married her. That's why the children are Nicholsons. George suffered a stroke over it. He lingered for a few years, angry and resentful every single minute of every one of them. His speech was so garbled, you could hardly understand what he was trying to say, his hands shook too badly to hold a book, and he couldn't walk more than a couple of paces from his wheelchair.

"Ira finished his degree and came home for good, but father and son hadn't liked each other from the day the boy was born. Effie turned up on the doorstep when the tutor abandoned her with two children born on the wrong side of the blanket and a mountain of debts she couldn't pay. From what I heard, there was a godawful fight, but Ira had always been fond of his sister and he got his way. Effie was the only person he was ever kind to. There are folks around here who still think it was unnatural that he preferred a sister to a wife."

"When was the last time you saw them?" Prudence asked.

"Alexander and Annabelle?"

"Yes. And why did you write that notice about them for the *Record?*"

"Not much happens in Francton, Miss MacKenzie. People get married, have babies, and die. In between they grow gardens, attend church, and tittle-tattle about their neighbors. That little tidbit about Alexander going off to boarding school and Annabelle maybe getting a new governess came straight from the horse's mouth, from Ira Nicholson himself. You could have knocked me over with a feather when he walked through that door and gave me the story. Made a big fuss about wanting it in the paper."

"Don't talk yourself down, Pearl," Olney interrupted. "She's as good a reporter as they come," he assured his visitors.

"Local gossip and advertising are what's keeping the *Record* alive right now. There's no point denying it. As it turned out, Alexander didn't leave until a couple of months later."

"What do you know about the boarding school?" Prudence asked.

"Brereton Oaks Military Academy? Fathers send their sons there to have them made into men. I imagine it's modeled after one of the institutions in a Charles Dickens novel. Cold water, merciless canings, miserable food, sadistic teachers, competitive sports no matter the weather, and the kind of headmaster who believes in beating an education into his pupils. It has an excellent reputation and is highly recommended."

"How long was Alexander there?"

"As far as I know, he's never left."

Prudence passed her the Jacob Riis photograph.

"That's him. That's Alexander. Annabelle always called him Zander. He called her Bella."

"Are you sure? Take a second look."

"I don't need to look twice," Pearl snapped. "That's Effie Nicholson's son. Without a doubt. And the girl who looks like she's been made over within an inch of her life is Bella." She tapped angrily on the picture. "What happened to them? You told me the gist of it, but that's not enough."

"We're hoping you can help us figure out the rest of the story," Prudence said.

"Whatever you need. Ira was a mean boy and he grew into an even more vengeful man. To everybody but his sister he was something of a bastard. Probably a bogeyman to the two children Effie left in his care when she passed. It wouldn't bother me at all to see him carted off to prison if he's neglected or harmed them. The men of that family have a lot to answer for."

"You wrote that Annabelle might have a new governess," Prudence continued.

"But nothing came of it," Chester said. "And precious little else changed at Lanternlight after Alexander went off to school. Ira made his trips down to the city every couple of weeks or so like he's been doing for years. The only live-in staff are the butler, the housekeeper, and the cook. All the maids and grounds-keepers are from town or nearby family farms."

"What about Bella?"

"Every now and then I'd run into one of the maids and ask how the girl was doing. I never got a straight answer. If a maid wanted to continue working at Lanternlight, she knew to keep her mouth shut. The housekeeper is one of those women who wouldn't tell you the time of day just for pure meanness." Pearl picked up the Riis photograph, holding it close, staring at the frightened girl in the alleyway. "The thing is, Miss MacKenzie, I can't remember when I last saw Bella. Except that it's been a long time. I'm a good reporter. I can burrow down until I get an answer. But until you showed me this picture, I would have sworn Bella Nicholson was somewhere in that house. Lonely perhaps, but not abused. This photo tells a whole other story."

"Can we read through some of the *Record*'s back issues?" Prudence asked.

"As many as you want. For as long as it takes. What are you looking for?" Chester's cigar had gone out again.

"Anything and everything about the Nicholsons, especially Ira and his sister, Effie. Something happened to make Alexander run away from his boarding school. We need to find out what made him do it. Annabelle was kidnapped. At some point she managed to escape her captors. But why wasn't the abduction reported?"

"Ira isn't the kind of man to take kindly to police nosing around in his personal affairs."

"We've seen that before," Prudence admitted ruefully. "The girl I told you about, the one who identified Bella for us? Her parents hired private detectives after the police failed to find her. I'm not sure how much cooperation they provided the city officers to begin with."

"Let's get started," Pearl Olney said. "You've got a paper to get out, Chester, so let me take care of these good people."

"Have you got the jail notes?"

"Of course I have the jail notes." She tossed her reporter's notebook down on her husband's desk, scattering the debris in his huge glass ashtray.

"There's nothing here," Chester complained as he opened it to an empty page with the single word *JAIL* scrawled across it.

"I told you, Chester, this place can be a reporter's worst nightmare. Nothing worth writing about ever happens in Francton."

CHAPTER 21

Danny Dennis and Mr. Washington wove their way expertly through the busy traffic of Lower Manhattan, driver and horse so well attuned that Danny's whip was mainly for show. He'd kept a straight, expressionless face at Geoffrey's request to take him to one of the better and more private brothels in town, holding back a grin until his passengers had settled themselves and the hansom had begun to roll. He hadn't been the one to drive her, but Danny's network of cabbies had been quick to report that Miss Prudence had been to see Madame Jolene earlier in the week. With Mr. Hayes. The only thing he hadn't puzzled out was whether Mr. Hunter knew about the visit. He nudged the trapdoor beneath his feet slightly open.

"It's probably better if I tell you before we get to Madame Jolene's," Ned Hayes began.

"Tell me what?"

"I couldn't stop her, Geoffrey. You know how she gets when she's made up her mind about something. I tried to talk her out of it, but nothing I said made any impression." Ned paused as long as he dared. "Prudence and I called on Madame Jolene a couple of days ago. That's where she got the idea to go to Nellie Bly."

He hoped Danny was listening and would stop the cab before Geoffrey threw him bodily into the street. Or worse.

"We went early in the morning," Ned explained. "The ladies were all still asleep."

The silence in the hansom cab was as deep and black as midnight on the East River.

Then, unbelievably, a chuckle. Geoffrey's cane rapped on the trapdoor, and Mr. Washington picked up speed.

"She told me all about it, Ned."

"God almighty, I thought you'd be fit to be tied." Ned's Southern turns of speech were never stronger than when he was well in his cups or trying to talk his way out of an embarrassing dilemma.

"I was. But we've been through this more than once, Prudence and I. She's right not to want to be coddled because she wears skirts. She's made herself into a good operator. But I'm also right in trying to keep her from getting herself killed."

Geoffrey managed a wry smile, largely for Ned's benefit.

"For what it's worth, I really did try my best to dissuade her."

"It's done." Geoffrey turned to meet Ned's worried frown. The knuckles gripping his cane turned briefly white, then both men nodded. Subject closed.

Not quite.

"You should know that Madame Jolene warned us off the case." Ned wasn't sure Prudence had remembered to tell him that, but he knew for sure Jolene would.

"Advice I'm sure she wasn't about to heed."

"I think Jolene sent her to Nellie Bly as a way of keeping her out of danger. Bly can handle herself in all kinds of situations. Jolene was reasoning that if a reporter went undercover for the sake of a good story, Prudence would be protected."

"That makes an odd sort of sense," Geoffrey conceded. "But only if you don't know Prudence."

"I couldn't let her go by herself." Ned had a tendency to worry over a thorny discussion long after it should have died a natural death.

"Give me a few minutes. Don't say anything more. Just give me a few minutes."

Madame Jolene's house was in the final throes of gearing up for a busy night to come. Unlike some other brothels, she kept strict hours, and as a result the premises were cleaner and the girls healthier than could be found almost anywhere else. The main parlor had been freshly swept and dusted, the last of the previous night's debris carried away, and the windows opened wide for an hour's worth of fresh air to dispel the lingering haze of cigarette and cigar smoke. The working girls who would soon be servicing the first barrage of customers were finishing up an early dinner under the watchful eye of Big Brenda, the cook. There was a strict rule against liquor not bought by a client; any girl who broke it could find herself out on the pavement with only her suitcase for company.

The bouncer who let them in led the way to Madame Jolene's private parlor and went off to advise his mistress that the former NYPD detective and his ex-Pink friend had arrived without warning. George Bright's short boxing career had given him a bad taste in the mouth for cops; Ned Hayes was the only exception.

"I thought you'd be back, Ned." Madame Jolene swept into the parlor, sparkling from head to toe in black jet beads over black silk and feathers. Skillfully applied makeup made the wrinkles on her face less noticeable, but she'd taken to wearing high-necked chokers to conceal the ropey skin on her neck. She needed the pair of spectacles pinned to her still-formidable bosom to countersign the bills some of her long-standing clients ran up in a business operated for efficiency and profit. A collection of shrewd real estate purchases and the bank account she kept under her real name guaranteed a worry-free old age.

"It's been a while, Mr. Hunter. Not since that gentleman butcher made a mess of one of my best rooms. Not to mention the girl who got in the way of his knife." It wasn't Jolene's way to linger overlong on calamity; she never allowed emotion to override the smooth running of the house. Only a very few people realized there was compassion beneath the hard exterior. And they knew better than to remind her. "Almost two years."

"Sally Lynn Fannon was her name," Geoffrey said, rising to his feet as he would when any lady entered a room.

"That was a bad time. Best forgotten." Madame Jolene settled her skirts, her feathers, and her glittering beads into the elaborately carved armchair a grateful banker had given her. Then she waited.

"We've learned a lot more about the girl Miss MacKenzie tried to save," Ned began.

"I take it Nellie Bly wasn't interested in the story?"

"She told Miss MacKenzie it wasn't the kind of story she could sell."

"I warned her, didn't I, Ned? I told her this was big business. One of the city's most profitable, and likely to remain that way. Half the houses are owned by politicians and men with more money in their back pockets than you or I will see in a lifetime."

"You did offer to help," Ned said.

"I did what I said I would. I showed Miss MacKenzie's sketch to everybody in the house. And I talked to some business acquaintances."

They waited, but Madame Jolene seemed to have said all she was going to divulge.

Geoffrey made a decision based on nothing but instinct, a feeling in his gut that the feather- and bead-bedecked woman in front of him was throwing up barriers that might crack under the truth of what they'd discovered so far. He told her about

Prudence and Detective Lowry's visit to the Five Points tenement, described the doll that had arrived anonymously at his hotel, recounted the visit to The Doll House, and then the rescue and death of Ottilie Urquhart. "Our girl's name is Annabelle. Bella for short."

"I think I knew right from the start, Ned, that you and Miss MacKenzie wouldn't give up," Madame Jolene said. "Nor you neither, Mr. Hunter. All three of you are like badgers. You dig and dig and dig. You never let go once you catch hold of something."

"This is important," Ned said. "You may be the only person who can help us find the thread that will unravel this knot."

"I already did. You just haven't seen it for what it is."

"The doll," Geoffrey murmured. "You were the one who sent it."

"It got you started thinking, didn't it? I told Miss MacKenzie there wasn't anything a man could dream up that he wouldn't be able to buy somewhere in New York City."

"You can't leave it at that, Jolene." Ned had been one of the best detectives on the force in his day. He'd never had to resort to the third degree to get what he wanted out of a witness. It was all in building rapport, he'd often told his skeptical cohorts. He hadn't lost the touch.

"One of my girls left that doll behind when she decided to go elsewhere. The name she worked under probably wasn't the one she was born with, but I'll keep that bit of information to myself just in case."

"Why not tell us?"

"A name is an important thing, Mr. Hunter. It's as rare as hen's teeth for a girl in the life to cross over into respectability, but it has been done. I'd like to think my girl made it, and if she did, the last thing in the world she needs is a policeman looking for her."

"Neither one of us is a policeman," Ned argued.

"Close enough." Madame Jolene stroked her feathers and

polished some of the larger jet beads with a saliva-dampened forefinger.

"That's fair," Geoffrey agreed.

"All right then. I'll call her Gloria so you can follow along. But that's not her name. *G* isn't even her initial. She'd been on the streets before she showed up here. And in more than one other house, from the stories she told. But I make it a practice not to ask too many questions. Just the important ones. Everybody deserves a fresh start, even a whore."

"When was this? When did Gloria come to work for you?" Geoffrey asked.

"Not quite a year ago. Never any complaints from the clients. Did her job, met her quotas, got along with the other girls, mostly kept her mouth shut."

"But . . ."

"But she talked in her sleep, Ned. Not the best habit a girl in her situation can have. You know I rarely let a client spend the night. When I do it's because he's on the brink of setting a girl up in her own place. Just needs a little nudge. Gloria wanted that security, but she knew she couldn't trust herself when she was asleep. Having a drink or a noseful made things worse. About four or five months ago, she had a client who nearly bought us dry celebrating his engagement to a young lady of considerable fortune. Gloria made the mistake of enjoying too much of the champagne he was buying. I'm a light sleeper. She woke me up at four o'clock in the morning, talking to beat the band. I might have just turned over because I knew she was alone, but I heard crying, too. I know the sound of despair; I've listened to it often enough. I went into her room, and there she was in bed, sound asleep but eyes wide open, having a conversation with that doll, tears pouring down her cheeks. I could have shaken her awake, but I didn't. I sat down and listened."

"I don't see how you could have done otherwise," Geoffrey said.

"I do have a care for them, you know," Madame Jolene offered. "The doll wasn't Gloria's, to answer your first question. It was given to her by someone she called Margie, though I never learned whether she was a relative or a friend. At any rate, this Margie seems to have taken up with a man who died unexpectedly of a heart attack. In his own home. That's the vital piece. When she realized what had happened, Margie grabbed the doll and the box it was stored in and fled, emptying his pockets on the way out. She went to Gloria's boarding-house to hide until she could figure out what to do. Terrified for her life. Gloria said she'd never seen anything like what Margie had done to herself. She didn't look anything like a real woman. She could have been that porcelain doll's twin. Except that she was alive and breathing. Gloria couldn't get anything out of her. In the end, Margie borrowed the few dollars Gloria had put aside, left the doll and the box in her bed, and got the next train west. Gloria never saw her again."

"You got all of that from a sleep-talking working girl?" Ned was incredulous.

"I picked up enough clues to know what questions to ask the next day. She answered most of them. Margie was where she shouldn't have been the night her john died. She told Gloria that the brothel where she was usually kept had strict rules about letting the girls leave the premises. But money can always buy an exception to any edict. The point of all of this is that what you now have in your possession is the genuine article—and if you can learn where or who made it to look the way it does, you'll be two steps closer to finding the man or men you're after."

"Why did Gloria leave?" Geoffrey asked.

"Why do any of them go?" Madame Jolene smoothed her black silk skirt. "Always dreaming of something better. Always restless for a different place to be. Sometimes it's a terrible thirst or a hunger for the white powder. A sensible girl would find a decent house with a fair madam, bank the money she earns, buy a small property, and set herself up in business. But that takes planning and self-discipline, something very few of them have."

"What happened when you showed the sketch around?" Ned asked.

"It was a good likeness of the girl in the photograph, but nobody here recognized her. Most of them worked other houses or the streets sometime in the past; they get to know one another. They see things. They hear things. But this girl and what I was able to piece together from Gloria and the evidence of the doll—this was as if it had never happened. My own opinion is that no one who knows anything will talk. The madams I told Miss MacKenzie I'd contact were a little less guarded, but only after I assured them no names would be mentioned. One of them said she thought I was talking about a place she called The Doll Club, but she couldn't or wouldn't tell me where it's located. You can hide anything in this city. You know that, Ned, from your time on the NYPD. You could spend your whole life looking for someone or something or someplace that didn't want to be found."

"I wonder how many of the doll-girls have escaped," Ned mused. "Three that we know of, including Margie, if that's even her name."

"It's not," Madame Jolene assured him.

"There have to be more than just those three."

"There have been," Madame Jolene said enigmatically.

"You're sure?" Geoffrey asked.

"Rumors. Stories. Nothing anyone can prove. But The Doll Club isn't new. It's been around for a long time. As secret as the Masons but harder to join."

"I wonder . . ." Ned looked at Geoffrey.

"What are you planning, Ned?"

"You've been to The Doll House with Prudence. Go back alone, Geoff. Spend some time looking at those dolls you said were in glass cabinets. Take one out, run your finger over the face as though you're caressing it. Make up some nonsense about wishing a real woman could be as beautiful as the doll."

Madame Jolene shook her head. "You'll get better results telling a few of the madams what you want. We charge extra for finding something that isn't available in our own houses."

"How does that work?" Geoffrey asked.

"A regular client tells me he's ready to experiment. He wants a certain type he hasn't had before. Maybe it's a specialty none of my girls will perform. He's comfortable here, doesn't want to go to a strange house. So I check around, find what he's asking for. If the girl isn't turning tricks on the streets, if she's working another house, the madam gets paid for lending her out. Like I told Miss MacKenzie, you can get anything you want in New York City. You just have to know where to go or who to ask."

"I can't come right out and ask for a girl who looks like a doll."

"I'll go with you to The Doll House," Ned offered.

"Neither one of you is doing anything that dangerous," Madame Jolene declared. "That foolish. You may be an ex-Pinkerton, Mr. Hunter, but right now you're a man getting over as close a brush with death as you ever want to have. You can't walk without a cane, and you've got pain lines engraved so deep on your face, they look like dry riverbeds.

"Ned, you haven't got the strength or stamina of a goat. I know Tyrus has been building you up and keeping you off the booze and whatever you can stuff up your nose, but it's not good enough. You've flushed too many bad things through your body for it to ever forgive you." Madame Jolene's cheeks were a mottled red. "I don't want to be responsible for either of you two dying. And that's what'll happen if you go after these men out in the open like that. The Doll Club has only lasted as long as it has by getting rid of anyone who might threaten it.

Girls who get away, men who can't keep their mouths shut, inquisitive outsiders asking questions. You won't see it coming, but it will come. I can promise you that."

"Then why did you send the doll?" Geoffrey asked.

"Jesus, Mary, and Joseph—I wish I hadn't." Jolene made a sign of the cross the way only an impassioned Irish Catholic could do it.

Ned smiled. Jolene was deep into this, more deeply than she wanted to admit. And despite everything she'd told them, despite the cautions, she'd end up helping them if they needed her.

He wasn't sure of many things, but of that he was certain.

CHAPTER 22

Pearl Olney remembered every story she'd written during her more than thirty years as the *Record*'s only reporter. "There's not a lot on the Nicholsons," she told them, flipping through back issues so rapidly that Prudence caught only glimpses of the headlines flashing by. "We printed an obituary whenever one of his wives died, but other than that, you won't find much. His first wife, Ira's mother, had some notion about making a name in New York society; she persuaded her husband to buy a house in the city and then she sat in the parlor waiting for the invitations to pour in. They never did. She gave up eventually and swallowed a bottle of laudanum. George brought little Ira and Effie back to Lanternlight, hired a tutor for the boy and a governess for the girl, then set about trying to create that powerful dynasty he wanted. Unsuccessfully, as I told you."

"Did you know his wives?" Prudence asked.

"They were pitiful creatures. George wore them down as surely as he terrorized Ira. That boy was never so happy as when he went off to Yale. Effie was miserable without him. And lonely. Her governesses didn't last long in George's household, so there were months at a stretch when the girl rattled around without another female to keep her company. She wasn't allowed to be friendly with any of the maids."

"So she fancied herself in love with the most recent tutor and ran off with him."

"You won't find any mention of that in the *Record*." Chester Olney lit a fresh cigar. "It was the biggest story to hit this town since the end of the war, but we never published a word of it."

Josiah studied the twisted little man. Thick clouds of smoke wreathed his head and printer's ink had permanently stained the tips of his fingers. He looked, Josiah thought, like the caricature of an elfin creature reproduced on the frontispiece of an adventure novel. "Why not?" he asked.

"My father had to take out a loan to keep the paper running," Chester said, his face obscured by a cloud of smoke. "It wasn't much, but over time the interest more than doubled what he owed. George Nicholson owned the bank, so for as long as the loan was outstanding, he was our landlord." A bitter twist of his lips turned down the corners of his mouth. "We're free and clear now, but at a cost no newspaperman should ever have to pay."

"We'll go under rather than owe any man another cent," Pearl said. She touched her husband's shoulder lightly as she passed him to lay the small stack of papers she'd retrieved from the files on the desk where she wrote her copy. It was a gentle touch, consoling and reassuring, as though these two had reached a deep and abiding understanding strong enough to withstand any threat that came their way.

"How far from town is Lanternlight?" Prudence asked. She tugged on her gloves and picked up the reticule that held a handkerchief, a small purse, and the derringer Geoffrey insisted she carry with her.

"Do you think that's wise?" Josiah knew there was little chance she'd change her mind, but he had to make the effort.

"You'll need an excuse, if you go onto the grounds." Pearl's eyes gleamed with the challenge. "And you'll have to, if you want more than a glimpse of the house. It's set back from the road in a grove of trees. George had shards of glass cemented into the wall around the property to keep out casual intruders, but there hasn't been a gateman for the last few years. Ira prefers dogs. Big ones."

"It sounds like a fortress rather than a home," Prudence said. She wasn't sure why she felt the need to see Lanternlight in person, just that sometimes a structure gave a more accurate picture of the man who lived there than any portrait artist could create.

"Chester, do we still have any of those flyers we printed for the boys' home in Sadskana?" Pearl asked.

"About a dozen," her husband answered, scanning the file folders in a drawer marked CONTRACT JOBS. "Most of them have small ink smears or a letter that didn't print right, but they're usable." He handed one to Prudence. "Pearl says I'm a pack rat because I keep just about everything, but this way, if the home decides to ask for used clothing donations again next year, we've already got a flyer designed."

"That's your ticket into the house," Pearl said smugly. "I can get you past the dogs and as far as the kitchen door. You're on your own after that if the housekeeper is there."

"What's her name again?"

"Sybil Johnson. Meanest woman in three counties."

"You said you could get me past the dogs?"

"Us," Josiah corrected. "Get *us* past the dogs."

"We'll take the buggy. It'll be a squeeze, but we'll make it. The dogs know me because I went to school with the Nicholson cook. I take a piece of meat or a bone with me every time I go out there." Pearl grinned the smile of a fellow conspirator who has just hatched a foolproof new scheme.

"You didn't mention that before."

"I'm a reporter, Miss MacKenzie. In the normal way of things, we collect information. We don't give it out unless there's a very good reason."

"So you can get us inside the house?"

"I'm not promising anything," Pearl hedged. "It all depends on the housekeeper. My friend sometimes sends me word when Mrs. Johnson's not there and it's all right to come by for a cup of tea. I'm careful to be gone before the housekeeper gets back. Gertie's a good cook, but she'd be out the door without a reference if Sybil Johnson thought she was gossiping about the Nicholsons with a reporter. Which she rarely if ever does. We mostly talk about the old days before the war, when we were young, before my son was killed and she lost her husband. But she needs that job, so I'm careful not to be seen. The last time I was out there was a couple of months before Christmas."

"What about the maids? Or the gardeners? Don't they know when you're there?"

"The people who work for Ira Nicholson may take his money, but that doesn't buy loyalty."

"You might need this," Chester Olney said, handing Josiah a very old but well-oiled pistol. "It never hurts to have a surprise waiting in case you run into the unexpected."

Josiah wondered if newspaper people ever said exactly what they meant. He hid the gun in his coat pocket and asked himself how much more Chester Olney knew about Ira Nicholson than Pearl the reporter did.

The dogs running free on the Nicholson estate were bull-mastiffs, two powerful brindle-coated males with black muzzles that looked strong enough to seize and hold any prey.

"Don't get out of the buggy," Pearl instructed as she climbed down herself and unwrapped a butcher's bundle of soup bones. The animals were leaping against the closed iron gates of the estate, fierce barks alternating with deep, threatening growls. "Look what I brought you, sweet boys." She tossed small pieces of bone through the bars.

"They know me," she told Prudence and Josiah as she vaulted into the buggy, handing what was left of the butcher's package to Josiah. "But it's best not to take any chances. They expect a treat, so I give them one. Let's go on up to the house while they're busy. I'll close the gate again once we get through."

A graveled road wound through a thick grove of towering oaks before breaking out into the open to allow their first good look at Lanternlight. The gray stone mansion reminded Prudence of some of the eccentric homes being built along Fifth Avenue, a flamboyant American mixture of classic European styles, not large enough to be called a palace, but far too big for the family that lived in it.

"What happened to the dogs?" she asked as Pearl brought the buggy to a halt.

"They're loud and dangerous-looking," Pearl said, "but not very well trained. Once you're on the grounds and away from the gates and the wall, they think you belong here." When no one came to lead away their horse, she set the buggy's brake and slid a feed bag over the animal's muzzle. "That should keep him."

"We didn't see anyone as we drove in," Prudence remarked since it was obvious that Pearl had expected to be met.

"I've got a feeling about this," she said, leading them down a set of steps to the mansion's kitchen door. "It doesn't look to me as if there's anybody here." The heavy iron knocker echoed in the stillness.

The woman who opened the door to them wore a cook's white apron and starched mobcap. A streak of flour decorated her nose, one of the lenses of a pair of spectacles, and a round cheek that testified to the quality and quantity of the food she prepared. The scowl beneath the flour disappeared as soon as she recognized her friend.

"Pearl! You must have read my mind! I was just thinking I needed a sit-down and a cup of tea."

Then she caught sight of Prudence and Josiah.

"We didn't run into anybody coming up the drive," Pearl said.

"Come in, come in," Gertie ordered, swishing them past her, giving a careful look at the deserted grounds before closing the door behind them and folding Pearl into a hearty hug.

They resembled one another, Prudence thought. Both tall, physically powerful women. Sensible looking, inspiring confidence, radiating hard work and good humor.

"And who might these be?" Gertie asked, nodding at Prudence and Josiah.

"That depends," Pearl answered, fishing around for one of the orphan home flyers in the large bag she carried everywhere. "Where is everyone?"

"Mr. Nicholson went to the city. We never know when he'll be back. Mrs. Johnson, too, so she can roust up the servants there and see to his comfort. He does like exactly the same routine in both his houses." Gertie nodded in the direction of a dark hallway leading off the kitchen. "Mr. Quinn is in his parlor, nodding off over the master's brandy. The maids and gardeners won't be back to work until Monday." She dusted off her floury hands with a spotlessly clean towel. "I've baking to do, but always time for a visit."

Pearl settled one of the flyers on the table where a recipe book lay open. "Just in case your butler toddles out from under his brandy," she said. "Miss MacKenzie and Mr. Gregory are looking for Miss Annabelle." She signaled Prudence to show Gertie the Jacob Riis photo.

"Dear God in Heaven!" Gertie exclaimed. "What have they done to her?" She collapsed into a kitchen chair, dropping the photograph faceup onto the table. "She's the sweetest child. Never a moment's trouble."

"When was the last time you saw her?" Pearl asked. She draped one arm comfortingly around Gertie's shoulders.

Josiah and Prudence drew up two more chairs. Josiah had his notebook out and pencil at the ready as Prudence slid the Riis photograph closer to the cook. She tried to see the girl in the picture through Gertie's eyes, a woman who had known and obviously loved her. It made what had happened to Annabelle, to Ottilie, to the unknown Margie, and who knew how many other girls, all the more horrifying.

"Gertie," Pearl prompted. She held out the clean dish towel.

The streaks of flour on Gertie's face were themselves streaked with tears. "She used to come down to the kitchen whenever she thought her uncle wouldn't catch her doing it. I taught her how to make lemon cookies and roll out biscuits." Gertie wiped her face dry, sat up taller in her chair, twisted the dish towel in her fingers. "After the New Year Mr. Nicholson sent Master Alexander off to that boarding school he'd been talking about. The boy didn't want to go, didn't want to leave his sister alone. They've been close all their lives, poor things. Their father wasn't worth two sticks to rub together and their mother, Miss Effie, was the loveliest, most foolish girl you'd ever want to meet. It wasn't her fault she didn't know how to be a mother. The only ones who looked out for those two children were the children themselves. Alexander protected his Bella like a tiger and Bella poured out on her brother every bit of love she had to give. She called him Zander whenever their uncle wasn't around to hear. He hates the nicknames they have for each other.

"On the day he had to go to that school, Mr. Nicholson dragged the boy out of here kicking and shouting, and shoved him into the carriage like a sack of laundry. I walked out the kitchen door to the back courtyard to watch them leave. I could hear Annabelle crying and screaming in her room. Mr. Nicholson had locked her in. Nobody was supposed to get to her until the next day, when Mr. Nicholson came back. He'd taken the key with him."

"She was all alone that night and the following day?"

"One of the gardeners, Jerry is his name, put a ladder up against the side of the house as soon as it got dark. The butler takes to the brandy whenever Mr. Nicholson leaves, and Mrs. Johnson's room is on the other side of the house. I gave Jerry some food and drink to carry up, which he did, and then I stood out in the yard with a candle so Miss Bella could look out her window and see my face. Know she wasn't really alone. We didn't dare get caught, so the ladder came down as soon as Miss Bella finished her food."

"Was that the last time you saw her?" Pearl asked.

"I heard her from time to time, crying, but I never saw her in the flesh again."

"Not even at the window?"

"He ordered the shutters nailed closed over the windows in her room."

"How long did that go on?"

"Close to a month. Meals were served on a tray. Mrs. Johnson took them up and brought the tray back down. Miss Bella ate hardly anything. I fixed all the dishes I knew she loved, but it wasn't any use. She'd lost her appetite. Maybe lost the will to keep on fighting."

"Why didn't you try to get word to me?" Pearl asked. "I could have gone to the police."

"What good would it have done? Mr. Nicholson is her guardian. We were told that Master Alexander was making good grades at his school and that Miss Annabelle was being stubborn about going off to school herself. We didn't know what to think, except that we needed to keep our jobs.

"Then Mr. Nicholson came back from one of his trips to the city and announced that he'd hired a governess and Miss Annabelle would be leaving Lanternlight. Moving into the New York City house with the governess. We thought the bad times were over, Pearl. Honestly, we did." She touched the Riis photo lightly, as if to smooth away the fear from the girl's startled face. "What did he do to her?"

"Gertie, this is important," Prudence began, reaching for the hand that held the damp, twisted dish towel. "Can you take us up to Annabelle's room? Do you have the key?"

"I have keys to both the children's rooms," the cook said.

"They're hanging on a hook in Mrs. Johnson's parlor. Nobody's allowed in there, but I figure she's got to know more than she should. She acts like Mr. Nicholson walks on water. You ask me, he should drown in it for what he's done."

"We need proof," Prudence said.

"Where are they?" Gertie asked, wiping fiercely at her eyes. "Who took that picture, Miss MacKenzie?"

"A very good photographer named Jacob Riis. He's a reformer who spends hours every night taking photographs in the tenements to show people how bad the conditions are there." She held Gertie's hand tightly. "I've told Pearl all about how I met Bella. And she'll tell you. But right now we need to search those rooms and get out of here before your butler wakes up."

"I'll show you the rooms," Gertie said. "Take your shoes off so Mr. Quinn won't hear you on the staircase. Wait here while I get the keys."

"What are we looking for?" Josiah asked, bending over to unlace his boots.

"I don't know," Prudence answered. "Anything and everything."

"You'll know you've found it when you see it," Pearl Olney predicted. "There's been plenty of times I didn't realize a story was there until I stumbled into it."

"No stumbling," Josiah muttered.

Bella's room was furnished as luxuriously as that of any pampered daughter of an important and wealthy family. Everything was pink and white and pale yellow, like the petals and pollen-laden stamen of a summer flower. The four-poster bed was sheltered by a lace canopy and piled high with down-filled coverlets and pillows. A satin-covered stool sat before a mirrored dressing table, its surface immaculately clean and empty, not so much as a grain of powder or a stray hair on its gleaming top. The pale oak floor was waxed and buffed, lain over with small Turkish carpets in shades of cream, pale rose, and gold. Filmy lace curtains covered the shuttered windows, bracketed on each side by heavy, lined drapes that would capture sound as well as exclude daylight.

"It's like what I imagine being laid out inside a coffin would be," Prudence breathed. "All soft cushions and pale colors, but nowhere to go and no way to escape once the lid has been screwed down." She shuddered.

"Only the housekeeper and one of the maids has been in these rooms since Alexander went off to boarding school and Bella went to the city to meet her new governess," Gertie said.

"Do you want me to tackle Alexander's room?" Josiah asked.

"Not yet," Prudence decided. "I think we'll be more efficient if we remain together." Pearl had volunteered to stay outside to quiet the dogs if they approached the house and warn if anyone came up the drive. "We'll divide each room into sections and Gertie can tell us if anything has changed recently."

It was a proven Pinkerton search strategy that Geoffrey had taught both Prudence and Josiah. Eyes moving slowly and methodically from left to right, you worked your way visually through a section before touching any item within it. And while you performed this preliminary inspection, you put yourself in the mind of the person who had lived or worked in that room. You searched for hiding places just as he or she would have done. It was a simple, logical approach that had proved itself many times over.

"There's nothing of Miss Bella left," Gertie declared angrily after Prudence had opened the doors to the tall armoire that dominated one wall and Josiah had pulled out the drawers of the bedside tables and dresser. Not even a sachet of dried lavender remained, thought the faint scent was unmistakable.

"Did she keep a journal?" Prudence asked. She'd returned to

the center of the room for a last perusal of the walls and furniture. Everyone she knew had been trained from childhood to create a daily record of thoughts and events.

"Burned," Gertie said. "Along with all of her books and the watercolors she painted."

"When did that happen?"

"After Mr. Nicholson had taken her down to the city to live. Mrs. Johnson ordered them gathered up and carried to the burn barrel that's out behind the gardener's shed. She stood there until the last bit of paper had turned to ash."

With Gertie's help, Prudence and Josiah searched under Bella's bed, taking the mattress off and putting it back on again after looking for rents where she might have hidden something. Nothing had been taped to the slats, no floorboard was loose.

"Sybil Johnson did a thorough job." Gertie smoothed the bed linens and replaced the pillows and cushions so that everything looked as untouched as when they'd entered the room. "She started out as a chambermaid, so she'd know how to strip and scrub a bedroom. Most big houses do a thorough clean twice a year."

"Alexander's room next," Prudence said, standing for a moment in the doorway. She'd been so hopeful of discovering something that would lead her to Annabelle. It was heartbreakingly disappointing to leave with nothing.

"This is a very different kind of space," Gertie said, unlocking the door to Alexander's room. "Mr. Nicholson believes a boy should live a spartan kind of life. It toughens him, he says, and a boy who doesn't grow up to be a hard man is a failure. He used to lecture Alexander all the time against showing emotion. The boy wasn't allowed to feel anything. Or if he did, he risked a beating if he showed it."

The room in which Bella's brother had slept was as bare as a monk's cell. Hard mattress on a narrow, pillowless bed. Rugless floor and curtainless windows. Furniture that would have looked more at home in an attic. Empty drawers and armoire. No books, balls, or art on the walls. Not even the lingering scent of boy.

Nevertheless, they gave it as thorough a search as they'd performed in his sister's room. This time it was Josiah who lingered in the doorway when they had finished. And found nothing.

"So sad," he murmured as Gertie turned the key in the lock.

"I'll get us back to town in time for you to catch the next train to the city," Pearl promised as she sent the carriage rumbling toward the gate. The two bullmastiffs ran alongside, barking happily in anticipation of more bits of bone.

"Things look bad, Miss Prudence," Josiah said. He stared at the trees whipping by and wondered where Bella and Zander would hide tonight. In what fetid alley or damp, moldy cellar they would collapse in nightmare-haunted sleep.

"Geoffrey always says that just when you think matters can't get any worse, they do," Prudence replied. She ventured a quick touch to Josiah's sleeve. "And then they take a turn for the better. Something unexpected happens. A clue you weren't looking for turns up. Something."

She devoutly hoped he was right.

CHAPTER 23

Geoffrey sent for Amos Lang, an ex-Pinkerton known as "the ferret" for his ability to get to the bottom of a case while disappearing so effectively on a stakeout that even fellow Pinks had difficulty spotting him.

"We don't have much information," Prudence said, handing over Ira Nicholson's address and the scant few lines Josiah had penned on the train back to the city. "His father was a wartime speculator and his sister eloped with a tutor who didn't marry her, even after she bore him two children."

"Do we know the tutor's name?" Lang asked.

"Clyde Mitchell. He abandoned her shortly after Alexander was born. Vanished into thin air and left Effie without a dime. She made it back to Francton, where Ira took her in and helped raise the children. When Effie died of pneumonia, she named Ira sole guardian of her son and daughter."

"I know this street. Tree-lined, townhomes on both sides. No businesses. Very quiet. Entirely residential." Lang handed back the piece of paper Prudence had given him. He never kept anything that might betray the job he was on, just in case. He lived his whole life like that. Just in case. It was one of the qualities that made him a good operative. And had gradually led to the cork-stoppered brown bottle in his jacket pocket and the white powder in his bedside table.

"We want to know where he goes. When he leaves the house, what time he returns. Whether he meets up with anyone. As far as we can tell, he's living off the fortune his father made from wartime commissary contracts," Geoffrey said.

"He brought the housekeeper with him from upstate," Prudence continued. "Mrs. Sybil Johnson. The story we were told is that she accompanied Nicholson and his niece to the city because he'd hired a governess for the girl and the former housekeeper in town had retired. The two of them travel back and forth between Lanternlight and the city fairly frequently. Usually together."

"Name of the woman Sybil Johnson replaced?" Lang asked.

Prudence shook her head. "Don't know. Neither does our source. We think Sybil Johnson helped keep Bella a virtual prisoner after Alexander was sent off to boarding school. When we searched the girl's bedroom, it was beautifully furnished, but the window shutters had been nailed closed from the outside. The uncle and Mrs. Johnson had the only keys to the door, which, according to the cook, was always locked. She claimed to have heard Bella crying, but didn't suspect any mistreatment other than being confined to her room."

"This is the only picture we have of her," Geoffrey said, removing the Jacob Riis photograph from the case file. "There were no likenesses anywhere in the Francton house. No portraits on the walls except of George Nicholson, the wartime profiteer. And this is the sketch Josiah drew."

Lang pointed to the artificially thin eyebrows and the painted-on lashes.

"It's even more dramatic when you see her in person," Prudence explained. "Frightening, really. It becomes obvious that the idea was to make her appear other than human. Her skin has been whitened, too."

"Clown white?"

"Something that changes the natural color of human flesh and can't be washed off," Geoffrey said. "Arsenic ingested in small doses can have that effect. Lead paste has been used also, but too much lead can cause an even more immediate and deadly reaction than the arsenic."

"Where do you think they are, Miss MacKenzie, these children you're looking for?"

"We believe they're hiding in the back alleyways," Prudence said. "We know they sheltered with at least one group of street urchins for a short while, and Riis's photograph is proof that they were scavenging behind restaurants for food."

"Three boys who look like Alexander have been murdered, their bodies left at the City Asylum for Orphan Boys and Foundlings. Someone is trying to eliminate him, someone who believes the girl is dead and that Alexander is a dangerous witness to what was done to her."

"And Ira Nicholson, the uncle, is our primary suspect?"

"Our only suspect," Geoffrey said. "So far, all we have on him is what the cook at his Francton estate was able to tell us. A judge would say he was a stern, authoritative guardian to his sister's children, but that there's no evidence of anything for which he could be indicted. If the children chose to run away, that only proves that a firm hand is needed to bring them back into line."

"Children are victims without advocates," Josiah said quietly.

Prudence would have liked to ask if he spoke from personal experience, remembering the way he had seemed unsurprised by what had shocked and dismayed her during their visit to the Asylum. The tightness of Josiah's lips told her now was not the time.

"I'm hypothesizing that Nicholson has hired someone to find and eliminate young Alexander. Zander, as he may be known on the street." Geoffrey summarized the bones of the case as he and Prudence had constructed it. "I don't know why no photograph or painting exists of him except the one we have, but the killer is operating on a verbal description only. Which would explain why all of the victims murdered or dumped at the Asylum had blond hair and dark brown eyes. They were also of very slight physical build, appearing to be about twelve years old. We know that Alexander is thirteen or fourteen but looks younger. Bella is fifteen or sixteen, but she also gives the impression of being at least two or three years smaller than the average girl of her age."

"Were they starved?" Lang asked.

"You mean like the chimney sweeps in Mr. Dickens's stories? Deprived of food so they wouldn't outgrow the shafts they had to clean?" Prudence's father had accumulated an extensive library where he encouraged his daughter to keep him company while he worked on legal briefs. Much of her childhood had been spent stretched out on the floor with a book in front of her and a cat purring at her side.

"Possibly," Geoffrey said. "It could also be that food was scarce and hard to come by in the years before Effie returned to Francton."

"But not whiskey," Josiah muttered. "I'll lay you odds the tutor was a drinker and a woman beater."

"I'll stake out Nicholson's town house," Lang said. "The man he's hired to do away with the boy will show up there eventually. He shouldn't be hard to spot in that neighborhood."

"Keep in touch," Geoffrey reminded him. "One or two of Danny's street sweepers will always be nearby if you need to send word."

"You can set a boy to trail after Sybil Johnson if she goes out," Prudence suggested. "The household supplies are delivered, so there's no need for a housekeeper to go anywhere except on her afternoon off. But we don't know how involved she is with whatever Nicholson has done to Bella. He could be using her as a messenger or a go-between."

Amos Lang left the office, Josiah settled himself at his desk again, and Geoffrey stepped out into the hallway, pacing off a measured tread that was meant to strengthen the bad leg until he could walk without the hated cane.

Prudence sat and stared into space, trying to ignore the ragged tap-tap of the Remington typewriter's keys and the steady thud of Geoffrey's awkward gait. The case seemed like an untidy pile of firewood, broken pieces of dry kindling sticking out in all directions. And every time she picked one up, it broke apart in her hands. The only promising lead she could hold on to was Madame Jolene's revelation that the doll she had sent Prudence had come to her brothel via a young woman who took refuge with a friend and left it behind when she decamped. Running over the details in her mind, Prudence took a piece of stationery out of her desk drawer and began to sketch out a diagram of the story Geoffrey and Ned had reluctantly revealed.

The girl she called Gloria had told Madame Jolene that a prostitute named Margie had escaped from a client she referred to as her master when the man suddenly collapsed and died of an apparent heart attack. Why Margie snatched up the doll when she fled, Gloria didn't know. But she'd sworn that her friend had borne an uncanny resemblance to the porcelain doll who'd been as elegantly dressed as one of the illustrations in *Godey's Lady's Book*. Once Gloria thought about it, she'd realized that the clothes Margie was wearing when she showed up at her door were the same as the doll's. Exactly the same. Did fancy dressmakers do that? Make small facsimiles of their work so their lady clients could tell what a sketch would look like translated into satin or silk?

What else had Madame Jolene said? Prudence tried to dredge from her memory all of the bits and pieces Geoffrey and Ned had communicated in what had been an awkward conversation.

Added them to what she had learned at the law school and in Madame Jolene's parlor.

There were brothels in the city specializing in certain forms of entertainment demanded by well-heeled clients whose appetites were whetted by the bizarre. Some specialized in girls of a certain nationality or race, as well as girls who would perform services unavailable at ordinary brothels. That was about as precise as her partner and Ned had been. What stood out was the doll itself and the fact that Margie, like Ottilie and Bella, had been physically reconfigured to resemble a porcelain plaything. Which came first? The doll or the girl? And hadn't Madame Jolene said that other madams knew of the existence of something called The Doll Club? Without ever specifying exactly what or where it was?

As Josiah tapped away unevenly at the keys of the Remington and Geoffrey returned from the hallway to walk the smaller cage of his office, Prudence made up her mind. When the typewriter fell silent and she heard Josiah knock on Geoffrey's door with whatever document he had prepared, she closed the door of the outer office behind her without a sound.

She was going back to The Doll House.

Ira Nicholson's doll had been badly battered, one side of the porcelain face smashed almost beyond recognition, the expensive, lace-frilled dress ripped and stained. It should never have been in his house, he knew that. Members of The Doll Club had recently been strongly encouraged to leave their china and porcelain beauties in the safekeeping of the club premises, but it was a request none of them liked. A man who wanted to have a physical reminder of his real-life doll with him always had only to slip a few folded bills into the hand of the guardian whose chief function was to ensure that the dolls required for a given night were available to the gentlemen who owned them. Repaired and redressed, if necessary. The current guardian had a ferocious thirst and a deep, all-consuming love of the horses.

The night the doll had been smashed 'and Bella disappeared from her locked room at the club's members-only mansion, Ira had been upstate at Lanternlight dealing with the aftermath of his nephew's latest breakout from the school which had promised to keep the boy securely confined to its grounds. A note had come from the headmaster. Brief and to the point. Regrettably, Alexander was no longer welcome at Brereton Oaks Military Academy.

Despite the institution's reputation for being able to reform the most recalcitrant miscreant, young Master Nicholson had proved too great a disruption to his fellow pupils and the staff. There followed a partial list of his transgressions, all of which had been dealt with harshly and to no avail. This latest escapade was the last straw. The local police had been summoned, as usual, and after several days search of the surrounding area, reported finding no trace of the boy. Since they and the school had more important things to do than mediate what was obviously a quarrel between guardian and ward, Brereton Oaks washed its hands of the matter. No doubt Alexander would turn up at his uncle's home, as had happened once before. When he did, Mr. Nicholson was invited to keep him there.

Ira was of a mind to let the boy go, to make no effort to find and rein him in. But he knew the headmaster was correct in predicting that Alexander would make his way back to Lanternlight, drawn by concern for the sister he loved as much as life itself. The first time he had run away from school, the boy had managed to sneak into the house and spend several days and nights in the attic before his noisy nightmares gave him away. Quick to understand what she was hearing, Sybil Johnson had locked him into the stuffy, cluttered, nearly airless space and in the morning told her employer of the prize she had captured. Bella confessed tearfully to smuggling food and drink to her brother, begging her uncle not to force him to return to the school where he was miserably unhappy. Brereton Oaks took him back that time. But not again.

It was only a question of time before Alexander turned up. Like a bad penny. He had not been told that Bella was no longer at Lanternlight, that Nicholson had removed her to the New York City town house. To the care of a governess no one in Francton had ever met and of whose existence the city servants were unaware.

Nicholson settled in to wait, telling none of the Lanternlight staff the real reason he was there, but alerting his groundskeepers to be on the lookout for anything that seemed out of the ordinary. The boy was clever and experienced in the devious arts of a runaway, but he was bound to leave some trace of himself where eyes trained to the hunt would find it. A pile of pine boughs in the woods or disturbed straw in the stable, food missing from the root cellar, a pair of pants or a shirt stolen from a clothesline. Ira spoke of sightings of vagrants in the woods, homes that had been broken into while their owners were away. He ordered the groundskeepers to clean and load their guns.

Jerry, the gardener who had carried food up a ladder to Bella's room when she had been locked in, waited in the shelter of the greenhouse through several long nights before Alexander crept stealthily across the grounds. "She's gone, son," he told the boy, filling his hands with the ham sandwiches he'd saved from his lunch every day since he'd begun to suspect that the tramps the master had warned them to watch out for was really the young master on the loose again.

"Where?" Alexander demanded, crumbs spilling down his chest as he chewed and swallowed and tried to talk all at the same time.

"The city. He's hired a governess to teach her to be a lady and make her debut with all the other young ladies of important families. Leastwise that's what we were told." He had no reason to doubt Mr. Nicholson's explanation of why Bella was leaving Lanternlight, but Jerry hated the way the man treated his own flesh-and-blood niece and nephew. Didn't trust him to do what he said he would. Hadn't he fired many a maid and stable boy for no reason? Without a severance packet of wages or a reference? And they always left with fear and loathing in their eyes, lips tight against the questions their friends on staff asked. Left the area, too, as though they'd been warned away. Or were afraid to stay.

"You'd best not try to go into the house," Jerry counseled. "I can find a place for you to hide out in the village until Mr. Nicholson leaves. Then you'll be safe here, as long as Mrs. Johnson is gone."

"She's not here, either?"

"Went to the city with Mr. Nicholson and your sister and didn't come back with him this time. Something about the other housekeeper retiring. Or outright quit, more like it. Your uncle is a hard taskmaster. But that's something I don't need to tell you, do I?"

"I've never been to the town house," Alexander said, wiping the last of the mustardy ham from his lips. "And I don't have any money for a train ticket."

"You don't want to go there," Jerry advised. "You'd have no chance of getting inside with Mrs. Johnson running the place. None of the other servants know you."

"I can stand out in the street and pitch pebbles at her window until Bella sees me down below and opens it."

"Then what?"

"I haven't thought any further than that," Alexander admitted. Except that in his good dreams they were running away together, smiles on their faces, money jingling in their pockets, and no one in pursuit. The ocean figured in his imaginings, seagulls squawking overhead, sand between their toes, and a motherly figure appearing out of the dawn mist to enfold them in her arms and take them home.

In the end he took the price of a train ticket and a little extra from the tea tin where Jerry stored his life savings, leaving an IOU in place of the bills he folded into his pants pocket. He was gone before the early-rising gardener stirred, a runaway armed with nothing but determination, courage, and hopeful ignorance.

Jerry decided it would be better not to tell Gertie that young Alexander had come and gone. No sense in her worrying. And he wasn't proud of the fact that he'd failed to keep the boy from taking off again. He should have been able to figure out how to help.

CHAPTER 24

Despite the cool cloths Alexander draped over her forehead, arms, and legs, Bella's fever continued to burn frighteningly hot. She tossed and turned in silent delirium, as if she knew, even in her semiconscious state, that the slightest sound would give them away. Lead to discovery and separation. Return her to the hell on earth from which she had escaped with only a fragile hold on life and sanity. Sometimes, when her brother dribbled rusty-tasting water between her lips, she opened her eyes and smiled at him. Recognition and gratitude sparked for a moment, then the dullness of whatever was killing her stole away the light.

Each time Bella retreated from a moment of consciousness, Alexander felt her slipping further away from him until finally he realized that the next time, or perhaps the time after that, she wouldn't return. She would die. The sister he loved more than anyone else on earth, the beacon that had summoned him from school so many times, the terribly damaged female creature it had been his brotherly duty to protect. Guilt overwhelmed him, failure paralyzed him, the pain of losing her was becoming too much to bear. When she breathed her last, he, too, would

die. He would lie down beside her and wait for the welcome
end that could not be far off.

The cat who had leaped through the window he'd opened
last night to let in a little fresh air curled itself under one of
Bella's hands. Her fingers made tiny stroking movements,
barely visible, but enough to set the animal purring. And as he
listened, Alexander remembered the cat that had been perched
atop one of the cupboards in the kitchen of the Friends Refuge.
Its green eyes had stared at him as he sat at the table, eating oat-
meal and resolutely not answering any of the questions put to
him by the woman whose sandwiches he had stolen.

There had been a dog there, too. Alexander's fingers curled
as he pantomimed clinging to the silky, reddish gold fur later
that evening in the stable where he had felt momentarily safe
and cared for. Until a shadowy figure pausing outside the open
door reminded him he was being stalked. And that once the
man discovered Bella was still alive, he wouldn't be content
with just the killing he'd been hired to perform. Alexander
knew he'd find Bella and take her back to the house of horrors
she'd told him she would willingly die rather than experience
again.

The reassuring purr of the cat and the memory of the comforting dog turned his thoughts to the gentle Quaker doctor,
the gray-eyed woman who'd cornered them in the basement,
and the Irishman who sang to the enormous white horse while
he rubbed him down. Alexander had known very few nurtur-
ing adults in his short life; he'd trusted no one after his uncle
had forced him into Brereton Oaks Military Academy. But a
small glow of something like hope began to ease some of his
heartache.

Very quietly, so as not to scare away the cat, he rose to his
feet and slipped out of the University Building apartment left
temporarily vacant by a mathematics professor who was attending a conference in Vienna. Zander had smuggled Bella in
at dusk, when the janitor was making his evening rounds and

the few students remaining in the hallways were in too much of a rush to their dinners to notice strangers who didn't belong. The lock had presented no problem; Alexander had trained on Brereton's well-secured doors. The professor's bed had been made up with clean linens for his return, and while there were no perishable food items in the tiny kitchen, his cleaning lady hadn't bothered with unopened boxes of crackers and cans of beans, peaches, and sardines. Two days of bliss. Then Bella had spiked the fever.

If she wasn't to die—and now Alexander was as determined that she wouldn't as he had been resigned that she would—he had to get medical help.

From a Quaker lady named Dr. Charity Sloan.

"I don't know where she's gone," Josiah said, running a hand over the clean surface of his desk. "She didn't say anything and there's no note. Come to think of it, I never saw her leave the office."

"I can't wait," Geoffrey declared, reaching for his hat and cane. He looked out the window to the busy street below. "Danny's down at the curb."

"I'll call the house," Josiah offered. "Mr. Cameron might know where she is."

"Tell him to make sure that if she comes home, he informs her of what's happened and that I'll meet her at the Friends Refuge."

"It's not like Miss Prudence to go off on her own," Josiah fretted. But he knew it was exactly the kind of thing she did whenever she thought someone would object to a plan she'd concocted. Rather than argue, she followed her own instincts. *Harebrained schemes*, he'd heard Mr. Hunter call them. More often than not there'd been elements of danger that she blithely ignored. The two men who knew her best worried that someday she'd get herself into a dilemma from which neither she nor they could extricate her.

Dr. Sloan's message had been tersely worded, the need for haste making her handwriting more difficult to read than usual. In the end, Josiah's Gregg shorthand skills had helped to decipher it. Alexander Nicholson had turned up at the Refuge's back door pleading for help. His sister had a fever that burned his fingers. She was dying. He had refused to allow her to be taken to a hospital, and when he explained why, Dr. Sloan had acceded. Bella was at the Refuge. Her condition was grave. Come quickly.

The girl was as pale as the sheets between which she lay, still and silent as Rebecca draped cool wet cloths on her burning skin and replaced them as soon as they turned warm.

"I've given her a mixture of tincture of willow bark and simmered cloves." Dr. Sloan sat at her patient's bedside, nearly as wan and exhausted-looking as the girl she was treating. "Rebecca got ice from the butcher's, and that's helped."

"I left word for Prudence," Geoffrey said before the question could be asked. "She'll be here as soon as she's told what's going on."

The private room in which Bella was being treated was at the back of the building, overlooking the delivery alleyway. Alexander stood at the window, alert to every sight and sound, following the path of every vehicle lumbering by, registering every person setting out refuse or stepping through a door to get a breath of air. After breaking his silence to summon help for his desperately ill sister, he had retreated into self-imposed mutism.

"What did he tell you?" Geoffrey asked.

"The fever started two days ago," Dr. Sloan began. "Thank goodness he realized they could shelter in one of University Building's empty apartments. If they'd still been on the streets, I doubt she'd be alive. He said he figured no one would think they'd go back there now that the janitor had been put on the alert and the basement locked up tighter than a drum. But when they were there before, he'd overheard students talking about a popular mathematics professor who was on sabbatical. He decided they'd be safer there than anywhere else. And he was right."

"He's a very determined boy," Geoffrey said, taking in Alexander's attentive posture, the clenched fists, the single-minded resolve strengthening every muscle of his undernourished body.

"It'll be the saving of both of them."

"What more did he tell you?"

"Only what I needed to know to treat his sister. He's said nothing about where or how he found her. But he obviously believes she's still in danger. Both of them, I think. He's like an animal who knows it's being stalked. Silent, watchful, ready to run at the slightest threat. Except that Alexander won't leave Bella behind." Dr. Sloan wrung out another damp cloth. The piece of butcher's ice in the basin of cool water had melted into a sliver.

"We need the whole story," Geoffrey said. "We have bits and pieces, but we're missing the glue to hold them all together."

"He won't leave his post at the window. Not for anything or anyone."

"Are the outside doors to the Refuge locked?"

"Rebecca saw to that right away. We've posted a quarantine sign on the front door. Patients know that in an emergency they can always go to Bellevue."

Charity Sloan had closed down the Refuge only a very few times since its inception, and each of those instances had been due to the threat of violence. Not to her, specifically, or her nurses, but to a woman or women sheltering within the clinic walls. She'd learned over the years that defiance wasn't always the best protection against a man bent on murder. Sometimes the police intervened, sometimes the frustrated woman-beater took his own life or sobered up enough to stand down. But hot-tempered barbarity was always a part of life in the Five Points.

"I'm hoping the fever will break tonight," she said softly,

knowing that with Alexander so close by, Geoffrey could not ask aloud if Bella would live. It all depended on the fever. It always did. Patients who sweated the fever out into their sheets often survived. Those who remained hot and dry never did. "She's breathing well." The dreaded pneumonia against which there was no defense had not yet begun to fill her lungs with watery pus and blood.

"Will he talk to me?" Geoffrey asked, keeping his voice low.

Dr. Sloan shrugged. She thought that if the boy opened up to anyone, it would probably be Prudence.

Geoffrey settled himself into a chair by the window where Alexander stood staring out at the alleyway. He folded his hands atop his cane, the way old men kept their balance on city park benches as they warmed themselves in the sun. Pigeons strutting through the peanut hulls at their feet. Unthreatening. Inviting casual conversation and the exchange of confidences. He eased himself into the role. Cloaked himself in patience. "I left word for Miss MacKenzie, Zander. She'll be here soon."

"When?" The boy never let his eyes wander from the window.

His voice sounded like a long untuned musical instrument. Rough. Unsure of its pitch and volume.

"I don't know precisely. As soon as she gets my message." Geoffrey cleared his throat. "Will you talk to me instead? While we're waiting?"

The boy shook his head.

"The doors are locked. Mr. Dennis is outside, keeping watch. Nobody's ever gotten past him who shouldn't have. You and your sister are safe. For the moment. But time isn't on your side. Sooner rather than later the man you've been running from will find out you and Bella are here. He'll come after you. And he may not be alone."

"We'll be gone by then." Desperation in his young, cracked voice.

"Where? Back out into the streets? She isn't strong enough for that, Zander. She needs the kind of care Dr. Sloan can give her. But the Refuge won't be the shelter it's meant to be as long as your uncle remains free to pursue you. It is your uncle who caused this to be done to Bella, isn't it?"

Alexander's face contorted in a spasm of nightmarish fear. His eyes darted around the room as if searching for the monster who inhabited his dreams. Quickly, before he could change his mind, he blurted out the answer Geoffrey waited for. "Yes. Yes, he did this to her. I'll kill him! I'll kill him!" When the tears came, Alexander could not stop them. He was only an undersized boy living in a world of adult horror.

Geoffrey let him cry. He sat motionless, as if unaware that Alexander's defenses had disintegrated like a sandcastle at high tide. The boy's sobs filled the small room, echoed off its bare walls.

Dr. Sloan, the back of one hand testing her patient's forehead, choked back tears. In every medical situation, she firmly believed there had to be one unshakable pillar of strength. Most times, it was she.

"Miss MacKenzie would want you to talk to Mr. Hunter," she said when the room had fallen silent again. "I know you're strong enough to do this for your sister, Alexander. What you've already accomplished for her proves it." Her measured tones and formal way of phrasing her sentences lent Charity Sloan an otherworldly aura that was more persuasive than any amount of bribery or pleading. "I'll keep an eye on the alley for you." She surrendered the damp cloths to Rebecca, then took up a watcher's post at the window as Alexander turned away to face Prudence's partner.

"Start at the beginning," Geoffrey urged. "Don't leave anything out. We don't know yet what's important and what isn't."

Danny had sent Blossom inside when a half-dozen of his street urchins arrived to station themselves unobtrusively around the Refuge, so familiar a sight in the Five Points that their presence on the street went unnoticed. The dog had lain across the threshold of the room, but now she padded over to the boy who had pillowed his head on her flank when they slept together in Mr. Washington's stable. She nudged one hand with her broad head, and when she felt his fingers entwine themselves in her red-gold fur, leaned in so he could feel the warmth of her body against his.

"I ran away from Brereton Oaks," Alexander began. "I knew something was wrong. Bella hadn't told me what it was the last time I saw her, but she was so pale and frightened, so beaten down, that I knew it had to be the very worst thing I could imagine. I had a plan. I would steal the money Uncle Ira kept in his safe and we would run away together with it. We would tell people that our father had sent for us to join him—somewhere—and that the reason we were traveling alone was because our mother had died on the journey."

"What went wrong?"

"Bella wasn't at Lanternlight when I got there. The head-master of Brereton had written my uncle, so he was waiting for me to show up. He knew I would. Someone at Lanternlight, I don't want to give away his name, warned me as soon as I got close to the house. He hid me overnight, fed me, and told me that Bella was to have a governess and be educated to make her debut when she turned eighteen. He promised to find me a place to hide out in the village if I didn't want to go back to the school. In the end, I managed to get the address of the town house from him, and then, while he slept, I stole money from his tobacco tin and caught the early-morning milk train to the city. I left an IOU, and I mean to honor it."

The shame of having no money burned in Alexander's cheeks. This man didn't have to be told that he'd stolen puckered apples and sprouting potatoes from market carts, begged for handouts from restaurant kitchens, and rummaged through garbage cans for edible vegetable peelings and bread from which the mold could be brushed off. Both before he found Bella and afterward. When despite giving her the best of what he could scavenge, she had fallen ill anyway.

"She wasn't at the town house, but Mrs. Johnson, the Lanternlight housekeeper, was. She was dressing down the cook when I knocked at the kitchen door, and as soon as the maid opened it, she recognized me. I ran, but I came back that night. There never had been a governess and Bella hadn't stayed there more than a few days. I talked to one of the maids and a stable boy. Nobody knew where the young mistress had gone. And none of the staff liked Mr. Nicholson, so I knew they were telling me the truth. I didn't break into the house, but I wasn't exactly invited in, either."

Alexander's hands clenched into fists. His lips blanched and his shoulders shook as he relived that night.

"What did you do?"

"I found a key hidden under a boot scraper by the kitchen door. One of the maids or a footman always hides a key outside somewhere for when they're back late from an afternoon or evening off and they need to get into the house without being noticed." Alexander grinned, and for a brief moment he looked like any mischievous boy of his age. As quickly as the grin appeared, it faded away. "At Lanternlight, we were never allowed into Uncle Ira's study unless he was going to discipline us. He kept all of his important papers there, so I knew that if the town house had a study, that's where I'd find his secrets."

"What did you find, Alexander?" Dr. Sloan asked, eyes still fixed on the alleyway.

"A doll," he choked out. "I smashed its head on the fireplace."

"Why?" Geoffrey waited. "Why did you try to destroy the doll you found?"

"It looked like Bella. It looked just like my sister except that the eyebrows were thin half circles and the eyelashes were painted on."

"Why did you try to destroy it?" Geoffrey repeated.

"It was evil. I knew he'd done a bad thing to her and that the doll was somehow a part of it. The smile wasn't right. It wasn't a happy smile. The lips were pursed in a funny way that looked all wrong. I didn't know what had really happened until later."

"You left the doll there so he'd know he'd been found out," Dr. Sloan said.

"I wanted him to know it was me. I found an address taped beneath a drawer and I knew right away that's where he'd hidden Bella. So I wanted him to know it was me who rescued her."

"Tell us what happened next, Alexander," Geoffrey urged. "You're almost done now."

"I found Bella. I picked the lock where she was being kept and then I got her out when everyone had fallen asleep. I don't want to say any more about it." Alexander's chin jutted out. "If she dies, I'll kill him."

"Let's pray the fever breaks," Dr. Sloan said as Alexander nudged her aside to take his place at the window again. She glanced at the small watch pinned to her shirtwaist, then at Geoffrey.

He'd been at the Refuge for almost two hours.

Where was Prudence?

CHAPTER 25

The Nicholson town house was one of a row of three-story brick homes within walking distance of Fifth Avenue and the opulent boutiques and department stores of the Ladies' Mile. Well out of the congestion of crowds of shoppers alighting from hansom cabs, carriages, and horse cars, the street was like a breath of country air. Trees in full spring growth spread canopies of green across the sidewalks, flowers bloomed in window boxes, and the stench of manure and garbage that permeated the rest of the city was barely noticeable.

Amos Lang lit a cheroot and leaned back against a wrought-iron railing inside which budding roses scented the air like a cloud of women's perfume. On days like today the dark years of working as an undercover Pinkerton operative seemed so far away, they might have been part of someone else's life. The worst of it had been cracking the skulls of laboring men like himself who asked nothing more than a decent wage and some measure of safety in the mines and factories never visited by the millionaires who owned them. He'd had to get out to save his sanity.

Pinks were well trained and in high demand wherever they turned. Amos resigned from the organization while he could still control the drugs and drinking that helped him forget what he'd done. He'd met up with Geoffrey Hunter after the Great Blizzard two years ago, and when Hunter and MacKenzie opened its doors to investigations, he was one of the first operatives hired. On a case-to-case basis, to be sure, but even so, he had all the employment he wanted. And the satisfaction of working for a man who understood what it meant to be an ex-Pink. He liked Miss MacKenzie, too, though he found it odd to remember that he was supposed to take orders from her as well as Mr. Hunter.

Two of Danny Dennis's street urchins lurked at the Fifth Avenue corner, running back and forth across the roadway wielding brooms that were bigger than they were, sweeping mounds of fresh horse dung against the curbs where carts drawn by more manure-dropping horses would eventually lumber along to remove them. Down in the Five Points, hardly anyone had indoor plumbing. In warm spring and hot summer weather the stench of outhouses, in addition to the muck rotting in the unpaved streets, led some people to cover their mouths and noses with scarves whenever they ventured out. It was another reason the toffs stayed in their own less-smelly part of town.

And there, at last, someone was leaving the Nicholson house. A woman, the housekeeper, Mrs. Sybil Johnson, by the look of her. Dressed in black, carrying a cloth bag, an umbrella or parasol dangling from one arm. Out shopping? But he'd been told that whatever the household needed was delivered. So this must be a personal errand.

He had a moment to decide whether it was worth following her. And if so, who should do it? Ira Nicholson and the killer he'd hired to eliminate his nephew were the focus of the investigation and likely to prove more important and more dangerous than a domestic employee.

Amos raised a hand to adjust his hat and watched in satisfaction as one of the sweepers tossed aside his broom and scampered along the opposite side of the street, shooting him a conspiratorial glance as he passed. He'd stay far enough behind Mrs. Johnson so she wouldn't catch a whiff of him, but he wouldn't lose her. Danny's boys were among the brightest in the city. Fast on their feet and lucky, too. Though most of them preferred to find their own sleeping places, Mr. Washington's stable and its piles of fresh hay was always open to them. Josiah Gregory fed them sandwiches and saw to it that there were boots, jackets, and short pants available in the office storage closet. Mr. Hunter and Miss MacKenzie never went anywhere without an abundant supply of nickels to hand out.

The sweeper boy disappeared around the corner.

Amos settled back to watch and wait.

Prudence didn't have a plan, other than to browse along The Doll House's glass-fronted cases admiring the beautiful creations within and listening to what other customers were saying. The idea that a mother or aunt could commission a doll to look like her daughter or niece was both intriguing and vaguely disturbing. Especially in view of what she had seen when Ottilie lay on an examination table in the Refuge and Rebecca placed Madame Jolene's doll beside her.

Only, it wasn't Madame Jolene's doll. It had come to the house through a working girl whose real name wasn't Gloria. Who had in turn been given it by another working girl whose name wasn't Margie. The whole thing was giving Prudence a headache.

Somewhere in the city was a brothel that existed only to serve the bizarre tastes of extremely wealthy men with a fetish for very young women made to look like delicate porcelain creations miraculously brought to life. From the circumstantial evidence they'd accumulated, the existence of such a place was undeniable though Prudence still found it difficult to believe. If wealth was the primary requisite for inclusion in this perverted club, what were the odds that a male acquaintance of her late father or one of his dissolute sons was a member? She had to force herself to consider that she might have danced or drunk champagne with such a creature. It made her shudder.

A very ordinary-looking woman wearing a plain black dress and unstylish hat came out of The Doll House as Prudence approached. Definitely not anyone who belonged to Mrs. Astor's clique or even the less exclusive world of the newly wealthy. *Godey's Lady's Book* was nothing if not up to the minute with its sketches of what the beau monde in London and Paris were wearing that season. No society lady worthy of the name would jeopardize her reputation by wearing an outdated outfit in public. Even Prudence's plain walking suit was beautifully tailored, sewn from the finest of lightweight wools, and sported the newly returned and much-reduced bustle.

What was a woman of ordinary means doing in an exorbitantly expensive shop that depended on word of mouth for its clientele and only announced its existence by a discreet brass plaque? If not to make a purchase, could she be on an errand for an employer? Prudence remembered the clerk who had introduced himself as Sebastian Marks saying that in addition to selling dolls of exceptional quality, The Doll House maintained a workshop for repair and refurbishment of its clients' collections. Could that workshop be somewhere on the premises? Perhaps at the rear of the building where large windows let in good light and the comings and goings of craftsmen were managed through the same back service yard and alley devoted to delivery wagons? It was an intriguing idea and one Prudence thought she would inquire about while dithering over which doll to purchase for the goddaughter she had claimed to have. Or had it been a niece? She'd have to be careful in case Mr. Marks had a good memory for the casual comments of his customers.

She rang the bell to announce her arrival, then opened the front door into the hallway that doubled as showroom for the glass-fronted case of baby dolls that had so thrilled Phoebe

Taylor on Prudence's first visit. A beautiful child, with silky red-brown curls, enormous hazel eyes, and a pale, unfreckled complexion. Prudence could still picture the innocent face smiling up at her.

"How delightful to see you again, madam," Sebastian Marks greeted her, inclining his head gracefully in the polite bow gentlemen made to ladies of their acquaintance. "What brings you back to The Doll House?"

"I've spoken to my niece's mother," Prudence began, before the slight twitch of one of Marks's eyebrows warned her that she'd gotten it wrong. "She's not really my niece, of course, but her mother is my dearest friend, so I think of her as one of the family and she is my goddaughter. She's quite thrilled that I should be the one to begin her daughter's collection." Eyebrow down and no longer twitching. Old friend then, who had chosen Prudence as her child's godmother. She wouldn't forget again since it was now obvious that the dapper Sebastian was also a good listener.

"And which of our many treasures have you chosen?"

"Well, that's just it. I hadn't made up my mind when I was here last. In fact, I was rather overwhelmed. So I think I shall have to look at all of them again. I do believe a doll with the same coloring as my dear goddaughter would delight her no end. What do you think?"

"How old is the little girl?"

"She'll be nine on her next birthday. Still a child. Not quite on the threshold of young ladyhood."

"An ideal time to begin a serious collection. Young enough to be thrilled by her first important doll, but old enough to appreciate the exquisite workmanship. Collectibles are not playthings."

"Perhaps I should think about purchasing two dolls. One for the collection, and another to keep on her bed. I assume you can also supply the less collectible models? I recall a little girl who was quite enamored of the dolls in your entryway cases. Perhaps something like that?"

"Our baby dolls are of very good, but not collectible quality," Marks agreed. "We've found over the years that they do quite nicely."

"Then I shall take my time," Prudence said, peering into one of the cases as though to inspect the stitching of every gown and the painting of every facial feature. When Marks made no move to leave her alone, she swished her skirts and shot him a look that clearly demanded privacy.

With another of the graceful half bows, he faded into the hallway. She heard the click of a door closing. The workshop? An office?

One doll looked pretty much like any other doll, Prudence decided as she paced along the row of cabinets. What thrilled other women and young girls bored her in a way rows of law-books and case studies would not have. She admired the superb artistry, but there was nothing human about the figures that spoke to her in the way a narrative of deception or victimization would have engaged her mind and touched her heart. She was here to do a job, so she assumed an expression of awed fascination and waited for Sebastian Marks to return.

"I'd like to see your workshop," she told him when he reentered the showroom with two of the distinctive red boxes under his arm. "I want to be certain that should an unforeseen accident occur, there would be someplace reliable where my friend could bring her daughter's prized possessions to be restored to their original condition."

"Our craftsmen are trained in France, madam."

"I do recall your saying that you imported your collectible dolls from that country. But where do the baby dolls come from?"

"Some of them are made in Germany. A very few, although created in the United States, are of good enough workmanship to be included in our stock." He stiffened, as though the inclusion of American and German products was a reluctant confession.

"I shall make my final choices after I've seen the workshop," Prudence declared. She set her shoulders in a way that said she would not be denied. Nor would she wait much longer.

"This way, then."

Setting the boxes on one of the display tables, Marks led her into the outer hallway, past the baby dolls, and through a door he unlocked with a key attached to his watch chain. "We wouldn't want any of our younger clients to wander into the work area," he explained, ushering Prudence down a long, dark corridor. "The paints can be dangerous if accidentally ingested, and some of the tools are as delicate as jeweler's instruments."

"Very wise of you," she agreed. "Children can be annoyingly intrusive when they become excited."

As she had suspected, the workroom at the back of the house looked as if a wall between two smaller rooms had been torn down to create a large studio flooded with natural light. Dolls needing repair lay in labeled boxes awaiting attention. Two men wearing black aprons and accountants' eyeshades looked up from their worktables as she entered. At a nod from Marks, they neither stood nor interrupted what they were doing. One of them, Prudence noticed, was noticeably broader through the shoulders than the other. He seemed to be holding his tools awkwardly, hesitantly. The other man, older and smaller, was performing an intricate operation on the head of a doll with cascading blond curls.

"As you can see, madam, we have what you might call a doll hospital here should our clients need such services."

The man with the heavyset shoulders dropped his slender scalpel-like instrument. It made a loud, clattering noise against a stack of other tools piled untidily in front of him.

Doll hospital? Where had she heard that expression before?

A row of stretched canvases leaned against the rear wall. Un-framed, ready for the artist's brush? She remembered that for a doll to be made to order, the child it was to resemble had to sit for a portrait. As she looked around the studio, breathing in the smell of paint and resin, noting the meticulously labeled boxes whose contents awaited renewal and the focused concentration of the craftsmen, she could find nothing amiss or out of place. Nothing to cause alarm or raise questions.

"Shall we return to the display rooms?" Sebastian Marks asked.

"Of course. I must thank you for indulging me. Seeing all of this sets my mind at ease." Prudence turned to go, casting a last glance toward the dolls currently undergoing repair, catching for the first time a good look at the badly battered head cradled in the skilled hands of the smaller of the two workmen.

The side of the doll's skull had been smashed nearly flat, as though it had been flung against a hard surface. The porcelain had exploded into dozens of small cracks, a spider's web of tiny fissures leaking fine translucent dust. The fractures spread across one side of the doll's face, leaving the other half intact. As Prudence's eyes followed them, she gave a horrified gasp of recognition. Without thinking, without realizing what she was saying, she blurted out, "Bella!" And immediately knew she'd made a mortal mistake.

Before she could take more than a few steps toward the door, a pair of thickly muscled arms closed around her from behind, lifting her feet from the floor, holding her as though she were weightless. She caught a glimpse of the face of the man who'd seemed so ill at ease with his tools, then a black bag was shoved over her head, and she felt her reticule snatched out of her hand.

"A derringer, a dollar's worth of nickels tied up in a handker-chief, a set of picklocks, and a business card," Sebastian Marks said. "Prudence MacKenzie. Hunter and MacKenzie, Investigative Law," he confirmed to the man restraining her. "She played a good game the first time she was here. Pity for her she couldn't keep it up."

The bag was loosened for a moment, then a strong hand thrust a wad of crumpled rags against Prudence's nose and mouth. The unmistakable smell of chloroform was the last thing she remembered before darkness fell.

CHAPTER 26

Annabelle's fever broke before the evening Angelus bells of nearby St. Marcellus Church ceased pealing. Her hot, dry skin poured out a salty flood of pent-up fever fluid, and as the poison left her body, she opened her eyes and recognized the brother who had come to stand beside her bed.

"Zander," she breathed.

"Don't try to talk, Bella," he said. "I've told them everything they need to know."

Dr. Sloan lifted Bella's head and cradled it like a baby's. She held a glass of cool water to her lips, urging her to drink as much as she could. But slowly. Slowly.

The golden dog who had never left the girl's bedside thumped her tail on the floor, nestling her head where one of Bella's hands could find and caress a velvety soft ear.

In the hallway outside the room whose door had been left cracked open, Danny Dennis gave Geoffrey the worrisome news.

"No one's seen her since she left the office hours ago. All of my boys know her by sight, but none of them remembers her being out on the streets today. I sent a note to the butler, Mr. Cameron, but he's as much in the dark as we are. Wherever she went, she didn't first go home to change clothes. That's according to Colleen Riordan, Miss Prudence's lady's maid." Danny frowned and twirled the cap he clutched in one calloused hand. "I don't like this, Mr. Hunter. It's not natural for someone like her to disappear without anybody noticing something."

"There's one other place we can try, though I can't imagine why she'd spend an entire afternoon there," Geoffrey said. "Annabelle's fever just broke. According to Dr. Sloan, that means she'll probably live."

"I'll take you there," Danny offered. "The streets will be crowded right now, but Mr. Washington can make short work of any horse that tries to get by him."

"How do you know where I'm going?"

"There's nobody in the pleasure business who can keep a secret from Madame Jolene. If Miss Prudence has stepped on a toe she shouldn't have, and someone's decided to retaliate, Jolene will know about it. Faster than Billy McGlory, though he'd be next."

"I'll tell Dr. Sloan what we're doing, then I'll meet you outside."

It was an indication of how worried he was that for once Geoffrey didn't utter a word of complaint about his new cane. Ned Hayes had introduced him to a craftsman whose stiletto sword walking sticks were both superb examples of artistic design and deadly weapons. All the more effective for being concealed.

It was nearly dusk by the time Danny pulled Mr. Washington to a halt in front of Madame Jolene's discreetly ordinary-looking brick house. Geoffrey waited impatiently for an elderly gentlemen to alight from his carriage and make his way inside before telling George Bright that he urgently needed to talk to Madame Jolene. Alone.

The bouncer ushered him through the reception room where clients waited for the ladies to make their appearances, then down a hallway to the private parlor-cum-office where Geoffrey had met with Madame Jolene in the past. The deeper they went into the house, the quieter it became as the sounds of laughter, clinking glasses, and piano music faded into the distance. Madame Jolene preferred doing her serious business where she would not be interrupted.

"I haven't seen Miss MacKenzie since she was here with Ned Hayes. That was three or four days ago, Mr. Hunter." Madame Jolene paged through the coded appointment book where gentlemen callers were referred to by their initials. "Here it is. Tuesday." She closed the ledger with a decisive snap. "You'd better tell me what's wrong."

"She left the office without telling anyone where she was going. She didn't come back and there's no sign of her at her home."

"Maybe she just wanted some time alone. Women need to get away from men occasionally. Especially independent ladies like Miss MacKenzie."

"Josiah was supposed to let her know that the girl she's been looking for was brought to Dr. Sloan's Refuge in a very bad way and that I'd meet her there. He left messages with everyone she might have visited, including Nellie Bly. Prudence never showed up."

"I take it the girl is either dead or has decided to live. Otherwise you wouldn't be here."

"Her fever broke a little while ago. I stayed at the Refuge because I knew Miss MacKenzie would expect to find me there. If her disappearance has anything to do with the girl and her brother, or with Ottilie Urquhart, she could be in real danger."

"The police are well paid to look the other way when it comes to this business," Madame Jolene said. "A madam might be responsible for the day-to-day running of a house, but the original investment to purchase the best properties and furnish them to meet the tastes of a discreet clientele is almost always too much for her to manage."

"Meaning?"

"That if you have a contact you can trust on the police, now may be the time to reach out to him."

"Not Billy?"

"McGlory isn't the power he once was. He's back in the game, but nobody's forgotten that he was closed down and forced to sell the Armory building to a furniture factory. You never entirely recover from that kind of defeat, especially in his business. No matter what the reformers may think, it was never the same as mine. Saloons thrive on public drunks and the sort of disorderly mayhem that ends up with bouncers throwing customers out into the street. A well-run house of pleasure can exist for years without its neighbors realizing it's there." She smiled and cocked her head. "Except for the parade of expensive carriages stopping at the front door. That's what usually gives us away."

"What do you know about Detective Warren Lowry?"

"The reason he's wearing a badge is because the police failed to find the sister who disappeared. He bought his detective's shield, but he's more than earned it. He's good at what he does and he has a reputation for closing the cases he handles. Except for that one. The thing about Lowry is that he's never given up, never admitted defeat." She hesitated for a moment. "If Miss MacKenzie struck a chord with him, he'll be the best ally you could hope for."

It was a hard truth to tell an ex-Pink like Geoffrey Hunter. Madame Jolene did not doubt for a moment that he was as much in love with Prudence MacKenzie as a man could be. He'd have to admit that despite his years of training and experience, the bullet that remained in one leg and the damage that necessitated the use of a cane to get around meant he needed a fully able-bodied presence to back him up if things turned bad. Which they probably would.

"The word's out that Lowry rewards any beat cop who can

provide new information about young women of a certain age who work the streets."

"I don't believe Lowry's sister was ever on the streets," Madame Jolene said. "There's another world behind the façade of respectability our bankers and stockbrokers and captains of industry erect around themselves. But it's just as real as the one you see down at Mulberry Bend. That's where she is. In a high-priced, exclusive bordello. If she's still alive."

She was talking about Bettina Lowry, but she might as well have been describing the fate Geoffrey feared had befallen Prudence. Who had committed the dangerous and foolhardy act of caring enough about another human being to want to rescue her from a life of forced degradation and a downward spiral into the hell of addiction.

Madame Jolene had no illusions about the profession that had enabled her to rise above the status of poorly paid household drudge, which was the best she could have expected when she got off the boat as an immigrant. The city had been peppered with signs advertising that NO IRISH NEED APPLY. Sometimes the message read NO DOGS OR IRISH NEED APPLY. She'd escaped the fate of thousands of women who lived short, brutal lives threatened by yearly childbirth and abusive husbands, but she'd never closed her eyes to what might have been and what was. The advice she had given Geoffrey was sound and practical.

Difficult to hear, but unwise to discount.

The chloroform had given her a vicious headache. Prudence's eyes stung, her mouth was dry and foul-tasting, her lips had cracked and swollen under the savage force of the hand that had silenced her.

She lay on a narrow bed in a darkened room feebly lit by a single wall-mounted gas light. From the pain in her wrists and ankles, Prudence realized that she must have been tightly bound during the journey from The Doll House to wherever she was now. The last thing she clearly remembered was seeing the shattered head of the doll that Bella Nicholson had been made to resemble, followed by the sudden realization that she had been right all along. The expensive boutique patronized by a wealthy, respectable clientele operated as a front for one of the most sadistic and cold-blooded trades in the city.

Then had come the blackness of a heavy hood, the nauseating stench of chloroform, the sensation of falling. Impenetrable nothingness.

She lay still until the angry throbbing behind her temples eased into a dull pounding. Moving cautiously, she flexed her fingers and wrists, rolled her shoulders, tensed and released the muscles of her legs, relaxed her feet and ankles. Feeling gradually returned, and with it the overwhelming need to explore her prison. She forced herself to wait, to listen, to try to identify the faint sounds she could hear on the other side of the solid door where a splinter of light shone for about six inches along the side of the frame. Warped, she thought. Which meant more than ordinary dampness.

Could she be somewhere along the East River where there were docks, Bellevue Hospital, old stockyards, and decaying slums falling into filthy water? Every now and then a small strip of park? She replayed numerous carriage rides in her mind, trying to picture riverside areas of the city that flashed through her memory. Weren't there areas of Manhattan Island where green lawns stretched from private docks to imposing mansions the rapidly encroaching city had not yet swallowed up? A mansion where The Doll Club existed in safe, isolated splendor? The headache surged back with hammering intensity.

Never mind. It didn't matter *where* she was, only that she had to escape before it was too late. Chloroform deprived you of consciousness, but unlike laudanum, it didn't eat into your soul and rouse the monster of addiction until nothing else mattered and reality receded into a haze of dreamy lethargy. She could overcome pain; she could use it to force herself into action and to plan a survival strategy.

Whatever she did would have to be accomplished in silence. If someone was standing guard outside the door, he must not hear a sound from within. For as long as possible, whoever had taken her had to believe she was still unconscious. She needed time to build her strength, clear her mind, toughen her resolve. Very slowly, she untied the tapes that bound her silk petticoats around her waist. Slid the garments down over her legs, let them settle on the end of the bed. Silk rustled when you walked, a calculated enticement of wealthy, respectable women whose hips could not be allowed to sway. The day suit she had put on that morning was of soft wool, ideal for spring weather, and blessedly quiet.

The most important thing was not to fall. Prudence sat on the edge of the bed, breathing deeply to clear out the last trace of chloroform from her lungs, fighting back the waves of dizziness until her vision cleared. The room's single window had been closed to light and air by shutters nailed to the frame. The only item of furniture was the bed. No armoire for clothing, no chair, not even a bedside table on which to place a candle. An unlidded metal bucket stood against one wall. No china chamber pot that a captive might smash into dangerous shards. Or use to slit her own wrists. Whoever decreed she should be held captive here knew what he was doing.

Moving slowly, cautiously, Prudence inched her way to the door. Pressed her face to the crack outlined by light from the hallway. *Don't forget the sense of smell.* Was it Geoffrey who had taught her that? Prudence breathed in a mixture of women's flowery perfumes, the scent of dusty carpet, the odor of heavily applied Macassar oil. And tobacco. Whiffs of old cigar smoke, the more acrid stench of cigarette ash. The faintest suggestion of whiskey and the smashed grape bitterness of sour wine. No sense or sound of a living presence standing guard.

Madame Jolene had warned her. By whatever name its members called it, The Doll House was a brothel, and Prudence had been selected to be its next victim. If they didn't decide to kill her first. She racked her brain to think of who might be behind the abduction. Was it one person or had she gotten so close to the truth of what was going on that she became a threat to the entire enterprise? If she knew who her enemy was, she reasoned, she stood a better chance of besting him.

She remembered suggesting to Nellie Bly that the reporter go undercover into a house of ill repute without taking full account of what that would mean. And then she'd been horror-struck by her own stupidity.

If she couldn't get out of this place, she was about to find out for herself just how loathsome that experience could be.

Warren Lowry met Geoffrey and Amos Lang on the corner of Fifth Avenue and the quiet side street where the Nicholson town house was located. Two sweeper boys had been set to cleaning the tree-shaded cobblestones out front, with strict orders for one of them to bring word if anyone entered or left the premises. Another pair worked the alleyway behind the house. Extra nickels jingled in the pockets of their ragged pants.

"The only person who's gone out all day is the house-keeper," Amos reported. "She left with a shopping bag shortly after lunch. Loopy Dick followed her to her destination and back. Said he never let the woman out of his sight."

"How many stores did she visit?" Lowry asked. "And how long was she gone?"

Amos consulted his notes. "One shop only. She stayed inside just long enough to drop off whatever she was carrying in the bag. Ten or fifteen minutes. She'd folded the bag up and stuck it under her arm when she came out. Didn't dawdle and didn't window-shop. She was gone for about forty-five minutes. Home again, into the house, and there she's stayed."

"What was the name of the shop?" Geoffrey asked.

Lowry, who'd started to walk away, stopped to wait for the answer.

"The Doll House."

The plan was sketched out within minutes, each of the men weighing the options available to them.

Amos was to continue watching the front entrance of the Nicholson pied-à-terre, but with an added sense of urgency now that a link had been established between The Doll House and Bella and Alexander's uncle. He was armed, but under orders not to interfere with Ira Nicholson or his hired thug unless his cover was blown and he had no other choice.

"It doesn't look as though telephone lines have been strung along this street," Lowry pointed out. No telltale wooden poles and tangle of wires stretched down the alleyway and above the elegant townhomes. Some of New York's prosperous householders were reluctant to have either telephone or electricity installed in their residences until it could be proved that the mysterious new inventions didn't increase the risk of fire.

"That works in our favor," Geoffrey agreed.

"And practically guarantees that if Nicholson has orders to convey, there will have to be a face-to-face meeting," Amos mused. "I think a telegram can be ruled out. My guess is that Nicholson has set up a regular time and place for reports. Probably shortly after dark and almost certainly here to avoid any casual witnesses. It won't be the back alley because that door gives onto the servants' hall and kitchen where there's bound to be someone working or resting between chores. No, whoever he is will be anticipated. Nicholson himself will be waiting just inside the front door so there's no need to ring the bell. Nicholson or the housekeeper, if she's colluding with him. The meeting will be short. I'll follow when our target leaves, station a boy to keep an eye out, and send another to let you know what's happening. That's about the best we can do."

"I don't want any of my officers at The Doll House," Lowry said. "Not while there's time to leak information and warn off the men we're looking for. The department's rotten with informers on the take. But one of these sweeper boys should let Danny know where we're heading."

"I'll take care of that," Amos promised. "And I'll see to rousting out a few more ex-Pinks. I'll tell them they're on standby, in case we need them."

"The Doll House it is then." Geoffrey swept his cane upward like the weapon it was, brought it down onto the pavement with a metallic click. "Let's get going."

His leg ached and the spot where the bullet had lodged itself into bone occasionally flamed a crippling pain, but he matched Detective Warren Lowry stride for stride. Anyone seeing them walk purposefully along the street would have assumed they were two prosperous men of business hurrying home to a good dinner.

Both of them knew that Prudence's life might depend on how quickly they found her.

CHAPTER 27

The Doll House had closed for the day. No lights shone from within except a low gas flame sending dim illumination through the transom window onto the stoop and the doorbell.

"Let's try the alley," Geoffrey suggested, limping down the front steps with the aid of a handrail and his cane. The walk from the Nicholson town house had been more taxing than he'd expected. More painful and exhausting than he wanted to admit.

"I'll go," Lowry volunteered.

"We'll both go." It would mean walking to the end of the block, around the corner, and down an unpaved alley almost certainly littered with spilled trash and hardening mounds of horse dung, but Geoffrey would not be pushed aside or condescended to. He might be slow on his feet at the moment, but he'd been one of Allan Pinkerton's best agents in his day.

And he'd find Prudence no matter where she was or who had taken her.

The rear entrance of The Doll House was protected by a high wooden fence pierced by a wide double gate for deliveries.

Unlike the alley sides of some properties, both appeared solidly built and maintained.

"Locked from the inside," commented Lowry. "No key left in it, and there's a chain for added security."

"Give me a moment," Geoffrey said. He took a slim leather case from an inner pocket of his coat and removed a slender pick. Cane balanced over one arm, he slid the pick into the lock and probed delicately until a faint click told him he'd been successful. The looped chain was even simpler once the gate had been opened enough for him to ease a hand through the narrow gap.

Lowry raised one eyebrow and gave an appreciative nod.

The back door took a little longer because there were two locks to pick, but they were inside before dusk had deepened into darkness. Enough light penetrated the shaded windows to guide them from what had once been a kitchen area into a workroom where studio windows stretched from midway up the walls to the ceiling.

"Very neat and tidy," Geoffrey commented. Unlike most of the behind-the-scenes shops he'd investigated, this one looked to be obsessively clean. Except for one doll laid out in pieces on the single long worktable, there didn't seem to be any other repairs or refurbishments in progress.

A wall of shelving contained rows of the distinctive red boxes, each one labeled in elegant cursive script. Lowry opened them methodically, finding more examples of the expensive, imported bisque dolls displayed in the glass cabinets of the public display rooms. He held a few of them up for Geoffrey's inspection, but the inventory contained nothing unexpected or suspicious.

Geoffrey looked for a desk or filing cabinet where he might find invoices, orders, or correspondence, but it didn't appear that anything of that sort was kept in the workroom. There must be an office elsewhere, he decided, perhaps on an upper floor. Before he left the workroom to explore the rest of the premises, he drifted over to the table. Finely crafted instruments, much like those used by watchmakers, lay lined up on a dark green felt cloth. A hinged case contained a jeweler's loupe, and a small but powerful gas lantern could be lit to shed bright, focused light on the project in hand.

Someone had been restoring and repairing a doll whose detached head and body showed evidence of a heavy blow. Perhaps a fall over a balcony to a marble floor below. Or a slam against a wall by an ill-tempered owner. He almost chuckled, picturing to himself a small tyrant venting anger or frustration on its defenseless victim. Then he picked up the head that was cradled facedown in a velvet-lined wooden holder. Turned it over. And froze. Lit the lantern to be sure.

"Lowry," he called out, quietly but urgently. "Take a look at this."

Half the doll's face had been crushed, but it was the undamaged portion that Geoffrey recognized. Above one dark brown eye was a stenciled eyebrow, a perfect half circle painted on with hair-fine brushstrokes. Around the eye, as regular as spokes on a wheel, radiated stylized eyelashes, thick where they joined the lid, tapering out to a single thin brushstroke at the end. The cheeks were rosy in a determined sort of way, and the rest of the face had been painted to resemble exceptionally pale human skin. No freckles. None of the heart-shaped beauty spots that occasionally marked fashion dolls. On the undamaged portion of the head pale blond curls cascaded like a very young girl's hair. A small bag lying beside the velvet cloth contained strands of matching blond hair waiting to be attached to the reconstructed portion of the skull.

"I recognize the coloring," Lowry said. "You don't often see natural blondes with those exceptionally dark brown eyes."

"It's a Bella doll," Geoffrey agreed. "And if there's only one to represent each kidnapped girl, this could be *the* Bella doll."

"Could this be what the Johnson woman carried in her bag

earlier today? The doll Zander smashed when he realized what had been done to his sister?"

"I think we have to presume it is." Assumptions made without good evidence were something Pinks were warned to avoid, but in this case circumstantial was all they had.

"There are a few of those red boxes not stored on the shelves," Lowry said, gesturing toward a counter he hadn't examined. "I'll take a look at what's inside them. Maybe more repair projects like this one."

"Look for a doll that resembles Ottilie Urquhart. Light brown hair, pale blue eyes."

"Do you think they reuse a doll when her human facsimile is no longer available?"

"It's a possibility. It would be considerably easier to replace just the head rather than start from scratch every time a girl dies from abuse or has to be eliminated for any of a dozen reasons." Geoffrey's throat tightened in disgust for what had been done in the past and fear for what might happen to Prudence. "We have to hurry."

"Wait!" Lowry commanded.

"What is it?" Geoffrey whispered into the shadowy room. He loosened his Colt revolver in its shoulder holster.

"I can smell the chemicals I know they must be using to repair the dolls. But there's something else." Lowry stood very still.

Geoffrey closed his eyes. Seconds ticked by. "Chloroform," he said finally.

"Too sweet and nauseating to be anything else," Lowry agreed.

Both men's eyes fell to the floor beneath their feet. A floor that had been swept clean of the day's debris.

Except for a very small, nearly disintegrated piece of rag that had fallen from or been kicked beneath the table on which the Bella doll lay. Geoffrey snagged it with the tip of his cane. Held it away from his face with one hand, fanned it lightly. The un-

mistakable odor of chloroform hung in the air. Faint, but iden-
tifiable.

"Miss MacKenzie?" asked Lowry.

"They've taken her," Geoffrey said. There was no proof
she'd ever been there, but instinct would have to do. He
clenched the hand holding the ragged piece of chloroformed
cloth. Raised his fist as if the man who had held it over Prudence's face stood before him.

The hinges to the slightly warped door standing between
Prudence and her freedom were on the *inside*. It took a few
moments of heavy staring at what she knew had to be signifi-
cant before her chloroformed brain registered what that meant.
If she could shove the pins up and out of the hinge knuckles
holding them in place, there would be nothing but the bolt on
the outside to keep the door in the frame. That should prevent
it from crashing to the floor and making a noise that would
alarm one of her captors. But would it swing wide enough to
allow her to squeeze out?

She didn't have a chair to stand on to work the topmost
hinge, but her fingers could reach it if she stretched. She wouldn't
be able to see what she was doing. She'd have to rely on touch
alone. Leave that to last. Attack the lower hinge first. When she
tugged on the pin, it didn't budge. She needed something to in-
sert into the open bottom of the hinge or under the head of the
pin to force it upward. But her captors hadn't obligingly furnished her with a screwdriver and hammer. The heel of her
boot? Maybe. She laid a fold of her skirt over the head of the
pin to dull the sound, then tapped upward repeatedly with the
edge of her leather-soled walking boot.

Ten quick blows. Prudence listened for anyone who might
be approaching her room or passing in the hallway. Nothing.
The pin hadn't moved. No use trying a hairpin on it. You could
pick a lock with one, but it wouldn't stand up under repeated

pounding. She needed something much stronger. A building nail?

She ran her hands over the shuttered windows, searching for a poorly driven nail she could pry loose. There wasn't one. The only other possibility was something from the bed frame, a piece of wire from the heavy webbing on which the thin mattress rested?

She pulled the bare mattress from the cot, dumping it unceremoniously on the floor. And then she started examining the legs, the frame, the metal webbing. Every time something sharp bit into her hands, she caught her breath, only to be disappointed over and over again. Nothing long or loose enough to double as a nail. Until, finally, a piece of rusty bedspring broke off when she'd almost given up hope.

She doubted it was strong enough to serve as a nail or a punch, but it might be pushed as a lever under the head of the pin. What was it Geoffrey had told her during the lessons on lock-picking and getting out of tight places? *It might seem unlikely, but try it anyway. You never know.*

Ten more taps and the sharp edge of the bedspring slid beneath the head of the pin. All she needed was enough room to be able to use the bootheel as a hammer. Ten more taps. She withdrew the bedspring and tried to wedge a finger into the space between the head of the pin and the first hinge knuckle. Surely there was more space than when she'd started?

Back went the rusty bedspring. Ten more rapid blows. Pull out the piece of metal and tap upward against the underside of the pinhead. Now she was sure it was working. She could slide almost the whole of one finger into the space. All she had to do was take out the lower pin, then start on the upper hinge. She was slender; even though the door was bolted, she'd slither through the gap like an alley cat squeezing into an impossibly small hidey-hole.

Ten more taps. This time the bootheel caught the finger

holding the skirt hem in place. She choked off a cry of pain, then sucked the ripped nail bed until the stinging faded and it bled less. Then she chewed on her discarded silk petticoat until she was able to rip off a narrow strip of fabric. *Never leave a trail that someone can use to track you.* She twisted the improvised bandage around her finger and tucked in the end to hold it in place. There would be no drops of blood on the floor to show where she had gone.

She didn't think too much time had passed since she'd swum back to consciousness, but there was no way to tell how long she'd been insensible after breathing in the chloroform. The gold watch she usually wore pinned to her shirtwaist was gone, and no light penetrated the window that looked to have been shuttered from without as well as within. She had to hurry. There might not be much time left.

What had Ottilie called it, the place where every hair had been plucked from her body, eyebrows and eyelashes tattooed on, and her skin bleached to the stark whiteness of a piece of paper? *Something* hospital. The doll hospital. That was it.

No matter what it took, Prudence couldn't end up there. She couldn't. She wouldn't.

Ignoring the wounded finger, she picked up her boot and began tapping again.

The Doll House was like a museum of ghosts in the darkness.

Bright glass eyes from the cabinets reflected a glimmer from the small lantern that had stood on the workroom table. Lowry turned the flame down as low as it would go without sputtering out, shielding the glass mantle with one hand as he and Geoffrey made their way from room to room in the display area, searching for the desk they knew had to be somewhere on the premises.

The lantern cast a soft glow that might be visible from the street even though dark curtains had been drawn over the windows, but it couldn't be helped. If they didn't find some reference to where Prudence had been taken, they would have no choice but to continue the watch outside the Nicholson town house. Sooner or later Sybil Johnson was bound to come out, or Nicholson's hired killer would show up. But either of those alternatives would take time, and that was a commodity Prudence was surely running out of.

"Nothing down here," Geoffrey confirmed. They'd found a small desk containing a pot of ink, a few pens, and blank sheets of paper on which clients could presumably sketch out the details of what they wanted. But no records of any transactions either in progress or completed. "They're very careful."

"Not as careful as they should be," Lowry said, plucking a set of keys from a small hook set into the wainscoting of the wall beside a narrow staircase leading upward. "Can you manage?"

"Lead the way," Geoffrey growled. "I'll follow." It would take every ounce of strength and endurance he possessed to navigate those steep steps, but it had to be done. He'd thought from the beginning that if there were an office in which customer records were kept, it would be on an upper floor where clients never ventured. But the presence of a ring of keys was disconcerting. It was too late to comb through ordinary sales receipts, and surely the location of the ultimate destination of the kidnapped girls would not be carelessly noted in easily accessible customer correspondence or a ledger. There had to be a concealed safe. He flexed his right hand, picturing in his mind the dial he would have to twist, readying himself by rubbing the tips of his fingers lightly against each other to increase their sensitivity. He could pick locks and crack safes as well as any skilled housebreaker. That's what it had once meant to be a Pink.

The second floor of the converted town house was largely inventory. What had been a series of small bedrooms had been turned into storage space filled with shipping containers bearing French and German labels and cartons of the distinctive red Doll House boxes. Weatherproofed trunks revealed layer upon layer of imported silks, multi-hued velvets, yards of handcrafted lace, and spools of ribbon.

The imported fashion dolls sold to the public were too valuable to be stored in what was essentially an attic space, but there was one bin that spoke volumes. In it were piled the naked bodies of featureless dolls whose torsos had been sculpted to resemble those of young girls. Faceless and without their human hair wigs, the dolls were curiously menacing. They reminded Geoffrey of the corn husk voodoo likenesses he'd seen throughout his childhood on the family plantation in eastern North Carolina and on Bradford Island last year. Emptiness waiting for a spell to transform it into a weapon.

They found the office they were looking for at the end of what had been the bedroom corridor. One of the keys on the ring Lowry carried opened the door. He swung it wide on noiseless hinges, taking one tentative step inside, revolver in hand. "All clear."

The rolltop desk beside a curtained window was locked, and although Lowry tried every key on the ring, none of them worked. He looked quizzically at Geoffrey, shrugged his shoulders, then stepped over to the window, twitched back the drape, and looked into the street below. "Be quick," he said quietly. "Someone across the way is going to glance outside and wonder why they're seeing a light over here."

"Keep an eye open."

"It looks as though they cleaned up downstairs after drugging Miss MacKenzie. They won't be back tonight. The bit of rag we found is the only mistake they've made so far."

"Not a very good lock," Geoffrey said as he slid open the desk's barrel top. "Second mistake."

"There's no one coming." Lowry turned his attention to a row of wooden file cabinets. "There probably won't be anything in here that will tell us what we want to know, but I'll take a look just the same. I've a mind to compare their client names to our police records and newspaper accounts of missing girls." He slid open the first drawer and began flipping through the files, occasionally writing down a familiar-sounding name. "Each file has notes about the transaction, including the name and address of the purchaser, dates of order and delivery, and a detailed description of what the doll looks like, including clothing. It's as complete a provenance as you could wish for." He took out one of the papers in a file that was slightly thicker than some of the others. "Here we are. This one describes not only the doll, but the child for whom it was supposedly destined. A very detailed catalog of what the girl looks like. What are the odds that some of the children with this kind of portrait in their files have disappeared?"

"Look for an address that keeps repeating itself," Geoffrey ordered, methodically sifting through the contents of rows of small drawers before turning his attention to the ledgers stacked in a cubby beneath them. "They have to meet somewhere and we know now that the physical transformations Ottilie described to us are not being done here. I'm betting the shop is a front for locating the type of girl a member dreams of turning into his personal doll. That business of having a portrait painted so a doll can be created that looks just like its young owner has always bothered me. I'm wondering if the portrait is the final decisive factor in whether a girl is kidnapped or not." He set aside a telegram that had been folded into one of the drawers, found another slipped between the pages of a ledger.

"That sounds like the portraits medieval kings commissioned of prospective brides."

"This is all I've been able to come up with," Geoffrey said, holding up the two yellow telegrams. "The messages are unremarkable. *Expect delivery tonight.* The other is just as cryptic. *Delivery canceled.* What's interesting is that they were both sent to the same address."

"But not here?"

"No. It's an address I'm not familiar with. Whoever signed for them had to have brought them back here at some point. But why?"

"He stuck them in a pocket, forgot they were there, and found them when he sat down at the desk to make an entry in the ledger," Lowry said, reaching for the telegrams Geoffrey held out to him. "The simplest explanation is usually the right one." He stared off into space for a moment. "Before Fifth Avenue became the fashionable location to build your mansion and Newport the only place to spend the summer season, there were estates on the bluffs along the East River. Some of them are still there, despite the commercial docks and the stench of the water at low tide."

"You said estates?" Geoffrey asked.

"I remember them from childhood," Lowry said. "Very private and very remote. We children thought the carriage ride to get there would never end. But there were woods to run and play in, huge stretches of lawn going right to the edge of the bluffs, stairs down to boats tied up at private moorings. Every property fenced and gated, the homes hidden behind winding roadways and tall trees."

"How many of them are left?"

"As private residences? I don't know. I haven't thought of them in years."

"But your family once owned an estate there on the East River?"

"My grandfather liked the privacy. He was an irascible old man, not fond of his wife, his children, or his grandchildren. So he built this enormous enclave on the outskirts of the city where they'd be too busy amusing themselves to bother him. That was in the days before train travel made life easier for everyone."

"We can't afford to get this wrong. Prudence is running out of time."

Neither man wanted to say aloud what each was thinking.

That it might already be too late.

"We're staking her life on this," Geoffrey said.

They had no other choice.

CHAPTER 28

The telegraph boy appeared just as dusk was spreading pale gray shadows over the tree-lined street where Amos Lang kept watch.

He was pedaling furiously, uniformed body bent over the frame of his bicycle, leather pouch slung around his neck. Western Union paid its fleet of messengers by the mile. The faster they cycled, the more telegrams they delivered. The greater the distances covered the more they earned. It was dangerous work on the congested New York City streets, dodging lumbering delivery wagons, rattling hansom carriages, the cumbersome horse-drawn trolleys, and the crowds of fast-moving pedestrians. Messenger boys could start as young as ten years of age. By eighteen their careers were over.

Amos stepped out from behind the plane tree where he was sheltering as the messenger swerved toward the sidewalk in front of the Nicholson town house. This was what he'd been waiting for.

"Just a minute." Lang's grip on the handlebar held the bicycle upright while his body blocked the boy from dismounting.

Startled features below the bill of the uniform cap stared up at him. He judged this messenger to be about fourteen years old, long enough in the business to have figured out ways to increase the pittance the company paid for hours of hazardous cycling from early morning to late at night.

"I got a telegram to deliver, mister," the boy said.

His eyes glimmered in the reflected light of the gas street lamp. Fearful, slightly belligerent, determined. Amos figured the messenger boy had a good idea of what was coming next. And that it was something he'd done before.

"Two bits for a look at the telegram before you deliver it."

"Four."

"That's highway robbery," Amos said, keeping his voice friendly and conspiratorial.

The boy shrugged.

Amos dug two quarters from the pocketful of change he kept on the ready. He tossed the coins in the air, caught them in a swiftly clenched fist just out of the boy's eager reach. "The telegram," he ordered. Only when the flimsy yellow envelope was in his hand did he relinquish the four bits.

The envelope should have been sealed shut, but as with most of the communications leaving the Western Union office, time was of the essence. A quick swipe of glue moistened sponge, and the missive was off.

Amos blew on the envelope's flap, and when it fluttered, slid an experienced finger into the opening. Intercepting correspondence and scanning the contents without the addressee's knowledge was an elemental part of Pinkerton training. The message was short and to the point. *Tonight. Ten o'clock.* No salutation. No signature. No indication of where the meeting was to take place. He'd have to get word to Mr. Hunter and Detective Lowry, arrange for another of Danny Dennis's boys to take his place, and follow Nicholson when he left the town house.

Which, he decided as he looked at his pocket watch, was likely to be soon. Depending on how long it would take to get wherever he was going. Stops along the way?

"Ten minutes," Lowry said, handing over another two bits. "Fiddle with your bicycle chain as though something's wrong with it. Wait until you see me come back before you deliver the telegram."

He walked casually toward Fifth Avenue, then sprinted as soon as he was sure he was out of sight of any of the Nicholson town house windows. The boys he was looking for were sweeping industriously at the corner. One of them took off in the direction of the stable where Danny boarded Mr. Washington. Another slipped through the dwindling sidewalk traffic toward the side street where The Doll House was located, and a third appeared out of nowhere to gather up the brooms and continue with the sweeping.

Standing in the concealing shelter of the plane tree again, only slightly out of breath, Amos watched the Western Union boy climb the Nicholson stoop and lift the brass lionhead knocker. The sound echoed along the length of the quiet street.

A woman dressed in housekeeper black opened the door, stuck out her hand for the telegram, handed over a coin, and disappeared from view before Amos could get a good look at her face. No white maid's cap or ruffled apron. It had to be Sybil Johnson. No butler. Interesting. Housekeepers didn't usually receive visitors in well-staffed households. Was Nicholson making do with a cook, a couple of maids, and perhaps a single manservant for the heavy lifting?

That could make a difference. Servants who felt put upon because their employers stinted on hiring additional staff could usually be counted on to complain to anyone who cared to listen. Information was the lifeblood of the inquiry business. Depending on what happened tonight, Amos decided, the next servant to leave the house would pocket a few extra coins in exchange for whatever particulars he or she could deliver.

In the meantime, Lang remained a slightly darker presence in the lengthening shadows.

The sweeper boy was waiting in The Doll House rear delivery yard when Geoffrey and Detective Lowry closed the back door behind them, relocked it, and walked silently toward the double gate that gave access to the alley.

"Figured you'd be coming out this way," the boy whispered, one finger lightly touching his cap in respectful salute. All of Danny's urchins knew that Mr. Hunter, the ex-Pinkerton with the mysterious past, was limping around with a bullet in his leg. There were bets laid on when or if the piece of flattened metal would work itself out of the bone and inch its way upward through muscle and skin.

"What is it, Tommy?"

"Mr. Lang sent me. Said to tell you he'd be following the toff he was staking out. A telegram came for him." Tommy wrinkled his face into the semblance of a serious scholar. "Something about tonight at ten o'clock. Mr. Lang said to tell you he didn't know what it was, but he'd find out."

"Can you get us a cab at the corner?" Detective Lowry ordered. He handed Tommy a pair of nickels.

"Danny should be waiting up there now, sir." Tommy touched the brim of his cap again.

"Tell him we're on our way."

The boy sped out of sight, skinny legs flashing as he tore through pools of gaslight.

"Why the telegram?" Lowry asked as Geoffrey secured the gate and they set off up the alley toward Fifth Avenue.

"Nicholson has put the entire operation in danger," Geoffrey said. "His doll escaped or was rescued by her brother, which brought the whole nasty business some very unwelcome attention. Think about it for a moment. Two private inquiry agents, a New York City police detective, a Quaker doctor and her medical staff, the most famous investigative reporter in the world, and the madam of a highly successful brothel with political connections. All of us asking questions and exchanging information. It's too much to believe there hasn't been a leak somewhere along that chain. They have to know we're on to them. We're not dealing with amateurs."

"So they've summoned Nicholson to a reckoning," Lowry mused. "He has to clean up the mess he's made."

"At the very least."

"And then he has to disappear. Permanently."

"But in such a way that no one suspects anything."

"Miss MacKenzie also." Lowry glanced over at the man limping beside him, face set sternly against the pain he must be experiencing.

"Tell me everything you know about these river bluff estates. What the grounds are like, the roads into them, the gates, the mansions themselves."

A hansom cab blocked the mouth of the alley. Danny Dennis, driving one of Mr. Washington's dark stablemates. Even without much of a moon tonight, the gigantic white horse couldn't be hidden.

"That's a bit of a drive," Danny commented when Lowry had given him the address.

"They've got Miss MacKenzie," Geoffrey said.

Danny picked up his whip and pulled his hat down tightly over his ears.

"Hang on, gentlemen. It'll be a rough ride."

The pin to the bottom hinge had come loose and now lay in the pocket of Prudence's skirt.

But the topmost hinge almost defeated her. Working by touch alone, she used the rusty bedspring as a lever beneath the pinhead again, but twisting, turning, and tapping with arms raised above her head strained her shoulder muscles until she wanted to scream with the pain of it.

Slowly, slowly. Twisting, pulling, twisting again, pulling again. Counting to ten. Bringing her arms down for another count of ten. More twisting, pulling, tapping. Over and over until the hinge was stained with Prudence's blood, bits of skin had been shredded from her fingers, and the bandage she'd fashioned from a ripped piece of petticoat had fallen off.

And then, miraculously, the pin popped free of the hinge knuckle.

Boot back on her foot, she dragged the mattress onto the bed frame. There was nothing she could use to suggest a body lying there, but by the time someone came to check on her, she hoped to be long gone. And the unhinged door would be a dead giveaway. Nothing she could do about that either.

She pushed the door open, edged her way into the corridor, replaced the door in its frame as best she could, then took stock.

A row of eight doors, four on each side of the dimly lit hallway. Eight separate rooms then. She'd have to assume they were like the one she'd just escaped from, empty of everything but a cot. Punishment cells? She knocked tentatively at each of the other doors, moving quickly and as quietly as she could. Not a sound from the other seven rooms. Were they empty? There wasn't time to find out.

A door at the end of the hallway opened onto a landing where the brightness of the gaslight made her hold up a hand to shield her eyes.

She had to get out, but she didn't dare attempt the wide, curved staircase carpeted in crimson with brass rods stretched across each step. If this was a mansion converted into a brothel, there would be a servants' staircase somewhere toward the back of each floor. Narrow, probably not carpeted, but perhaps her only hope of not meeting up with the men who had abducted her. Or their loathsome clients.

Prudence found the servants' staircase where she expected it to be, where a maid with broom and dustpan in hand could pause to survey the corridor before venturing out to perform her duties. Servants were trained to be invisible.

Edging her way downward on tiptoe to avoid the thud of bootheels against bare, splintery wood, Prudence reached what a glance out a narrow window told her must be the second floor. She stood for a moment by a green baize-covered door listening for voices and movement. Heavy footsteps. What sounded like an argument. Was that music somewhere far off? She caught the scent of something that smelled like the alcohol Dr. Charity Sloan used to clean patient wounds at the Friends Refuge. Could this be the floor on which the suite of rooms Ottilie had called the doll hospital was located? Was another victim undergoing the torturous procedures she had described? Or were preparations underway to transform Prudence herself?

She had to find out.

The footsteps she'd heard had been moving away, the raised voices growing fainter as she listened.

When all was silent, she eased the door open and slid through the narrowest gap she could manage, standing motionless to listen for the sound of returning footfalls. The gaslight on this floor had been turned down to a low glimmer. She could make out Turkish carpets, mahogany tables holding bouquets of fresh flowers, mirrors in heavy, gilded frames. And all along the walls, row after row of portraits in identical frames. Faces of such stylized young female beauty that it was difficult to believe they had been painted from life.

She retreated into the staircase, and as she followed its downward turns, the smell of alcohol grew stronger.

If this mansion was like the one in which she had grown up,

the basement would be a warren of storerooms and work-rooms. Kitchen, servants' hall, butler's office, housekeeper's parlor. Laundry rooms, pantries, wine cellar, boot room. Had one or more of these spaces been transformed into the pseudo operating theater Ottilie had described? That would only make sense if every servant employed by the club knew what was going on. Or if none of them lived in, and the ordinary cleaning work of the public areas was done on a rigidly structured schedule.

The stairway giving access to the basement floor ended abruptly. Darkness faintly illuminated in patches by gaslights turned low spread off to the right. Prudence could make out simply furnished rooms, doors without formidable locks or bolts drawn across them. This, then, was where the ordinary household work was organized, where servants probably entered early in the morning and left at the end of the day. It looked very much like the staff quarters of her own home.

But the hallway stretching off to her left had been barred halfway down its length by a heavy steel door secured by one of the supposedly unpickable locks used in many banking establishments. Geoffrey had taught her to make short work of their pins, but the set of tools she usually carried had been taken, along with her reticule and the small derringer it contained. For some reason, her kidnappers hadn't seen fit to remove the hairpins from her elaborately coiled coiffure when they'd stripped off her jewelry.

It took several minutes with the hairpin, her ear pressed against the steel, but the lock finally snapped open. Prudence closed the door behind her but did not secure it. If she had to make a hurried exit, she wouldn't have time to work her hairpin feat again.

The first room she came to was clearly where the extravagantly embellished doll costumes were made for human girls and young women. Rolls of silk, taffeta, velvet, and chiffon in all colors of the rainbow lay on shelves beside small bins of sequins, lace, ribbons, buttons, artificial flowers, and feathers. Silk undergarments and sheer stockings that could only have been made in France filled other bins, as did boxes of delicately heeled shoes and dancing slippers labeled as to size and color. Heaps of jewelry glittered next to white gloves; waterfalls of curled human hair decorated a forest of wig stands. Dress dummies lurked in the corners, a long cutting table took up the center of the room, and a bank of sewing machines stood beneath shaded lamps hanging from the low ceiling. A sketch had been left on the cutting table, identified by a jumble of letters and numbers. Code to avoid revealing a name. Prudence memorized the sequence.

She took a long white doctor's coat from a changing room and used the wall mirror over a hand sink to pull her hair back into the stern bun she imagined would be worn down here, adding a piece of white cloth tied to resemble a nurse's scarf. If she had to go back up into the public rooms of the house, it might be the disguise that would buy her time until she could find a way out.

The suite Ottilie had called the doll hospital was as well-equipped as Dr. Sloan's treatment rooms. Or, Prudence imagined, the mortuary parlors where it had become the fashion to embalm bodies before burying them. Trays of instruments gleamed behind glass cabinets, but there were also hairbrushes, combs, manicure kits, bottles of alcohol, laudanum, and other chemicals she couldn't identify. And glass jars of a white powder that she suspected could be the arsenic or lead used to whiten skin.

Each of the two examination tables had thick straps attached at head, middle, and foot. So what was done here was painful and not always under the dulling effect of laudanum or chloroform. She imagined tortured bodies writhing helplessly against the straps. Were the victims gagged to stifle their screams? She saw needles, tweezers of all sizes, razors and strops, scissors with curved blades, and pots of what she thought must be the inks used to tattoo eyebrows and eyelashes. Permanently color lips and cheeks.

It was a nightmare made real.

Prudence tasted bile in her mouth and wiped tears she hadn't known she'd shed from her face.

She'd seen enough. Time to go. Time to find a door to the outside, make her way across the lawns and into the trees she'd glimpsed through the stairwell windows, climb the fence that was bound to enclose the property, and reach the safety of whatever road lay on the other side. She didn't know where she was, but she was counting on stars in a clear night sky to guide her once she decided which direction to go.

She heard nothing above her as she regained the servants' portion of the basement, relocking the steel door, quickly realizing that the barred gate securing the kitchen door to the delivery yard could not be picked. The windows were barred, too, the whole lower floor as well secured as a prison. She had to risk the staircase again.

There was no other way to save herself.

CHAPTER 29

Sooner than Amos Lang expected, the basement areaway door to the Nicholson town house opened, sending a beam of light into the darkness. A footman sprinted up the stairs onto the sidewalk and ran off in the direction of Fifth Avenue. Minutes later he was back, a hansom cab trailing in his wake.

Amos left the concealment of his plane tree as soon as the driver pulled his cab to a halt. The footman had disappeared inside, presumably to let Nicholson know that his transportation had arrived. Odd, though. A gentleman usually kept his own carriage, even in a city like New York where stable space was expensive. Where was Nicholson going that he preferred anonymity to comfort?

Whispers in the dark, mention of Danny Dennis's name. Coins changed hands.

As Nicholson climbed into the hansom and banged shut the half door, Lang vaulted up onto one of the large wheels and into the driver's seat above and behind the passenger compartment. It was a tight squeeze, not meant for two men to occupy, but Amos was as thin and pliable as the ferret after which Allan Pinkerton had nicknamed him.

"Where to, sir?" the driver asked Nicholson through the trapdoor.

"Out to the bluffs overlooking the East River. I'll let you know where I want you to stop."

As the cab pulled away from the curb, Lang searched the shadows for one of the urchins who should be lurking there. He saw the flash of a dirty white hand raised to signal that all was well. Someone would stay on guard and someone else would convey the message that Lang was on Nicholson's trail. He doubted the boy could have heard the destination, but it hardly mattered. A relay of runners would presumably follow, hopping on and off the back of the cab as necessary.

When Geoffrey Hunter planned a surveillance operation, he left nothing to chance.

Ira Nicholson was puzzled and annoyed, but not overly concerned that he had been summoned without warning to the mansion where The Doll Club met. There had been three escapes so far this year, two more than during the previous twelve months. The owners of the missing dolls had been exhaustively interrogated, each of their suspicions investigated as the searches widened. His own loss had been accounted for and he'd shared with other members his decision to augment the club's security force with an addition no one could object to. An ex-Pink who'd turned his considerable skills to the lucrative field of murder for hire. He'd reported that both Nicholson's doll and the boy who had freed her were dead.

Which left the streetwalker who never should have been recruited in the first place and the girl who'd been abducted from a park when her governess was distracted long enough to chloroform the young woman and drag her off. Nicholson hadn't been interested enough in either of the other runaways to bother learning the details of the incidents, but he supposed he'd find out about them tonight. Whenever potentially dangerous or embarrassing cases were resolved, the council gathered to debate how to prevent anything similar from happening again. Nicholson had recently been elected to fill a vacancy on the seven-member council.

He let his thoughts drift away from the meeting he was on his way to attend. There was a more pressing issue to address. A replacement for wonderful, darling little Bella. He'd been lonely for so long before Effie returned, wandering aimlessly between the memories that bound him to Lanternlight and the delights that beckoned him to the city. Everything changed when he looked into Bella's deeply dark brown eyes and ran his fingers through her bright blond curls.

Such a surprise Bella turned out to be. She was the reincarnation of her mother, but a dozen times better. The only fly in the ointment had been the boy. Alexander. So protective of his sister that until Effie died and he could send her son away to boarding school, Nicholson had had to worship Bella from afar. Every time he urged her to sit on his lap or allow him to play with her hair, the brother appeared at her side. As if by magic. And just having him there was enough to spoil the moment because Bella paid no attention to her uncle when she could share Alexander's company.

Out of desperation, Ira had begun spending longer and more frequent stretches of time in the city, reacquainting himself with The Doll Club's lures and possibilities. Alexander and Bella thrived at Lanternlight without him; their mother indulged their every whim and showered them with gifts and attention to make up for the hard life they'd known under the tutor. Who drank. And gambled. Beat Effie senseless. Knocked his two children around when they tried to interfere. Where he was now, Nicholson had no idea. Nor did he care. The man had had no legal claim to Effie's children while they were alive; he couldn't demand a share of the Nicholson estate in their name now that they were dead.

The ex-Pink he'd hired had been graphic in his reports, especially the final one. He'd unrolled a piece of dirty rag to display the crooked little finger hacked from a young boy's hand. As pale as pig's fat and just as smelly. Zander's.

"You required proof," the man had reminded him.

"Get rid of it," Nicholson had replied. He'd kept the tuft of golden hair clipped from Bella's sweet head, enshrining it within his watch fob where he could look at it whenever he consulted the time. Bella would never have left him if it hadn't been for her brother. He was as sure of that as he was that he would replace her with another pale-haired, brown-eyed angel.

Ira Nicholson flipped open his pocket watch, rubbed an affectionate thumb over the curved glass beneath which nestled the precious lock of hair, and noted the time by a passing flare of gaslight. The escaped dolls he knew about aside, he wondered again what urgent matter could have persuaded this year's Doll Master to summon the council with so little warning.

At the last moment Prudence picked up a folder from the cutting table. She paged through the sketches it contained, each of them labeled with the name of the doll for which costumes were being designed. Miranda. Was it the girl's real name or one the man who owned her had chosen? No matter. If she succeeded in destroying this nest of vipers, Miranda, whoever she was, would be set free. As would every other young woman or girl kidnapped and ill-treated by men who deserved the most severe punishment society could mete out.

She smoothed her features, assumed an expression of stony-faced determination, and began to climb the servants' staircase. Her plan was to walk boldly through rooms and hallways until she found a door to the outside. Wearing the white coat she had found in the hospital and carrying what was clearly a case folder in her hands, she thought she had a good chance of managing it. If anyone accosted or questioned her, she'd snap out a reminder that time was of the essence and clients didn't like to be kept waiting. *Masters,* Ottilie had called them. Masters then. *Masters don't like to be kept waiting.* If she could deliver the line with the right degree of impatience, she should get away with it. *The successful agent is bold and self-assured.* Who had taught her that? Geoffrey. It had to have been Geoffrey.

Best not to think of him now. She couldn't afford to let herself become distracted. *Mind on the mission at hand. Attention focused on the present.* He was with her even though he wasn't.

The door to the first floor opened onto a magnificently black-and-white tiled, two-story foyer, a broad staircase spiraling upward to the club's private rooms. Were all houses of ill repute alike? Madame Jolene's brothel had had a series of opulently furnished parlors where clients were entertained as they waited. She remembered walking through them when she'd called on the madam, slightly shocked at the previous evening's debris sitting on tabletops and draped over chairs. But that was a much more public establishment than this exclusive playground.

She heard a carriage roll up outside, the horses snorting and blowing as the coachman reined them to a stop. A driver or passenger in a hurry. Prudence stood for a moment, debating whether to slide behind a thick drape or duck back into the staircase before someone came to open the front door.

She waited a fraction too long to make her move.

A heavily muscled man strode across the foyer and came to an abrupt stop when he spotted Prudence in her white coat, folder held in front of her like a protective shield.

"What are you doing here?" he asked. "We don't have any transformations scheduled tonight."

"Masters don't like to be kept waiting," she replied, then turned back toward the staircase, shrugging her shoulders as if to dismiss any blame for delay.

She heard the slap of his boots on the tile and felt his hand seize her upper arm before she had taken more than a few steps. He spun her around so viciously that she dropped the folder she was carrying. Its contents spilled out over the floor.

"I've never seen you before," he snarled. "Who are you?"

"What's going on, Fleming?"

The front door stood open to the night, on its threshold a well-dressed older gentleman with the distinguished bearing of a judge, a senator, or a banker. The carriage rolled away as another burly individual appeared from the interior of the mansion. Like the man holding tightly to Prudence, he wore a dark blue suit tailored to look like a uniform. Boxer's muscles bulged beneath the shoulder pads and his face was scarred with the evidence of bare-knuckled bouts.

"Fleming?"

"I'm not sure yet, sir. She's wearing one of our lab coats and carrying one of our case histories, but I don't recognize her and we don't have anything scheduled for tonight except the council meeting."

"Let me take a look," the dignified gentleman said. He tilted Prudence's head up with one finger beneath her chin, scrutinizing the features of her face with the scientific appraisal of the medical man he was. "Too old to be one of the dolls," he said. "Too fine-featured for a seamstress or a laboratory attendant."

"Someone was brought in earlier," the newly arrived muscleman said.

"On whose order?"

"I'd rather not say, sir."

"Very discreet of you, " the gentleman commented. "Though hardly necessary under the circumstances. I doubt this one will be leaving us."

Amos Lang leaped down from the hansom cab in which Ira Nicholson was riding as soon as the driver slowed his horse to a walk in front of a pair of iron gates set into a high stone wall. From the far side of the cab Lang faded into the darkness, then darted forward into the prickly hollies that discouraged passers-by from walking too close to the wall and adventuresome boys from attempting to scale it.

Four carriages arrived in the next twenty minutes, the passengers inside each one making themselves known to the two gatekeepers who, Amos decided, were armed guards. Their unbuttoned suit jackets promised quick access to the guns he caught a glimpse of in their shoulder holsters, and their heavy gait spoke of the muscled strength common to ex-boxers, ex-wrestlers, and gang members. One man alone didn't stand a chance of getting past them. He'd have to scout the perimeter of the wall to find a spot where an unpruned tree would be as good as a ladder.

As Amos moved off beyond the gate, bending low to weave through the shrubbery, he heard another conveyance behind him. One horse. So probably not a gentleman's carriage. He waited, crouched as low as he could get, and as the hansom cab drove by, he recognized Danny Dennis in the driver's seat, his top hat with its Irish green feathery plume unmistakable even in the semidarkness of the gas lit street. Lang stepped out of his hiding place, careful not to startle the horse, who wasn't the distinctively enormous Mr. Washington.

"How did you know where I was going?" he asked as Detective Warren Lowry and Geoffrey Hunter climbed out of the cab. "I presume you got my message."

"Jimmy found us as we were leaving The Doll House," Geoffrey explained. "Someone got careless with a couple of telegrams. What do you know so far?"

"I'd lay odds Nicholson wasn't planning to go out until he got the telegram I intercepted," Lang began. "The house had that look of settling in for the night, not many lamps lit downstairs or up on the bedroom floor. He didn't order his own carriage, if he has one, which to me signals that he didn't want anyone knowing where he was heading. He got here not more than about twenty-five minutes ago, but four carriages have come through the gates since then."

"Not hansoms?"

"Private carriages only. Two armed guards on duty to check each carriage and its passengers. I doubt they'd let a hansom cab onto the property. Nicholson didn't seem to expect it. He told the cabbie to pull over in the street, then he got out, paid him, spoke to the guards, and walked up the driveway by himself."

"No sign of Miss MacKenzie?" Geoffrey asked.

"Miss MacKenzie?" Amos whispered the name, shock and a sudden flash of alarm in his voice. "What would she be doing here?"

"She's been missing for most of the day. There was a piece of chloroformed rag on the floor of The Doll House workroom."

"We believe she's been taken," Lowry said. "It's the only way to explain why she hasn't contacted anyone. Why she's vanished into thin air. And we also think Nicholson has been summoned to answer for putting the operation in danger."

"He wasn't acting like a man who thought he was being called on the carpet," Lang said.

"I doubt he suspects anything. But if Miss Prudence *was* on to something that got her in trouble, they probably believe it can be traced back to his doll's escape." Geoffrey pointed at the wall with his cane. "How do you propose we get over that thing?"

"I'm looking for a tree," Amos said.

"They've been too careful for that," Danny Dennis contributed, looming out of the deserted roadway, bridled horse in tow. "I drove up the street a way, but there aren't any branches hanging over the wall and nothing close enough to it to risk a jump." He laid a calming hand on the dark chestnut's muzzle. "Morgan isn't as big as Mr. Washington, but he'll do the trick. I'll hold him still while you gentlemen get up on his back one by one and hoist yourselves over the wall."

He didn't bother asking if they were armed. He'd worked with Mr. Hunter before and knew he never went anywhere without a loaded Colt tucked into a shoulder holster. And he recognized the cane for the thin, deadly sword it was.

If Miss MacKenzie *was* inside the house whose rooftop loomed in the distance, and if anyone *could* rescue her, it would be Mr. Hunter.

Nevertheless, while he waited, he'd say the rosary he carried in his pocket, its string of beads wound around the barrel of the pistol he'd been given years ago when he was a lad in Ireland. Before a failed mission against the hated British occupiers landed him in Kilmainham Gaol.

The organization to which he'd sworn allegiance never acknowledged surrender. No matter what. Neither did Danny.

Chapter 30

Prudence regained consciousness slowly, vaguely aware of skilled hands stripping and then redressing her, painting her face and lips, securing curls and coils of hair atop her head. They slipped jeweled bracelets onto her wrists, rings on her fingers, a necklace around her throat. Threaded hoops of gold into the lobes of her ears. Patted a heavy, sensuous perfume onto her skin, encased her legs in silk stockings, forced her feet into high-heeled satin dancing slippers.

"I think that's the effect we want to achieve," a satisfied voice proclaimed.

"A pity we have to lose the jewelry," another voice said.

"Can't be helped. The stones aren't of the first quality."

"Not that the country bumpkins up there know the difference."

"Isn't that the point?"

Each of the two women working on her wore the same type of white coat in which she had tried to make her escape, their hair bundled beneath starched white linen kerchiefs that gave them the look of nuns or nurses. Keeping her eyelids lowered as awareness of her surroundings gradually returned, Prudence could make out frowns of concentration on their faces.

"What about the others?"

"They're all dressed, made up, and ready to go. Enough laudanum to keep them docile but not put them to sleep. They'll be brought down to the council room when the gong strikes."

"What do you think they'll do to her?"

Prudence felt a disturbance in the air above her face as a hand waved in her direction. She listened intently when the speaker lowered her voice.

"Best not to speculate. But I doubt we'll see her again. Not alive anyway."

"I've never prepared a dead body. Have you?"

They were forbidden to discuss their pasts, but so many rules had already been broken tonight. "I had a job applying cosmetics to dead ladies in a funeral parlor for a while."

"I don't think I'd like that."

"You wouldn't. I was always afraid one of them would open her eyes and stare at me."

"That's why you quit?"

"The money wasn't as good there as it is here."

"Nobody pays better than The Doll Club."

And then silence. Neither of the women who tweezed and plucked, waxed and tattooed, rouged and whitened skin had ever observed what happened after their creations left the basement room that was always referred to as the doll hospital. They knew better than to ask, better than to speculate aloud. Nobody could be trusted not to repeat what they heard. There was as much money paid for spying as doing the job you'd been hired to perform.

"We're done here."

"Not much to clean up. I'll ring to let them know they can come get her."

"I think she's coming around. I saw her eyelids flutter."

"Strap her down again. No point taking any chances."

Before Prudence could think to roll herself off the table on which she lay, heavy straps were thrown across her upper body and legs, buckled so tightly, she couldn't move. It wouldn't have done any good. The scalpel she'd slipped into her pocket had disappeared when her clothing had been taken off. She had no weapon but her mind. And that was clouded by the chloroform they'd used to knock her out.

At least, thank God, they hadn't dosed her with laudanum.

Which must mean they wanted her alert for whatever was going to happen next.

She started counting backward by threes from a hundred. It was a trick Geoffrey had told her he'd used more than once to clear a fogged brain.

Geoffrey. Surely by now he'd know she'd gone missing. Where was he?

Morgan's broad back was as steady as a rock. With Danny holding the horse's bridle, whispering whatever it is coachmen tell their animals to quiet them, first Detective Lowry, then Geoffrey, and finally Amos Lang clambered up and over the wall, dropping softly onto a carpet of thick, well-tended grass.

Geoffrey had thrown his cane down, then followed it without any more difficulty than either of the other two men. Or so it looked. The darkness hid the grimaces he could not suppress as pain bad enough to make a man pass out shot through his bullet-ridden leg, up his hip, and into his spine.

Amos Lang knew his fellow ex-Pink was suffering. It was why he'd positioned himself as the last of the three to go over the wall. With Lowry already inside the grounds, he could lend the assistance Geoffrey would not ask for to haul himself onto Morgan's back. He'd seen courage in his days with Allan Pinkerton's men, but nothing like the silent fortitude his employer was displaying tonight. Bravery could backfire, make a healing wound flare up again, aggravate almost healthy flesh and turn it gangrenous. Mr. Hunter would need a doctor as soon as this rescue was over. Danny Dennis shot him a nod as Amos vaulted onto the horse's withers. Danny would see to it that a doctor would be waiting at the Fifth Avenue Hotel when tonight's job was finished.

When, not *if*. The Pinkerton way was to think positive while preparing for the worst.

"We need to take out the guards by the gate," Detective Lowry said as they gathered beneath the sheltering branches of a towering pine. "In case we have to make a quick exit."

"I only saw two," Lang said.

"One for you and one for me." Lowry took a blackjack from his pocket, slapping its pouch filled with lead pellets against the flat of his hand. A solid enough tap against the side of the head brought a man down without a sound. And kept him there.

Amos flexed his fingers, then extracted a narrow-bladed knife from his boot. Noiseless, and if used properly, almost bloodless. A quick upward thrust beneath the shoulder blade, a twist to speed things along, and you were done. Once the heart was pierced, blood stopped flowing. An expert knifeman could kill without spilling a drop on himself.

When the bodies had been dragged into a clump of dense growth, Geoffrey unlocked the gates and stepped outside for a moment to signal to Danny Dennis. The cab would be in position when the time came.

There were no guards on the mansion's veranda, but they made out at least one silhouette inside the foyer.

"Careless," commented Lowry.

"Amos and I will go around back," Geoffrey whispered. The faster their entry and the fewer men they encountered making it, the better. Criminals about to be captured were prone to making foolish and deadly decisions. Innocent bystanders and hostages died. He could never allow himself to forget for a moment that Prudence was almost certainly inside. Alive, but a likely target if the men they were after saw no hope of getting away. "Lowry, give us ten minutes, then come in the front door. Quietly."

The New York City Police detective smiled. He wasn't sure his notion of going in quietly matched the ex-Pink's, but he'd have the guard in the foyer stretched out on the black-and-white tiles unable to make a sound before anyone else inside knew their security had been breached. That would have to do.

The chamber in which the council met had once been the mansion's ballroom, an achingly beautiful space with floor-to-ceiling windows on three sides, an intricately patterned wooden dance floor gleaming with hand-rubbed polish, and chandeliers that could hold hundreds of pure beeswax candles. But that had been in the home's glory days.

After it passed into possession of The Doll Club, heavy black velvet drapes that were opened only when the room was empty hung over the windows, massive sofas and small tables lined the walls, and a raised platform on which the dolls performed and paraded stood in the center of the room.

When the council met, the platform was encircled by a ring of canopied armchairs carved to look like massive medieval thrones. If a judgment was to be rendered or discipline dispensed, the entire membership and their dolls stood in the stretches of open space surrounding the council, every man and his plaything having a clear view of the drama to be enacted before them. Harsh discipline witnessed by all ensured that fear ruled behavior. The pleasure that followed punishments was all the more intense for the terror they inspired.

Tonight's meeting was of a different tenor. The general membership had not been summoned, so the voices in the ballroom echoed in its vast emptiness. There had been some discussion about whether all of the dolls should attend to witness the lesson meted out, but in the end it was decided that only those belonging to the six councilors and the Dollmaster need be present. For form's sake, but also because they could be counted on to spread word of what took place. Dolls were forbidden to gossip among themselves and supplied with regular doses of laudanum to dull their wits. But everyone knew that nothing on earth could keep a girl entirely silent and that the stories grew more terrible and therefore more effective with each retelling.

So there they assembled. Human statues with gleaming white porcelain skin, reddened cheeks, plucked and tattooed brows and lashes, hairless bodies. Dressed in each master's favorite costume. Eyes glazed or bright with dread, depending on each doll's tolerance of the amount of laudanum she had ingested.

Two dark-suited guards blended into the black drapes. Each was armed with a short-handled whip and a sheathed knife. Pistols were only carried where there was no danger of ricochet or shooting blindly with disastrous results. When it was all over tonight, they would be paid in gold, white powder, and the use of any doll whose master no longer wanted her. The guards were bestial, short-lived men, angry and disillusioned from birth, steering a haphazard course toward early and violent death for lack of anything better to expect.

One by one the masters filed into the ballroom, each taking his place in the chair beside which his doll stood waiting. Last to enter was the member who had been elected to serve as Dollmaster for a term of three years, the aristocratic doctor who had held a finger beneath Prudence's chin to better examine her face—Master Ocelot. They knew each other's real names, of course, saw one another in the normal course of their lives as respected scions of society, but at the mansion they were always called by the sobriquet each had chosen at the time of his initiation. It was part of the mystique, an element of the allure of secrecy to assume an identity associated with animal danger and death.

When all of the masters had been seated, Master Ocelot raised two fingers toward the platform. A ripple of surprise electrified the air. Two to be judged at the same time? When had that last happened? Could anyone remember?

A guard shifted from one foot to the other, recalculating the amount he might expect to pocket at the end of the night. One of the dolls, whose eyes were brighter than the others, had steeled herself to endure degradation without benefit of laudanum, surreptitiously pleasuring the male attendant who prepared her body for her master's demands. So close, she was so close to enlisting him to help her escape. Surely her dream wouldn't be shattered tonight. She nerved herself to deny everything, commanded herself not to give in to the fear, not to betray herself by trembling should the Dollmaster point to her.

And then a stranger was led into their midst, a woman no one had ever seen before, an outsider dressed as if for a ball at Delmonico's.

Head held defiantly high, Prudence MacKenzie walked to what she immediately realized would not be a quick or easy death.

And decided that when the moment came, she would fight it with every bit of strength she possessed.

She would not go down without taking someone with her.

CHAPTER 31

The two women who had prepared Prudence for her ordeal made a pot of coffee to help them stay awake until they were needed to undress tonight's dolls. Sat down at the worktable to chat and pass the time. Never heard the faint snick of the steel door opening. It should have been locked. They hadn't bothered.

The first hint they had that something had gone terribly wrong was the sight of Geoffrey's Colt revolver pointed at them. Cocked and ready to fire. Two coal-black eyes stared with a stony and unrelenting accusation that told them faster than words that this man knew everything.

"Where is she? Where is Miss MacKenzie? She was brought here tonight."

A small, slender man appeared with lengths of leather strapping he had taken from the hospital room. He snapped them viciously as he approached the chairs in which the two transformers had thought to have a bit of a breathing space before setting to work again.

"Hands behind your backs," he ordered.

"I asked you a question," Geoffrey said, voice devoid of any hint of mercy or forgiveness. "I won't ask it again."

He leveled the gun at the younger of the women, the one who had talked about washing dead people in a funeral parlor.

She'd seen what a gunshot could do to the human face. How impossible it was to repair the damage. You placed a cloth over the wreckage and counseled a closed coffin.

"In the ballroom. Upstairs. On the second floor."

"What was done to her?"

"Nothing. I swear it."

The older woman sat stolidly silent, more afraid of what the masters would do to anyone who betrayed them than she was of this intruder who should have shot them at first sight. He wasn't a contract man. That type killed without bothering to ask questions. She could wait out being tied up. Someone would find them eventually. After the guards had dealt with whoever these interlopers were. Some relative of the MacKenzie woman? It rarely if ever happened that a kidnapping went awry, but there were contingencies in place to deal with unexpected circumstances. The masters were ruthless and thorough. They'd been in existence for years with no one the wiser.

The money was good. She'd take her chances. Play dumb.

The Dollmaster arranged the folds of his black gown to cover the bespoke suit that impressed patients with his ability to heal them. The richer the doctor and the more exclusive his practice, the greater his medical knowledge must be. It made sense that prosperity was the result of talent. Like Phineas T. Barnum, he knew better than most that spectacle and oddities captured more people than careful plodding. His offices were opulent, the nostrums he prescribed liberally laced with laudanum, and his handsome face radiated concern and confidence. What more could you ask of a medical man?

"Welcome, Miss MacKenzie." He waved her to one of the stools set in the center of the circle.

"Dr. Kagle." She'd recognized him immediately, this society charlatan who preyed on gullible women and the husbands who had much to conceal from their wives. The MacKenzie family physician had warned her father off him when the consumption ravaged her mother's lungs and the judge was desperate for a remedy. Kagle had been society's favorite doctor for years, attending the same balls and dinners as his wealthy clientele, comforting family members when a patient died. Prudence had considered him a clever quack. Now she knew he was so much more.

"I wondered whether you'd recognized me."

Her eyes must have given her away, she thought. She'd been shocked to see him in the black-and-white foyer, repulsed when he touched her. It was well-nigh impossible to keep strong emotions concealed. She'd thought she might have managed it. She'd been wrong. Whatever he was planning, her fate had been sealed the moment he walked through The Doll Club's front door and saw her standing there in her useless white coat.

"Master Jackal, please take your place beside Miss MacKenzie." It was a command, not a request.

The two guards shifted their gaze from the woman to the member who was being called to account. He would be restrained, if necessary, but most ex-masters who broke the covenant they had vowed to uphold recognized the inevitability of their deaths and chose the poison they were offered. In return, one of the club's physicians would sign the death certificate, attesting to a bad heart, a seizure of the brain, a cancer of the blood. The body would be consigned to consecrated ground and the family's reputation remain unstained, its place in society assured. Men who gambled with the devil knew the consequences of losing.

Ira Nicholson blanched as white as the Bella doll he no longer owned. Rose from his hollow throne, removed the black cloak that marked him as a master, and went to sit beside Prudence on a stool that reduced him to the status of condemned captive.

He had never seen her before. Nor she him.

"You broke one of the covenant's most basic tenets." The Dollmaster no longer addressed Nicholson either by title or by name. "You went outside our purview to hire a private agent in the matter of your doll. By so doing, you revealed our existence. The punishment is death." The punishment was always death.

Nicholson bowed his head and clasped his hands to stop their trembling.

"You passed on to the council the lies told to you by the ex-Pink whose dupe you became. You had no irrefutable proof that the doll and her brother were dead when you swore to us that it was so."

"The boy's finger," Nicholson stammered. "He brought it to me."

"Who can tell one crooked finger from another? You should have demanded the head. Heads don't lie."

But even Nicholson's stomach hadn't been strong enough to entertain the vision of his nephew's severed head tumbled onto the floor from a bloody sack.

"Your ex-Pink bungled the job you gave him. Attracted attention when he should have done his work in deepest anonymity. The woman who sits beside you is proof of his ineptitude. For which both of you must answer. As your defective tool already has."

The killer who had murdered the orphan boys was dead, Prudence realized. Whoever he had been.

And they were next.

Lowry waited the ten minutes Geoffrey had instructed, then knocked authoritatively on the mansion's front door, stepping to one side to shade his face. The idea was to pass for a late-arriving member demanding immediate admittance. He turned his back for good measure, staring out over the dark lawn as if he owned it, gambling that at least one of the men expected tonight would be over six feet tall, broad-shouldered, and unmistakably athletic. They couldn't all be pot-bellied moguls whose only exercise was defrauding their competitors and standing at the helm of a yacht.

A shadow darkened the light from within, and then a moment later he heard the distinctive rasp of a bolt being drawn back. The man who opened the door to him never realized his mistake. Lowry's practiced slash across his throat sent blood cascading over his shirtfront. He made a gurgling, grunting noise like a steer gone to slaughter.

Lowry caught the body before it could fall and stain the black-and-white floor tiles. He dragged the dead guard outside across the veranda, and dropped him into some freshly trimmed shrubbery. Kicked the legs well out of sight under the leafy branches. Wiped off the knife he had used and slid it back into its sheath. The whole silent operation hadn't taken more than a couple of minutes.

"The kitchen door had a bar drawn across it on the outside. There weren't any guards and no one from within could have opened it," Geoffrey reported as he and Amos exited the servants' staircase to the basement and joined Lowry in the foyer. "The council is meeting upstairs in the ballroom. Second floor. How many guards were down here?"

"Just the one man on the front door. I've checked the rest of the rooms. They're empty."

"Two at the street gate. One here. How many more?"

"It'll be an odd number so they can work in pairs if need be," Amos said.

"Three then," Geoffrey agreed. "They aren't expecting anyone but the members who were sent telegrams. Like Nicholson."

"Not more than half a dozen of them, judging by the number of carriages I saw arrive before you got here," Lang said.

"However many, the guards will be armed," Lowry said. He'd taken a pistol and a knife from the body under the bushes.

Faint footsteps paced above them, toward the back of the house.

"That's the guard outside the ballroom," Geoffrey said, voice barely above a whisper. Listening. "He's alone."

"And dead." Lowry bent to remove the knife from his boot. "I shouldn't have bothered to put it away," he said.

And then he was gone, springing like a large cat up the beautifully curved staircase into the darkness of the upper floor.

"Your carelessness has already totted up a number of casualties. And there are other threats to reckon with now," Master Leopard said. He sat to the right of the Dollmaster, the senior and first to speak among the others who had been summoned to act as the night's justices. "This woman before us brought your doll to a Quaker doctor whose assistant helped care for her. Both of them observed and will remember the transformative work accomplished in our hospital. They will be found to have been asphyxiated by a malfunctioning coal stove."

The masters called out a single word. "Agreed."

"The order will be given," the Dollmaster said. He nodded permission for the next member to speak.

"This MacKenzie woman has partnered with an ex-Pinkerton in a private inquiry agency. He, too, has seen evidence of our work. He's dangerous, but he needs a cane and walks with a bad limp. I suggest a runaway hansom cab, death beneath the horse's hooves."

"Agreed."

"The order will be given."

"A city police detective who has a special interest in our practices has joined forces with the ex-Pink and the woman." Master Panther was as well-known to New Yorkers as their current mayor, but far more powerful.

No one asked what that special interest might be. Prudence knew it had to be Warren Lowry the member was talking about, and the special interest could only be the sister who had been stolen from the family home. Surely she was dead by now. Surely no doll could long survive what Prudence knew she herself would rather die than endure.

"We know the detective entered the Friends Refuge while the doll was there. And that he's intensified his efforts to find us. I recommend a gang fight, a knife, and a lonely street at night. He's known to wander the alleys down by the Five Points."

"Agreed."

"The order will be given. Are there others?" the Dollmaster asked.

"None who saw the doll with their own eyes."

"And we are certain she and the boy are both dead now?"

"We are. The man hired to do the job swore he eventually accomplished what he was paid to do. And there have been no more sightings of either of them. But that doesn't exonerate the master who set in motion the series of events that have endangered us."

"We have chosen a murder-suicide pact." The oldest master had a fondness for ritual. "In the manner of Crown Prince Rudolf of Austria and his mistress. Last year at Mayerling. It was in all the newspapers. A marvelous scandal. He shot her and then himself."

And now Prudence understood why she had been dressed in a ballgown, why she was coiffed and bejeweled as though for a formal dinner or lovers' rendezvous. It was all part of a staged event that she was helpless to prevent. A bullet to the brain. And she could not run. Her ankle had been chained to the footstool as soon as she'd sat down. She was as helpless as an organ grinder's tethered monkey.

One of the dolls detached herself from her master's side.

When she returned from the long table that had been laid with tonight's feast, she was carrying a tray on which stood two crystal glasses.

"We have decided against a shooting," the Dollmaster informed them. "Poison will do the job just as well, and with far less observable damage. We want the Francton-on-Hudson police to believe that our two lovers mutually agreed to take their own lives together. Rather a nice touch, don't you think?"

"A carriage is waiting. You will be found in one another's arms, she lying on the bed, you on your knees beside her. As Prince Rudolf knelt to say farewell to his baroness. The newspapers will be quick to point out the parallels."

"But will they believe it?" It was only the second time Prudence had spoken since she'd been brought to the ballroom. "No one has ever seen the two of us together." Most society affairs were gossiped about long before the wronged partner became aware of spousal infidelity.

"We've prepared love letters, Miss MacKenzie. Expressions of despair. Despondency. The hopelessness of keeping your affair a secret. We have to thank the Crown Prince for establishing the precedent. The press and the public will *want* to believe it. So they will."

"You are allowed to speak. One last time. It's the custom." The Dollmaster gestured to the doll who was holding the tray. She stepped forward, offering the poisoned wine.

"I have nothing to say." Ira Nicholson reached for one of the crystal glasses. He could choose his own death or be thrown to the men who would not hesitate to carve him up for fish bait. He'd known from the beginning that this could happen. Known in the abstract. Never dreamed it would be he who died.

"The poison is fast-acting. I can assure you of that. You will not be in any way disfigured," said the master who taught history to awed undergraduates and loved ritual. "I chose it myself."

The two guards who had been standing motionless in the far corners of the room moved closer as Ira Nicholson hesitated. They unbuttoned their uniform coats, revealing sheathed butchering knives. The choice was clear. A quick, relatively painless death or the horror of a blade slashing into flesh.

The masters would not wait long for him to make up his mind.

Nicholson raised the crystal glass in a silent toast. He had witnessed ceremonial deaths before. The Club expected nonchalant grace. The member who wanted his memory untarnished and his family legacy preserved complied. "You'll see, Miss MacKenzie. It will be like falling asleep. A choice I perhaps should have made years ago."

He took a tentative sip of the rich, dark wine, then drained the glass in three swallows. For a moment, after he replaced the empty goblet on the tray and sat like an expectant diner waiting for his next course, nothing happened.

Then his fists clenched, his eyes bulged, he gasped for breath, his body arcing and twisting in desperate need of oxygen. The masters sat as if oblivious to the dying man a few steps away from their polished boots.

Prudence dropped her head into her hands, unable to move from the stool on which she sat because of the chain around her ankle. She could hide her eyes from the sight of Ira Nicholson shaking uncontrollably, but she could not block the sounds from her ears. He choked and wheezed, fought for breath and struggled for air.

Just before it was over, she heard a low whimpering as if puppies were shivering in a cold wind, and realized it was the dolls trying not to scream at the horror they were witnessing.

When silence fell, Prudence raised her head and opened her eyes. Nicholson lay on the floor, curled up like a child, right hand clutching his neck, the left still tightly fisted. One of the guards straightened his arms and legs, ran curved fingers from the dead man's forehead to his chin, stepped back to inspect his handiwork. "If we leave right away, we can get them to Francton before they stiffen too badly."

"Most of the staff no longer lives in," the Dollmaster said, rising from his chair to lay two fingers on one of Ira's carotid arteries. "Good. He's gone. You see, Miss MacKenzie, it's a matter of a very few minutes."

If she struggled, they'd hold her down and pour the poison into her throat. Or use a knife on her. Two strong, experienced killers. She didn't stand a chance of fighting them off. But she had to try. She wouldn't go down without using her nails to scratch out an eye or her teeth to bite off an ear. What good was false dignity in the face of a death she didn't deserve? She would kick and shout and raise high holy hell before she'd submit to her own murder.

And then she smiled. She'd heard the tap-tap of something metal, a tiny faraway familiar sound that was almost lost in the concentrated tension of Ira Nicholson's convulsions. No one else around her seemed to have noticed. Not the guards who were moving the body away or the masters who had leaned forward in their seats to watch her die. Certainly not the dolls whose freakishly perfect faces seemed incapable of expressing emotion.

She bent over at the waist as if to pull herself together, as if reaching within for the strength to claim the remaining crystal glass and drink its contents as unflinchingly as Nicholson had done. A small sip to taste the wine, then a flick of the wrist to drain it of its deadly liquid. It had been an almost elegant gesture when Bella's uncle did it. She had to fool the masters into believing she had decided to go out with gravitas. She needed time.

A minute? Two minutes? How long would they wait?

"Come now, Miss MacKenzie. It's getting late. We need to speed you on your way."

This was it then. She had one more chance to buy a few additional seconds.

She sent Dr. Kagle the arch glance of a debutante about to slide into her first dance with an elderly male relative, smoothed the skirts of the ballgown she wore. Tightened her back into the perfect posture her governess had insisted upon. Lowered her lids for a moment as if in silent prayer.

She could feel their eyes on her, following her every move, drinking in her last actions of life.

Then she reached for the crystal glass on the tray being held out to her.

The doll's face swam into view. It was like looking at one of the soulless poppets she had once seen in a voodoo queen's cabin. Blank, because it contained no human spirit.

Prudence's fingers brushed the cut crystal, then she swept her open hand across the glass as though it were a croquet ball she was hitting with a wooden mallet. The goblet flew off the tray and sailed through the air, dark red liquid streaming. It smashed against the floor, scattering crystal fragments like a fall of diamonds.

And at the precise instant that the poisoned wine began to seep into the ballroom's inlaid parquet floor, the rescue party whose leader's cane she had heard signaling her as they climbed the stairs barreled through the door, revolvers raised and cocked to fire. Amos drilled the guard who bent over Nicholson's body; Lowry shot the other man dead center through the forehead.

Geoffrey had eyes only for Prudence, but when a glance and a nod from her told him she was well able to take care of herself now, he tickled the Dollmaster's throat with the wickedly sharp point of his cane sword. It was sheer pleasure to watch the man wince as blood trickled from the long, shallow cut carved skillfully into his neck.

"The key is in that guard's pocket," Prudence told Amos, who had the chain around her ankle unlocked before she could finish giving him instructions.

The six dolls stood as if turned into pillars of salt, except for the one with the bright eyes who had never given up planning, never believed that escape was beyond her grasp. That doll turned to the man she had had to call *master* and slapped him so hard across the face, that he slid to the floor before he could stop himself. She lifted a high-heeled foot and landed the most agonizing blow she could manage on the tender spot between his legs, grinding down for good measure as he howled in outraged pain.

"I recognize two of these faces," Detective Lowry said, peering at each master in turn. "If we try to lock them up, they'll be let go before I get the paperwork done."

"Take them down to the basement," Geoffrey ordered. "Put them in with the women you'll find there, then lock the steel door behind you."

"What about them?" Amos asked, gesturing toward the dolls.

"We'll drive them to the Friends Refuge. Dr. Sloan will look after them. God knows, I have no idea where to begin."

Geoffrey watched as Lowry and Amos herded the six strangely compliant masters from the ballroom. They were too submissive, these warped men who had reigned like absolute monarchs over their loathsome kingdom. Was another shift of guards supposed to arrive tonight? Was that what they were counting on? He strode over to one of the windows, breaking the glass with his cane. Then he tossed a lit lamp out onto the lawn below, throwing as high an arc as he could. Signaling Danny Dennis to bring his cab onto the grounds.

The carriage that would have transported Ira's and Prudence's bodies to the Hudson River village where they were supposed to be found in a last, tragic lovers' tryst waited in the driveway. As soon as Lowry and Amos got back, they'd start loading the women into it. The sooner they got them into Dr. Sloan's care, the better.

And then Geoffrey would fold Prudence into his arms and never let her go. Say the things he'd been too proud to tell her for fear of rejection. Keep her safe from harm forever. And if she refused him, he'd find some way of making her change her mind. No matter how stubborn she was, he was ten times more obstinate.

There she was, across the ballroom, talking to the dolls as though everything was perfectly normal and they had never been kidnapped, never had their physical appearances changed, their identities stolen, and the light of the inner spirit quenched.

He raised an arm in salute. She nodded, then turned back to the girls who needed her now more than he did.

"What's your name?" Prudence asked the doll who had meted out swift punishment to the man who thought he owned her.

"Faithann," she said. "I never forgot who I was, no matter what they made me do. I would have gotten out of here eventually, you know. I know of at least one other girl who escaped, and so did my friend Ottilie." She caught the look on Prudence's face. "They're dead, aren't they? That's why you look that way. You're afraid I'm not strong enough for you to tell me they didn't make it."

"One of them disappeared, presumably to safety," Prudence said. "But Ottilie is gone. You should know that at the end she was being taken care of by some very kind women who did all they could for her."

"We can't cry," Faithann said. "They do something to our eyes so we can't cry. Dolls aren't allowed to have tears."

"We need to get you out of here. Are there other girls in the house?"

"Not anymore. They were moved two days ago. Still in the city, but I don't know where, only that they think this house is too close to the river now that the docks are being rebuilt. It's no longer private enough." Faithann's perfect face twisted into a poor facsimile of a grimace, the most her tortured features could manage. "There's an office on the first floor where records are kept. I heard the attendants talking about the supplies that had to be ordered for the new house, so there's bound to be an address there somewhere. We six were supposed to go to-morrow. After the ordeal and what was to follow. That's what they call it, when someone is punished. The ordeal."

"How many of you are there?"

"I'm not sure. The last time I counted, there were more than twenty of us."

Madame Jolene's brothel housed less than a dozen women.

"How long have you been here, Faithann?"

"A year, I think. There's no way to count the days. It was spring when I was taken. It feels like spring again."

"It's early May. Flowers are blooming in all the parks."

"It's time," Geoffrey said. He'd put away his pistol and resheathed his cane sword.

The dolls lowered their heads to stare fixedly at the floor as soon as he came close. Even Faithann, brave as she was, feared what this unknown man might have in store for her.

"Can you get them to follow us out?" Prudence asked her.

Faithann nodded.

"He won't hurt you," Prudence said. "No one is ever going to hurt you again. No matter what. I'll see to it. I promise."

As the carriage and Danny's hansom cab rolled out of the grounds onto the narrow road that ran along the bluffs, flames exploded behind them, sending a fountain of red and yellow sparks upward like fireworks into the night sky.

Danny reined in the big gelding who was Mr. Washington's stablemate, gentling him to the side of the unpaved street. Detective Lowry and Amos Lang, who were driving the carriage, pulled over also.

All of them, the dolls and the men who had rescued them, Prudence and Geoffrey, walked to the edge of the bluff over-looking the East River. The promontory on which The Doll Club mansion sat jutted out like the prow of a ship. Aflame. Belching clouds of smoke into the cool night air, sending the sound of crashing timbers, shattering glass, and cracking bricks along the shoreline. By morning there would be nothing left but ash and skeletal chimneys.

In the rush to the carriage and the cab, no one had kept track of anyone else. So while the dolls squeezed themselves into the vehicles that would carry them to safety, Geoffrey had searched for and found the office and the stack of orders with the all-important address Faithann had told them about. Detective Lowry had disappeared toward the rear of the house, shoulder-ing a heavy sack when he returned. Then he went from floor to floor inside the mansion, telling an impatient Geoffrey when he came out that he'd checked one final time, and they were empty.

"There was a secret tunnel from the hospital area behind the steel door out to a root cellar where they'd stored boxes of dy-namite. That's why they went down to the basement without an argument. I could hear somebody picking the lock. It was just a matter of time," Lowry told Amos after they had driven away from the inferno blazing above the murky East River. The distinctive burnt sugar odor of dynamite dust clung to the fingers handling the reins. "Somebody had left a heavy metal bar lying on the ground by the root cellar door ready to be slid into place to keep out stray foxes and racoons."

"There's still a lot of wildlife out here, even though we're in the city."

"Animals won't break into that cellar. I guarantee it."

And nobody would get out, either.

CHAPTER 32

Prudence was still wearing the much-wrinkled evening gown when the carriage into which she'd squeezed herself arrived at the Friends Refuge. It was well past midnight, but crowds of gamblers, drinkers, saloon habitués, prostitutes, and their clients thronged the streets of the Five Points neighborhood. Gaslights flickered and flared on every street corner, turning the dark night yellow. The air was almost too thick to breathe. It stank of unwashed bodies, heavy perfumes, cheap hair oil, the day's uncollected horse manure, rancid cooked meat, and overripe boiled vegetables. Everywhere the pervasive reek of raw whiskey and the yeasty scent of newly brewed beer.

The Refuge was dark and silent. Dr. Sloan kept early hours, as did the women she sheltered.

"I'll go," Prudence offered, climbing out of the carriage with soiled skirts bundled in one hand. Despite the horror of the past few hours, she'd dozed off to the sound of horses' hooves and carriage wheels over dirt roads and then cobblestoned streets. Dozed off, awakened with a start, dozed off again. And judging from the sleep-wrinkled faces around her, so had the dolls. Emotional exhaustion had taken its toll. The ending of the frightful atrocity of their lives could not be faced all at once because the future was still unknown. Sleep brought a longed-for escape that reality still denied them.

A deep woof greeted Prudence's knock. "That's all right, Blossom," she called out. "Go easy, girl. It's just me." She raised her fist to knock again, but before she could bring it down, the door opened.

Dr. Sloan. Hair braided and hanging down her back, wrapper cinched tightly around her waist, slippered feet peeping out from beneath her white cotton nightgown. She clutched Prudence to her as tightly as though they were sisters. "I was so worried," she said, fingers automatically checking Prudence's pulse, roving over face and upper body searching for cuts to be stitched and bruises to be poulticed. "When Mr. Hunter told me you'd gone missing, I didn't know what to think."

"I'm all right, Charity. But I've brought you six new patients who are desperately in need of healing." Prudence stepped back to the carriage, extending a beckoning arm within, gesturing out its passengers.

One by one they stepped into the gaslight, tattooed and painted faces eerily inhuman despite the wide open, frightened eyes. Rebecca appeared behind Dr. Sloan, clucking and patting as she wrapped each girl in a blanket and ushered her inside where two other Quaker nurses waited for them. Blossom's feathery tail waved back and forth, brushing animal comfort against cold hands and numb legs. Clenched fingers opened to welcome the push of the dog's firm muzzle and the lick of her tongue. Bella and her brother were safely asleep in their beds upstairs or Blossom would not have left her post outside their door.

"Detective Lowry?" asked Dr. Sloan. "Why isn't he with you? Is he all right?"

"No casualties on our end," Geoffrey reassured her. "But we

were told that two dozen young women had been moved to another location. He and Amos Lang and Danny Dennis are on their way there."

"Will they be able to free them?"

"They won't be alone. Amos has rousted out the other ex-Pinks we sometimes use. All good men. And they'll have the advantage of surprise." Cane in hand, Geoffrey clambered down from the carriage he'd been driving since the rescue party had split up. His face was gaunt with pain and fatigue, but Prudence was safe. And that was all that mattered.

Charity Sloan slipped a supporting hand under Geoffrey's arm. "You won't be of use to anyone if you don't let me look at your leg. That bullet you're carrying around might have dislodged itself with what you did tonight."

Dr. Sloan didn't inquire what had become of the men who had victimized the young women now sheltering within the Refuge. Over the years she had learned that it was best to leave many such questions unasked. In time, she would find out their fate. She and the volunteers who worked with her could not change the past; they could only hope to shape the future with the kindness of their hearts and the healing power of their hands.

Cups of hot, sugared tea were handed around, and if a doll stared vacantly into space and seemed not to know what to do with what she had been given, Dr. Sloan sat beside her, holding cup to lips and murmuring reassurances as her keen diagnostic eyes assessed the mental damage that had been done. As each cup was emptied, the doll was led away by one of the nurses, to be gently washed, clothed in a clean white nightgown, and tucked into one of the six beds that had been hastily moved into a contagion room.

"They shouldn't be separated," Dr. Sloan had decided. "Not yet. Nothing will be familiar to them when they wake up. Nothing except each other. They'll be afraid and confused."

"They were given laudanum," Prudence said. "To keep them quiet and obedient."

"Do you know how much? Or how often?"

"We found enough laudanum in one of the basement storage rooms to supply a small hospital for months," Geoffrey contributed. "They were probably dosed on a regular basis. Perhaps even without their knowledge if it was slipped into their food or drink."

"Laudanum becomes a craving," Prudence said quietly. "The sense of euphoria it brings is preferable to the reality the addict is trying to escape. They may have taken it voluntarily."

Dr. Sloan nodded. She knew Prudence's history and had treated countless women whose dependence on alcohol or opium was all that made their miserable lives bearable.

"We'll deal with it tomorrow. They'll be all right until the morning." The pupils of their eyes had told her what she needed to know. "We'll make plans then. But now the two of you need rest."

"I'd like to stay for the remainder of the night," Prudence said. "In case help is needed."

Dr. Sloan shook her head and briefly held Prudence's hands in her own. "You're going home to sleep in your own bed. I insist. There are four of us on staff here. And Blossom. We'll manage. We'll need you and Mr. Hunter in the days to come. We mustn't have another tragedy."

"Like Ottilie?"

"She pinned all her hopes on being accepted by the family she believed would love and cherish her. When her father and brother rejected what she had become, against her will, she saw no reason to live. That must not happen to any of the girls you rescued tonight. Or the others Detective Lowry will find and save."

"How will you prevent that?"

"I have an idea," Dr. Sloan began. "I've been thinking about it for weeks, but tomorrow is time enough to discuss it. Now I'm going to be firm with you. Sidewalk Andy chops our wood and does the heavy lifting we can't manage. He'll drive you home and see to the carriage and horses. No more arguments."

"What do you think she meant?" Prudence asked as she and Geoffrey climbed into the carriage. "How could she have a plan already?"

"Look," he said, pointing to a sign tacked to the building next door to the Refuge. "It's for sale. And didn't you tell me that the last time you volunteered down here the clinic was so full, women had to wait outside on the sidewalk to get in?"

"The Refuge never has the kind of money it would take to buy that house." Prudence paused, one hand on the carriage's open door. "It looks as though it was a family home at one time. Years ago, and probably broken up into tiny apartments now. Likely to need everything from plumbing to a new roof."

"We'll wait for Dr. Sloan to confirm it," Geoffrey said, "but I think she started dreaming about purchasing that property the day the For Sale sign went up. She could easily double the size of the clinic and add more dormitory space." He was thinking of the photographs Jacob Riis had taken of alleyways filled with desperate orphans huddled together for warmth, of the prostitutes who plied their trade in dingy rooms where a blanket was hung from the ceiling to shield children from the sight of their mother servicing a customer in order to put food in their mouths.

"It needs to happen *now*, Geoffrey. Before the premises get turned into a saloon or a brothel."

"The morning will do, Prudence. I'll have Josiah contact the seller."

The funds to buy the house adjoining the Friends Refuge came from Jay Gould, via his daughter, Helen. Prudence shared the good news with Geoffrey on Sunday afternoon as they waited in his hotel suite for Detective Lowry and Amos Lang to supply the details of the second of the previous night's raids.

"Mr. Gould looks terrible, Geoffrey," Prudence said, thinking her partner had also seen better days. "Helen had already told me in confidence that he was diagnosed with consumption two years ago, but I wasn't prepared for how quickly the disease has ravaged him. He's kept it from everyone; not even his late wife knew. The doctor is sworn to secrecy, but all you have to do is look at him to sense that something is very wrong. I only planned to stay long enough this morning to drink a cup of coffee with Helen and tell her what we needed. I never expected her father to join us in the breakfast room."

"I imagine he'll be a silent partner. From the little I've been able to find out, he supports a number of charities, always on condition of anonymity."

"He said he'll have his lawyers make the purchase and draw up the papers immediately. And you're right. Jay Gould's name won't appear on any of the documents. Helen will oversee a trust to renovate the building and permanently fund the expanded Refuge. She's desperate for something to do that will distract from the deathwatch she's keeping over her father. She needs hope in her life, but she can't leave his side. And she's also raising the two youngest children."

As soon as the small team of Detective Lowry, Amos Lang, and Danny Dennis arrived, Geoffrey ordered coffee and sandwiches sent up to his suite. Reports needed to be made and next steps discussed, but pale faces and drawn features testified to the fatigue and heaviness of heart that afflicted each of the rescuers. Dr. Sloan had dispatched Quaker volunteers to begin the healing at the newly secured house, and three of the ex-Pinks remained to guard against no one quite knew what or whom. Only that the dolls shouldn't be left alone.

More than two dozen additional victims had been found. The men guarding the estate just outside the city and the women who transformed the girls into dolls and saw to their daily care deserted their drugged charges as soon as they learned that the East River house had been raided and burned to the ground. Detective Lowry, Amos Lang, Danny Dennis, and the ex-Pinks they brought with them discovered locked rooms as small and comfortless as jail cells, hastily abandoned supplies of laudanum, arsenic, theatrical cosmetics, perfumes, elaborate costumes, and glass jewelry that imitated the precious stones worn by society beauties. But no staff, no money, and no incriminating papers.

"Who warned them?" Geoffrey asked.

"We found a telephone in an office on the first floor at the rear of the house. I doubt we'll ever discover who made the call, but I think we can assume it was a member who saw the East River house burning. It lit up that whole bank along the bluffs." Danny Dennis had installed a telephone in the stables where Mr. Washington and his other horses were kept. He had a feeling the instrument would change lives the way electricity and the elevator were already doing.

"There was evidence of documents having been burned in the kitchen stove," Detective Lowry said. "Not a lot of ash, so there couldn't have been many, but I'd bet my badge that anything a prosecutor could use as evidence has disappeared forever."

"Aren't the girls themselves all the evidence a jury would need?" Danny asked. Hardened as he was by what he'd seen and suffered in Dublin's Kilmainham Gaol and on the streets of his adopted country's largest city, he'd never imagined the sustained, coldhearted cruelty he'd witnessed during the last twenty-four hours.

"They won't know the names of the men who abused them," Prudence predicted.

"Without identification that can be sworn to in court, we have no one to charge," Detective Lowry said. One of the most bitter disappointments a dedicated officer had to swallow was that many of the criminals he arrested or knew without a doubt should be detained walked free. It happened over and over again. If he hadn't clung to the hope of someday finding his sister, Lowry would have quit the department within the first year of joining it. "Sybil Johnson managed to slip out of the Nicholson town house without being seen by any of Danny's lookouts. Whatever she knew disappeared with her into the night."

"Is this the end of it then?" Danny asked. "Miss MacKenzie?"

"I wish I could say it wasn't," Prudence answered. She looked around at the faces of the men who had put so much time and effort into solving this case. Amos Lang, with his Pinkerton training and years of undercover work; Warren Lowry, who had put his life on hold to find a precious sister he wasn't sure was still alive; Geoffrey, who combined Pinkerton skills with a keen legal mind and a thirst for justice that meant he never gave up, no matter the odds; Danny, who had asked the question and looked to her for a response. "Geoffrey?"

"It may take years, but an evil this malevolent won't stay contained forever. One of the men will crack eventually. His unslaked lust will overcome any sense of caution. He'll blame what's happened on a weak link—Ira Nicholson. He'll convince himself that enough time has passed to ensure the secret is so deeply buried it can never be discovered. He'll contact one or two of the members he trusts, suggest each of them recruit a few others. If we stay alert, we'll pick up the early stirrings. Nothing happens in this city without people being aware of it."

If that happened, Madame Jolene would know it long before anyone else. She'd sent Prudence the doll that triggered the initial visit to The Doll House and sparked the first suspicion of the hideous barbarity they'd uncovered. Despite her profession, Prudence had sensed a kindred spirit.

In the months to come, Prudence decided, she'd find ways to

remain in touch. Once you'd done something that shocked everyone around you to the core, it was easier to do it a second time. And a third.

"I'll get back to the stables then," Danny Dennis said. "Blossom can stay at the Refuge for as long as Dr. Sloan needs her."

"Won't Mr. Washington be lonely?" Prudence asked. It was meant to be a lighthearted comment to distract them all from the gloom of failure.

"She'll be home before that happens," Danny predicted. He nodded at Amos Lang to come along if he wanted a ride to wherever he was going.

"Josiah will be in touch," Geoffrey said.

"There's a note here for you." Danny stooped to pick up the envelope that had been slid under the door. If a bellboy had knocked, none of them had heard it. "It's addressed to Detective Lowry."

"The only one who knows I'm here is Dr. Sloan. I sent a message to the Refuge as soon as we got back to the city." Lowry slid a finger under the flap and removed the single sheet of paper.

She's here. Come as quickly as you can. Charity Sloan.

CHAPTER 33

"Do you want company?" Prudence asked.

"I'd be grateful if you'd come with me," Lowry answered. "You, too, Mr. Hunter. If it hadn't been for your investigation, I might never have found her."

"She'll have changed," Prudence warned. "She won't be the sister you remember."

"I haven't forgotten Ottilie Urquhart," Lowry said. He slipped Dr. Sloan's note into his pocket and started for the door. "Nor the choice she made. I can't allow that to happen to Bettina."

Prudence had seen a studio portrait of Bettina Lowry taken on her fifteenth birthday, and she knew now that she'd sat with her for more than an hour in the closeness of a carriage. Yet she hadn't recognized the girl among the six rescued dolls. How could a young woman change so much? And why hadn't Lowry's sister cried out when she'd seen her brother among the rescuers? Surely she'd noticed him. Surely she'd prayed every day since her abduction that he would find her? How terribly and deeply damaged was she?

She could tell by the apprehensive frown on the detective's face that he was asking himself the same questions. And remembering that there had been no family members at Ottilie Urquhart's graveside. Would he be the sole mourner to bury another victim of The Doll Club?

"She's with the other girls." Dr. Sloan had ushered them into her private office. "We've been keeping them together as much as possible and never separating only one from the group. Always two, even when it's to perform an examination. Being singled out can be perceived as a threat."

"How did you learn her name?" Lowry asked. He was holding himself tightly erect, the brim of his hat crushed in a clenched fist. He trusted Charity Sloan to know when and how Bettina could be returned to his care. But the waiting was almost more than he could bear.

"She inked her initials into the sole of her right foot," Dr. Sloan explained. "Tattooed *BL*. You'd think at first glance that it was a tiny scar. Just under and half hidden by the big toe. But something made me take a closer look. I'd say she used a pin and soot from a fireplace. She must have thought of it very soon after she was taken, before the laudanum and what was repeatedly done to her affected her mind. She meant for someone to be able to identify her."

"How badly is she injured?" Lowry held out the small cabinet photo he carried with him. He'd shown it to the doctor once before, when he'd first told her his sister's story. "Please. Look again. Are you sure it's Bettina?"

Charity Sloan traced the beautiful fifteen-year-old's face with a light touch. She held her forefinger over the eyebrows and eyes. "Same nose, same mouth. Even with the changes, I'm certain it's your sister, Detective."

"How could I not have recognized her?"

"You mustn't blame yourself," Prudence said.

"It was dark," Geoffrey reminded him. "Everything happened very quickly. There was neither time nor opportunity to talk individually to the girls we rescued, and Prudence was the only one they weren't afraid of."

"But surely she saw me. Surely she knew who I was." Anguish roughened Lowry's voice.

"She's not herself," Dr. Sloan said quietly. "It won't be a quick or an easy recovery, Detective."

"I won't have her confined to an institution."

"I wasn't going to suggest that."

"Please, Dr. Sloan. I must see her."

"Come with me." Dr. Sloan nodded her consent and approval when Prudence and Geoffrey joined her and Detective Lowry as she led the way toward the contagion ward where the six dolls had spent the night.

"Have you contacted any of the parents?" Prudence asked.

"Not yet. Only two of them have been able to tell us their names."

"The others?"

"It will take time. As I told Detective Lowry, the recoveries will be neither swift nor without considerable difficulty." She stopped outside the contagion room. "Are you ready?"

Lowry nodded.

Six heads snapped toward the doorway where Dr. Sloan stood, blocking from sight the three figures in the hallway behind her. For a moment it was as though all the air had been sucked out of the room in a single frightened inhalation. Neither the dolls nor Dr. Sloan moved.

One girl breathed a sigh of relief. Then another. A third and a fourth. Charity Sloan stepped into the room and smiled. Five timid faces smiled hesitantly back, then turned questioning eyes on the three visitors a few paces behind her. The sixth doll had ducked her head, covering her features with one hand so that only blond curls were visible.

And Detective Lowry knew. Bettina *had* recognized him. Fear and shame would destroy her unless he could pierce through what she believed herself to be and reach the innocent girl child she had once been.

Moving as reassuringly as his height and muscled frame would permit, he approached the bed on which she sat. With every step he took, Bettina hunched over a little more deeply, until it seemed as though she would disappear snail-like into herself.

He had to get it right. There would be no second chances.

The foot of the narrow bed creaked beneath his weight as he sat down. Five pairs of eyes stared fixedly and not without fear. No one said a word.

"Bettina," Detective Lowry murmured. "I've come to take you home." He reached out one large hand to touch and stroke the bowed back, smoothing the quivering shoulders with a gentling, repetitive motion that soothed and comforted. "You don't have to tell me anything you don't want to. I won't ask any questions. We'll just be together, the two of us. And no one will hurt you ever again. I promise."

Bettina uncurled herself so slowly that at first no one could be certain she had moved at all. But then Detective Lowry's hand withdrew from where it had lain on her back. She raised her head cautiously, as if she feared that the sight of her would bring revulsion to her brother's eyes. Tattooed eyebrows and lashes, artificially whitened skin and reddened cheeks, lips permanently stained bright red.

Gaze locked on his face, she waited. He smiled as broad and unjudgmental a welcome as any man greeting a much-beloved and long-lost sister. Opened his arms. And hugged her tightly to his broad chest when she flung herself against him and tucked her head into the warmth of his embrace.

Tears streamed down Prudence's cheeks. She reached out blindly and found the hand that Geoffrey held out to her.

* * *

"There's not much I can do to reverse what was done to the girls' faces," Dr. Sloan informed Prudence several days after Detective Lowry had taken custody of his sister. "It's a great pity, but if their eyebrows and eyelashes do grow back, in time the tattooing will be less noticeable."

"What about the excessive whiteness of their skin?"

"Again, only time and a healthy diet without any more of these." Dr. Sloan opened the lid of a box marked *Dr. Rudolpho's Herbal Salts Wafers for Whitening the Skin*. "They're arsenic-laced crackers. I don't know how much arsenic each wafer contains, but even a very small amount is dangerous. Danny Dennis and Amos Lang brought back some of the products they found stored in the basement of the house they raided." She handed a jar of thick white cream to Prudence. "You rub this on before applying a layer of enamel face paint. Then again in the evening so it can be absorbed overnight."

"What's in it?"

"More lead than anyone should be able to tolerate. We've known for years, centuries, that arsenic and lead were dangerous to use as beauty products, but for women desperate to achieve some unnatural ideal of perfection, they've always been worth the risk. Small doses of ingested arsenic and applied lead do eventually result in extremely pale skin. But the lead pits so badly that more and more of the cream and enamel has to be used to hide the damage. Eventually the arsenic and lead combine to kill the woman foolish enough to have used them. It's not a pretty or an easy death."

"Will they recover?" Prudence asked. It was one thing for a grown woman to act stupidly in pursuit of elusive physical beauty, but quite another to have poison forced on young girls who could neither resist nor protect themselves.

Charity Sloan shook her head. "Everything depends on how

much poison their systems have absorbed. Probably none of them will heal entirely."

Prudence waited.

"I think many of the dolls will have difficulty conceiving. And if they do become pregnant, they may not carry to term or the infant will die soon after birth."

"That's always supposing they're able to marry," Prudence said. It would take an enormous dowry to overlook the fact of deflowerment and what had followed. A man who could be bought was unlikely to bring anything but a lifetime of neglect to the woman whose fortune was the only thing about her he valued.

"Miss Gould and I have talked," Dr. Sloan said. "She can tap into assets I've only been able to dream about."

"What does that mean for the Refuge?"

"The Refuge and its medical mission won't change. I insisted on that. Miss Gould won't manage things herself, but she will direct a board that will oversee an expanded vision of what the Refuge has come to mean to the girls and women of the Five Points. Rehabilitation, Prudence. It's always been the missing piece of what happens to a patient once I've treated her medical problems. More often than not she went back into the situation that nearly got her killed in the first place. We can't allow that to happen to the dolls whose families won't accept them. We can't turn them loose into a life of prostitution because they have no other way to survive. Miss Gould's help will be a burden lifted from my shoulders."

"Dare I say you already look more rested?"

"I slept well last night. For the first time in forever, I didn't wake up sick with worry about how the bills would get paid." When Charity Sloan smiled, years fell away. The tertiary syphilis that would someday kill her had not yet manifested itself in any symptoms a lay person would recognize. The man who had abused her as a child was long since dead.

"Now if only we could engineer a happy outcome for Bella and her brother," Prudence said. "I've felt responsible since I first found them in the basement of University Building. But they need a home and a family, and that's something I can't provide."

"You won't have to."

"What do you mean?"

"I didn't want to say anything until I was sure. Now I am. That's why I sent the note asking you to come by the Refuge this morning." Dr. Sloan consulted the small gold watch pinned to her shirtwaist. "They should be here any minute."

"You're smiling again."

Dr. Sloan rose to her feet as a knock sounded on her office door. "Dr. and Mrs. Mitchell," she greeted the couple she ushered into the small room. "I'd like you to meet the person who's responsible for finding and saving your niece and nephew. Miss Prudence MacKenzie." Charity shook her head warningly. *Wait*, she seemed to be saying. *Don't ask any questions yet. Give them time.*

"We're grateful, Miss MacKenzie," Dr. Mitchell said. "You'll never know how appreciative we are."

His wife reached out with both gloved hands. "I haven't the words to thank you enough."

"Please sit down," Dr. Sloan said. "I've asked Rebecca to bring us some tea while we talk."

"I have so many questions," Mrs. Mitchell said. She was small, with bright blue eyes and the clear, unlined skin of a woman content with her life.

"We thought it best not to force Annabelle to relive what she's been through." Dr. Mitchell extracted a card from his wallet. *Samuel Cooper's White River School.* "It's not an orphanage, Miss MacKenzie, although many of our pupils have lost their parents."

"Samuel Cooper was my brother," Mrs. Mitchell explained.

"He was an ordained Congregationalist minister who served in the Union army as a chaplain. He had a great love of children, so when we founded our school, we named it in his honor."

"I've shared with the Mitchells what you told me about finding Annabelle and Alexander," Dr. Sloan began.

"They must have been half-starved for Alexander to steal your sandwiches," Mrs. Mitchell said. "But I'm so glad he did." She added a sugar cube to the cup of tea Dr. Sloan handed her. "Won't you tell us everything, please, from beginning to end?"

"I'm not sure . . ." Prudence hesitated.

"There's nothing we haven't already heard about the cruelties done to innocent children," Dr. Mitchell said. "I'm a medical doctor, Miss MacKenzie, as well as an educator. We believe in treating the body, mind, and soul at White River. You won't shock us, and nothing you can say will dissuade us from giving Annabelle and Alexander the loving care they deserve."

"I was sitting in Washington Square Park with a dog named Blossom," Prudence began, persuaded by Charity Sloan's encouraging look that these two ordinary-seeming people were worthy of trust and able to accept the ugly truths she would tell them. "Alexander came out of nowhere, like a whirlwind. He'd grabbed the packet of sandwiches and run halfway through the park before I realized what had happened."

Cynthia Mitchell laughed, a tinkling sound of simple joy. Braxton Mitchell put down his teacup and took one of his wife's hands in gentle reassurance that what must follow next would not be impossible to bear.

The tale poured from Prudence as effortlessly as though she'd known these strangers all her life. Even when she fumbled for the right words to recount what was most painful or distressing, they did not interrupt. It was as though they had decided that her narrative was too important, too sacred, to intrude upon.

When Prudence finally finished, dry-mouthed and emotionally exhausted, Cynthia Mitchell wiped tears from her cheeks and turned to her husband.

"We must tell her about Clyde," she said. "It's time. Both Dr. Sloan and Miss MacKenzie deserve to know the whole truth about him."

"Clyde Mitchell is the children's father," Dr. Mitchell said. "And my brother. He was seventeen when Fort Sumter was attacked. Clyde went to Harvard that autumn, and when the time came, he bought himself a substitute. I don't think he ever seriously considered volunteering for the army, although many other young men of his age did." He reached for his wife's hand. "Clyde was as different from Samuel Cooper as night from day. He was a drinker and a con man from the time he could tip a bottle and throw the dice until the day he died. It hurts me to say it, but the only decent thing he did in his life was to marry Effie Nicholson."

"We were told he abandoned her and that the children were born out of wedlock," Prudence interrupted.

Dr. Mitchell passed her a much-creased and well-worn document. "He showed this to our father when he came asking for money. It's not a forgery. I checked."

"Then why did Effie tell her brother that he'd refused to marry her?" Prudence asked.

"To protect the children," Geoffrey said. "To deny her husband custody of them should he ever come looking."

"My brother was a drunkard with a violent temper," Dr. Mitchell said. "Our father turned his back on him very early on. Wrote him out of his will, disowned him. But Clyde had a way of turning up when least expected, like a bad penny. If begging and pleading didn't work, he threatened."

"How did he get the job as Ira Nicholson's tutor?"

"He wrote himself a letter of recommendation, Miss MacKenzie. And he never intended to stay very long in the post. As I understand it, Clyde was hired to help prepare Ira to retake some exams he'd failed. My brother had one of the keenest minds I've ever come across. He was brilliant. And deeply flawed."

"Effie fell in love with him right away," Cynthia Mitchell said. "We were told it was her idea that they run away together."

"I don't think we'll ever know the truth about that," Dr. Mitchell said. "But I can tell you that after Effie died, we offered to take Annabelle and Alexander and treat them as our own. We thought that being a single man, Ira Nicholson would accept our proposal. But he didn't."

"He allowed no more than a very few visits before sending Alexander off to that horrible boarding school," Mrs. Mitchell said. "He told us that Effie had signed over legal custody to him. Then our letters began to be returned unopened. No one had heard from or of Clyde for years, so we had to presume he was dead. It seemed we had no legal recourse."

"We only found out that Alexander had run away by the sheerest accident. I had written to him at Brereton Oaks, you see, but Ira had given orders that he was not to receive any mail. So my letters were kept in the headmaster's office and never delivered. But then, after he ran away that last time, the headmaster's secretary assumed that because we were listed as Alexander's paternal uncle and aunt in the school's register, we should be informed of what had happened. That the school had decided not to accept him back. It was a fortuitous mistake."

"We didn't warn Ira that we had decided to visit Lanternlight," Dr. Mitchell said.

"We thought he'd find some way of stopping us if he knew we were coming," Mrs. Mitchell put in.

"He wasn't there. But the cook told us what had happened. She gave us the address of the Nicholson town house and told us about your visit. She felt that something was very wrong."

"The rest was easy," Mrs. Mitchell finished. "A ragged little urchin intercepted us outside the town house and brought us here. To Dr. Sloan."

"We're taking them with us to White River," Dr. Mitchell said. "Giving them a home there."

"Blossom, too." Mrs. Mitchell's tinkling laugh filled the office again.

"We thought you would like to say good-bye," Dr. Sloan said, opening the office door.

Blossom led the way, plumed tail waving as she nuzzled Prudence's hand. Newly bathed and groomed, her golden fur seemed to shoot out beams of sunlight.

Fingers buried deep in the dog's coat, Alexander stood defensively in front of his sister. It would be a very long time, if ever, before he trusted the world not to hurt her.

"I wish you the very best," Prudence said, knowing better than to reach out to embrace this young survivor, treating him with the adult respect he had earned. "Mr. Hunter and Detective Lowry will be very glad you've found family again."

Alexander bobbed his head politely and met Prudence's gaze with a determined tilt to his head but did not reply. Speech had too often brought him the strap to feel easy with it yet.

Bella, lingering near the not-quite-closed door, glanced once at Prudence, then kept her eyes resolutely fixed on the floor. She wore a high-necked early summer dress of fine white lawn with lace-trimmed sleeves and skirt. Modest but fashionable. A dusting of powder softened the tattooed brows and lashes, dulled the permanently rouged cheeks. She might have stepped from the pages of *Godey's Lady's Book*, Prudence thought. If you didn't look too closely at her face.

"Our carriage is waiting." Mrs. Mitchell smiled her thanks one last time, then ushered niece, nephew, and dog from the office. They could hear her cheerful voice leading them out of the Refuge.

"This marriage certificate means Alexander and Bella are Ira Nicholson's rightful and legitimate heirs," Geoffrey said, handing it back to Dr. Mitchell. "Lanternlight, the New York City property, and whatever else he owned. It could be considerable."

"We'll be in touch when decisions have to be made." Mitchell picked up his hat. "Mrs. Mitchell and I feel very strongly that it would only be right and proper if you both were to continue to play a part in their lives. There's a tie among you that's as strong as blood."

Left alone in Dr. Sloan's office, Geoffrey raised Prudence's hand to his lips.

EPILOGUE

The death of seven prominent members of New York society in the blaze that destroyed a venerable old house on the East River Cliffs was a two-day sensation in the press. Although the original house had been expanded into a far more elegant structure over the years, the grounds dated back to a time when wealthy Dutch settlers carved out spacious summer retreats for themselves where they could escape the heat of the island's low-lying swamps. It was always a tug at the heartstrings of nostalgia when one of the city's historic homes was lost. In this case, everyone agreed, the fire must have begun in a blocked chimney or a carelessly cleaned stove.

The bones that were recovered could not be identified with any certainty, so they were quietly distributed to the families concerned and interred without ceremony. The coachmen who had driven their employers to the house above the bluffs were generously rewarded for having remembered where they had gone that night. And then let go. No one would be able to forget that had it not been for their excellent memories, the names of the important dead might never have been known. Memorial services were held, wills were read and probated, widows donned black, heirs wrestled with some odd paperwork and got on with their lives. In time, people stopped wondering what kind of association it was that favored such an out-of-the-way location for its meetings.

Prudence waved farewell to Warren Lowry and his sister, Bettina, as the steamship on which they were passengers pulled slowly and majestically away from its New York mooring for an Atlantic crossing to the French port of Le Havre.

"From Paris I've reserved a private compartment on the new Orient Express to Strasbourg," Lowery had told her. "We'll change trains there for Zurich, where staff from the sanitorium will meet us. Then it's a day's carriage ride to our destination."

"Are you sure this is the best thing for her?" Prudence had asked. "Surely we have skilled alienists here in New York."

"I don't want to read Bettina's name in a gossip column. That's what would happen if we stayed. It was difficult enough to resign from the police department without attracting attention."

Lowry had declined to give a reason for his departure and then refused reporters' requests for an interview. As far as anyone knew, another rich man had tired of a temporary fascination with the criminal world and decided to turn his attention elsewhere. A few scathing remarks had made headlines, but interest soon faded when Lowry ignored the slurs cast his way.

"Dr. Sloan said her recovery would be long and difficult," he had reminded Prudence. "At least a year. Probably longer. Switzerland is as far away and obsessively private a place as I could find."

"Will you write and let me know how she does?"

"I think not, Miss MacKenzie." He'd taken one of her gloved hands in his, then let it go. "Clean breaks make for the best recoveries."

"But you'll be coming back?"

"I doubt it. Europe is kinder to women than America. More tolerant. We'll travel, and eventually we'll find a place to roost."

He'd touched a finger to the brim of his hat, made his way up the gangplank, stood at the railing beside Bettina and the hired nurse who was sailing with them.

Prudence watched the steamship pull away from the dock, guided toward the open sea by squat tugboats.

When it had nearly faded from sight down the Hudson, she walked to the carriage where Geoffrey waited.

"So that's the end of it," he said. He'd shaken Detective Lowry's hand, wished him and his sister well, then left Prudence to say her farewells in private. "To the office? There's time to look at some of the new cases that have come in, if you're ready."

She settled herself facing forward, and when he would have taken the seat opposite, patted the tufted velvet bench beside her.

She took the cane from his hand and slipped one arm into the crook of his elbow.

"Geoffrey, what would you say if I told you that I've decided to sit for the bar exam without bothering to enroll in the Law School of the University of the City of New York?"

"You'll pass on the first go-round. And I predict your marks will be among the highest ever recorded." He leaned closer to her sparkling gray eyes and slightly flushed face. "What took you so long?"

AUTHOR'S NOTE

Prostitution and the casual exploitation of women have existed on the fringes or in the underworld of every society one can name. Gilded Age New York City was no exception.

While we focus in mesmerized fascination on Mrs. Astor's Four Hundred, the magnificent mansions built along Fifth Avenue and in Newport, Rhode Island, and the wasp-waisted fashions of corseted society women, we cannot forget that this opulence played out against a decidedly different national backdrop. Manufacturing was expanding at a breathtaking pace, as was transportation by rail, the availability of electricity and the telephone, private financial networks, and the implacability of corrupt and powerful political machines. Floods of immigrants swelled to bursting point the populations of already-overcrowded cities. The disparity between the very wealthy and the impoverished can be likened to a yawning, unbridgeable chasm.

Women without the financial support of fathers, husbands, or sons were often driven to barter their exhausted bodies in exchange for the few coins necessary to sustain life. Prostitution was both a business and a growth industry. Women could be bought on the streets, in brothels, and in rented rooms, often through the intermediary of pimps who promised physical protection and madams who provided a steady stream of clients in their houses of ill repute.

It shouldn't be surprising that kidnapping for the purpose of sexual exploitation was a part of this underworld commerce. Anything that can be sold will be bought.

Jacob Riis's seminal work *How the Other Half Lives: Studies Among the Tenements of New York,* published in 1890 by Charles Scribner's Sons, is as horrifying a read today as it was in the late nineteenth century. Perhaps even more striking than his written descriptions of tenement life are the photographs and illustrations of crowded, unsanitary living conditions. Barefoot children sleep in doorways and stairwells. Loitering men line alleyways choked with filth. Staring out at us are the huge, anguished eyes of the desperately impoverished subjects whose lives of overwork, little pay, rampant disease, and early death he chronicled. A precious cache of glass negatives stored and forgotten in the attic of Riis's Richmond Hill home was discovered and preserved some thirty years after his death.

Nellie Bly (Elizabeth Jane Cochran) was the celebrity sensation of her day, yet only five years after her seventy-two-day circumnavigation of the globe, at age thirty-one, she married a millionaire industrialist in his early seventies, retiring from the adventuresome public life that had brought her fame. After her husband's death in 1904 and the subsequent bankruptcy of the company she had taken over, she returned to journalism, reporting on the Eastern front of World War I and the Women's Suffrage Movement.

French bisque dolls were made of unglazed porcelain, giving them a smooth, dull finish that suggests the look of human skin. They were popular among the daughters of wealthy families, and while some of them were intended as expensive toys with wardrobes of fashionable clothing, many were treated as collectibles, too valuable to be casual playthings. They varied widely in size and design, ranging from baby dolls to be rocked and carried about to dolls intended to represent adult women wearing the iconic fashions of the era's most well-known couturiers. Like many of today's fashionable objects, knockoffs were both readily available and far less costly than the originals.

Any mistakes in interpreting the historical data are unintentional and entirely mine.

ACKNOWLEDGMENTS

Grateful thanks are due to the critique group with whom I have been meeting every Tuesday morning for the past six years. Being part of a loyal band of supportive, insightful, dedicated, and always perceptive fellow writers is an author's greatest delight and source of strength when the going gets tough. First drafts are not easy on anyone. Louise Boost, Joyce Sanford, and Carol Bondurant are cherished in my heart and roundly applauded in my head.

I found the Oro Valley Writers Forum a while back, an organization whose goals have never changed since the first meeting I attended. We read aloud what we have written, listen attentively to one another, and always, always provide a safe harbor where creativity flourishes and motivation is nurtured. Another treasure in the desert.

I count on John Scognamiglio to keep me on a steady editorial track and agent Jessica Faust to lead me through the shifting shoals of writerly inspiration. They are the professional base upon whose judgments I rely and build.

Special thanks to Pearl Saban, who found the things none of the rest of us did—and fixed them.

And to Richard, who has been there for more years than either of us cares to count.